MW01294004

THE WRONG HUSBAND

L. STEELE

*To all the good girls who
crave a man obsessed with you
who watches from the shadows —
and whispers: "You're mine."*

This is for you.

1

Connor

Classified Internal File: Case Study – Phoenix Hamilton
Alias: "The Doctor"
Objective: Surveillance and Protection per Directive J.H.
ENTRY 1: INITIAL OBSERVATION (Remote Surveillance)

- Name: *Phoenix Hamilton*
- Profession: Junior Doctor in the ER.
- Domicile: Narrow-terraced house on a tree-lined street in one of the more affordable corners of North London.
- Daily Pattern: Leaves at 06:50. Walks to The Archway Hospital. Returns 19:00–21:00.
- Behavior: Exhibits hyper-focus. Rarely interacts with neighbors. Reclusive tendencies.
- Noted Quirk: *Unconsciously taps her chest. ~~Self-soothing behavior hinting at underlying anxiety?~~*

- Emotional Tone: Appears fatigued. Possible depressive undercurrent. ~~Is she eating enough?~~

Notes: No visible threats in proximity. ~~Stalking~~ Surveillance to continue.

2

Phoenix

"I don't love you."

The words land like a scalpel in the silence. I look straight into Drew's face, watching the flicker in his eyes. "I care about you... But it's like chronic inflammation. Persistent, dull, the kind that simmers under the surface. Not the kind that stops your heart and leaves you gasping. Not the kind of passion I'm looking for."

He winces. "Are you breaking up with me?"

Sweat pools at my neck, sliding down my back. My heart pounds. I press a hand to my stomach, trying to hold it together.

"Yes," I whisper. "Everything happened so fast, and it was easier to just go along with it. You were familiar. I didn't stop to ask myself what I really wanted."

All true. I'm doing the right thing. Doesn't mean it makes me feel less horrible.

"What brought this on?" he rasps. "I thought we were okay."

I breathe out a humorless laugh. "When was the last time we actually spent an evening together?"

He blinks, clearly scrambling for an answer.

"I'll tell you. We haven't. Not in six months. We work opposite shifts. We barely text, let alone talk. We've become strangers. It's time we face the facts, Drew. I need more from a relationship. *You* need more."

"I'm happy as we are." He sets his jaw.

"I don't believe you. And anyway, I'm not. I want the kind of love that knocks the breath out of me. Consumes me. I want to crave my man like oxygen. I need to hear his voice just to function, ache for him when he's not beside me. I want to wake up and fall asleep with him on my mind, every single day. I want a love that makes me feel *alive*."

He scoffs, "That kind of love doesn't exist."

Tension coils at the base of my neck. *Maybe it doesn't, for him.* But I have to believe it does. Because if it doesn't, then what's the point of the endless ER shifts? Of leaving home at eighteen to build a future I could be proud of?

What am I working so hard for, if not for something more?

"Maybe." I turn away. "But if I shut myself off from it, I'll never know."

"You need to stop reading those delusional books that fill your head with nonsense," he snaps.

He means my books on manifestation. On choosing your future. On believing you deserve more.

"At least, I'm brave enough to face the truth," I say, curling my fingers into fists.

"And what truth is that?"

"That we were never meant to be anything more than friends."

He sets his jaw.

I take a shaky breath. "I didn't want to hurt you, Drew. That's why I couldn't say it before. But the longer we pretend, the harder it gets. I know what I want. And it's not this. That's why we need to end it; before we both get pulled deeper into something that was never real."

"*Now* I get it," he spits, his eyes flashing with venom. "You never wanted me to meet your family because, deep down, you always knew you were going to break up with me."

He spins on his heel and storms toward the back door.

"Drew, wait, where are you going?" I chase after him, stepping out onto the patio, the early morning air biting against my skin.

He doesn't answer. Doesn't even glance back. Just keeps striding toward his bike, like he can outrun the mess we've become.

"Drew," I try again, voice tight, "you shouldn't ride when you're this angry."

That stops him. For a second.

He throws a bitter look over his shoulder. "Why do you care?" His voice is a whip. "You'd probably be relieved if I crash and die."

"Don't say that!" I shout, throwing my hands up in frustration. "Don't you dare say that. Come back. Please. Let's just talk—"

But he's already unlocking the padlock, already throwing one leg over the frame. No helmet. No hesitation. No goodbyes.

And then he's gone.

I stand there, frozen, as the sound of his wheels fades.

My hands fall uselessly to my sides. I drag my fingers through my hair, tugging it loose from its messy bun so it spills down around my shoulders in a heavy curtain.

Every conversation we have is a battlefield, and I don't even know what we're fighting for anymore.

Thankfully, we no longer share a bed. He moved into the guest room, so our schedules at the hospital wouldn't disturb each other. It made sense at the time.

Now, it feels like foreshadowing.

I swipe at the moisture that clings to my cheeks, but the tears keep coming. I'll give myself this time to get a handle on the open wound that is my life. *Two minutes.*

I let the tears flow. When the choking sensation in my throat eases somewhat, I take deep breaths.

Then spin around and march into the kitchen. I splash water on my face, snatch a dish towel to wipe at my face, then toss it aside. I throw my hair into a messy bun and pull myself together. Because I don't have time to fall apart.

Reaching my room, I step into my favorite pair of sneakers. I prefer to buy a new pair of footwear only when the previous ones wear out. It's a game I play with myself, tracking how long each pair lasts and trying to get the next one to wear out faster. These are almost there.

I grab my oversized backpack on my way out, pulling out my phone as I walk down the short path to the sidewalk, then stop. A prickling at the nape of my neck makes me pause.

I look up and down the tree-lined street. It's quiet, except for the chirping of the birds. It's only 6:30 a.m. I step onto the sidewalk.

I used to love walking to work. The quiet. The early morning air. The way the sunlight trickles through the branches of the trees that line the pavement like sentinels. It made me feel grounded. Safe, even. At least, it used to. Until a few days ago, when I first had this sensation of being watched.

I glance over my shoulder. Cars line both sides of the narrow street. Compact hatchbacks, a weathered SUV, the silver antique that always leaks oil. And then there's that white van. *Again.*

I only noticed it because I like to watch the magpies feeding their young in the chestnut tree at the top of the street, and the van is parked in front of it.

Same position. Same smudged windscreen. With the name of a building services company painted onto the side.

Do workmen even show up before dawn?

I don't know my neighbors well enough to ask who's having what done to their kitchen or loft. But that van's been here for over a week, maybe longer.

I roll my weight from foot to foot.

It's probably nothing. Just another vehicle taking up space on an already cramped road.

I shake off the feeling of disquiet, hook my AirPods into my ears, and flick on the medical podcast I've been listening to.

I get immersed in it, and before long I'm crossing at the light in front of the hospital. The employees' entrance is separate from the main one, tucked away on a quieter side street.

A small knot of people has gathered beneath one of the trees lining the sidewalk. They're looking up at the branches of the tree.

I reach them just as one of them cries out, "She's going to fall."

I look up to find a small gray tabby, clinging to a branch, her body trembling with effort. She lets out a desperate yowl, claws scrabbling against the bark as the branch sways beneath her weight.

"Someone needs to rescue that cat." A man in jogging shorts and T-shirt nods sagely.

The same woman who'd cried out earlier clasps her hands together. "Mina, please, come down kitty."

The cat's back leg slips.

A collective gasp breaks the morning quiet.

The cat lets out another desperate cry and scrabbles for balance as the branch wobbles.

That's when he appears.

3

Phoenix

Tall. Commanding. He hijacks my attention like he's a force of nature.

I take in the battered leather jacket that clings to the breadth of his shoulders, the T-shirt which strains the width of his chest.

His blue jeans, too, have seen better days. Worn at the knees, pulled apart over those powerful thighs, between which is the unmissable outline of his dick. *Inappropriate. Don't stare at his crotch. So, what if he's packing?* Guess that explains the confidence radiating from him.

He has scuffed leather boots. Big boots. Size thirteen? Maybe fourteen? My gaze, once again, swings back to the space between his thighs. The zipper is tight and stretched and, surely, that tent is more substantial than before?

My breathing grows rough. My nipples under my T-shirt tighten into points of need. I'm aware, I'm close to panting, and I can't understand it. Sure, he's good-looking. More than good-looking. And yes, there's something about him that's vital. And real. And commands attention. And he's charismatic. But he's only a man. A man who moves so fast his feet don't seem to touch the ground. He reaches the tree, jumps up and grabs a branch which must be at least seven feet above.

A gasp runs through the crowd.

He pulls himself up with a flex of his biceps and deltoids that would do an anatomy chart proud. The kinetic coordination is flawless. His pectorals, latissimus dorsi, and core engaging in a fluid motion. Like a real-life vigilante sprung straight from a comic book panel.

Sweat breaks out on my brow. Moisture springs to life between my legs. I squeeze my thighs, not that it has any effect on the yawning emptiness I'm suddenly aware of between them.

Someone calls out, "Careful," but he doesn't hesitate.

He climbs with unhurried strength, scaling the limbs of the tree like he's done it a hundred times. The cat hisses, tail fluffed, her tiny body braced and trembling.

He doesn't flinch. Doesn't speak. He grasps the trunk of the tree and extends a hand, slowly, palm-up.

"Easy, sweetheart," he rumbles. Then, quieter, like a promise, "Good girl."

His voice rakes over me like silk over gravel. It's low. Rough. Heat-soaked. The kind of voice that curls around the base of your spine and plants roots.

I shiver. Something sparks low in my belly. Something wild and feminine and completely irrational. Because… Why is my body responding to those words like they were meant for me?

Ding-ding-ding. New level of pathetic, unlocked.

He reaches for the cat. She freezes. Then lets him lift her into the crook of his arm, nuzzling into his chest with a final, plaintive mew.

He climbs down just as smoothly. One-handed, if you can believe it! This man defies gravity; he bends it to his will, as if it's a mere inconvenience. It has no effect on his mission.

His boots land on the ground with a thud. The crowd claps. The woman rushes forward, tears in her eyes, and takes the cat from his arms. "Thank you, thank you. She's never done that before."

He nods. No flourish. No smugness.

And then he turns.

He wears sunglasses and a black baseball cap pulled low, casting half his face in shadow. But there's no hiding the hard lines beneath. A stubbled jaw cut from stone. Lips unsmiling. The cords of his neck stand out in relief, tension shearing through the tissue like taut surgical wire.

His shoulders are massive. Broad enough to carry the weight of the world without flinching. And that jacket, scuffed and worn, clings to a body built not just to break rules, but to break through walls. To break hearts.

Something in my chest tightens. My heartbeat speeds up.

Diagnosis: acute emotional arrhythmia. Elevated pulse, shallow breathing, catastrophic loss of rational thought. Prognosis: not good.

I step toward him—the sound of his voice still vibrating through me like a low-frequency hum—like gravity itself just shifted toward him.

His spine straightens. His shoulders lock. All of his muscles seem to freeze.

I lean forward to take another step, when a hand lands on my shoulder. I spin around.

"Phe! Thank God, I'm not the only one late." Emma pants as she rushes up beside me. "Took my daughter to the zoo on my day off. I need another day just to recover. Oh, did you hear about more staff cuts?" Her brow furrows. "I really hope I don't lose my job. I've got rent, student loans, daycare…"

Typical Emma. An open book. The complete opposite of me. Maybe, that's why we click.

She pauses, then frowns. "Wait. Aren't you off today? Why are you here?"

Because I'll do anything not to be home while Drew's there. Because the place which used to feel like a refuge feels suffocating with him in it.

Before I can think of an answer, she barrels on, "Let me guess.

They called you in, short-staffed again. You really need to stop saying yes. You deserve a break."

I let her voice fade into the background and glance back toward the man who rescued the kitten, but he's gone.

The crowd has already dispersed. The woman with the cat walks past me, fussing over her pet.

I pocket my earphones. *Where did he come from?* And when he praised the cat... *"Good girl..."* I shiver again.

The sentiment in those words resonates with a hidden part of me. A very secret, very forbidden part of me. One I didn't even know existed. Until today.

"What did you say?"

"What?" I glance sideways to find Emma frowning at me.

Ugh. Did she hear me mumble, *good girl?* "I said, good morning." I curve my lips into what I hope looks like a smile and not a grimace.

"Oh, right, good morning." She accepts my explanation without question. "Let's hope it stays that way."

It does not stay that way. Things go downhill from there. My shoe falls apart. It literally comes apart at the seams. Guess I wore them out.

I don't have a backup, so I change into a pair of borrowed clogs a size too big for me. Ugh! They're also a hideous yellow color. But needs must...

I shove the curtain aside and step into the cubicle. The air reeks of antiseptic and adrenaline. A teenage boy clutches his abdomen; his tracksuit soaked in blood.

"Stabbing?" I ask the nurse who hovers at the foot of the bed.

She nods. "Lower right quadrant. BP's dropping. Looks like internal bleeding."

I turn to the boy. "I'm Dr. Hamilton. You're safe now, okay? What's your name?"

He barely murmurs it before his eyes roll back. I slap the call bell. "Get the trauma bay prepped. *Now.*"

The nurse bolts. I press two fingers to his neck. His pulse is thready.

We wheel him through the swinging double doors, past cubicles spilling over with groaning patients, past a toddler screaming in his mother's arms, past an elderly man vomiting into a plastic bowl.

The trauma bay is more chaos. Machines beep. Monitors flash. A woman with half her scalp torn open is mid-suture on one side. A cyclist with a shattered femur moans on the other. I slide the kid in between them and snap orders. "Cannula, fluids wide open, cross-match six units. Page surgery, now."

The surgical registrar arrives just as we stabilize him. I hand over, peel off my gloves, and toss them in the trash. My hands are shaking. I don't have time to breathe.

Outside the trauma bay, another nurse flags me. "Dr. Hamilton, cubicle four's asking for a doctor again; head injury, belligerent, tried to leave."

Of course, he did. I hustle down the corridor, adrenaline pumping, pulse racing. On the way, a consultant I've worked with many times murmurs a sarcastic, "*Good* morning," as he passes, then leans into a registrar over a set of CT scans.

In cubicle four, a man in his forties sits shirtless, arms crossed, a gash over his left eyebrow oozing sluggishly. "Sorry to keep you waiting." I flip open the chart. "Head injury protocol says we need to keep an eye on you. And from the look of that laceration —"

"I'm fine." He coughs. "I have to get to work."

"You're not going anywhere until I stitch that up and clear you." I reach for the tray. "Or you'll collapse and end up back here."

He grumbles, but he lets me clean the wound.

That authoritative voice? Works every time.

Outside the cubicle, someone screams. Here we go. Not a moment's rest. My pulse ratchets up into higher gear. My vision narrows. The comforting thud of the blood at my temples tells me I'm in the zone.

Thank God for the chaos of the ER.

It gives me the perfect excuse to not dwell on the mess I've left behind at home. I spend so much time here—even overnight some-times—that the ER feels more like home than my own place.

Besides, everything I do here is for a good cause. I'm saving lives, aren't I?

"Need a doctor here!" another nurse yells.

My feet don't seem to touch the ground as I move in the direction of her voice.

A middle-aged woman is slumped on the examination table, one hand pressed to her side, her coat soaked with blood. Her face is gray, her breathing shallow. "I... Was mugged... Stabbed... Near the station," she gasps. "Hurts to breathe..."

I grab the trauma trolley. "Get her on oxygen. Start a large-bore IV—wide open fluids. I want crossmatch blood sent to the lab and a trauma panel drawn."

I press down on the wound with gauze, my gloves slick with blood. "Suspected internal bleeding. Alert the surgical registrar. And get a FAST scan in here, now."

My voice stays steady, even though adrenaline surges through me.

The crash team arrives seconds later.

By the time the rush of patients slows, it's past nine p.m. I've been on duty for more than twelve hours.

I've forgone my entitled breaks, barely pausing to grab a drink of water. My eyes are scratchy, and my throat hurts. The makings of a headache bang at the backs of my eyeballs. *Someone page me a nap and an IV drip.* I might have overdone it a tad.

I should have stopped for a bite to eat. My stomach feels so hollow, the walls of my intestines may have fused. Medically, an impossibility, I try to tell myself.

I stagger toward the changing room, too tired to do more than wash my hands and face. I grab my oversized bag and make my way out. Now that I have a moment to catch my breath, Emma's worries about the looming closure of the ER catch up with me.

The administration has been threatening to cut this department for months, but it's unclear whether they'll actually do it. I have to believe they won't, for the sake of the surrounding neighborhood that depends on it. And for my own sake.

I need the nonstop urgency of the ER to keep myself from examining too closely the disaster of my own life.

It's dark when I step past the main doors of the hospital. I draw in deep breaths of the cool night air, take a few steps forward, then come to a stop at the site of where Mr. Hot & Mysterious rescued the cat this morning. Interestingly, despite not having a second to spare all day, thoughts of his deep, dark voice have not completely faded from my mind.

That has never happened before.

I've never thought of Drew when I'm at work... Except when I run into him. But this unknown cat whisperer? I can't stop thinking of him.

I'm too tired to even hook on my earbuds and listen to my podcast. Instead, I allow my body to lead as I trace my steps back home.

At least, I'm not dreading going home. I checked the rotation in the hospital to make sure Drew's on shift. *Fringe benefits of working in the same place, huh?* I snicker. I won't have to tiptoe around my own living room. Hopefully, he'll move on soon, and I won't have to avoid my own home anymore.

By the time I reach the turn off to my lane, I'm ready for a hot shower and bed, when a noise reaches me.

The hair on the back of my neck rises. I jerk my chin up and stare in the direction of where the sound came from.

"Who's there?"

4

Connor

Bloody hell, she nearly caught me again.

This morning, I risked everything by breaking cover near her hospital to rescue that damn kitten.

She saw me. But I slipped away before she could make contact.

Now she's on her street again. Pausing. Looking around her. She scans the darkness like she *knows* I'm out here.

I freeze.

There's no way she can see me from this distance, not at this hour. Still, I hold my breath. My grip tightens on the steering wheel. I don't even blink.

Why did she stop like that? What exactly did she *feel*?

I'm parked far enough away. I've done this kind of surveillance a hundred times. Hell, a thousand. Most people never even get a twinge. But her? She picks up on me like I'm transmitting on a private frequency only she can hear.

A full ten seconds pass before she finally walks up her path and disappears inside. The front door shuts with a quiet click.

Only then, do I let the tension bleed out in a slow exhale.

She left the lights on again. She always does. All day, every day. Maybe it's a comfort to her, so she doesn't feel like she's coming home to an empty house?

I scan the surroundings of her house, my training as an undercover operative kicking in. Never let down your guard; that's the first rule.

The second? Never get involved with those who know you in your undercover life.

I'm on a sabbatical from MI5.

She is my current assignment. And I already crossed the line of being personally involved, considering it's my best friend who asked me to watch out for his little sister.

Still, I can only do my job if I keep some distance, which means, trying my best to ignore this draw toward her.

With half my attention still on her house, I reach for the tablet on the passenger seat. I ignore the open tab: a dense research paper on recent trauma protocols.

I already speed-read it, along with the core textbooks in emergency medicine.

Just enough to hold my own in her world.

When you've got an IQ north of 150, it's not hard to absorb the material. The real challenge is understanding how she thinks. What drives her, what keeps her tethered to a job that demands everything.

I want to know it all. That's the first step to getting under her skin. And staying there.

I pull up the report I worked on earlier for James and send it to him. As I've done over the last three weeks, I video call him.

He picks up on the second ring. "How is she?"

"She seems fine."

"What do you mean *seems*?"

I choose my words carefully, not wanting to let on how personally involved I already am on this assignment.

"Nothing's changed since my last report. She works all day.

Comes home so late, there's only time for her to sleep. Tomorrow is her day off, so I'm hoping she'll be out and about."

"Hmm." James rubs his jaw. "She *is* an ER doctor, and they work long hours, but you're right. The fact that she hasn't been out the entire week, except for the hospital and home, isn't very healthy."

He exhales hard. "I'm a shit brother. I should have been more involved in her life." He drags his fingers through his hair. "Thanks for doing this, bro. I appreciate it." His tone is gruff.

I feel guilty that I'm so invested; this has gone beyond professional. No way, can I tell James that… *Yet.*

If I do, he'll pull me off the surveillance and hand it over to someone else. The thought of any other man parked in my place and watching her ties my guts in knots.

Nope. No way, am I letting that happen. 'Course I'll let him know about my growing attraction to his sister—just not yet.

"I'll keep the surveillance going and report back." I hang up and settle back in my seat to wait.

My stomach grumbles. I skipped lunch, not wanting to vacate the parking spot I found near the hospital, and I'd give my right arm for some coffee to help me stay awake. But this is not the first time I've been on a solo observation job.

It *is* the first time I haven't had anyone backing me up as a base team. It's only me. And frankly, I'm glad.

I feel greedy for every single opportunity to catch a glimpse of her, so the physical discomfort I'm going through is worth it.

I move around and find a more comfortable position in my seat. Those years on recon missions have trained me to keep watch without falling asleep.

Still, when morning dawns and she leaves the house, I'm relieved. Even *I* have limits to my endurance. Only, I'd never vacate my post. Not as long as she's in there.

She's wearing a sunny yellow dress with a denim jacket and sandals today. And instead of her oversized backpack, she has a crossbody bag slung between her breasts. Hmm. I'm glad she's going out to enjoy her day off. She needs the downtime.

I wait as she heads down the sidewalk. Good thing, too. Because she suddenly stops, pivots and scans the road.

Thankfully, I'm parked at the top of the street, so she shouldn't be able to make out my figure. Still, the fact that she looks around tells me, I need to be more discreet in the future.

She's nearly caught me twice now. Once could've been chance. Twice feels like something else. *Could I have slipped up on purpose?* Some reckless part of me wanting her to see me. To stop hiding, to finally speak to her, to tell her the truth? No. That's not possible.

I've only been watching her a few weeks. Not nearly enough time to grow attached. And yet... I'm not acting like myself. I've handled riskier assignments without so much as a blink. Never once, have I let personal feelings interfere. Never once, have I begun to care for the person I'm tracking.

But this isn't an assignment. It's a favor to James. That's what I keep telling myself. I'm doing this for him. To watch out for his sister.

And that's exactly why I *can't* cross that line. He trusted me. I won't repay that trust by acting on something as stupid—and dangerous—as attraction.

Finally, she turns and keeps walking.

Only once she's gone, do I let myself breathe.

After she rounds the corner, I get out of the van, lock it, and follow—just in time to see her vanish down the next street.

She reaches the crosswalk and, as she waits for the light, taps her chest three times. Familiar ritual. I've seen her do this before. Is it a nervous tic, or something deeper?

The light turns green. She crosses.

Twenty minutes later, she steps onto Primrose Hill High Street.

She heads to the bookshop called The Sp!cy Booktok. I give it another ten minutes, then make my way down the street. I stop in front of a book display in the window. I feign interest in the book title—*The Unwanted Wife* by L. Steele—then let my gaze wander across the inside of the store.

She's at the shelf featuring books on sale. She's in profile, but I can make out the smile on her face. Her shoulders are relaxed. She runs her fingers down the spines of the books on the middle shelf.

A shiver curls down my spine.

Then she stops at a book, partially extracts the volume, and… I can imagine her curling those slender fingers around my cock.

The blood drains to my groin, and I groan aloud. I need to get a grip on my imagination. She pulls off her hair tie, moves to put it in her purse, but it slips to the floor.

Her thick auburn hair flows around her shoulders; I can imagine the whisper of the strands over my skin. My thigh muscles bunch. My blood pressure shoots up. I feel dizzy with longing and shake my head to clear it.

Then, because I've stood there long enough and don't want to attract attention, and because she's moved deeper into the store, and I reckon she's preoccupied and won't notice me, I step inside. The bell over the door tinkles. The assistant behind the counter is busy with someone else. Good. The less people who see me, the better. I pull down my baseball cap to avoid my features being captured by the security cameras inside.

I head for the secondhand section and locate the sparkly hair tie on the floor. Before pocketing it, I lift it to my nose and sniff: a trace of roses; deeper notes of jasmine; an underlying strain of vanilla. My already hard cock lengthens further. I want to roll around in her scent like a rutting canine.

My heart leaps in my chest. I feel like a five-year-old who's been told Christmas comes early this year. I have something of hers. *With me.*

I close my fingers around the hair tie, very aware that my behavior is not normal. That I'm acting like someone obsessed. That I have already crossed the line between surveillance and having a personal interest in my subject—some might call it stalking—and there's no going back.

I stop myself from groaning aloud, and speed-read the titles on the shelf in front of me.

Self-help books dominate the shelf: *Dealing with Grief. How to Recover from Burnout. Coping with Trauma.*

Why would she want to read these? Then again, given her line of work, it makes sense.

But right beside them—like a defiant splash of color—sit *Around the World in Eighty Days* and *Five Weeks in a Balloon* by Jules Verne, alongside *Balloonatics: How I Learned to Love the Air and Let It Love Me Back* by Richard E. Hamlin.

O-k-a-y, she may also have a thing for hot air balloons.

I can't resist touching the spines of the books. Is it my imagination or does her warmth linger on them?

"I love the classics!" A woman's high-pitched voice gushes behind me. "These are a great choice."

"Jane Eyre is my favorite. I have a weakness for independent, resilient heroines wary of relying on powerful men." Another voice—softer, more melodic—reaches me.

It's *her* voice. I've never heard her speak. But I have no doubt that's her. Like the tinkling of chimes in the breeze. There's an underlying sadness which is evocative, a haunting quality to her chuckle which makes me want to scoop her up in my arms, take her home, and make her laugh until whatever is bothering her fades away, leaving only sunshine and satisfaction in its wake.

"That's the transaction gone through for you." The shop assistant says brightly. Then I hear the crinkle of paper. That must be the books being handed over.

"Thank you so much. Say hi to Gio," Phoenix tells the woman behind the counter. Her footsteps fade.

I pretend to peruse the books for a few minutes more. When the bell over the door tinkles, I know she's left.

I spin around and make my way out. Just in time, as she's standing in front of a shop window. She stares at the display for several minutes, then seems to tear herself away. She walks down the sidewalk and enters a coffee shop at the end of the street.

I amble along, coming to a stop in front of the same shop window. It's Karma West Sovrano's atelier. The label now belongs to her husband Michael, who's a friend of the Davenports.

The display at the window is of a wedding dress. I don't know shit about them, but it's clear to me this one has been crafted with care. It's a vision of lace and tulle, and so ethereal, it feels like it would fall apart if you blew on it. I have no doubt; it would look spectacular on her. Imagining her in this dress, with the veil shimmering from where it's pinned to her hair…

Her, in a wedding dress? Why does that feel so right? Why does it feel like I've waited my entire life to stand here and picture this beautiful woman dressed in white walking down the aisle toward me? My breath whooshes out. It feels like I took a kick to the chest. Whoa.

Am I thinking of a future with her? Am I thinking of her as *my* wife?

Out of the corner of my eye, I see her step out of the coffee shop, a cup in her hand. I wait until she turns the corner, then head in her direction. I try to shut down the miasma of emotions the vision of her as my bride provokes in me. I draw in a breath. Another.

I draw on the techniques that help me ground myself on undercover missions, the same ones which helped me keep my composure in my life before that, as a biochemist working on life-changing discoveries in the laboratory. My sight clears. My world rights.

I turn the corner and find she's entering the gates of a primary school up ahead. I read the temporary sign at the gates.

Primrose Hill Farmer's Market

It runs on weekends. I walk in, take in the rows of stalls and the people meandering among them. Even in a crowd, she's the one my eyes go to. Like my mind's been rewired for it.

I keep a half-stall's length behind her, blending into the slow current of shoppers drifting between crates of heirloom tomatoes and bunches of strawberries.

Taking sips from her cup, she meanders past stalls selling handmade clothes, trinkets and paintings. She tosses her cup into a recycling bin and pauses near a candle stall. I hang back behind a trellis of hanging herbs, half-shadowed beneath the canvas overhead.

She lifts a candle jar. She uncaps it, brings it close to her face, then closes her eyes.

The world stops moving.

She's beautiful like that. Unaware. Open. Something in her face softens as she breathes it in. It's as if the sharp edges inside her have dulled. The tension seems to flow out of her shoulders.

Making sure to keep out of her sight, I step close.

She sniffs the candle. "Smells like secondhand books." She smiles at the vendor. "If I believed in indulgence... I'd get this."

She places it back on the table, slow and reluctant. Like it hurts to let it go.

That tiny gesture—that split-second flash of longing—punches me straight in the gut.

This woman barely lets herself *want*. I've watched her for weeks. She's always rushing, always working, always pushing herself past the point of exhaustion. Her hair's always scraped back like she doesn't have time to bother. Her clothes? Functional. Her meals? No doubt, she forgets to eat them. She gives her all to everyone else and keeps nothing for herself.

And now, here she is, denying herself a small joy. A damn candle.

I clench my jaw. *No.*

She should have everything she desires. Everything. And I want to be the one to give it to her. I *will* be the one. I want to be the reason she stops second-guessing her own worth. The reason she reaches for beauty, for comfort, for pleasure. And takes it without apology.

The desire to care for her grips me with a ferocity that makes my hands curl into fists. I want to protect her. Pamper her. Possess her. I want to be the only man she ever leans on.

That's it.

I'm done watching.

I'm done waiting.

I'm all in. *No going back.*

I wait until she's moved on, then step up to the vendor's table.

"That one." I point to the candle she touched. I resist the urge to touch it, to absorb the lingering warmth from her fingers, her scent mixed in with that of the candle.

The vendor eyes me. "The India Ink?"

Of course, she'd choose something related to the written word. Her first stop on a rare day off was the bookshop, after all. I nod.

"Should I wrap it up?"

I glance down the row of stalls toward where Phoenix is sampling a tiny paper cup filled with juice. A strand of hair falls over her cheek. My fingers itch to walk over and tuck it behind her ear. Then, she stiffens and begins to turn in my direction.

On instinct, I step to the side and out of sight on the other side of the stall.

The stall owner arches an eyebrow. "I'll take that as yes." He wraps it up.

I pay for it and accept the paper bag from the vendor. Then follow Phe at a safe distance.

I watch as she stops to sample some cheese, exchanges words with a vendor selling the kinds of trinkets that women seem to prefer, then buys some blueberries before she heads for the exit.

She begins to retrace her steps home.

I follow her, ducking behind an SUV parked at the bottom of her street. There's a VW van in front of it, so there's no way she can spot me.

She veers onto the path leading from the sidewalk to her house. She pauses mid-step, and my heart seizes in my chest. She turns and glances down the street, right toward my van, and *bam-bam-bam*, my heart explodes back into action. My breath comes in short pants, like I've run for miles.

This is the moment. *This* is when it all changes.

This is when she walks over, when she follows the pull, she doesn't even realize is guiding her. When she steps out of her world and into mine. When I stop being just a shadow at the edge of her life and become real to her.

I brace myself.

This is when she sees me. Really sees me. When I get to meet her gaze—those gorgeous hazel eyes that have haunted me for weeks— and say, *I'm the one who's been watching over you. I'm the one who knows you better than anyone else ever will.*

A weight lifts off my chest, so massive, it makes me dizzy. I'm done hiding. Done watching from a distance. Done pretending I can keep this professional.

If she comes over and looks into my face, I'll be reborn.

And if she doesn't? Fuck it. *I'm done waiting.* Because whether she's ready or not, it's time.

Time for me to step out of the dark. Time for her to finally see me. To know I'm not going anywhere.

Not now.

Not ever.

I wait... Wait... As she takes a step in my direction.

5

Phoenix

I take a step forward, scan the street, then stop. Once again, there's no one. But the hair on the back of my neck prickles. That now familiar feeling of being watched is back.

I take in the parked cars, including the VW van I passed earlier.

I look across the street. Other than the cars, and the lights on in my neighbor's house, there's nothing to be seen.

It's probably heightened vigilance. A response to the stress I face daily in the ER... Add to that, the situation with Drew, and yeah, it's probably my amygdala firing overtime after too many sleepless shifts and too much cortisol.

My mind isn't betraying me. It's just overcompensating. That's all.

I shake my head and turn toward my place. No one's following me. Maybe, I'm so exhausted that my mind is playing tricks on me.

Still, I hasten my pace and only let myself relax when I'm behind the locked doors of my house. I can tell it's empty.

The door to the guest room is slightly ajar. Drew must have left it that way. Thankfully, he's away on his shift. I'm glad he's not home. I'm not ready for another confrontation with him.

I head into my bedroom. A quick shower later, I heat up a microwave dinner, catch half a movie, and am in bed by 9:30 p.m.

I broke up with Drew, but my routine hasn't varied. Nothing feels different. This is why I told him we were barely a couple. Whether I'm with him or not, there's no discernable change to my life. Except for the guilt I carry around in my heart.

I fall into a troubled sleep, punctuated by dreams of someone watching me. I'm awake before my alarm goes off. I don't feel very refreshed. By 6:30 a.m., I'm showered and dressed.

Carrying my backpack, I head into the kitchen to get a coffee and come to a stop.

Drew sits at the tiny breakfast nook. He's hunched over a glass of water, staring into its depths.

He prefers to use the back door to come and go. He also parks his bicycle near the back of the house, where he can access a bike path to the hospital.

I've accepted it the way I've accepted the scratchy blanket he added to our—I guess, mine again—bed. Without complaint. Without emotion.

Maybe, it's because he's my superior in the hospital, and I've allowed that to influence my behavior toward him at home.

The one thing I was adamant about? That we not publicize our relationship. I didn't want anyone thinking I was getting special treatment at work.

I walk over to the other side of the breakfast counter. He looks up. His face expressionless, his eyes heavy with exhaustion.

Something tugs at my chest. Maybe pity. Maybe guilt.

I don't love him. I never have. But after nearly a year together, of which we lived together for nine of them, part of me feels responsible, for him.

This was my house. I found it, made it mine. Then he moved in and made it his too.

I didn't want that.

I knew from the start, he wasn't the man I'd spend my life with. But he was so sure, so convinced, that I went along.

Now, I want him to move on, but he's struggling. I can see it in the slump of his shoulders; in the way he clings to this place. I get it. Change is hard, especially when you're leaving what you've come to call home.

In some ways, this is my fault. If I'd told him no, back then—if I'd set that boundary—we wouldn't be here. And because of that, I want to see him land on his feet.

But wanting the best for him doesn't change the truth: we're over.

I have to make sure he understands that too. For his sake. *For mine.*

Keeping him here is only postponing the inevitable. He needs to leave. And if I don't tell him now—if I keep skirting around it—we'll both stay trapped in something that's already dead.

I take a breath that barely makes it past my ribs. My hands are clammy. My heart's pounding so loudly, I swear, he can hear it.

Still—I square my shoulders, count to three under my breath, and push the words out before they can claw their way back down my throat.

"I'm sorry it didn't work out." My voice shakes.

I wrap my arms about my waist to support myself.

"I know what I said came as a shock. Perhaps, I should've said it sooner. But I kept putting it off because… I didn't want to hurt you."

I meet his eyes, even though it makes my stomach flip. "You're upset now; I get that. But I think you'll be happier without me, in the long run."

He doesn't say a word. Just picks up his glass and takes a slow, measured sip, eyes locked on mine—expression blank, but sharp enough to cut. The silence isn't passive. It's pointed. Designed to make me squirm. Ugh! That's classic Drew.

He doesn't need to raise his voice or argue. Just sits there, looking wounded and disappointed, like I've let him down in some unforgivable way. But I'm not going to let him get to me.

I force myself to keep going, even though my throat's tight, and my legs are trembling.

I have to. Otherwise, I'll cave. And I can't do that—not this time.

"Given we're no longer together…" My voice dips. I swallow and try again. "I think you should move out."

My pulse is a freight train. My lungs can't seem to fill. I feel dizzy. Like I might throw up.

But I said it. The first real step toward disentangling our lives.

The one I should have taken months ago.

His lips curl into a sneer. "You're so anxious to get me out of your life; you don't care what happens to me."

Oh God. I hate these confrontations. I wish I could run out of here and not have to complete this conversation, but I've started it. It's best I see it through. *You can do this. Don't be a weakling. You're an ER doctor. You've faced far worse crises.* Somehow, saving someone's life feels so much easier than trying to salvage my own.

"That's not true." I tap my chest three times, taking comfort in the familiarity of the technique I use to get my emotions under control. "I *do* care about you. Just not in a way that I want to spend my life with you."

His eyes narrow, then the fight seems to go out of him. His lips turn down. "You break up with me suddenly. Now, you want me to leave the place I've come to call home?"

He looks so pathetic, I feel my resolve waver. I'm such a bleeding heart. I kept putting off breaking up with him… And see where that got me?

Trapped in this house I used to love—this place that was supposed to be mine, my sanctuary. But now, I can't breathe here. Not with Drew still under the same roof.

It's my fault for letting it go on this long. For not speaking up. For avoiding the confrontation.

Go on…give him an ultimatum. You owe it to yourself.

I manage to paste on a smile that I'm sure makes my face look sickly. "You don't have to do so today… But maybe…within the next month?" I lock my fingers together. "Once you find a new place?"

He sets his jaw.

Oh no, he's going to ask for more time. I don't want that, now that we're officially broken up. Seeing him around the house...is stressful. Not to mention, uncomfortable.

When Drew settles for nodding, relief fills me.

"Right then." I nod briskly. "I'm off."

If only he were gone by the time I return home. Clearly, that's not going to happen. Still, I can hope, right?

Deciding to forego the coffee, I spin around and walk out the door.

My mind is so preoccupied with our encounter that I forget to look out for the white van, or for anyone watching me.

Before I know it, I'm at the locker room in the hospital. I deposit my stuff and change into a fresh pair of scrubs. Damn, I forgot to buy new work shoes. I slip on the ugly, oversized, borrowed clogs.

The hiss of the automatic doors gives way to the low murmur of voices, the steady blip of machines, the quiet chaos that always simmers just beneath the surface in the ER. I draw in a breath—sterile air, laced with antiseptic and adrenaline—and step through.

The triage station is buzzing. The whiteboard's half-filled. I clock at least four patients waiting in chairs—one cradling an arm, another with blood trickling from a forehead gash.

"Dr. Hamilton." A nurse nods and hands me a freshly printed triage sheet. "Cubicle two. Shortness of breath, chest pain."

"Got it." I take the page and pivot without breaking stride.

My clogs cuff across the linoleum as I draw back the curtain to the first cubicle. I really do need to buy a new pair of sneakers. I push the thought aside and focus on the patient.

He's a man in his sixties, pale, sweating who meets my gaze with a haunted sort of panic. "Feels like someone's sitting on my rib cage." He swallows.

"Let's get that sorted." I grip his wrist gently, feel his rapid, shallow pulse.

Out of the corner of my eye, I see my colleague Sunita, appear with the portable ECG trolley. She moves with her usual competence, but her shoulders are slumped.

There's a tension in the way she tapes the leads, in the way she bites the inside of her cheek between movements.

I file it away. First, I need to stabilize the patient. "Let's run the ECG and get a troponin test. Stat."

"On it," Sunita murmurs, voice tight.

Minutes later, once the man is hooked up and monitored, I pull the curtain closed behind me and fall into step beside her.

"You, okay?" I ask, keeping my tone low, neutral.

She doesn't answer immediately. We pass the meds trolley, the crash cart. Then she exhales, a long, shuddering breath. "I'm fine," she says. Then — "No. I'm not. Sorry."

We stop near the break room. Her hand clutches the strap of her lanyard like it's the only thing keeping her grounded.

"My mum's getting worse," she says in a rush. "The caregiver quit, and the agency quoted me double for a replacement. If the ER shuts down—if they don't reassign us—I'm screwed."

"They can't just shut down the ER," I say with an edge of desper-ation because I want to believe that's true, though the hollow in the pit of my stomach tells me anything is possible during these times of price increases and budget cuts. I shove that thought away and nod. "This community depends on it. Look at how swamped we are."

I wave my hand in the air.

"And even if it does, I think they'd still reallocate us to other roles within the hospital?"

"*Maybe*, they'll redeploy us somewhere else. But where? Urology? Surgical ward? I can't go back onto nights. I'm the one who gets Mum sorted in the evenings, before she goes to bed. If I lose this schedule, I can't be there for her...and if I lose this job altogether, the mortgage doesn't get paid."

Her voice cracks, and she presses the back of her hand to her mouth like she can push the emotion back inside.

Someone calls out my name.

"Go on." She blows out a breath. "I didn't mean to unload on you."

"Anytime. I'll bring you a cuppa in a bit." I move on, but Sunita's teary face lingers in my mind.

As I head toward the assessment area, my fellow ER doctor, John nods in my direction. I've seen him put patients at ease with his calm voice and gentle manner. Today though, he appears stressed in a way I've never seen before.

"Rough night?"

He nods, then yawns wide enough for his jaw to crack. "Friday nights are always full on. Not to mention, the lack of doctors on call. The layoffs are taking a toll on us."

The hospital has always had funding problems. But things took a turn for the worse when they let go of support staff last month.

"I have two mortgages and three kids to put through college. If they shut down this ER, I'm going to be pissed." He yawns again.

When two of my colleagues bring up the issue within minutes of each other, I know things must be serious.

"Surely, they can't do that." I stuff my hand into the pocket of my scrubs.

He scoffs. "The management has no idea what it's like to be on the front lines." He shakes his head to clear it.

"There's an online fundraiser to raise money, which I contributed to." I shuffle my feet. "Hopefully that will help?"

"I'm afraid it's a drop in the bucket." A look of resignation settles on his features. "Besides it's not only about the money."

"What do you mean?"

His lips turn down. "Without someone advocating for us at the top-most echelons of the system we may not have a chance."

He walks away, leaving my thoughts racing in my head.

If this place shuts down, I'll be heartbroken. It's been more of a home to me than my own. I've spent so much time here, in many ways, I've come to know the people I work with better than my own family. And while I could find work at another hospital... I feel a certain emotional connection to this one, given the number of hours I've spent here.

Surely, the higher-ups will come up with a plan to save it. This is the only ER in the borough, and it provides vital services.

I compose myself and head back to where patients have been

triaged, ready for examination. I'm about to pull aside the curtain to the first cubicle when a nurse appears at my elbow.

"You're needed in another bay, Dr. Hamilton."

I must have been about to walk into the wrong one—it happens more often than I'd like to admit.

She leads me down the row to the last cubicle, pulls the curtain aside, and I step in. The rings scrape along the rail as she closes it behind me.

"I'm Dr. Hamilton." I walk forward. "What brings you here today?"

The man seated on the clinical table tips up his chin and looks straight at me.

There's something familiar about him. Where have I seen him before?

Blue eyes so pale, they seem to reflect my image. It feels like I'm drowning in his eyes. *Like he's drowning in mine.* His hair is cut so short, there's less than half an inch on top of his head.

I can see the brown of his scalp which, for some reason, I find appealing. He has an intelligent forehead, currently bisected by a cut on his temple with blood trickling down. His eyelashes are thick enough to elicit envy among beauty influencers. High cheekbones, sharp enough to double up as scalpels. Straight nose, stern upper lip. He's all planes and angles. All austere. His features are stern enough that they could be labeled as mean, but for that sensuous lower lip. One which is currently cut. And which only adds to his appeal.

I should be thinking of how to fix his wounds, but I can't seem to get past the shape of that mouth. Its pillow-like puffiness—accentuated by the cut—hints at forbidden pleasures. And long steamy nights. And wicked things he could be capable of. Things which could bring me a lot of gratification. And pleasure. *So much pleasure.*

I swallow. And then, there's that chin, with a hint of a dip in the middle, which only adds to his appeal. Those beautiful cords of his throat lead to the neckline of the T-shirt he's wearing.

A scarred leather jacket hugs the breadth of his shoulders. So massive, they block out the room behind him. The sleeves outline the powerful muscles of his biceps. *Biceps which threatened to burst the seams of his jacket's sleeves when he swung himself up the tree.*

Before I can stop myself, the words burst out, "You're the one who rescued the cat outside the hospital."

6

Phoenix

"Guilty as charged, Doc." His voice is pure gravel and sin—low, rough, with a dark edge—like thick, hot fudge you dig out with a spoon.

It rips through me like an adrenaline shot to the heart, flooding my veins before sparking outward, leaving even my fingertips aching for release.

I swallow to stop the moan that whips up my throat.

"What are you doing in my ER?"

Surely, it's not a coincidence that he's here now?

"*Your* ER?" he drawls.

That voice shouldn't be legal. It does things to my autonomic nervous system I can't explain. Makes my breath hitch, my pulse flutter, my common sense short-circuit.

Doesn't change the fact that he's right.

I wish I could play it cool. Wish I was one of the doctors who could shrug off the possible ER closure like it was another administrative hiccup. But I'm not.

I care too much.

I take on too much. I say yes when I'm already drowning. Maybe, it goes back to my mother. Wanting to make her proud. Wanting to be enough.

My siblings and I were all adopted, but it always felt like my mother held me to a different standard. Stricter. More alert. *The curse of being the only girl with a bunch of brothers.*

She tried to mold me into her mini-me. Ladylike. Prim and proper. *So not me.* So, I pushed back. I rebelled. I tried to prove I didn't care. But I did. More than I ever let on.

I've spent most of my life trying to earn something I never knew how to ask for her approval, her trust. Her love. I mean, I know she loved me, but it always felt conditional, like I was a disappointment. I don't need a therapist to tell me that's where my overdeveloped sense of responsibility comes from.

I left home at eighteen, thinking I was claiming my freedom… But the guilt followed me. It always does.

Maybe, that's why I pour myself into the ER. Why I jump into every crisis like it's mine to fix.

And I wish sometimes that it didn't cost me so much to feel everything this deeply. Life would be easier if I didn't.

I wave a shaky hand.

"I didn't literally mean it's *my* ER. Just that I've been here long enough to feel a sense of…ownership."

My voice cracks. I clamp my jaw shut. Yeah, that sounds weak. I'm not giving this walking daydream with a jawline and storm-colored gaze insight to my personality.

Although… Given the way he stares at me, cobalt eyes unblinking, makes me feel like he's able to read past the walls I put up against the world to the secrets I harbor inside.

A tremor spirals under my skin. I shake my head, trying to cast off the sense of disorientation gripping me.

I've just broken free of one relationship. The last thing I need is to be pulled into another man's orbit. *Or maybe, that's exactly what I need?* A diversion?

He nods slowly. "I know what you mean."

There's no hint of sarcasm on his face.

"You do?" I venture.

His gaze seems to turn inward. "When my team works on a biotech discovery that could make a difference to people, even though I may not be the one researching, I feel responsible for it. I take the outcome of every experiment personally—especially the ones that fail."

"You're a scientist?"

He smirks.

Ugh! It makes me want to slap it off. And, kiss him. Damn it, why did I ask? Why did I give him the satisfaction of knowing I'm curious?

"I'm a biochemist," he explains.

Huh. He looks more like he bench-presses bodies than test tubes.

"*And* I've worked undercover."

My eyes widen. That explains the cat rescue. The way he scaled that tree like he's done it while running for his life.

"Don't you people keep that kind of thing...secret?" I arch an eyebrow. "Or is that something you say to impress women?"

His eyes spark, lips curving like he's got my number. "Are you impressed?"

Yes. But hell, if I'll admit that.

"What I am"—I tighten my jaw—"is deeply skeptical about running into you again."

I glance at the gash on his forehead. "But first let's deal with that wound."

"Whatever you say, Doc." He tips his chin.

I survey his features once again, looking for signs of mockery, but find none.

Instinct tells me, it's rare for him to acquiesce so easily. That he's a man more accustomed to giving orders than taking them. Well, too bad. In this ER cubicle, I am the doctor, and he's, my patient.

A very sexy patient whose smirk triggers an acute spike in my core temperature.

Ovaries: on hyper alert. Blood pressure: elevated. Pulse rate: abnormally fast.

Every cell in my body seems to be in overdrive, completely fixated on him.

Then his gaze narrows. "You have an American accent."

"My mother's American. I went to the American school in London," I blurt out, then curse myself.

Why am I sharing personal information with this man? He must have shaken my composure to the extent that I'm not thinking straight.

His eyes sweep over me—slow, deliberate. A touch without contact, that leaves prickles of awareness in its wake; like powdered snow laced with shards of glass.

He could hurt me. Shatter me into something unrecognizable. Break me down and rebuild me in an image that serves his desire. And the twisted part? I'd let him. I'd want it. The idea of pleasing him—being remade for him—sends a pulse of heat through my chest.

I shiver. *God, what a thought.* But it clings to me, sharp and sweet. A new kind of anticipation unfurls inside me. Deep, primal, unfamiliar. It climbs my spine like a live wire.

I need to get on with treating him. Need to do my job.

I tear my gaze from his. Immediately, air fills my lungs. *Good God, surely this is how it must feel to be extubated without warning: raw, exposed, but finally able to breathe on my own.*

I pick up the paperwork, and scan through it. I'm not surprised to find my fingers are shaking. I compose myself.

"Connor Davenport. Thirty-five years. You were in a bar fight?" I ask without looking at him.

If I do, I'm going to be drawn into this strange chemistry between us again, and I don't want that happening.

"The triage nurse was thorough," he rumbles.

I ignore the instant leap to attention from various parts of my body and focus on the paperwork. Reading it until the end, I set it aside.

"Take off your clothes." My voice comes out husky. Like we're in the bedroom instead of this examination room with its harsh fluorescent lights and tiles made of vinyl.

He arches an eyebrow.

My flush deepens. I clear my throat and try again, pleased when my tone is brisk instead of breathy. "I mean, please take off your jacket and T-shirt so I can examine your wounds." I keep my expression impersonal. "There's blood on your T-shirt, under your jacket, which is ripped."

He glances down at himself, then unfolds his body and rises to his feet. And keeps rising.

The promise of the breadth of his shoulders and of the width of his palms is borne out when I tilt my head back, then further back, to see his features. *He's tall.* As tall as my brother James, who's six-feet-four-inches.

The man shrugs off his jacket, dropping it on the treatment table.

I have a brief impression of the blood blotting the side of his T-shirt. Then he reaches behind himself—winces—and pulls it off.

Holy serotonin overdose. I draw in a sharp breath at the sight of acres of golden-brown skin, tanned by the sun. His pectoral muscles are well developed enough to warrant a dip between them. Very male nipples, and corrugated abs form an eight-pack.

Yep, an honest-to-life eight-pack, marred by an ugly bruise over his ribs on the right side. The skin is mottled and turning purple. Blood from the cut has dripped onto his jeans.

My gaze slides down to take in the mouth-watering iliac furrows on either side swooping down to the waistband of his pants. He flicks open the button, lowering his zipper.

The r-r-r-i-pping sound ricochets off the walls of the room and seems to hit me in my chest. My pulse shoots through the roof. I want him to shuck off his jeans so badly. It's the hunger in me which brings me to my senses.

"S-stop," I croak. "You can keep your pants on." I stumble over the words like I'm thirteen, instead of a qualified trauma specialist. I need to get a grip on my emotions.

"As you wish, Doc," he drawls.

That last word feels like a caress coming from him. Another shiver squeezes my lower belly. Ridiculous. I close the distance toward him. With each step I take, expectation pitches in my chest. I am conscious of the fact he's watching me closely as I inch toward him.

Under that sharp astringent hospital smell is something dark and smoky, like a distant campfire on a star-drenched night, with a hint of leather, maybe, from his jacket. And something else unique. Intoxicating. The scent of his skin, perhaps?

Just as I'm congratulating myself on completing what feels like a walk of shame as I near him, I stumble and pitch forward.

7

Connor

I hold out my arms, and she falls into them. Against my bare chest, right over the wound. Pain zings up my spine, sharp and electric, but it's nothing compared to the jolt of her touch. Slim fingers. Pale. Nails short, unpainted. Unadorned. And yet, I've never seen anything more beautiful.

I pull her closer. Her hair brushes my cheek, and I dip my head, breathing her in. Lush roses. Sultry jasmine. A trace of vanilla. The scent hits hard—feminine, intoxicating, fucking lethal.

I caught it from her hair tie in the bookshop. It gutted me then.

Now, with her in my arms, it's more than scent. It's sacrament. It sinks into my blood, holy and overwhelming.

My groin tightens. My scalp tingles. I want to drop to my knees and worship her. Her scent, her softness, the quiet chaos she stirs in me. I grit my teeth to keep from groaning.

I've spent weeks watching her, imagining what it'd feel like to hold her. But nothing could've prepared me for this. She's soft, curvy, all temptation. I want to grip her hips, feel the give beneath my fingers. But that would ruin everything.

She just met me. I might feel like I know her, but to her, I'm still a stranger. I can't afford to fuck this up. Not when every cell in my body is screaming to claim her.

Our eyes lock. Her pupils are blown wide, just a rim of green circling the dark. And something inside me stills. Then detonates.

The space between us hums, molten and alive. The world narrows to her gaze—steady, open, unflinching—and the quiet truth it holds.

She sees me.

Not the biochemist. Not the operative. Not the heir trying to make his privilege mean something. She sees past the masks, the armor, the weight I carry.

And she doesn't flinch.

Awe unfurls in my chest, raw and unfamiliar. Like I've stumbled into something sacred I didn't earn. Like I've been cracked open and, somehow, she accepts what's inside.

And just like that, I know.

The world has shifted. I'm no longer the man I was five minutes ago. I'm standing in front of the woman who sees every brutal, broken part of me and fits anyway.

My other half. My reckoning. My redemption.

I must tighten my hold on her, because she winces. "Hey let go of me."

Her voice brings me back to myself. Reminds me I'm holding her close, sniffing her hair like a...creep.

Why not? She already turned me into a stalker.

To disguise the intensity of feelings she evokes in me, I set her aside. "You could have hurt yourself," I bite out through gritted teeth.

My blood pressure is still not normal from having seen her trip and almost face-plant.

"You could have knocked out a tooth, or broken your nose, or scarred your face." The thought sends another pulse of anger through my veins. My pulse detonates in my chest.

I cannot bear to think of how she almost left a permanent mark on her beautiful face. I can't. I lower my chin.

"Your clogs; get rid of them."

"Excuse me?" She gapes.

Goddamn, that came out too abruptly. I fight for composure and manage to calm my blood pressure somewhat.

"Your clogs are too big for you. Your gait changed right as your heel lifted. That only happens when the shoe's too loose—which means, they're new or borrowed—and your foot's trying to grip."

I glower at the offending yellow contraptions.

"And judging by the slight swelling at your ankle? You've been on your feet for hours."

I swivel my gaze up to her face.

"Did you skip your last break? You're a doctor; you should know better than that."

"I… You…" She seems to be at a loss for words.

"It's not a criticism. Just an observation." I try to soften my words.

"My clogs *are* borrowed," she says slowly. "Not that it's any of your business."

"You're my doctor. You're here to treat me. That makes it my business. If you hurt yourself, it'll have to be *me* taking care of *you*, not the other way around. And why not wear a pair of shoes that fit —preferably ones that don't look this hideous?"

I glower at the yellow, closed-toe sandals with the thick, rigid soles. What I don't tell her is that they emphasize the delicateness of her ankles, even swollen.

"What are you, the Sherlock-of-shoes?" She scoffs.

I nod at her feet. "Am I, or am I not, right about those?"

"I haven't had a chance to buy new sneakers, so you're right about that." She waves a hand in the air and takes another step back as if to put distance between us. "And you're very observant."

I see patterns. Connect dots most people don't even notice. Though, in this case, it was simple deduction. "It was nothing." I shrug.

"I can't tell if you're being sarcastic, or modest." She's talking a little too fast. Clearly, she's nervous. That only adds to her appeal.

Toe-to-toe, she barely comes up to my chest. I'm, at least, a foot taller than her. I've always been a big guy. I've learned, over the years, how to relax my body so I appear non-threatening on my undercover missions. But next to her curvy, petite form, I feel like a giant. I sink back onto the examination table.

She takes that as an invitation to get on with her examination. "You're going to need stitches." She peers at my forehead and begins gathering the items she'll need.

I slide my thighs apart in invitation. She hesitates. Then, because that's the best way to examine the wound I sport, she steps between them.

Her cheeks flush, but her fingers are confident when she pulls out a pencil-shaped flashlight and shines it in my eyes.

Blinded, I blink, then manage to keep my eyes open. She makes a humming sound which could mean anything, in the way that doctors often do.

She switches off the flashlight and places it aside.

Then moves her finger in front of my eyes. I follow the direction.

"No concussion." Movements brisk, she touches the skin next to the dried blood on my forehead. My muscles jump. Sensations zip up my spine. It takes everything in me not to groan. I curl my fingers into fists, press my feet into the floor, and will my body to relax. Impossible, when every tendon in my body seems to have turned to steel. And the muscle between my legs to granite.

She presses down on the skin, and pain shudders out from the point of contact. Still, I make no sound. She frowns, presses around a little more. "Does it hurt?"

Yes.

I shake my head. I'm not lying; I can bear it.

She shoots me a disbelieving look from under her eyelashes. Then presses down harder. This time, I hiss out a breath.

"So, it *does* hurt?"

"Just do what you need to," I say through gritted teeth. Sweat beads on my brow. She *is* hurting me. Just not where she imagines.

I've ached for her touch, but nothing prepared me for this.

My blood turns into lava, and my pulse rate kicks up. I want to divest her of those scrubs that do nothing to disguise the lush curves of her body and throw her down on the examination table, before I cover her body with mine.

But I don't do that. Obviously. I hope none of my thoughts show on my face. But she must hear something in my words because her movements speed up. Some more digging in with her fingers, which sends little points of pain racing under my skin, and she nods.

"No ribs broken; only bruised. So, you won't need an X-ray. You do need stitches for this, too, however."

Then she reaches over to grab the antiseptic spray from the small rolling table positioned beside us. The curve of her waist brushes my thigh, and I'm so turned on, I could come from the contact. *Damn.*

Then I'm gasping for air—this time, for real—as she sprays antiseptic on my wound.

I manage not to cry out. Which means, hopefully, I don't dispel the projection of my macho persona and impermeability to pain; *only so I can impress her.*

She straightens. "Close your eyes."

I don't let anyone order me around. But in this examination room, she's the expert. And apparently, her no-nonsense doctor's voice is a huge turn on, as evidenced by my hardening groin. I do as she says. She sprays the antiseptic on the cut over my eyebrow. Then on the one on my lower lip. The resulting burn is barely a twinge.

Eyes still closed, I hear her walk around to one of the shelves. When she asks me to lay down, I oblige, hoping the part of me that wants to stand at attention is impeded by my jeans. *Down, boy.*

Her footsteps approach. I feel the warmth of her body as she bends over to inject an anesthetic to numb the space around the cut on my eyebrow. Her scent intensifies, exacerbating the lust dancing through my veins. After weeks of watching her from afar, I'm close enough to touch her.

My fingers tingle, but I manage to keep my hands to myself. I open my eyes and see my fill of her. She must sense my gaze, for her cheeks redden. But her fingers don't stop moving. She finishes stitching my forehead, then turns toward the gash in my side.

When she touches the abraded skin around the wound with the cotton pad, I can't stop the groan which boils up.

"Sorry," she murmurs without looking up. Goosebumps pepper her skin. Interesting. And reassuring to know she feels this connection between us, too. That even though her touch is professional, the impact on her is far from it.

I sense her breathing roughen. Then she gets a hold of herself and begins to clean the wound. She follows the same protocol, numbing the space before she stitches it up.

I reach out and pocket the flashlight.

All too soon, she's done. Snipping off the thread, she steps back.

"Keep the stitches dry. They should start dissolving within ten days. You'll probably have a scar, though." She pulls off her disposable gloves and drops them in the bin. "It's only going to add to your good looks, I'm sure."

"You think I'm good-looking?" I swing my legs over the side and sit up.

She stiffens. Then, rubbing antiseptic onto her hands, turns to me. "You know you are."

"It means a lot to me to know that you think so, too."

Her expression turns cautious. "Why is that?"

"Because you're the most beautiful woman I've ever met."

She flushes and her eyes grow wide, then she tosses her head. "It's just gratitude for having stitched you up that's kicking in." She pulls a tablet from her pocket, and her fingers fly over the surface. "You're going to need to use a prophylactic antibiotic. A prescription has been sent to the hospital pharmacy. You can pick it up there. Make sure you apply it daily until the wound is healed."

She pockets the device, hooks her stethoscope around her neck, then looks around, no doubt, searching for the flashlight.

Then she gives up and levels me with a calm, clinical, no-nonsense look. One I'm coming to classify as her 'doctor' look.

A look which amps up the pulse in my chest...and in my wrists...

and in my balls. *I might have a doctor kink I was unaware of—but only when it comes to her.*

"Now that we have *that* out of the way..." She folds her arms across her chest. "Are you going to tell me why this is the second time I'm seeing you in such a short period of time?"

"I absolutely intend to." I lean forward until I'm peering into her eyes. "Over dinner."

"Dinner?" She blinks, the surprise evident on her face. But she doesn't step back. Which means, she's not averse to the idea. *Yes! I can work with that.*

Then she tosses her head. "That's very forward of you, isn't it? I barely know you."

"Have dinner with me, and I'll tell you everything you want to know, including...why you're going to marry me."

She bursts out laughing. "That's some ego you have."

The mirth in her voice makes me smile. *It's not ego. It's the truth.* As she's going to find out.

She pivots and moves toward the curtains drawn around the cubicle.

I should let her go, but after weeks of having watched her from a distance, we're in the same room, and I can't do it. I snake out my hand and wrap my fingers around her wrist. "Would it help if I said please?"

She stiffens, then stares down at my fingers, before looking up at me. "You're overstepping the doctor-patient relationship."

"You've treated my wounds; that relationship is now over." I hold onto her for a few seconds more. Then, I slowly retract my hand. "You also haven't told me your first name."

Of course, I know her name, but I feel compelled to keep up appearances... for now.

She heads to the curtains, pulls them aside, then turns to look at me over her shoulder. There's challenge in her eyes. "I'm not looking to date anyone right now."

8

Connor

Classified Internal File: Case Study – Phoenix Hamilton
Alias: ~~"The Doctor"~~ Doc
Objective: Surveillance and Protection per Directive J.H.
ENTRY 2
•Name: Phoenix Hamilton

- Age: 26 years. Would have trained straight through medical school, likely in her second year of foundation or early specialty training, to become a junior doctor in the ER so quickly.
- Eyes: Hazel. Irises shift to golden-green under direct light.
- Height: ~5'3"
- ~~Other distinguishing characteristics: Gorgeous curvy figure.~~

- Initial Response: Professional detachment, masks instinctual curiosity.
- Tactile Response: When her palm touched my chest, subject's pulse elevated. ~~Mine too.~~
- Vocal Pattern: Slight rasp clipped when emotionally flustered.
- Behavioral Tic: Avoids direct eye contact when aroused.
- Scent Profile: Jasmine. Roses. Vanilla.
- Notable: Uses medical terminology in conversation as defense.

Notes: Subject unaware of my identity. Initial contact successful. ~~Affects me more than anticipated.~~

9

Phoenix

> Drew: I don't believe what you told me. I
> don't believe you don't love me anymore.

I stare at the message that came through a few hours ago.

The knot of tension at the base of my neck tightens. If I reply, it'll only encourage him.

I told Drew we're over, but he shows no signs of having accepted it. I always knew he was more dependent on me, but surely, he should have begun to come to terms with it by now.

I rub at my temple. I should have told him I didn't feel the same way when he asked to move in with me. *No, I should have cut off this sham of a relationship before it even started.* But I'm so used to going along with things to keep the peace... *Not anymore. Not the new me.*

"Phoenix, did you hear my question?"

I look up with a start.

My friend's faces stare back at me around the table. I'm at The Fearless Kitten, a coffee shop in Primrose Hill where my friends hold their book club meeting. They've been begging me to join them for months, but I've resisted.

What with work and the situation with Drew, I've barely had the energy to finish my shift, come home, and fall into bed. Of course, it would help to talk through my Drew situation with them...but I haven't felt ready.

Perhaps, meeting the walking bad decision with ocean eyes and a smirk built for trouble this morning made me feel alive again.

It reminded me I have a life outside of just the ER and my home.

I do have friends who care for me.

And they've been wanting to meet up with me for months. So, I accepted their invitation.

"You asked how my day was?" I turn to Zoey.

She nods.

"High-intensity, prolonged exposure to high tension situations, with intermittent periods of caffeine administration. My prognosis: survival, but barely," I deadpan.

She chuckles. "An understatement, given the black circles under your eyes and the hollowed-out cheekbones. I'd wager you've lost weight since I last saw you...which was—" She frowns. "More than six months ago."

Well, duh! I've been stressed out enough about the situation at home to not eat or sleep properly, so it's not surprising I look terrible. And damn, has it been that long since I met up with them? I'm a terrible friend.

"It's been intense." *I'm also the master of understatements.*

But I don't want to whine about my life. Really, compared to the starving millions in the world, I have it easy—not withstanding troublesome ex's and gorgeous walking-orgasms—I mean, strangers.

I take a sip of my dirty chai latte and savor the taste of the spices. Cinnamon and star anise. It's almost as heady as the scent of the man I treated at the ER.

It's true; I'm not looking to date right now, not when I'm still not over my last relationship. But I'm tempted to make an exception, for *him.*

The two times I met that stranger, it felt like I'd been knocked off my feet. Like I'd been shot up with a cocktail of dopamine, oxytocin, and endorphins, and was spinning into the stratosphere.

It's like nothing I've experienced in my life. It would get complicated with him very quickly. Which is why I told him I don't date.

Now, I'm regretting it. *I wish there were a way I could see him again.*

If for no other reason than to confirm to myself that I didn't imagine my physical reaction to him.

Besides, I'd love to know if it was a coincidence he landed in the ER just a few days after I saw him rescue that cat. Thinking about him is a distraction. One I welcome, as it takes my mind off the possibility of the ER closing.

Not to mention, I have no idea what to do about Drew not moving out of my place.

My other friend, Grace, looks at me closely. "Zoey's right. If exhaustion were an aesthetic, you'd be the poster child."

"Thanks?" I wince. "It's been nonstop at the hospital." I drain the cup of tea and place it back on the table.

"That's because you're too busy saving the world," Zoey says in a soothing voice.

"When I'm in the ER, I'm too busy trying to survive." I raise my shoulders. "Any altruistic notions about my chosen profession were dismissed the day I dissected my first cadaver."

There's silence around the table. I look around their faces and stifle a chuckle. Their expressions vary from shock to horror to plain disgust.

"You do that to get a reaction from us," Harper complains.

I bat my eyelids. "Do what?"

Zoey chuckles. "I'm glad you're back to using medical terminology in everyday conversation. You were so morose when we last spoke, I was worried you'd lost your sense of humor."

I take in the happiness and surprise in her eyes.

"I don't think I lost it. Not completely. It was buried for a while, under the weight of everyday life, I suppose." I manage to keep my tone light.

"So, what changed?" Grace surveys me with a shrewd look in her eyes.

Of all my friends, she's the one who dislikes Drew the most. It doesn't help that they haven't met him.

I never felt serious enough about Drew to want to introduce him to my friends. But I've shared enough about him that they know I haven't been happy with him for months.

"Guess I found my mojo." I raise a shoulder.

More likely, it's the feeling of well-being from being with my friends, combined with the leftover buzz from having run into that mystery man, which is, oddly, making me feel like I've been given a new lease of life. My friends are right in saying I was lackluster the last time I saw them. I really have been avoiding them. I knew they'd ask me about Drew, and I wasn't ready to talk about him. But I am now.

"Also, I broke up with him."

Silence.

Zoey and Grace exchange a knowing look.

Harper gasps, her expression softening. "Oh no, sweetheart. I'm so sorry." She reaches for my hand. "Are you okay?"

"I am," I say, and to my surprise it's true. I feel it. In my bones.

"Are you through with him? Is there a chance you'll get back together?" Grace scans my features.

"No, there's no chance we're getting back together."

She blows out a breath of relief. "Good riddance, if you ask me. That man made you a shadow of yourself."

"Grace," Harper scolds, scandalized.

"What?" She frowns. "Life is short, and I call it like I see it."

"No kidding," Zoey mutters, then turns to me. "She's blunt, but she's not wrong. That man bled you dry."

"Zoey!" Harper shoots her a warning look.

Grace shrugs. "Come on, Harper. Phe's not made of glass." She turns to me. "We all saw it. He had a sweet gig. Moved into your place and coasted. Didn't even contribute to the mortgage, did he?"

I hesitate. "I didn't ask him to."

"Oh, honey." Grace leans in, her voice gentler now. "That's the point. A real partner *offers*. He steps up. From everything you told me he didn't."

Heat rushes to my cheeks. She's right. I let it slide. I let *everything* slide because I didn't want to start a fight. Because I felt sorry for him. Because he needed saving, and I needed to be needed. I needed him to like me. I needed his approval.

Just like I tried to do everything to gain my mother's approval growing up.

"He knew you'd hold him up, no matter what." Frustration laces Grace's voice. "He took advantage of your accommodating nature."

Zoey cuts her a glance. *Enough.*

Grace sighs, then her features soften. "Look, relationships are messy. But from where we stood... He made you doubt yourself. And you, Phe?" Her eyes shine. "You're not meant to feel small in love."

I swallow hard. A lump rises in my throat. Because she's right.

I *was* shrinking.

Drew chipped away at me—inch by inch—until I believed I wasn't good enough. For him. For anyone.

He made me think letting him go meant ending my last shot at love.

He didn't just spot my insecurities. He played on them. And I let him.

But somewhere deep down, the part of me that still believed I deserved better finally clawed its way to the surface. Things got so bad, I couldn't *not* speak up. And thank God I did.

For the first time in forever, I can breathe.

Still, hearing my friends say aloud what I've been too scared to admit... It stings, while at the same time, it validates my feelings. I shift in my seat, the truth of it stamped across my face.

"Oh, sweetie." Harper squeezes my hand in both of hers. "We're sorry you went through that. But I'm *so* proud of you for ending it."

Even Harper—our resident romantic—is relieved he's gone.

I force a laugh. "Wow. I didn't realize it looked that bad from the outside."

They exchange looks. Guilt flashes in Grace's eyes.

"Maybe I should've said something," she admits. "But we all agreed it was better you realize it on your own. We didn't want to push you away."

My gaze bounces between them. "You talked about me?"

Harper and Zoey both wince.

"We were worried," Harper says gently.

"Especially when you kept turning down plans," Zoey adds. "And when you didn't want us over at your place? We knew something wasn't right."

"Nothing was right." I curl my shoulders. "Not even close."

Harper leans in, eyes searching mine. "We didn't want to push. We just wanted you to know we were here. On your side."

"I knew that." I half smile. "That's, partly, why I stayed away. I knew, if I saw you, I'd crack. I'd spill everything. And that would mean I'd have to do something about it. I wasn't ready... So, I avoided you."

"It's okay." Zoey exhales. "Breaking up is brutal. Even when you *know* it's the right thing."

"Tell me about it." I let out a laugh. It comes out bitter, brittle. "Truth is, I was just as much to blame."

I glance at Grace, then back at them. "I chose Drew because he didn't ask much of me. I didn't have to open up. Didn't have to be real with him. It was easy... Safe... And honestly, kind of lifeless."

I swallow. *It's so difficult to say this aloud.* "It wasn't love. I knew that. And I still stayed."

There's a beat of silence. Then I add, more to myself than anyone else, "I should've ended it a long time ago. And I probably shouldn't have stayed away from you guys."

"What made you decide to meet us today?" Grace fixes me with a shrewd stare.

Of course, Grace would ask that. I look away, "Umm —" I hesitate. "I —I..." I stumble over the words, trying to form them. "I —"

Her eyes narrow. "Hold on, did you meet someone?"

"What?" I whip my gaze back to hers.

God, they're fast. I'm just starting to process what that brooding masterpiece with shoulders who could carry my emotional baggage stirred in me—how alive he made me feel. And already, they've clocked it.

With Drew, too, everything moved quickly. I told them early, made them promise to keep it quiet, since he was my boss. I knew they weren't thrilled. Especially Grace.

When he asked to move in, I buried my doubts, pretending everything was fine. But my friends saw through me.

If I'd seen them sooner, they would've pulled the truth out of me. And maybe, that wouldn't have been such a bad thing.

But I wasn't ready to admit it. Not to them. Not even to myself. So, I stayed away.

Now, I've ended things with Drew but...I'm still not completely rid of him. Ugh.

It seems like every time I go home, he's there, waiting to pick a fight with me, or just try to make me feel guilty for asking him to leave.

If I tell my friends that... I doubt they'd understand... And I get it. I need to get him to leave stat.

Meanwhile, I can't stop thinking of the man with the ice-blue gaze. I would be insane to even consider a relationship with him. I'm not ready to be involved with anyone else.

I wasn't lying when I told Drew I want to experience the kind of love that I can feel to my marrow. But now that I am on the cusp of an attraction waking up my nerve endings, sending my heart racing, and threatening to turn me inside out—the *kind of animal pull I never felt with Drew*—I'm scared of how vulnerable it's making me feel.

I'm *definitely* not ready to acknowledge it. Let alone, talk about it.

"Just so you know, if you have met someone, that's okay," Zoey says gently. "You deserve to be happy."

"And if you're thinking it's too soon?" Harper squeezes my hand. "Don't."

Grace's gaze pins me. "Knowing you, you're probably blaming yourself for everything with Drew. And if—*if*—you've met someone new, I'm guessing you feel guilty for even thinking about moving on."

She's so on point, I suck in a breath. "Wow. Don't sugarcoat it or anything."

Grace's expression softens. "Babe, cut yourself some slack. You don't get to choose when the right person walks into your life."

Harper nods. "You know what they say—falling in love never happens at the perfect time. Just the right one."

Their kindness only makes it worse. My throat burns. I look away, blinking fast.

Grace is right. I am drowning in guilt. Guilt for letting things with Drew drag on when I knew I wasn't serious. If I'd been honest from the start, we wouldn't be stuck in this mess.

And I haven't even told my friends he's still living in my flat.

The idea of moving on so soon feels... Cruel. Cold. Especially when I don't feel ready. Not for something real. And definitely not with him.

That stranger—the one who rattled me without even trying. I know he'd see straight through me. He'd tear down my walls, force me to be honest. No hiding. No playing small.

It's exhilarating. And terrifying. So, so terrifying.

"Thanks." I manage a tight smile. "But I... I'm too busy to start a relationship."

Grace's forehead furrows. She's about to comment when the woman behind the counter walks over to us and places a tray of various desserts on the table.

Finally, a distraction!

"These look amazing," Harper breathes.

"This one's a lemon slice with a crunchy base and an icing which has spikes of saffron and lemon zest." The woman points to one of the desserts. "Try it."

Harper and I each reach for a slice.

"Cheers." She raises the cake in my direction. I mirror her action.

We bite into our pastries in unison.

It's light and fluffy, and not too sweet, at all. It's so good.

Harper moans. So do I.

The woman laughs. "That's my version of a lemon tart."

"It's so good." I finish off the rest and lick my fingertips.

"I call it Zest Friends." The woman nods and smiles at the crumbs on my plate which, by the way, I'm seriously considering devouring. "I'm so happy you enjoyed it."

A shiver runs up my spine. Goosebumps pepper my forearms. A feeling like I'm being watched, once more, assails me. I glance around the warm, cozy bakery and dismiss it. Just my imagination, working overtime again.

"Skylar, meet Phoenix. Phoenix, Skylar." Zoey introduces us.

I shake Skylar's hand and smile. "Is this your place?"

She nods, her smile broadening.

"It's amazing."

"I'm glad you could join us." Skylar drops into a chair. "The girls kept telling me you were coming to try the sweets. I'm so glad you could finally make it."

"Me too." I smile back.

"You work in the ER over at Archway Hospital, don't you?"

"Guilty," I say lightly.

I don't like talking about my job. Not because I don't like what I do, but the opposite. I'm dedicated to my job. When I'm there, I give it one hundred percent. I dissociate from the world for the hours I'm there.

Which is why, when thoughts of the devil with sapphire eyes distracted me at work, I was taken aback.

I shove those thoughts aside and focus on the cakes and pastries on the tray in front of me.

"Skylar's baking skills are unrivaled. Within six months of opening the first branch of the coffee shop in the East End, she opened this one," Harper enthuses.

"Help yourself." Skylar pushes a square-shaped, chocolate-topped concoction in my direction. "I'm trying out a few new recipes."

I reach for the treat. It looks like a brownie but when I bite into it, something gooey and filled with caramel and cherry and an overlay of mint explodes on my tongue.

"Oh my God," I exclaim with my mouth full, so it comes out as 'Aw-mah-ghod!' I chew, swallow. Take another bite. Don't stop until

I've consumed the entire slab. My mouth, my stomach and everything in between feels like it's going to explode with happiness. "Pretty sure I'm presenting with rapid-onset cardio-excitability."

Skylar laughs. "Glad you like it."

"I love it." I look at the woman with new eyes. Anyone who can bake like that is truly a domestic goddess. Especially since, I'm rubbish when it comes to cooking. Sadly, my skills as a doctor don't seem to stretch to interpreting recipes.

"I think I'll call this one *Heart Stopper*," she says with a smug smile.

Harper laughs. "That's so apt."

"I do love the names of your other desserts, too." I noticed a Clitasaurus, a Honey Pot, a Moist Goodness, and a Sweet Bits in the display cases.

She chuckles. "I wanted to differentiate my offerings. And since I love reading spicy romance novels, I couldn't resist."

I'm so taken in by her joie de vivre. Her spirit. The happiness flowing off her in waves. I'd give anything to feel that way again.

I did feel that way again, briefly, when the stranger with bedroom eyes and the body made for sin, touched me in the ER.

It made me feel young and giddy, and foolish again. It made me want to straddle him and feel that thickness in his crotch rub up against my core. Made me want to rub my cheek against the whiskers on his and feel the pinpricks of pleasure pinch at my nerve endings. Made me want to rub up against his chest and feel that unforgiving wall of his muscles digging into my softness.

I have no doubt, he would have made me feel small and delicate and protected. It's been so long since I've felt anything other than sad inside. And guilty. I've spent so long berating myself. Not allowing myself to feel anything other than self-reproach. I forgot how it felt to...feel.

It took that life-sized dopamine surge wrapped in muscle to blast through that numbness. He awakened desires I never thought I'd experience again.

Zoey turns to Skylar. "And how's that husband of yours?"

Skylar's features light up. "Nathan's doing great." Her voice softens, and her eyes gleam. Clearly, she's in love with her husband. Very much in love, based on the dreamy expression crossing her face. "We're hoping to go away on holiday soon."

"Another honeymoon?" Harper sighs. "That's so romantic."

Grace rolls her eyes. "You've been averaging a honeymoon a month."

"Just because you don't believe in love, doesn't mean others feel the same way," Zoey points out.

"It's not that I don't believe in love... I'm just—" She shrugs. "Okay, I'm a cynic. I don't believe in Happily Ever Afters."

"And yet, you're part of a spicy book club, where HEAs are guaranteed." Harper snickers.

"I'm in it for the 'happy endings.'" Zoey makes air quotes.

We chuckle.

"No wonder, you keep suggesting we read the spicier romances with BDSM themes." Grace wags her eyebrows.

"Exactly." Zoey slaps the table. "Give me lust over love, anytime."

"If not HEA, then what do you believe in?" After all, I briefly thought I'd gotten my HEA, and then, it turned out, I didn't... So, I'm halfway to agreeing with her.

"I believe in transactions"—she thinks before continuing—"and mutually beneficial arrangements."

"Which is how my marriage started out, but then we fell in love." Skylar lifts her hands. "He was very persuasive. And I was willing to be persuaded. I was willing to do anything to save my business." She glances around. "I never expected to fall for him. It didn't hurt that he was the CEO of a Davenport Group company. Nathan had that entire powerful-man-in-a-suit, boss-in-charge-who-knows-what-he-wants thing going for him, and hey, I found it irresistible."

I stiffen. "Did you say Davenport?"

Skylar tilts her head. "That's my husband's surname. And the name of the group of companies he and his brothers run."

"Hmm." I drum my fingers on the table.

Is it *another* coincidence that the dangerously high dose of testosterone in human form shares the same surname as Skylar's husband?

This can't be an accident. I should ask Skylar if she knows of a Connor Davenport.

But before I can open my mouth, the bell over the entrance to the bakery jingles. And almost as if thinking of the man from this morning has conjured him up, those wide shoulders I've been thinking about fill the doorway.

10

Connor

Yes, I did follow her here. And no, I shouldn't have walked through the door of the bakery.

I was watching her through the lens of my camera, in my van from down the street, where I had a clear view of the shop. I should have been content with that.

I saw her smile, and a strange sensation gripped my chest. Warmth, and an effervescent sensation like… Happiness? Like *I* was happy because she was? How fucking weird is that? I should have left right then. I did try to leave. My brain ordered me to go.

Some self-preservation instinct deep inside insisted I hustle out of there as quickly as possible, before things get more complicated.

I've asked her to have dinner with me. Things are beyond complicated.

Not to mention, I got involved in a bar fight — on purpose — so I could walk into the ER and have her tend to me, which took a little bit of arranging on my part but worked out fine.

Except, coming face-to-face with her was a punch to the gut. One which is repeated as our gazes meet.

"Oh, we're about to close—" Skylar begins, then she realizes it's me. "Connor?" She smiles. "What are you doing here?" A frown creases her forehead. She nods toward the bandage on my forehead. "What happened to you?"

"Got into a fight." I stop in front of their table, unable to take my gaze off the sultry siren who's occupied my mind over the past few days. "Dr. Hamilton"—I nod toward her—"stitched me up."

Skylar turns to me. "I didn't realize you'd met Phoenix already."

"She saved my life," I say softly, not looking away from Phoenix.

"Anyone in my position would have stitched you up." Her tone is casual, but her eyes flash little darts of anger at me. "And it's not like you were bleeding out."

"I might have, if you hadn't intervened." I take in her flushed cheeks. The way her chest rises and falls. It reassures me that she's attracted to me. It's a testament to how taken aback I am by this unexpected pull between us that I needed to see her again to confirm it's not one-sided.

"I was merely doing my job." She refuses to look away, and fuck, if her spirit doesn't turn me on further.

"I believe I have something of yours."

Her eyebrows knit. "You do?"

I pull out the flashlight—the one she used to check my pupils. I hold it out, making it clear it's hers.

She stiffens, then lifts a shoulder in a casual shrug. "So, that's where it went." She takes it from me. "Thanks." She slips it into her bag, then fixes me with a look.

"You could have turned it at the registration desk, and they would have returned it to me. Come to think of it, how did you find me?"

Her tone is belligerent enough for the others around the table to take notice. Skylar frowns. The others watch us with avid attention.

If I tell her the truth, it'll only raise more questions about my behavior. But if I want any kind of relationship with her, honesty— or something close to it—is the only way forward.

"I took the flashlight, so I'd have an excuse to see you again."

I lift a shoulder, offering a crooked, almost sheepish smile, trying to strike a balance between self-deprecating and unapologetic. Hoping I come across as more foolish than threatening.

Her lips press into a firm line.

I let the smile fall, then meet her eyes; this time, with full transparency, voice low but even. "I also waited until you finished your shift... And followed you."

She stiffens. Coughs. Reaches for a glass of water, buying herself a moment. Surprise flashes in her eyes, quickly overtaken by alarm.

"You've got a nerve admitting to that."

I need to tread carefully. Find a way to stick as close to the truth as possible, but also, not piss her off.

I raise my hands. "I wanted to see you and return your flashlight, is all."

"In which case, your job here is done," she retorts.

The other women, including Skylar, turn to me, waiting for my rebuttal with avid interest.

"Or just starting." I slide my hand into the pocket of my jeans. I changed out of the blood-splattered T-shirt and jacket in my van. Then waited outside the hospital with patience honed by years of having to do the same on other assignments, until she left the hospital.

She searches my features. "You're trying to tell me that's the only reason you waited outside the hospital, then followed me?" The expression on her face indicates she doesn't believe me. "What if I was delayed and didn't come out for another few hours?"

"I'd have waited as long as needed."

Our gazes meet. The air heats between us. The chemistry between us is thick enough to set fire to our surroundings.

Her pupils dilate. Her cheeks flush. She feels this connection too. Having that confirmation again makes me want to thump my chest and growl my delight. Then one of her friends clears her throat.

I blink, coming out of the trance. Goddamn. Meeting her again has turned my world upside down. But I can't show her how much she affects me...yet... "I don't mean you any harm. The fact that I approached you in front of your friends should confirm that to you," I say smoothly.

"It doesn't answer how you've managed to keep crossing paths with me since I saw you rescue that cat." She sets her jaw.

"I'll be happy to reveal that to you, over dinner."

The light in her eyes changes to one of challenge. I have no doubt, she's going to turn me down, regardless. Best to change the topic...for now.

"I don't believe I've met everyone." With practiced ease I hold out my hand to the woman on the doctor's right. "Connor Davenport."

"Zoey Malfoy." She shakes my hand.

"Harper Richie."

"Grace McFee."

"Good to meet you again, Dr. Hamilton." I level a slight smile at her.

Disregarding me, she turns to Skylar. "You know him?"

"He's my brother-in-law." Skylar casts a shrewd look in my direction. "Who's *rarely* in town."

There's a question in there, one which would be rude not to acknowledge.

"A friend needed me, so I scrapped my travel plans and stuck around." I glance at Skyler but make sure Phoenix hears every word. "Besides, I'd forgotten how irresistible London can be."

The corner of my mouth lifts as I say it.

When I glance at Phoenix, there's a spark in her eyes. She knows exactly what I'm talking about.

"I'm sure everyone is happy to see you home for a longer stint, especially Arthur," Skylar offers.

I wince and turn my attention back on her. "Gramps is happiest when he's plotting the demise of us brothers."

"Demise?" Phoenix murmurs.

"Since Arthur's brush with the Big C, he's very aware of his mortality. He wants to see us, his grandsons, settled ASAP."

"Which is natural." Phoenix finally meets my gaze. "He sounds like my mother, who constantly frets about all her children."

Taking advantage of the thaw in her demeanor, I nod to the chair next to her. "May I?" I address my question to Phoenix.

She hesitates.

"I only want to explain the sequence of events which brought me here," I plead.

She firms her lips.

"And I'm sure, you want to find out too?" I lower my voice to a hush and am rewarded by a subtle shiver of her shoulders. I love how responsive she is. Not that it sways her, for she juts out her chin. "Have dinner with me and I'll tell you."

She glowers at me, then tosses her head, before turning to the group. "If you ladies are okay with it…"

She's greeted by a chorus of assent.

"Thanks, ladies, I owe you all." I flash them my most charming smile. I'm rewarded by Skylar's speculative look, Zoey's piercing one, and Grace's curiosity-filled expression. Only Harper smiles back.

Tough crowd, but I'm glad her friends are protective of her. I fold myself into the chair.

It's like a trigger for her friends to excuse themselves.

"Uh, I think I have somewhere to be." Zoey rises to her feet.

"But we haven't even started talking about our newest book," Harper protests.

"Let's postpone it to our next book club meeting…" Grace sends her a warning look, then grabs her bag and hooks it over her shoulder. She pushes her chair back and holds out her hand. "I'd say it's good to meet you, Connor, but that's going to depend on whether you're able to convince Phe about your intentions."

Harper seems to finally get the message that the other women have been trying to signal to her. She pushes her chair back, rises to her feet, and grabs her handbag. "It's so lovely that you made it, Phoenix. I hope you'll make it to our next book club meeting."

"I don't think I'll have time to read a book in advance," Phoenix warns.

"The book club is only an excuse. It's more a chance for us to

meet and catch up. I promise, we won't spoil any of them for you."
Zoey squeezes her shoulder.

"You can spoil them. It's the only way I'll find out what they're about." She hugs Zoey, then Harper and Grace. "I'm so glad I made it today, you guys."

Zoey signals that she's watching me.

With a chorus of goodbyes, a wink from Harper, a speculative glance from Grace, and a final warning look from Zoey—which I interpret as *don't mess with our friend*—the three women leave.

"I'll be in my office tallying the proceeds," Skylar says, giving me a long, unreadable look before heading to the front door.

Yeah. Message received. My sister-in-law just made it very clear, Phoenix isn't alone.

I try to convey—wordlessly—that she has nothing to fear from me. Skylar just widens her gaze, her expression cool and cautious. She's reserving judgment.

She flips the sign to Closed and locks the door. "You can unlatch it when you leave. I'll hear the bell and come out to lock up."

Then she disappears behind the counter and through the kitchen door, leaving us alone.

Silence descends.

Phe turns to me. "Of all the ERs in London; you walked into mine. Were you already following me?" Her gaze narrows. "Is that why you were there at the very moment the cat needed to be rescued."

Woman's smart. Sooner or later, she's going to put things together and figure out how I came to be here. It's best I keep ahead of her.

I pull out my phone and message James to let him know that I'm about to share everything with his sister.

If I want her to really see me, I can no longer keep her in the dark.

Then I pocket my device, take a deep breath and tell her "You're right. I've been following you."

11

Phoenix

What the—? He confessed that he followed me. Hadn't expected to hear that from him. *Or perhaps, I had?*

Perhaps, my hindbrain was alerted the moment he walked into the coffee shop that, surely, I wasn't likely to see this man who made such an impact on me so soon again?

Perhaps, it's my subconscious that feels there's more here than meets the eye. But asking him is one thing.

And him confessing that he orchestrated our meeting in the ER is…not what I'd bargained for.

"I… I'm not sure I understand." I clear my throat.

"I don't mean any harm." He raises his hands in a gesture that's meant to reassure me.

I notice how wide his palms are, how thick his fingers are, how broad his wrists are… And my mind automatically goes to how big that tent at his crotch was. *Big hand. Big…thang, and his feet are big and wide, too. Definitely big thang.* Ugh.

Also, big hands can be dangerous.

And, strong. And capable. My brain, traitorous as ever, still drags up the image of those same hands peeling off his shirt in the ER.

No. Focus.

I can't let myself be distracted by his voice, his shoulders, the way his gaze coils around mine like a rope. Because what he's saying isn't just sexy. It's *unsettling*.

He didn't just stumble into the ER. He planned it. He didn't just see me again. He orchestrated it.

And now he's standing here, in my space, acting like it's all perfectly reasonable.

I should be panicking. *A lot.* Blame it on the fact that I face life and death situations daily. Or perhaps, it's the fact that he introduced himself to my friends, and that Skylar is within earshot. Either way, I don't think I'm in any real danger from him… Even though he has a dangerous edge to him. I'm more intrigued. I want to understand the reason behind his actions. And yes, I'm a tiny bit alarmed. But mostly, I'm curious. *Why would he follow me?*

"I know you won't hurt me." I jut out my chin.

"Oh?"

"Call it instinct, but I don't feel threatened by you." Not physically, that is. *Emotionally and mentally…? Things are more complicated than they should be.* I shove that thought aside.

"What I don't understand is how you managed to arrange things, so I'd be the one treating you in the ER."

"I pulled a few strings. Made sure that when my turn came, I was assigned to you." He raises a shoulder.

"You can do that?" Then it dawns on me. "The nurse… She directed me to your bay. Was that…was that you?"

I can't believe he'd pull something like this. Surely, he can't manipulate hospital systems.

But then he tilts his head. "If you know the right people—and are able to motivate them in the right way—anything is possible."

I gape, more stunned than alarmed… And God help me, more than a little intrigued. The confidence rolls off of him in waves, that calm, dangerous certainty that says he'll always get what he wants.

It's reckless. Unpredictable. And there's a strength there—a steadiness—that whispers I could lean on him if I let myself.

I shake it off. He's run undercover missions. Of course, this would be easy for him. I will not be impressed by his resourcefulness. I will not be flattered that he's set his sights on me. What he did was wrong, and I need to remember that. I set my jaw.

"By your own admission, you followed me prior to today?"

"I did." He places his palms face-down on the table.

"Oh."

I should feel upset and pissed off that this guy stalked me. And I *am* upset and pissed off, because I'd been sure my imagination was playing tricks on me.

"Do you know how many times I felt like someone was watching me? Good to know I'm not going crazy." I glower at him.

"No one I've followed before this has ever been alerted to my presence. *Ever*." His forehead furrows. "But you… I could tell you were picking up on my presence, and that it was upsetting you to think someone was watching you. I knew, I had to come out and tell you."

"Should I be grateful?" I throw up my hands. "You infringed on my privacy."

"Technically, I didn't. I watched you from afar, and only when you were in a public space. I never once investigated inside your house. Never infringed upon your privacy—"

"Thank you so much," I snap.

"—and if things had gone according to plan, I'd have reported to James that you were fine, and you never would have been aware of my existence."

"James?"

His expression takes on a tinge of discomfort, then he leans back in his seat.

"Your brother was worried about you. He wanted me to keep an eye on you."

What the hell?

"James sent you?" I blow out a breath. "I've sent his last calls to voicemail, sure. But I always meant to call him back."

For a moment, I feel guilt for not staying in touch with my big brother. But it's quickly replaced with rage.

"I can't believe he sent you to spy on me." I throw up my hands. "Typical, overbearing, older brother bullshit."

I pull out my phone and begin to dial James' number, but Connor places his hand on mine.

Electricity zings up my arm from the point of contact. This awareness between us is ridiculous. It seems to have multiplied since we met in the ER this morning. I pull my hand out from under his, my fingers trembling. The phone slips from my grasp and onto the table.

"I didn't mean to startle you," he says softly.

The concern in his voice does funny things to my composure. If he were rude, I could handle it better. The fact that those startling blue eyes are looking at me with concern and apology touches a chord inside me. It feels like he's melting through the resistance I've built up around my heart. I clear my throat and look away.

"You can understand why I'm pissed off at James, and at you. I'm a grown woman. A doctor. A professional with my own life. An adult." I rub at my temple. "And you were following me, and stalking me—"

"I wasn't stalking you." He shifts uncomfortably. "Not in the strict sense of the word."

"And I'm supposed to believe you because—?" I spear him with a look like he's a misdiagnosis I plan to correct. "Oh right, because *stalking* people is your *profession.*"

"On occasion," he says, maddeningly calm.

That non-answer snaps something in me. Seriously? He follows me for weeks, and *that's* the tone he takes?

"You have good instincts," he offers, like he's doing me a favor.

The *nerve.*

"If you think a few compliments are going to win me over—"

"I'm stating a fact." He shrugs. Like we're talking about the weather, not the fact that he's been shadowing me.

Anger coils in my chest, tight and sharp. My heart's pounding, and it's not just from rage. It's him. His calm. His arrogance. That infuriating confidence that should repulse me—*but doesn't*.

God help me, I find it hot.

I hate that I do.

He's been watching me. *Me.* Not just in passing. He's been *focused* on me. For weeks. And now that I know, I can't un-know it. There's something twistedly intimate about it.

Moisture gathers between my thighs. My armpits are damp. My thoughts are a mess of fury, confusion, and something that feels suspiciously like arousal.

This is wrong. So wrong.

And yet the idea of him disappearing from my life makes my stomach pitch. I'd *miss* him.

The thought slams into me like a punch to the chest. It's a full-body jolt. I shoot to my feet.

"I think I've heard enough."

Because if I stay one second longer, I'm afraid of what I'll say. Or worse. What I'll give away by my actions.

He rises calmly; which means, he towers over me. It also means, he's able to show off those massive shoulders, and that gorgeous neck, and that superb, sculpted chest across which the T-shirt stretches, and which now doesn't show any sign of blood. It's a twin to the one he was wearing earlier, but it's new. For that matter, his jacket is, too.

"You changed?"

As soon as the words are out, I curse myself.

It shows I'm paying attention to what he's wearing. And that I'm not serious about getting away from him. *Which I'm not.* But I don't need him to realize that.

Not that it gets past him. He acknowledges my comment with a nod. "I wanted to look my best when I take you out to dinner."

Huh. A warm feeling squeezes my chest. I bat it away. Yeah, okay so he changed his clothes for me. Big deal.

"I don't want to have dinner with you."

I move to step around the table, but he shifts with me. Smooth, fast, blocking my path. Hands raised again, like that could possibly make him look harmless.

"I think you do," he says, calm and cocky.

Confident. Arrogant. And devastatingly sexy.

God, help me.

I *could* brush past him, but that would mean getting close. Too close. And I'm not entirely sure I can do that without doing something reckless—like touching him. Or worse, sniffing him. So, I hold my ground and summon my most bored expression.

"Why would I want that?" I snap.

"Because I have an offer you'll want to hear."

I roll my eyes. "Yeah, I doubt that."

"I don't." His voice drops. "In fact, I'm sure of it."

Right on cue, my stomach growls. Loudly.

His lips twitch, smug. Of *course*, he heard that.

"It's just food," he says casually. "And conversation. And maybe, a little more about who I am."

I tap a finger to my chin, pretending to consider it.

Truth is, I *am* hungry. Despite stuffing my face with dessert, I never turn down a full meal when I know one's guaranteed. And uninterrupted. ER life trains that instinct into you.

Besides, I *am* curious about him. Not that I'll ever admit it out loud.

"Please?" His smile turns charming. The kind that makes women lose their minds. *And probably, their underwear.*

Mine, unfortunately, are already damp. I press my thighs together, refusing to let that smug bastard see the effect he's having on me.

"Fine." I tip up my chin. "Dinner it is."

Something flickers in his eyes. *Satisfaction? Victory?*

But he's not getting the last word. I smile sweetly. "On one condition."

12

Connor

ENTRY 3

- Emotional Response: Smile frequency: record high. First unguarded laughter observed.
- Social Circle: Special bond with 3 female peers. High emotional trust with one of them.
- Consumption: Dirty chai (1), 1 piece of what appears to be a brownie. 1 slice of lemon tart.
- Quirk Logged: Sighs contentedly after dessert, eyes flutter half-shut.
- Memory Anchor: Tilt of head when tasting something pleasurable = identical to clinical focus expression.
- Caffeine Tolerance: High. Three cups/day minimum.
- Laugh Frequency: Rare (baseline) but increases by 17% in group setting.

- Physical Marker: Left cheek dimples faintly when genuinely amused.

Notes: Third encounter at The Fearless Kitten. Subject profile recalibrating. Smile has lingering effect.

13

Connor

"She'll have the wild mushroom tartlet to start, followed by the fillet of turbot. I'll take the hand-dived scallops and the roast loin of venison. For dessert, we'll share the dark chocolate delice with orange sorbet. Coffee for me. A glass of white for her."

Turns out, she had not one condition, but two.

She chose the restaurant, and I was paying. The latter? Did she seriously think I'd take her to dinner and not pay?

The former? She chose James' restaurant. *Smart woman.*

She means to force a confrontation between the three of us. I say, *bring it on.* Of course, I took the precaution of messaging James to let him know we were headed here. He's going to be furious enough with me when he finds out I have designs on his sister. I didn't want to spring another surprise on him and take him unawares.

I hand the menus back to the waiter.

Phe arches a brow. "Presumptuous of you to order for me."

"How did I do?"

"Perfectly." A reluctant smile curves her lips. She reaches for her water and takes a sip. "How did you know what I wanted?"

I lean back, letting a slow grin unfurl. "Your pupils dilated when you read the word 'mushroom.' You tapped your finger—twice—when the waiter mentioned turbot. Subtle cues. Pattern recognition. It's my thing."

You're my thing.

I've been watching her for weeks, observing her so closely, I could write a thesis on her. But the truth? I haven't just been observing her. I've memorized her. Every twitch, every breath. Every soft, infuriating, fascinating part of her.

She lets out a breath that's half-laugh, half-groan. "I can't decide if you're showing off or just being your infuriatingly confident self."

I tilt my head. "I admit, I was trying to impress you."

"By rolling back years of female agency?" she scoffs.

"By taking care of you."

That gives her pause. Her forehead creases.

"You're exhausted. It's been another long day. I'll bet you haven't had a proper meal in days. Today was the first time you saw your friends in…how long?"

I pause, watching the subtle clench in her jaw.

"All I did was spare you one more decision. So, you could breathe. Eat. And maybe—just for a second—enjoy yourself."

"And you say, you did not infringe on my privacy?" She lifts her chin.

"Maybe I did… A little. Having the chance to run surveillance on you gave me a head start in terms of piecing together much of your personality. On the other hand." I incline my head. "It wasn't difficult to deduce that, based on you being an ER specialist."

"Hmph." She folds her arms across her chest. "Your point being?"

"I ordered for you, so you didn't have to make yet another decision. This way, you can relax and enjoy the dinner. And the company."

She takes another sip of the water. "I shouldn't find the argument compelling. Because really, everything you've done has confirmed to me that, while you're handsome, you're also a wanker. A stuck-up, egoistical wanker who has a very high opinion of himself."

"You think I'm handsome?"

She chokes on the next mouthful of water, then places her glass down. Her lips twitch, but then she seems to bring her mirth under control.

"Seriously?" She huffs. "Do you want me to answer that?"

"Sorry, that was me behaving like an arsehole." I raise my hands.

"It was." She nods.

"But I stand by everything else I said."

She tosses her head. "You have a big opinion of yourself."

"In this case, your observation is warranted."

She chuckles.

"If by ordering for you, I took you for granted, I apologize."

She blinks, then shakes her head. "Wow, okay. Now, you shatter my poor opinion of you with an apology."

I laugh. "Good, right?"

"Wait, is this a game for you?" She scowls.

I sober. "I'm as serious as a ruptured abdominal aortic aneurysm."

She gapes—then lets out a reluctant laugh. "How do you even know to call it that?"

"I might have been reading up on medical terminology," I admit.

"Hmm." She narrows her eyes. "Am I supposed to be impressed by that?"

I shake my head. "I did it because… I wanted to understand the world you live in. I wanted to get a feel for how it is to work in the ER."

"Why is that?" Her voice softens.

Because I want to know everything about you. Because I'm haunted by images of you when I close my eyes. Because I want to understand this very important facet about your life.

But I can't say any of that. Not yet.

So, I go with the safer version: "It's part of the research I do when I surveil someone. I read up about their profession. It helps me tailor my approach."

Our gazes meet and hold again. The chemistry sizzles. The air between us shimmers with lust and need.

I sense that connection between us, the one which has thrummed between us from the moment I first saw her. And from the flush in her cheeks, I know she feels it too.

Is it possible she reciprocates my feelings? I almost reach for her hand, but the waiter returns with my coffee.

I blink; so does she. On her face is that punchy, bowled-over expression which must mirror the one on my face.

The waiter pours her some wine to taste. She sips and pronounces it satisfactory. He tops off her glass and retreats.

"Coffee?" She stares at my cup.

"I'm still on duty." As soon as I say that I realize it wasn't smart to point that out to her. Me, the undercover spy who's adept at taking on new roles, is making rookie mistakes.

That's how unsettled I am in her presence.

She narrows her gaze on me. "I plan to confront my brother about that."

"I assumed that when you chose his restaurant for dinner."

She sips from the wineglass. Sighs. Some of the tension I've noticed in her shoulders since the first time I followed her seems to bleed out. I can take credit for that. And damn, if I don't feel happy.

"What happened at the bar fight?" She looks at me with frank curiosity. "Your enemies catch up with you?"

"Actually, yes," I concede.

"So, you're a spy, and your foes are onto you?" She waves a hand in the air. "Seems a bit far-fetched, don't you think?"

"I can assure you, it's true."

"What does that have to do with me?"

I drain the cup of coffee, needing that burst of adrenaline from the caffeine. My heart begins to thump in my chest. My pulse rate spikes. Damn, I'm nervous. In none of my missions where I've been in life and death situations have, I felt this unsure of myself. I shake off my anxiety, forcing myself to adopt a casual tone. "I have a proposition for you."

"Proposition?" She places her glass of wine on the table. "What do you mean?"

"Your hospital needs an infusion of money, and someone championing its cause in the corridors of power; without both, the ER will shut down."

She stiffens. "How do you know about that?"

"James mentioned you were an ER doctor at Archway Hospital. It only took a few calls to find out the hospital is struggling."

She regards me steadily. I can sense her mind beginning to join the dots.

"I also researched you online."

She stiffens. "You looked into my past?"

"Only what's publicly available, like on your social media feeds."

Some of the tension seems to go out of her. "I'm too busy to have much of a social media presence."

"You did share a fundraiser for the ER," I point out.

Her forehead furrows. "So?"

"The ER is your world. You have friends there. You care for your co-workers. You've built a community there which you value. I'd say, you'll do everything possible to ensure the hospital doesn't shut down the ER."

She surveys me steadily, then realization filters into her eyes. "Connor *Davenport*," she says slowly, rolling my name across her tongue.

And goddamn, it's as if I can feel the vibrations all the way to crown of my cock.

"Your family is very wealthy, not to mention, *connected*." She tilts her head and draws her cheek inward. A classic gesture to indicate she's thinking hard. "Are you saying you can help with the hospital's funding issues?"

I stare at her meaningfully, letting the silence do the talking.

She sits up straight, keen interest in her features. "You *are* saying that. You can stop the ER from shutting down?" Her cheeks flush with excitement. The embers in her eyes crackle.

Damn, she's beautiful. I can't take my gaze off her.

Also, I have a very small window within which to put my case forward.

"I am saying, unless there's a fresh infusion of money, not to mention, systemic changes, the hospital is going to shut down the ER within the month."

"That soon?" She gapes. "I had no idea things were that critical."

She looks so worried that, for a few seconds, I feel a pang that I've upset her. But I'm not telling her anything that's not true. Maybe, it's a good thing I brought it to her attention? And yes, I'm using the opportunity for my own selfish motives, but I can't let go of her. I need her in my life, and I'll do anything to ensure that.

"They are, unfortunately." I compose my features. "But, I may have a solution for you."

Her gaze turns wary. "You do?"

I take in the doubt in her features, and realize I need to lay out my proposition, before she jumps to any conclusions.

I raise my hands. "Before you read into my motivations, let me tell you a bit about myself."

Interest ripples across her features again, before she reins it in. "You mean, you're not as narcissistic as some of your earlier words led me to believe?" She scoffs.

"Guilty as charged. My ego gets in the way sometimes."

I allow myself a small smile.

"Hard not to when I've created biotech patents that save lives, *and* I was recruited as a government agent."

I shift my weight and tap my fingers against the table.

"Only, the missions I cared about weren't the ones the government prioritized. So, I became a private contractor, built my own team, and started funding the work I believe in—rescue operations, med tech for underserved areas, trauma relief in conflict zones."

"But even with the royalties from my patents, it's not enough to save those who'd never show up on an official priority list."

She curls her fingers around the step of her wineglass. "Is there a reason you're telling me this?"

I lean forward.

"I'm funding a charity that provides medical treatment for children caught up in war and other disasters. I need access to my trust fund to make a difference."

A surprised look comes into her eyes. "A billionaire with a conscience? Who'd have thought."

"First" — I hold up a finger — "it's my grandfather who's a billionaire, not me. And second, I'm doing it for my own selfish reasons."

"Which are?"

I run a knuckle along my jaw, before letting my hand fall to my thigh. *Hadn't expected to have this discussion so soon.* "I realized that money alone doesn't guarantee happiness."

Again, her gaze widens. She surveys my features as if trying to figure out if I'm telling her the truth, which I am. For once. After living a life undercover, it feels liberating to share my thoughts without having to hide.

"You're a spy who moonlights as a CEO?"

I raise a shoulder.

"I'm also a qualified biochemist. It provided a front for the missions I undertook in the field."

She shakes her head. "You don't choose the easy route, do you?"

I chuckle. "Wouldn't be sitting here if I did."

"Hmm." There's a pleased look in her eyes, again, quickly banked. "So, you have a pet project — a mission to save children — for which you need money."

"A *lot* of money. Which I can access through my portion of the Davenport fortune."

"So, what's the problem?"

"The problem is... I can only access my trust fund when I get married."

She blinks. Color flushes her cheeks. She wriggles around in her seat, looking half-ready to leave, but she doesn't. A fighter. Someone who isn't scared off easily. Damn. My heart gives a big thump in my chest. My balls tighten further. This perfect harmony between the emotional and the carnal in response to her is an irresistible seduction of my senses.

"And what's that got to do with me?" she asks slowly.

I meet her gaze head-on, my voice steady. "I want you to be my wife."

14

Phoenix

My hand jerks, and my fingers slip on my wineglass, which tips over. The wine blots the tablecloth. Before I can react, he reaches over and straightens my glass, then drops his napkin over the spill.

I look from it to his face, suddenly breathless. "I don't think I heard you right…" I clear my throat. "Did you say—"

"Marry me." His voice is light, but his tone is intent.

"What?" I cough. "What are you talking about?"

"It would help the both of us."

My head spins. "You'll have to explain this to me slowly."

"I need the money for my rescue mission. You need someone with influence to lobby the government from shutting down the ER."

I try to make sense of what he's talking about and fail. "What does that have to do with getting married?"

"By marrying you, I get access to the money in my trust fund. My grandfather will be happy I'm settling down. He'll agree to put the considerable weight of the Davenports behind liaising with the powers that be to stop the ER from shutting down."

"Ah." I swallow around the heaviness in my chest. I should have realized this wasn't a proposal for a real marriage. Not that he could have proposed to me after knowing me for so little time. This is a proposition which could result in mutual benefit.

That heaviness in my chest seems to sink into my belly. My entire being seems to turn into stone.

Why did I think this man felt something for me? He wants to marry me, but not because he loves me.

"You're talking about a liaison…of convenience?"

"Call it a strategic alliance." He drags his thumb under his lips. "I'm not offering you a fantasy. I'm offering you a partnership. With total transparency, and no strings you don't agree to. Call it unconventional. But what I'm offering is a win-win arrangement. No one gets hurt. There are no emotional traps. We walk into this with our eyes open. What's at stake is bigger than your happiness or mine. We're going to save the lives of many people by agreeing to this."

His voice seems to come from far away. He's couching his proposition with very reasonable words, but at heart, it's still a transaction. A fake liaison. I shouldn't be surprised by this suggestion.

He comes from a background I'm familiar with. Where money is used to negotiate your way into what you want. There's no reason to believe Connor is any different.

The silence stretches. The expression on his face is untroubled… and expectant. He's waiting for an answer.

I look away, needing some time to gather myself.

I walked away from Drew because I wanted more. And the way my emotions for Connor seesaw, I feel much more for him than I did in every second of my short-lived relationship with Drew.

But a pretend relationship?

I should turn him down. But the part of me that feels like it owes the world, which recognizes that he's right, that we could make a difference to the lives of so many, pushes me to consider his proposal carefully.

The Emergency Room has been my refuge from my personal life.

I've spent more time there than at my own home over the last few months. To find out there's a timeline to the ER shutting down brings home how serious the situation is.

My heartbeat accelerates; my stomach twists up in knots.

What would *I* do if the ER closed? *What would my colleagues do?* We could find other jobs, but it wouldn't be the same.

Connor's offering me a way out, a chance to stop it from shutting down. It means, the borough will continue to have access to the vital services the ER provides. It means, Emma can afford childcare, Sunita can help her mum, and John can keep saving for his kids' future.

And Connor's charity can keep helping children.

All I have to do is say 'yes.'

But to agree to be his wife? Despite it being a marriage in name only? *Nope.*

I broke up with Drew because I wasn't in love with him. I deserve love, and I won't marry for less.

I shake my head. "No, I can't agree to marry you." I throw up my hands. "I don't even know you."

"Hmm." He drags his hand over his mouth. The speculative look in his eyes makes my heart beat faster. "But the ER…"

I set my jaw. "If I needed the money, I'd go to my parents."

"No, you wouldn't."

"Excuse me?"

"You strike me as someone who's independent. I'll bet, you decided not to take any help from your parents for your education. In fact—" He leans forward. "I'd wager you put yourself through medical school by taking on loans and even pushing yourself to take on jobs on the side."

I flush, half-amused, half-angry that he's read me so easily. I don't reply to his assertion, but my expression must give me away, for he nods with satisfaction.

"Don't look so pissed off. It's a fine thing you did. A commendable thing. After all, I did the same."

"You did?"

He nods. "I also had a fierce need to make it on my own. So, I made sure I got scholarships to put myself through university on my own merit."

"Scholarships, huh?" I scan his features. He's so good-looking, it's easier to believe he isn't so intelligent.

Again, he reads me correctly. A smirk twists those beautiful lips. "Never judge a man by his looks."

My flush deepens. "I wasn't. I didn't think that because you're so handsome you don't have brains."

His grin widens. "You think I'm handsome?"

Not again. I see what he's doing and decide to play along. "Is that all you took away from our conversation?" I roll my eyes.

"Also, that I know you better than you give me credit for."

I toss my head. "We've barely met a couple of times. You don't know me, at all."

"That's where you have it wrong. As you pointed out, I've been watching you for almost a month and filling in the blanks, so I've formed a very detailed profile of you in my mind."

I'm still not sure how I feel about that. He may not have broken any legal rules... But I have mixed feelings about him getting to know so much about me, while I wasn't even aware of his existence.

"You profiled me?" I ask slowly.

"It's what I do when I'm on a surveillance job."

"And he's, no doubt, told you already that I'm the one who asked him to follow you." My brother's voice interrupts him, and I find him standing next to the table. *When did he get here?* "I hope you'll forgive me for that. I was worried about you."

I tear my gaze away from Connor's face with difficulty.

My brother looks contrite as he bows his head slightly. His hair is longer than when I last saw him, underscoring how six months have gone by since we last saw each other. But to hire someone to tail me? That's beyond the pale.

"What on earth is wrong with you?" I fight to keep my voice low so as not to draw attention. "Who does this kind of thing? Are you insane?"

"I was worried about you, Phe. You didn't call, didn't reply to my messages. You completely dropped out of sight." He drags his fingers through his hair.

"I've gone months without calling you in the past."

"Not like this. I haven't heard a peep out of you in six months."

"I've been on my own since I turned eighteen. I don't need to check in with you like you're my warden."

I narrow my eyes at my brother, and his shoulder slump even more.

"I can, and do, take care of myself, James. This was way out of line."

"I didn't mean to upset you, I only have your best interests at heart," he says softly.

I can see the apology in his eyes and the lingering worry. Damn, he really was trying to make sure I was okay. Some of the anger in my chest fades.

"You could have come by the hospital. You know where I work."

He firms his lips. "And you'd have been so pissed off about my checking up on you, that you'd have stopped talking to me completely."

He's right. But I shove that aside.

"I'm even more pissed off that you asked your best friend to watch over me." I wave my hand in the hair. "Who does that?"

We stare at each other.

My brother's features grow soft. "I know, you can take care of yourself. But that doesn't mean I can stop worrying about you, despite the fact you've always known what you wanted. Hell, when I returned from being in the Marines and floundered around, trying to figure out what I wanted to do with my life, I was jealous of you."

"Of me?" I gape.

"Of how focused you were. How you were intent on becoming a doctor, and on your own steam. I wished I had half as much of an idea of where I was headed."

My older brother has always been so confident. When he joined the Royal Marines, my admiration for him escalated. A decade later, when he took early retirement, I know he struggled with fitting back into civilian life. I was surprised when he decided to open a restaurant, but I figured he'd discovered a passion for food. He made it look so easy when his restaurant was a success. He captured the popular imagination in no time. I didn't realize how difficult this journey must have been for him.

I fight against the empathy that overwhelms me.

"Are you telling me this in the hope I'll forgive you for your over-bearing, overprotective, getting him"—I jerk my thumb in Connor's direction—"to watch over me, bullshit."

I scowl at him.

"I needed space. Surely, I'm allowed that?"

"Of course, you are. But you can't blame us for wanting to make sure you were okay. Especially since, none of us could get through to you."

"Yeah." I hunch my shoulders. He's making good points. And it was I who didn't keep in touch with anyone. The fact that my family noticed I had dropped out of sight? It reinforces the fact that I'm not alone.

Emotions squeeze my chest and must show on my face, for James' features soften.

"Hey, I didn't mean for you to get upset. And if you felt like your privacy was infringed upon, I take responsibility for that." He goes down on his haunches in front of me. "Either way, it brought you to my restaurant, so it was worth it. Again, I'm sorry, Sis, if I over-stepped, but *you!*" He rises to his full height and rounds on Connor. "Is this what you meant when you said you were going to reveal yourself? Because this doesn't look like the end of a mission, it looks like a date. With my little sister. What the hell?"

"Wait, what? You messaged him?" I turn on Connor.

"When I realized I was planning to ask you out for dinner, I reached out to James and told him I was going to tell you every-thing." He says this without taking his gaze off of James' face. "Why don't you take a seat, James. I think there's something we need to tell you."

Ooh, here it comes. This is going to be good. I lean back and prepare to watch how Connor's going to handle this one.

James' nostrils flare.

"We?" He looks from Connor to me, then back to Connor. "What do you mean *we?*" Not sure what he sees on our faces, but his jaw tightens.

My brother was always perceptive. It's what saved his life in the Marines, and he hasn't lost any of that ability to read the room.

A nerve pops at his temple. "No fucking way," he growls.

"Why don't you sit down?" Connor's voice is unperturbed. He kicks out a chair.

James ignores it. "What the fuck are you up to, Davenport?"

"I just asked your sister to marry me."

For the second time in the last half an hour, I'm struck speechless. This man... Will he never cease to amaze me? Also, it's stupid of him to tell James that. I count back from ten, nine, eight, seven—my brother reaches forward and grabs Connor by his collar.

"I told you to keep an eye on her, arsehole. You took advantage of my trust."

"Actually, I didn't. Nothing's happened between us. In fact, take this as my way of asking you for permission to court your sister."

"Court?" James blinks.

Permission? What the hell? Who is this guy?

"It's like going on a date, but with the intention of finding a life partner?" Connor drawls.

"You're looking to marry my sister?" James snaps.

"That's what I said." Connor's voice is patient, in an exaggerated fashion.

"Hey!" I jump up, shove my chair back. "I'm still here." I look between them. "You know—the woman you're talking about like I'm some item on the auction block?"

James looks stunned.

Connor's lips curve into the kind of smirk that should not be sexy but absolutely is. And I hate that I notice.

Enough.

I wave a hand. "Let's get one thing straight—I don't need anyone's permission to date, let alone marry. Especially not my brother's."

I swing toward Connor. "And you? What kind of caveman asks

for permission to 'court' a woman in the twenty-first century? Are you planning to exchange goats while you're at it?"

He doesn't flinch. If anything, his smirk deepens.

"And who said I'd even consider marrying you?" I add, stabbing a finger in his direction. "I barely know you."

"I'm going to change that." Connor nods. "We're going to get to know each other in a respectful, structured way. And I'm going to win your attentions. To show you..." His eyes flash. "That I'm the man for you."

A treacherous warmth tugs on my insides. My thighs clench. Despite the fact that my brother is standing over us, I can't stop my nipples from growing hard. The possessiveness in Connor's tone, the intent in his eyes... All of it is so hot. I have no doubt, he means what he's saying. And it makes me feel cherished. Wanted. Seen.

The way he's focused on me makes me feel special in a way that Drew never did. Thinking of my ex-boyfriend dampens my spirits at once.

I glance away. "I'm not interested."

James stiffens. "You heard her." He folds his arms across his chest.

"I don't need you to speak on my behalf." I lower my chin.

"But—"

"But nothing. I'm a grown woman. And yes, I'm aware I ignored my family, so you felt duty-bound to look me up. You can let everyone know I'm fine, but from here on out, you have no reason to be involved in this."

"So, there is a 'this?'" Connor quips.

I throw him a dirty look, but he's unperturbed. He leans back, his ridiculously big frame overshadowing the chair and making it look like a toy.

"Somehow, I feel responsible." My brother glares at Connor.

"You should feel that way, considering you asked him to look out for me, which I still can't believe you did."

"And which I'm glad you did," Connor murmurs.

James looks even more pissed off at that.

"Will you stop riling him up," I admonish Connor. "And you—" I turn to my brother. "It's time you back off."

James shifts his weight from foot to foot. "I didn't mean to upset you," he finally offers. "I was merely looking out for you."

Some of the tension slides from my shoulders. A warm sensation squeezes my chest. My big brother has always been overprotective. As have my other four brothers. It's James, however, who has never stopped himself from getting involved in things where he doesn't need to.

"I'm aware." I blow out a breath. "But this is my life, and I have the right to live it how I see fit."

His brow furrows. He looks like he's about to protest but then nods. "You're right, Phe. I was out of line with you. As for this bastard—" He nods in Connor's direction. "I'm watching you. If you hurt her, you'll have me to contend with."

Before I can say anything else, he turns and stalks off. We watch him head to the back of the restaurant and through the door that leads to the kitchen.

"Well, then…" Connor turns to me. "Where were we?"

"*We* weren't anywhere." I jut out my chin. "I'm going to leave and *you?* Are going to be too busy looking for a change of clothes."

"A change of clothes?" Connor looks askance. "Why is that?"

How dare he look so relaxed, when he's upended my whole life? Not a hair out of place, not a wrinkle in his shirt… Hot anger flashes though my veins.

"Because of *this*." I jump up, grab the jug of water on the table, and pour the contents over his head.

15

Connor

Classified Internal File: Case Study – Phoenix Hamilton
Subject Code: HPH-7869
Alias: ~~"The Doctor" Doc~~ Fever
Objective: ~~Surveillance and Protection per Directive J.H.~~
Subject to be protected at all costs.
ENTRY 4
•Stress Response: Displaces weight onto left hip. Touches base of neck.

- Reaction Time: 1.4 seconds to visual threat stimulus (hand reach). Hyper-aware.
- Micro-expressions: Forehead crease = truth conflict. Lip twitch = suppressed anger.
- Attachment Pattern: Deflects praise. Reframes vulnerability as humor.

- Psychological Markers: High empathy index. Martyr complex.
- Personal Risk Profile: Elevated. Prefers to exhaust herself to avoid emotional confrontation.
- ~~Additional quirk: Medical speak in conversation. *Fucking turns me on.*~~

Notes: No longer purely protection. Emotional contamination: 51%.

Note to self: Coax subject to snack healthier. *Must carry carrot sticks on hand to tempt her to eat it, instead of chocolate bars.*

16

Connor

"What did you do after?" Brody, my middle brother, drawls. He's the most controlled of all my brothers. For him to ask a question means something about my story must have struck a chord. I don't blame him. How many women would dump a jug of water on their date before leaving? *Uncomfortable?* Yes, but she earned my respect.

That was a week ago.

We're in the den in Sinclair Sterling's home, where this week's poker session is being hosted. The game started past midnight, so Viktor, the Crown Prince of Verenza and my brother-in-law, could join. He came straight from the airport, having just flown in from Verenza.

It's 4:30 a.m., and the game shows no sign of slowing down. The room is dimly lit, a single antique chandelier casting a warm glow over the poker table.

"What *would* I do?" I survey my hand. *While the other patrons sniggered and a couple of them applauded, she walked away, leaving me to grab a napkin and try to dry myself.* "By the time I looked up, she was marching out of the restaurant." *What a woman!*

I caught sight of her straight back and ample backside, which stretched the dress she was wearing and captivated me, until she pushed the door to the restaurant open and disappeared.

I also had to contend with James walking over to me with a smirk and a satisfied expression on his face. I glared at him, cautioned him not to say a word, then paid my bill and left.

James said he doesn't need me to keep an eye on her anymore. I told him I agreed.

I lied.

Because the truth is, I'm not ready to stop.

Not now. Not after all this time. Not after she's become a part of my routine, my day, my life.

Sure, James asked me to start the surveillance. But the decision to continue? *That's all me.*

Now that she knows I was watching her, it only makes sense to bring in someone else.

Someone I trust. Someone I've trained. Someone discreet enough to blend into the background but sharp enough to keep me informed. Because I need to know where she goes. Who she sees. How she moves through her days.

It's obsessive. It's stalker behavior. I know that. But I also know it keeps her safe.

And it gives me the one thing I can't seem to let go of—*access to her.*

I tell myself it's for strategy. That I need intel to woo her properly. To understand her rhythms. Her habits. Her tells.

But the truth?

I can't stop watching her. Can't stop thinking of her. Can't stop obsessing about her.

Because I meant every word. I want to marry her.

The idea sparked the moment I saw her staring at that wedding dress in the shop window. But it took root when she leaned over me in the ER—her fingers brushing my skin as she stitched me up, her scent cutting through antiseptic like it was meant only for me.

Even in those shapeless scrubs, her body called to mine. The steadiness in her hands, the sympathy in her eyes, the way she made pain feel like something I'd earned—Hell, I never stood a chance.

She didn't just tend my wounds. She carved herself into my bloodstream.

There's a pull toward her I can't explain, only feel. Raw. Unavoidable. Like gravity.

I've been searching for her without knowing it. And now that I've found her, I'll do whatever it takes to keep her close. I'll use every advantage to make sure she's in my life.

So, I made her an offer. Laid it out like a business deal. Logical. Strategic. Safe.

Because I couldn't risk a no.

Because I'm not confident that what I feel for her is enough for her to agree to be with me. Not when she doesn't know me well enough, and because... Feelings alone aren't always enough to move people.

Sometimes, it scares them away.

And m-a-y-b-e, it's fear that what I said wouldn't matter. That my words wouldn't be enough. That she'd walk—even if I handed her my heart.

So, I gave her what I knew she couldn't ignore. Something solid. Concrete. A reason to stay. Marriage with benefits that she couldn't turn down.

That buys me time to show her what she means to me. How much she needs me. Because she may not know it yet, but I'm the one thing she can count on.

Viktor leans back in his chair, blue eyes narrowed as he studies his cards.

Across from him, Toren Whittington yawns. A deliberate move. Once a sworn enemy of our family, he became an unlikely ally after helping us fend off a Madison takeover. Then his sister married Tyler, and his entry into the family was official.

He slouches like he's bored, but his eyes are razor sharp, scanning the table.

To my right, Sinclair—our host—stacks his chips into surgical little towers.

Toren makes the opening move.

"I'm in." He flicks chips into the pot. "Try not to cry when I take your money."

Viktor snorts. "Keep dreaming."

"He's funding our entertainment," Brody drawls, sipping his whiskey. "A generous donor, really."

"Charity work," Sinclair adds dryly, not looking up from his cards.

Toren puffs on his cigar. "You're all just jealous of my optimism." He shoots a grin at Sinclair. "Besides, I heard you lost your shirt last week."

"That was strategy," Sinclair cracks his neck. "Long game."

"You look tired. Way past your bedtime, old man." Toren smirks.

Sinclair scoffs. "After 3 a.m. wakeups and diaper duty? Poker night's downhill skiing."

I glance at my cards, toss in a stack and, "Call."

Viktor watches me. "Confident, are we?"

"Trying to make things interesting."

Brody grins, adding his chips. "I'm in."

Sinclair matches the pot. "Wouldn't want to miss this showdown."

Toren taps ash into a tray and tosses in more. "In."

Viktor completes the circle. "Let's go."

My phone buzzes on the table. I glance at it. It's a message from the team watching her. I flip the device face-down.

Brody's eyes flick to the screen. "Business?"

"Personal." I grind my jaw.

Toren smirks. "That wouldn't be the good doctor, would it?"

"Play the damn game," I mutter.

Viktor leans forward. "You're rattled. That's new."

"Oh, he's definitely off his game," Brody says with a grin.

"You don't strike me as the kind to let personal distractions in," Viktor notes. "She must be something."

I glare. "Stay in your lane."

Brody laughs. "That's basically a confession."

I toss in more chips. "Enough talking. Play."

Viktor raises an eyebrow. "When Connor's curt, he's hiding something."

Toren chuckles. "Or someone."

"You'll crack eventually," Brody murmurs.

"Put your chips where your mouths are," I retort.

Sinclair lifts a brow. "Touchy tonight."

"It's refreshing," Viktor adds. "The great Connor Davenport—undone by a woman."

Brody leans back, satisfied. "Speaking of... Any word on Michael?"

He means Michael Sovrano, Sinclair's brother-in-law. Michael's wife Karma, suffered a massive heart attack during childbirth. We were all told she died as a result.

But rumors persist that Michael took her and the kids and moved back to Italy.

Sinclair calmly pushes his entire stack into the pot. "All in. Let's see who's bluffing."

He avoided the question. Interesting. Maybe he knows more than he's letting on?

"All in." Viktor meets the raise

Toren hesitates, then sets his jaw. "Screw it. I'm in."

"Let's go." Brody's grin widens.

I push my chips in. "Game on." Then I lay down my hand.

"You've got to be kidding," Toren growls.

Sinclair curses aloud. Viktor shakes his head.

Brody lifts his glass. "Should've seen it coming."

I rake the pot toward me with zero humility. "Next time, stay out of my personal life."

Viktor chuckles. "The night's still young."

"Good." Brody tips his glass. "I'm just getting warmed up."

For a second, surrounded by my brother and friends, I feel almost content. Almost. I've always been the outsider—too sharp, too fast. School, university, research—never belonged.

Even in biochemistry, peers resented how quickly I cracked what they couldn't. That's what made the Secret Service so appealing. New names. New roles. Control.

But Phe changed everything.

She's had me heated since I met her. My own personal fever. My *Fever*.

She gives me purpose. Something real. She's mine. And I'm not letting her go.

My phone buzzes again. *Another update.* The lights are on in her house. She's up. She normally leaves for work around 6:30 a.m.

I check the time; it's 5 a.m. *Time to move.*

"Gotta go," I say, rising. "Try not to bankrupt each other."

"Hey, I thought you were giving me a chance to recoup my losses?" Viktor protests.

"Next time." I nod at Brody. "You can donate my winnings, as usual." I pocket my phone and run out of there. I slide behind the wheel of my Aston Martin.

It's luxurious, yet practical for high speeds, and doesn't stand out in London's traffic. And now that she knows my identity, I no longer have to use the van as a disguise. I can't use this car when I'm under-cover, so it is with great pleasure that I ease the vehicle onto the road.

I drive up the road leading to her home and slow to a crawl to keep pace with her walking on the sidewalk.

She notices me and keeps walking. She's dressed in her usual yoga pants and T-shirt... And her yellow clogs. She still hasn't bought new shoes. She's enroute to the hospital.

I pull ahead of her, come to a stop, then open the door to the vehicle. When she draws abreast, I call out, "Get in the car, Doc."

She ignores me.

"Doc. Get. In. The. Car."

17

Phoenix

I get in the car. The question of disobeying His Royal Bossiness doesn't even arise.

Sliding into his car feels like slipping into a warm yet erotic embrace. His extraordinary eyes rake over me, checking for any sign of injury or hurt, and damn my traitorous heart, it skips a beat. His full focus on me is like the sun coming out after a week of dark clouds. I hadn't realized how much I wanted to feel its warmth again.

To stop that treacherous line of thought, I firm my lips. "What's so important that you scare the daylights out of me when I've not even had my coffee—"

"Here." He offers me the cup I hadn't noticed in the cupholder next to my seat.

"What's that?"

"You have a fondness for dirty chai latte, so—"

"Thank you." I take the cup and sip from it. The heady taste of cinnamon, cloves, and star anise, mixed with tea, milk and sugar explodes on my tongue and slides down my palate like honey.

"It's still hot," I breathe.

"It's an insulated cup."

Because, of course, he'd think of everything.

"Coffee shops aren't open this early." I skipped my coffee because I didn't want to face a glowering Drew in the kitchen. I opted to forego my morning caffeine rush, again.

Having a dirty chai, first thing in the morning, is more decadent than being gifted diamonds.

"I know one that is." He shrugs.

Like it's not a big deal that he went to the trouble of finding it and then turning up at my place before daybreak.

I take another sip of the caffeinated nectar and feel myself slip a little more in 'like' —*not going to use the other L-word*—with this walking dopamine hit with a jaw that seems to be carved by someone with a scalpel knife and too much time.

"Happy to see me?" he drawls.

"Of course, not," I try to huff, but my words come out soft and melting.

"Liar," he says in a husky voice, carrying within it the implication of all the dirty things he could do to me. I shiver.

I become aware of the butterflies in my stomach… And all because I'm sitting so close to him. Ugh!

To disguise how turned on I am just by being in this enclosed space smelling of his dark scent, I toss my head. "Did you just diagnose that with zero lab results? Impressive."

"So, you *were* lying."

"What gives you that idea?" I take another sip of the chai, then place the cup in the holder.

His lips quirk. "You have a tell."

"A tell?"

"When you're trying to be evasive, you like to use medical jargon to confuse the other person."

"I do?" I chew on my lower lip.

"Also, when you're nervous you wrap your arms about yourself."

"Oh." I look down to find my arms are, indeed, around my waist. I drop my hands in my lap.

As for the medical jargon? He's right. It's my fall back. Something I do by default. It used to annoy Drew, but I would laugh it off. Because, as I've recently come to realize, I was trying to drive him away.

"Where did you go to?" He leans over and tugs on my lower lip, pulling it free from my teeth. His touch shoots an incendiary signal across my nerve endings. Like a distress flare from a stowaway marooned on an island who's spotted a ship on the horizon. Is that why he came into my life? Because he heard my cry for help and responded to it?

He must sense some of my conflicting emotions, for his eyebrows knit. "Are you okay?"

I lean away, so he's forced to drop his arm. "Being with you confuses me. It makes me want things I didn't think I could have."

"You can have anything you want. You deserve *everything*."

The vehemence in his words makes me raise my gaze to his. I see the sincerity in his eyes, and a pressure knocks behind my eyes. It's ridiculous that this man, whom I barely know, can move me so deeply with his words. When the man I tried to convince myself I loved never once evoked such feelings in me.

"Hey." He reaches over and pinches my chin, so I have no choice but to turn my head in his direction. I keep my gaze averted, though.

"What is it, Phe?" His voice is tender, and there's a gentleness to his tone that further undoes me. Why does he affect me so much? And this, despite the fact he was sent to spy on me by my brother, and he didn't share that with me earlier. I try to pull away from him, but he doesn't let me. "Tell me what you're feeling."

Oh, I want to. *So much.* Perhaps, it's the understanding in his eyes. Perhaps, it's just him taking up all the oxygen in the enclosed space of this car.

"Fever" — he lowers his voice to a hush — "talk to me."

That edge of dominance in his voice spurts a frisson of need under my skin. My blood heats. My lower belly clenches. Before I can stop myself, I murmur, "You don't even know me. How can you surmise that I deserve anything?"

He notches his knuckles under my chin, so I have no choice but to look up and into his eyes. The burning intensity in them makes my heart stutter. My breath comes in small pants.

How is it that a simple look from him has me wanting to obey him?

It wasn't like this with Drew. I never felt this need to make him happy. I never cared enough to want to please him.

With Connor, it's different. He doesn't just stir something inside me. He unleashes it. Every look, every touch, every word from him crashes into me like the monsoon breaking over parched earth. Sudden. Overwhelming. Impossible to ignore. He doesn't wash over me gently—he drowns out everything else. And I want to let him.

It's wrong to compare them. My guilt where Drew is concerned is only amplified by how powerfully attracted I am to Connor.

"I may not have known you long, but the unhappiness in your eyes tells me you've been through a lot."

I open my mouth to protest, but he places a finger over my lips.

"I am going to do my best to lighten those shadows. My instinct tells me you deserve every happiness possible. And I plan to do everything in my power to deliver on it."

His words are overwhelming. I glance away, trying to get a grip on my emotions. Then, to buy myself time, I go on the offensive, again.

"How did you know to drive by my place to pick me up as I was leaving?"

"You leave for work every day around the same time. It's not difficult for me to drive by in time to pick you up."

He does have a point.

"And you're right. I do also have someone watching you, to make sure you're okay."

I jerk my chin around to stare at him. "You have someone watching me?"

"The gray sedan parked at the top of the street, then the janitor who works the ER, among others."

Anger squeezes my guts. I curl my fingers around my backpack, which I placed on the floor of the car earlier. "I can't believe you'd do that again; and after you know how much I hate surveillance on me."

"Better you be pissed off at me than unsafe."

"Why would I be unsafe?"

"The Davenports are a wealthy family with enemies. We have security on all family members. It's discreet, so unless something goes wrong, none of us would ever know there were people around guarding us."

"That's *your* family. I'm not a Davenport—"

"But you will be."

Argh, the arrogance of this man. I don't know whether to be impressed or upset with him. Or both? I throw up my hands. "But I'm not *yet*, so why the security?"

"Our enemies will have clocked that I'm interested in you."

I begin to protest, but he raises his hand. "And even if they haven't, I can't take the chance." He stops at a red light and turns to me. "I cannot... Will not let anything happen to you."

His words land with surgical precision.

A part of me registers the shift in my own physiology—elevated pulse, tightened breath, a warmth in my chest I can't quite classify.

I assumed he stepped back the moment he told my brother I was safe. That he'd done his duty and moved on. And maybe, part of me resented it—his silence, his distance. It felt like I'd lost something vital.

I felt his absence like a phantom limb.

Now, hearing this? Hearing how much I still matter to him? It hits somewhere deep. The intensity in his voice, the way he says *interested* like it's code for something far more dangerous, far more intimate. It coils heat through my chest.

I should dismiss it. Compartmentalize it. Log it as irrelevant to the situation at hand.

But I can't ignore the effect it has on me.

Not as a woman. Not as someone who's been seen by him—in ways I didn't know I wanted to be seen.

I don't say anything. *Can't.* Because I'm not supposed to want this. Not his protection. Not his obsession.

And definitely not this reckless, magnetic pull toward a man who sees everything, misses nothing… And still chooses me.

Hearing him declare how much I mean to him makes me realize how much I crave his attention.

Not trusting myself to voice the words, because it'll give away the changing state of my emotions toward him, I continue to look ahead.

We ride in silence, until he misses the turnoff to the hospital.

"Umm, you're going the wrong way," I point out.

"I'm not," he says with a smile that makes me think he's hiding something.

"What do you mean? The hospital's in the other direction." I jab my thumb in the direction we came from.

"You're not going to the hospital."

"Excuse me?"

"Check your messages."

With a scowl, I pull out my phone, and sure enough, a message from the Clinical Director informs me that, as per Health & Safety rules, I have the day off and I should not come in. What the— I drop the device back into my bag. "How did you manage that?"

"What makes you think I did anything? " His voice is innocent, but the twist in his lips says otherwise.

Anger begins a slow burn in my gut. "You do realize that if you're trying to woo me, this isn't how to do it? My job is sacred to me. And by interfering in it, you're pissing me off."

"Firstly, I'd never jeopardize your calling. I respect that you're a doctor. You save lives, and I don't take that lightly. And secondly"— he shoots me a quick sideways glance—"do *you* want me to woo you?"

Damn, I shouldn't have used that word.

I lean back in my chair. "A slip of the tongue. Ignore it."

"Hmm." His smile widens further, enough for me to see the slight indentation in his cheek. It's so not fair that everything about him appeals to me. Even when he's acting like a domineering asshole. *Especially when he's acting like a domineering asshole.*

Which says something about me. Something I'm not willing to examine deeply.

I clench my jaw, count to five, then blink slowly. "Seriously, I don't know how you managed that, but I don't appreciate you getting involved in how I do my job."

"I'd never do that. I simply wanted to make sure you had some time off. Which will only help you do your job better. I didn't mean to upset you. I'm sorry if I did." He stops the car at a traffic light.

Damn, he apologized again. It shouldn't surprise me. It's the decent thing to do. But it still surprises me that he does. Given his good looks and privileged background, plus my perception that he's definitely the kind of person more used to giving orders and being obeyed, I expected him to be an asshole. And I'm not used to him acting to the contrary. He's one of the most thoughtful men I've come across.

I really shouldn't stereotype him.

And he's right. I've been working nonstop without a break. I know, I've been flouting guidelines. But given the situation at the hospital, I figured the management wouldn't notice. Apparently, I was mistaken. I blow out a breath.

"It's all well and good that you're apologizing, but it doesn't change the fact that you interfered in my career. In *my* life."

"Only because I was concerned about you."

"You don't need to be. Also, you *could* have had the conversation with me first."

"Would that have prompted you to take the day off?"

"Umm…" I wriggle about in my seat. "Probably not."

He gives me a look which implies, *I rest my case.*

I toss my head. "It still doesn't excuse what you did."

"You needed time off. This was the only way to get you to take it. Also"—he softens his tone—"you should know, I would never compromise you in any way at your place of work."

He's so confident and so calm, I deflate a little. The light changes, and he eases the car forward.

"Doesn't change the fact that this is very high-handed of you," I say stiffly.

"I didn't mean to upset you, but it's my prerogative to make sure your health is not compromised."

When I stay silent, he blows out a breath. "I really am sorry if I come across as overbearing." His tone softens further.

I cross my arms across my chest. "You don't just come across as overbearing, you *are* overbearing."

"I am," he agrees.

"And controlling."

"True."

"And pushy, *and* domineering."

"All true." A hint of a smile plays around his eyes. And *holy endorphin ambush*, he looks incredible.

With his T-shirt stretched across his shoulders, close-cut hair, and that square jaw, he resembles a Hollywood superstar on his day off. And he smells incredible. It's nice to think I don't have to go into the ER. With a huge sigh, I lean back in my seat.

"Feel better?" he asks softly.

I toss my head, feeling the rest of my ire slip away. "Where are you taking me?"

He pulls up at another traffic light, then pulls a black silk scarf from his pocket and holds it out.

"What's that?" I ask warily.

"Remember what I said about you deserving every happiness?"

"Umm, yes?"

"Well, this is me making a start at it."

"How do you mean?" I look up to find his eyes gleaming with mischief. His features are lit up with a half-teasing smile that makes me pause. Combine his dominance and his tenderness with his touch of humor, and I'm a goner.

He glances at the silk scarf, then back at me. "Wear it over your eyes."

A flutter of excitement pools in my belly. "Pardon me?" I fold my arms over my chest, trying to ignore it.

"Trust me," he drawls, that infuriating half-smile curving his lips. "Just for a little while. Just until I can surprise you."

Surprise me?

I hesitate, the logical part of my brain screaming that I barely know this man and should probably run the other way. But my brother knows him well enough to call him a friend. And that magnetic pull in his gaze, and the way his presence seems to wrap around me like a physical force, tells me that Connor would never do anything to hurt me. Still, something inside me insists I resist his demand.

"Is this some kind of kinky fuckery?"

His eyebrows shoot up. "My, my, Ms. Hamilton, four letter words from your mouth sound like the background to my most erotic dreams."

I suppress a laugh. "If you think you can talk me into following your orders"—I tip up my chin—"you're absolutely right."

A surprised chuckle wells up his strong throat. The masculine sound plucks at my nerve endings. I'm so turned on, I have to look away, so he doesn't see the reaction he's drawing from me.

That's when he leans over and looks into my face. "Close your eyes."

I do. That edge in his tone insists I obey him.

He wraps the silken fabric over my eyes, his fingers brushing against my cheek as he knots it gently behind my head. A shiver runs through me. Electricity seems to hum between us. My thighs quiver. My scalp tingles. The world is blanked out, darkness in front of my eyes. The sound of my breathing is too large in the space.

Unable to see, everything else is magnified. His scent in the car grows more intense, until it surrounds me, wraps about me, pins me in place.

Then the car moves forward. I'm unable to stop the shivers of anticipation flaring in my cells.

"Where are we going?"

18

Phoenix

"If I tell you, it won't be a surprise."

A warmth squeezes my heart. *It's not arousal.* It's this traitorous sense that he cares for me…enough to have planned this. The anger I felt at his somehow causing me to have the day off has fled. In its place is a sense of relief. Like someone cut the weights I've been dragging behind me, letting lightness flood my chest.

"Fine." I toss my head, trying to hide how easily I've given in. "But if you drive us into the Thames, I'm dragging you down with me."

He chuckles, low and amused. The drive is longer than I expected, and with each turn, my curiosity grows. When the vehicle stops, I hear the crunch of gravel, then Connor helps me out.

"Can I take this off now?" I demand.

"Not yet." His voice is close to my ear, sending shivers racing down my spine. He keeps his hands on my shoulders, steering me gently forward. "Almost there."

A minute later, he unties the scarf, and I blink against the sudden glow. My jaw drops. In front of me stands a massive, hot air balloon, its colorful fabric billowing in the wind, lit up from within like a giant, glowing lantern. "You've got to be kidding me," I whisper.

Connor's hand settles on my lower back. "I thought you could use a change of perspective. Something to clear your head, something to prompt you to leave work behind, so you can relax."

"And you thought of a hot air balloon?" I ask in disbelief.

"I thought it would help to have something to break your daily routine."

I can't take my gaze off the multicolored sphere. "How did you know I've always wanted to ride in one?" I ask slowly.

"I'd say it was a lucky guess, but—" He takes my hand and helps me into the basket. It's wide and sectioned into compartments, the kind used for larger flights with groups.

There are padded partitions separating passenger sections. Connor steers me toward the last one—set apart by a high woven wall that blocks the view from the rest of the basket.

This corner is different. The floor's layered with a thick blanket. A small picnic basket is tucked into the corner, and above us, a canvas panel hangs loosely—a partial screen for added privacy. Only the open side of the basket looks out over the field below.

"But?" I prompt him.

"One time, I followed you into a bookshop. You spent a long time looking at a bookshelf. I went in after you left and realized most of the books featured hot air balloons."

"Oh." I remember the outing. It was a wonderful day—my first day off in a while—and I enjoyed walking around Primrose Hill and entertaining myself. "I thought I was being followed that day but put it down to my mind playing tricks on me."

He takes my hand in his. "I'm sorry I made you doubt yourself, but I'm not sorry that I followed you."

"You and my brother both have a nerve." I try to pull my hand away.

He holds onto it. "We have your best interests at heart."

I open my mouth to protest, but he shakes his head. "I understand, that doesn't justify the fact that I had you under surveillance, but I have to point out, there's no law against that."

"And how about the fact that you know far more about me than I do about you, huh? Isn't that unjust?"

His eyes glitter. I realize the error of what I said. I implied I want to find out more about him. Which reveals that I'm interested in him.

"What do you want to know?"

He runs his thumb across my wrist, and my limbic system does cartwheels.

Someone alert the endocrine board—my hormones have launched an unauthorized Formula One race through my bloodstream.

I don't want to give in to the treacherous warmth that shoots up my arm from where he's touching me. "I—" I glance around. "I want to know who's flying this balloon."

"Hmm."

I sense his amusement but refuse to show how disconcerted I am. This man watched me from afar. He checked out my social media feeds. He knows things about me which I've forgotten I've shared with the world. He hasn't done anything illegal but... It makes me feel vulnerable and... Yes, flattered. I feel giddy that this incredible man is so focused on me. *What is wrong with me?* Why am I not more upset about this?

To my relief, Connor doesn't comment about my abrupt change in subject.

Instead, he nods toward the far end. "The pilot's up front." Now that he mentions it, I can make out the operator, half-shielded by the metal frame of the burner at the center. He's in a small cabin with a window, through which I can just about make out his outline. We're far enough from him that we have complete privacy.

As the balloon begins to rise, the ground drifting away beneath us, my pulse kicks up—a shiver of fear chased quickly by the thrill of being airborne.

I don't realize I'm holding my breath until Connor slips his arm around my waist, pulling me closer.

"Hey," he murmurs. "You're safe. Just look."

The balloon begins to float up, putting more distance between the ground and me. I feel my worries drop away. He was right about that. I focus on the breathtaking sight of the city sprawling below us. The world seems to stretch infinitely, a vital part of the larger tapestry.

"It's beautiful," I whisper, barely noticing when he pulls a thermos from the picnic basket and pours steaming hot chocolate into a mug.

He hands it to me, brushing his knuckles against mine as he does. I take a sip, the warmth sliding down my throat, grounding me. We stand, wrapped in blankets, cocooned together in the morning air.

"Sometimes," Connor says softly, his lips brushing my temple, "you just need to see things from a different angle. Life doesn't always have to be about fixing everyone else. Sometimes it's about just...being. About taking care of yourself. About letting someone else take care of you."

I don't answer. Words feel too fragile for what's blooming inside me. So, I lean into him instead. I turn my face into the solid warmth of his chest, letting his steady heartbeat ground me. I breathe him in. All strength and heat and quiet protection. For the first time in what feels like forever, I let myself exhale. Like I'm home. Like I'm his to protect.

When I tilt my head up, his gaze is already on me—steady, unflinching.

There's something stripped bare in his eyes. A kind of raw vulnerability that knocks the breath from my lungs. We look deeply into each other's eyes. The connection is so intimate, it feels like our secret selves are reaching out to each other, entwined in a slow dance neither of us fully understands, but both of us crave.

He dips his head, until our eyelashes entwine. His lips brush mine. Whisper soft. His breath tastes of mint and that darkness I've come to associate with him. The one calling out to the part of me I've hidden from everyone, especially myself.

The kiss is tender but underlying it is a charged promise.

One which speaks of long nights spent with my skin sliding over his. Of sweat-beaded brows, and heaving chests, and choppy breaths. Of his mouth on my swollen breasts, in the dip of my navel, the rock-hard bud of my clit. Of unspoken promises that he seems to feed to me as his tongue slides over mine. A shudder spirals down my back.

He takes my now empty cup and places it down on the blanket next to us, along with his.

He straightens, and when he pulls me up on my tiptoes, and then even closer into his broad chest, I melt into him.

The city below blurs into a kaleidoscope of color. I thread my hands through his hair and tug. A growl rumbles up his throat. He grips my hip, the other large hand sliding down to take a handful of my butt. He squeezes. A moan trembles from my mouth. *Oh God.*

My arse should not be such a collection of sensitive nerve endings sending signals to my brain, causing my thoughts to meld into each other.

Just when I think I can't take more of the emotions enveloping me, he deepens the kiss. He holds me firmly against his crotch, where the evidence of his arousal lays heavily against my lower belly. A hormonal storm is brewing in the quadrant of my lower abdomen.

Uterine contractions: imminent. Hypothalamus to ovaries—stand by for launch.

The kiss goes on and on. The electricity from the meeting of our mouths zips around my chest, circles my nipples, and arrow to my pussy. My clit throbs with such intensity… I ache for so much more.

When we break apart, I rest my forehead against his chest.

The quiet hum of the burner above us is a contrast to the wild boom of my heart. "Talk about changing my perspective."

He chuckles, then tips my chin up and surveys my features. His own are filled with satisfaction. "I hope you're hungry. I am."

Then the world tilts. He lowers me onto the cushions and follows me down to cover my body with his.

19

Connor

"What are you—" She gasps as I slide down her body and press my face into the apex of her thighs.

A shiver runs up her body. Her breath hitches. "Connor, the balloon operator—"

"He's called the balloonist. He can't see or hear us. He's also signed a non-disclosure agreement, so he won't talk about this trip to anyone."

A small smile curves her lips. "Are you always this thorough?"

"You ain't seen nothin' yet." I grab her hips to hold her in place. "You smell decadent."

She whimpers.

The sound turns my blood into a river of lava, my cock a volcano swelling with the pressure of the shifting tectonic plates deep below the surface.

I glance up into her flushed features, her parted lips, the red streaked across her cheeks. "If you want me to stop, tell me. Now," I order her.

She blinks, then in the next breath she raises her hips, bringing that sweet, delightful flesh between her thighs closer to my mouth.

"Good girl."

She shudders, the anticipation flowing up her body like the tips of waves flush with the promise of a tempest. One I intend to surf and harness for her pleasure, and my own. I squeeze the tops of her thighs, pulling them apart. She groans. And when I fasten my mouth around the ripe fruit of her cunt, she cries out.

"Connor." She digs her fingers into my hair and tugs.

The pain ricochets down my spine and clamps around my cock, making it swell. It's a preamble, a taste of how incredible it's going to be when I'm finally seated inside of her. But first, I need to tease her, to taunt her, to show her the power of pleasure, the rightness in making her come. The absolute ownership I have over her body. Only, she doesn't know it yet. I'm going to teach her what it's like to revel in the kind of sensual gratification the poets have written about, and icons have sung about.

Something tells me, my hard-working doctor has drowned herself in work because she hasn't been satisfied in other aspects of her life. Which is where I come in. The thought of anyone else holding her, kissing her, loving her, brings out my inner beast. My chest swells with anger. My lungs feel like they're on fire. I intend to wipe away the memory of anyone who came before me. So that she only remembers my touch, my feel, my scent, the way I tug on her pussy lips and make her jolt. The way I lick my way down her slit to her forbidden hole, wetting the fabric covering her center.

"Connor, please," she cries. "Please. Please. Please."

With a wicked grin, I fasten my teeth around the button of her clit outlined through her yoga pants and panties, and tug. She bows off the floor of the hot air balloon, the action making the basket rock gently. She moans, spreading her legs further apart. "Help me, Connor."

"What do you want?"

"I want —" She swallows. Then, as if unable to voice the demand trembling on her lips, she throws her arm over her eyes. "I want to come," she mumbles under her breath.

I sit back on my haunches, and after a second, she peers out from under her arm and stares at me with a panicked expression. "What are you doing?"

"What do you want me to do for you, Doc?"

"I told you, didn't I?" She presses her lips together.

"I need you to say it louder, and slowly, please."

Her eyes flash, then she lowers her arm, her fingers bunched into a fist. I merely tilt my head, enjoying the flush deepening across her cheekbones. She seems like she's going to refuse, then she tips up her chin. "I want to come. I want *you* to make me come."

"How?"

She stills.

"How do you want to come? On my fingers? My tongue or my —" I lean in slightly. "Cock?"

"On your —" She swallows. "On your cock."

"Hmm..." I nod. "That's good. But you haven't done anything to deserve it yet."

"What?!" Her jaw falls open.

I manage to stifle the chuckle crawling up my throat, enjoying her shock and surprise. Not that I don't want to be inside of her. I want nothing more than to feel her snug walls close around my throbbing shaft. But not yet.

First, I want her to enjoy the foreplay. I want every part of her body to feel like it's awake and open to receiving. I want her cells to tremble with yearning, the way I feel inside. I want to see the stubbornness that's such an inherent part of her awaken. I want to see the fight in her stance. For every time I challenge her, she rises beautifully to the occasion. She comes alive like a flower opening its petals to the sun. Allowing herself to live in the moment. That is the woman I want to see more of. So, I nod.

"What are you willing to do for this orgasm, baby?"

She frowns. I wonder if it's because of the nickname I used, but then she bites out, "Anything. I'll do anything for it. Please use your fingers or, preferably, your tongue, or even better, your big fat cock on me, please?"

I bark out a laugh. "You surprise me at every turn."

The skin around her eyes softens. "And you... Are a bundle of contradictions. Diamond hard on the outside. Oozing with softness inside."

I reel back as if she's struck me. "Soft? You must be mistaken."

"Am I?" A knowing look comes into her eyes. "You dropped everything to help out a friend. My brother, in this case. Never mind, it was to do something not strictly legal. Still, you couldn't turn down his plea. Then, you found out about my ER being in trouble. You took advantage of it to spring that crazy scheme about marrying me —again, it's an idea in a gray area—but underneath it was this desire to help me."

I stalked her because I was obsessed with her. I used her weakness—the fact that she needs help and would not ask her own family for it—against her. Yet she sees it as evidence of my caring disposition.

A part of me is angry that *she* can be so gullible.

That she chose to give me the benefit of the doubt throws light into the darker corners of my soul. This curvy, intelligent, sensuous woman sees through the mask I wear for the world.

Deprived of the love of a mother, with a weak father, and an overbearing grandfather who equated nurturing with enforcing his brand of exacting discipline, my brothers and I grew up in a loveless atmosphere.

My brothers found solace in the discipline of the Marines—the rules honing them into weapons effective in times of conflict.

My older brothers have been lucky to meet women who've redeemed them.

But I haven't held out such notions for myself. I've taken on enough missions where I had to hide my true self, so I haven't had to face my own ghosts. It's much easier to subsume myself in a character.

The fact that this woman has seen through my façade makes me panic. And angry that she sees me so clearly. The need for her builds to a crescendo.

The need to punish her... To punish myself for wanting her so much. For becoming dangerously addicted to her in a way I swore I'd never allow myself to depend on another.

I slip my fingers under the waistband of her yoga pants, and in one smooth move, I jerk them down her legs and off, along with her clogs.

She gasps and begins to close her thighs, but I grip each one and stop her. I stare at the wet patch on the crotch of her panties, and a fierce satisfaction grips me. "Look at you, already so wet and ready for me." I cup her pussy. "The heat from your core could melt the devil himself. And I am but a man."

She makes a sound at the back of her throat, and when I jerk my chin up to look at her face, it's to find her panting.

Her pupils are blown, the hazel having turned to a thin circle of gold blazing around the black infiltrating them. Her lips are parted, pulse beating wildly at the hollow of her neck.

"You're a goddess." I jerk my chin. "Raise your arms."

When she does, I pull off the T-shirt, then lean back on my heels. I take in the black lacy bra, with demi cups over which her breasts spill. Her aureoles are a shadow against the fabric, her nipples buttons of delight that peak the longer I stare at them.

My eyes move down to her narrow waist, the flare of her hips encased in the sheer panties forming a pair with her bra. "Did you wear this for me, hmm?"

She moans, then shakes her head. "Why would I?"

"Because you knew I'd come for you. Because you knew I wouldn't keep away. Because you knew you'd spun your web, and I'm caught, and I wouldn't be able to rest until I have you."

20

Phoenix

I wore this for him.

His eyes flash. Those arctic irises of his turn into winter steel. Hard. Unyielding. With riptides of fury beneath the surface that call to me to get lost in them.

If I give in, I'll never find myself again. He'll drown every logical thought in my head and make me subsume myself in him, until I forget who I am. It's my last bid at some kind of freedom. A desperate attempt at holding onto a part of me I've never shared with anyone else. *Not even Drew.*

But watching his nostrils flare and the anger fill every crevasse on his face, I know genuine fear. It's a reminder that he has many hidden parts. He's only shown me the profile he thinks I can cope with. Of course, I meant it when I said the softer parts of him are hidden inside. I feel them. Sense them. Know I am right, but to see his features turn to marble, and his expression freeze, sends a chill up my spine.

"What did you say?" He leans in close, until our noses bump, his eyelashes tangle with mine, and his breath is hot on my cheek. Sleet and magma. How could he be two completely opposing forces of nature at the same time?

"Repeat it to my face." He bares his teeth, the incisors sharp, the gleaming white teeth reminding me of the predator trapped under his skin. The one he's kept on a leash.

It didn't occur to me until now, he must be exercising a great deal of control by holding his emotions in check. The frozen countenance he presents to me hides an inferno inside. Or maybe I did know but chose not to acknowledge it, until now.

"I..." I swallow. "I said—"

He cants his head, the tic of a savage beast waiting to pounce on me. A tremor grips me—a mix of being scared and being so very turned on. Moisture trickles down my inner thigh.

I'm sure I've gone past the stage of soaked panties to dampening the blanket that lines the floor of this basket we're in.

"I said... I might have worn it for you," I admit grudgingly.

"Hmm..." A wicked look flickers in his eyes. "Good save, but perhaps... It's a little too late?"

Before I can react, he snaps the thin panel that connects my bra cups. I gasp. Then he reaches down and tears off my panties. Cool air flutters over my exposed nipples and cunt. "What are you doing?" I rear up.

He flattens his palm on my sternum, so I'm pushed back. He holds me there, then surveys my flushed and naked body, taking his time. Dragging his gaze from the top of my hair, which must be haloed around my face, down to my toes, which I've curled in a vain bid to try to draw into myself.

"You're magnificent," he rumbles. The anger in his gaze is replaced by a worshipful glint which draws some of the tension from my shoulders.

I've never been defensive about my curves. I love my body just the way it is. It's helped me withstand the rigors of training to be a doctor, and the demands of my job as an ER specialist. It's helped me help people and save many lives. Not even Drew's occasionally thinly veiled barbs where he'd imply I'd be better off on a diet, so I'd have no qualms about my plus-size figure.

But for a second there, as I was bared to his gaze, I felt a moment of worry that I wouldn't measure up to his expectations. Not when he's tall and broad, with sculpted features and a body fashioned from bricks of muscle. But the admiration in his gaze, the lust in his eyes, and the hint of red that laces his cheekbones tells me I needn't have worried. He finds me irresistible, given how he's unable to take his gaze off my body.

It's intoxicating to have his full attention. He looks at me like I'm the only thing that matters, and I drink it in like oxygen.

He straddles my hips, then cups both my breasts in his palms and squeezes. Tendrils of heat lasso around my center. He squeezes my nipples, tweaking them with enough force that I cry out.

"Who do these breasts belong to?" He presses them together, then leans down and draws one of them in his mouth. He sucks deeply. Enough for my womb to contract in response. Then moves his mouth to the other and treats it similarly. He releases it with a pop, then stares at me.

"Tell me," he demands. "Who do these belong to?"

"You," I shudder.

Satisfaction is fierce in his eyes. Without releasing his hold on me, he slides down my body, so his shoulders force my thighs apart. Still keeping his eyes on me, he licks up my pussy lips. I cry out, throw my head back, and pant loudly. *Ohmigod.* The sensations, the feelings, the way my womb feels ready to ignite turns my veins into liquid flames.

He continues to knead my breasts and pluck at my nipples, then stabs his tongue inside my melting slit. My hips bow off the floor. I push my pelvis up so his tongue slides further inside of me and his nose brushes against my clit. A whimper is drawn from me. I dig my fingers into his hair, tugging on the short strands. Wanting to hold him closer. Wanting to push him away. The contradictory feelings I have for him are not a surprise. Everything about this man puts me in conflict with myself.

He swept in and turned my life upside down. I'd resigned myself to a life where I would never find love, and then he appeared. He draws the kind of pleasure from my body I didn't think I was capable of feeling.

An intensity of emotions seems to give rise to a war beneath the surface. Hope and dread in the same breath. Desire laced with guilt. Longing wrapped in fear. A gown made of satin and thorns. Love mixed with...

Hold on. Love? What makes me think of love?

Everything between us has been carnal. Lust. The rush of endorphins must have addled my brain. My vitals must be off. The increased capillary profusion must be carrying an overflow of blood to my non-vital regions. Specifically, the one between my thighs. That must be the reason I'm thinking of this four-letter word so quickly after meeting this man. I must grow still, for he notices the change in my body language.

"What's wrong?" he growls against my swollen cunt.

When I don't reply, his eyebrows knit. Determination turns his jaw into sculpted marble. He swipes his tongue up my pussy, from puckered hole to clit, and my thighs tremble. He curls his tongue around the swollen bud, then bites down gently on it. My entire body jolts.

"Connor!" My eyes flutter in response to the pain that whiplashes through my cells.

"Eyes on me," he orders.

I can't disobey him. My eyelids open as if they're linked to the command in his tone. I watch as he continues to eat me out. He curls his tongue around the diamond hard nub of my clit; I moan. He licks his way down to my weeping slit, thrusts his tongue inside and does something indescribable; my eyes roll back in my head. The combination of him eating me out and pinching my nipples has every part of my body vibrating with tension. Little balls of fire erupt in my bloodstream, in my cells, from each pore in my body.

Surely, this is an acute sympathetic nervous system response, which only happens in times of extreme arousal. My libido seems to spike like a cytokine storm, sending alarm bells ringing through my brain. "I'm close," I gasp. "So close."

The pleasure is too much, the waves of sensation flooding my body with dopamine. It blends with the red lashings of pain that radiate out from my nipples, which he continues to pluck. He maneuvers my body like a fine surgical instrument he's going to use in an operation aimed at cutting me off at the knees and turning me into a blubbering mass of need. Of yearning. Of hope. Of pleasure. Of everything I've denied myself all my life.

"Connor," I groan. "Please. Please," I warble, half out of my head with the sensations, not caring if I make sense or not.

"Who does this pussy belong to?" His words vibrate against my core, pushing that tsunami of feelings further up my spine. Up toward that edge. The horizon I'm aiming for.

"You." I lock my ankles around his shoulders. "Only you."

A shiver grips his big body, a trembling signaling that I pleased him. The tension coiled under his skin turns his muscles into a vibrating pillar of strength. All of which is focused on where his lips are on me, between my legs. He doubles his efforts.

Licking. Sucking. Biting down on my cunt. Then squeezes my nipples with such intensity that pain lashes across the backs of my eyes, turning my eyeballs into circular blasts of delight.

My breathing fractures. The tension along my sacrum tightens, and heat coils low in my abdomen.

My pelvic floor contracts in spasms I can't control. My inner muscles clench involuntarily, a reflexive cascade driven by the over-stimulation of sensory afferents.

Pressure peaks at the base of my spine, and a full-body tremor arcs through me—autonomic, unrelenting. The edges of my vision blur as blood rushes to my head, and a rush of dopamine ignites behind my frontal lobe.

"Come for me, right now," he snaps.

I shatter. My climax crashes over me, the pleasure laced with fury roaring through me, ripping through the chains I placed around my emotions. Myself. My heart. My very soul. Sweeping away the woman I was. The one who blamed herself for everything that happened in her life. It sweeps me over the edge and then, I'm in free fall. Without gravity. Weightless. I float back to earth. Through white space. Through timelessness.

When I come back into my body, it's to find he's licking up the moisture on my inner thighs.

I flush, the honeyed heat crawling through my veins to settle in parts of me he's awoken. His eyes are molten, a myriad of emotions in them which I dare not question. I feel raw. Like he tore off the bandage I've wrapped myself in for so long.

He crawls over me and presses his lips to mine. I taste myself on him, the sweetness of my cum overlaid with his muskier taste. It's a concoction which goes straight to my head. Is there a me and him in any other way than this? *There could be, if I agree to marry him.*

"Eyes on me." His growl slices through my thoughts as precisely as a scalpel. But not to cut. To claim. "When I'm with you, I demand your complete attention. You will not think of anything else when you're with me. You feel me, Fever?"

"Fever?" I ask thickly.

"You're in my veins. A virus without a cure. You've infiltrated my blood. Taken residence in my cells. I don't think I can be rid of you."

I allow myself a chuckle. "You sure know how to romance me."

He nods, his expression serious enough to burn. "I know your language. I know what turns you on. I know what you like. I know the words that mean so much to you." He kisses me again, his lips hard, the contact sweet. His taste sinks into my palate. Coats my tongue. Laces my bloodstream.

He's taken residence inside of me as much as he claims I have in him. And the feeling is... A lot. Overwhelming. It suddenly feels like too much. I tear my mouth from his and take big gasps of air. And when I push at his shoulders, he instantly pulls back.

"What's wrong?"

I shake my head, ashamed of my reaction. It's not anything he did. In fact, I love his possession. His dominance. His ability to command my thoughts and make me forget. Too bad, he can't change the past.

He cups my face, and my gaze is drawn to his. "Whatever it is, I'm here for you. I can help you. I'll make sure no one ever harms you again." His words are soft, but his tone is steely. His gaze piercing. All knowing. Like he's looking into my soul, discovering my secrets.

I wish I could tell him everything. I wish I could share what's holding me back from opening myself up to him. But I can't. This is something I need to deal with myself. This guilt which is eating away at me—I need to come to terms with it myself. So, I pull away from him.

"I'm hungry." I glance past him at the packed basket in the corner of the balloon. "Are you going to feed me?"

21

Connor

ENTRY 5

•Touch Tolerance: High. Lingers when feeling safe. Avoids when conflicted.

- Breathing Pattern: Shallow, chest-based when flustered.
- Voice: Drops half an octave when aroused.
- Skin Reaction: Blush pattern – starts at clavicle, rises to cheek.
- Observed Behavior: Talks to self when anxious. Uses medical metaphors in personal reasoning.
- Additional quirk: Addicted to chocolate bars from hospital vending machine.
- Internal Conflict: Still grieving. *A past betrayal?* Projects confidence to mask emotional scarring.
- Coping Style: Overwork. Detachment. Sarcasm. Book immersion.

- Book Preferences: Spicy romance with redemption arcs.
- ~~Notes: I know her laugh, her pulse, the way she smells when she's just left the hospital. I know how she trembles when she's scared. I've never known anyone this way. Or wanted to.~~

Note to self: Subject holds secrets. *How can I make her trust me enough to share them with me?*

22

Connor

I tuck her torn bra and panties into my pocket before helping her back into her clothes.

Watching her come undone beneath my mouth—feeling her shatter and lose every last thread of control—was a deeper, rawer satisfaction than chasing my own release could ever give me.

We eat on the blanket, surrounded by the clouds and the sight of the city below. The sun brings out the strands of red in her auburn hair. Her hazel eyes, dilated earlier, regain their color. As she relaxes, the golden flecks in her eyes sparkle. She looks around, taking in our temporary position, far away from everything and everyone. But her swollen lips and the remnants of red on her cheeks, along with her hair, which is down from her messy bun, declare exactly what we've been up to. A surge of pride fills me.

I'm responsible for relaxing her, thanks to the orgasm I gave her. It's clear, something is bothering her. I hoped she'd confide in me. And I'm disappointed she hasn't.

But I have faith in myself…and in this connection between us. It's only a matter of time before she tells me. I'll coax it out of her. I'll win her trust, so she'll feel comfortable enough to share everything with me. For now, I want her to take this time for herself. To enjoy this interval where there are no other demands on her time… Except for mine, that is.

"This wine is amazing." She takes another sip, then beams at me. The openness in her features, the curve of her lips, the softness around her eyes… All of it makes my heart skip a beat.

"*You* are amazing." I raise a glass in her direction.

She blushes. "You…you don't need to sweet talk me."

"I'm not." I take her flute and place it on the floor, along with mine. "It's not every day that I skip my responsibilities and plan a trip in a balloon with a beautiful woman." I take her hand in mine.

"Oh." She lowers her chin. "It's not every day that *I* skip my responsibilities and get to ride in a balloon with a handsome man."

"You think I'm handsome?" I smirk.

"I knew that was coming." She groans. "And you know that you are."

I bring her hand to my lips and kiss her fingertips. "It's different hearing it from you."

She swallows. "You're turning on the charm, aren't you?"

"Is it working?"

She laughs a little. This time, when she tugs on her hand, I release it. She locks her fingers together and places them in her lap.

"I know you come from a very wealthy family and you're James' friend. I didn't hear much about you because—" She hesitates. "Because James is ten years older than me. He left home when I was eight. He joined the Marines, traveled the world, then became very busy trying to make his career as a chef."

So, she's taking me up on asking me questions about myself. Good. I want her to get to know me better. Enough that she begins to trust me.

"When did the two of you meet?" She tilts her head.

"He was in the same platoon as my oldest brother, Nathan. He came home a few times, and we hit it off. When he left the

Marines and was trying to launch his restaurant, I invested in his business."

"James didn't draw on his inheritance to get started?"

"Like you, he was independent enough to want to make it on his own. He used the money he'd saved from his career and raised the rest."

"That must have been difficult," she says slowly.

"It was bloody hard. But he's a stubborn son-of-a-bitch. He persisted."

"And look where he is today." She takes another sip of her wine. "It's quite inspiring. Gives me hope that if I keep persisting in my chosen career, one day soon... Perhaps... I'll see the light."

"And what's that?"

She shoots me a sideways glance.

"Where do you want to be five, ten years from now?" I prompt.

"I've never been one to plan that far out, but if I had a choice—" She looks into the distance. "I hope I can get more experience with trauma situations and keep helping people. I don't necessarily count growth as rising through the ranks, but more in the richness of experience I get along the way."

"That's mature of you." I can't help but look at her in a new light.

"You expected me to outline a career path, huh?" She laughs. "I've never been the kind attracted to linear advancement. It always felt shallow to mark my progress in that way, you know?"

"So, what satisfies you?"

She chews on her lower lip. I watch, fascinated, wishing I could feel her mouth wrapped around my cock, then force my gaze away. The attraction to her may have started out as physical, but the more I get to know this woman, the more I'm turned on by her intelligence, her quirky personality, her generosity in wanting to help her colleagues, her community. I've never met someone so multifaceted.

"This might sound like a cliché but"—she looks up at me from under her eyelashes—"bringing someone back from the verge of death, knowing I've helped to give them a new lease on life is the most incredible feeling in this world. It's also made me aware that I can't take all the credit for such miracles. There's a bigger force out there playing a role. Which is the only explanation for some people surviving."

Our gazes meet and hold. I'm struck by the determination in hers, plus the awe and this absolute captivation. One day, she's going to look at me in the same way. And it's going to be for more than an orgasm.

I tug on her hand. She loses her balance, and I pull her into my lap.

"Hey," she says breathlessly.

"Hey." I tuck a loose strand of hair behind her ear.

"You made me talk about myself again," she whispers.

"I love hearing your voice. I want to know everything about you."

"This was supposed to be *me* getting to know *you* better." Her lips part.

I fix my gaze on her plump mouth. "Ask me anything."

She licks her mouth. "What's your favorite color?"

"Black."

"No surprise there." She snorts. "Favorite movie?"

"Zero Dark Thirty."

"Good choice."

"And The Notebook."

"No," she gasps.

I chuckle, "You're right. It's not. But it was worth saying it to see the look in your eyes."

"You're a jerk." She shoves at my shoulder.

"I'm *your* jerk," I correct her.

"Oh." She draws in a sharp breath.

Once again, the chemistry between us flares. The air thickens. A gentle breeze wafts over us, turning the entire scene into magic. I lean in closer to her as she moves toward me.

When our lips are mere inches apart, she murmurs. "What scares you more—being alone, or being seen?"

"Being seen. Because if someone sees you... *Really* sees you... They know where to hurt you."

Like you can.

She nods, her expression serious. "Deep answer."

"It was a deep question." I trace my thumb over the curve of her eyebrow, down the slope of her nose.

She trembles. "Here's a not-that-deep one." Her pulse beats at the base of her throat, "What would your ten-year-old self think of you now?"

"That I'm the luckiest man in the world for sitting next to the most beautiful woman in the world.

"Aww." She sighs. "That's so cute. And I don't believe you, but I appreciate the sentiment."

"I mean it"—I hold her gaze—"and you know it."

Something flickers in the depths of her eyes. She nods almost imperceptibly.

"Can I ask you a question?" I hold her gaze. Without waiting for her to reply, I ask, "Why do you sometimes tap your chest three times?"

She seems taken aback. "Was it that evident I do that?"

"Only to me. And only because I watch you so closely."

She lets out a soft chuckle. "My own personal stalker. Of course, you'd notice something like that."

Her gaze flicks away, as if sorting through her thoughts, then returns to mine. "It's a self-regulation technique. Something I picked up along the way."

I tilt my head. "Do you often need help staying regulated?"

"When I became a resident," she says slowly, "the hours were brutal. Constantly on my feet, juggling impossible demands. I started snapping. Losing my patience. This tapping exercise helped me stay calm under pressure—kept me from unraveling."

She pauses, then nods, like she's made a choice to let me in. "But honestly? I think it goes back to my mum. She wasn't cruel. Just... Demanding. Precise. I was always on edge around her, terrified of messing up, of disappointing her. I don't think she meant to be harsh. But the pressure to be perfect? That was real. And during med school, it built up. I found myself more reactive than others, more easily triggered. This"—she taps her chest again—"keeps me centered."

I watch her closely. "I want to be that for you. Your anchor. The one who steadies you. Who helps you come back to yourself... If you'll let me."

Something shifts in her face. The sharp edges soften. Her eyes shimmer.

"And there you go again," she says, voice tight with emotion. "Always raising the bar on what a romantic gesture should be."

She swallows, offering me a shaky smile. "I've got another question for you."

"Ask me."

"What's the one thing you've always wanted—but never let yourself have?"

"This. You. A place to land." I close the distance between us, until our eyelashes tangle. "I've always been better at walking away, but not this time."

"Wow," she breathes, "that's intense."

"I'm an intense person."

"No kidding." She lowers her gaze to my lips. "Are you going to kiss me again?"

"Do you want me to?"

She leans in until her lips are a millimeter from mine. "Don't you?"

"Do it," I speak against her lips.

This time, I want her to take what she wants. I want her to initiate the kiss.

She raises her eyelids, and our gazes clash. I look deeply into her eyes drowning in the green, the gold, the silver that makes me feel like I'm skiing down a slope and losing control. Then her mouth touches mine. Soft. Sweet. It's like the gossamer wings of destiny have brushed up against me. My heart stutters. My balls tighten. I hold still, barely allowing myself to breathe.

She licks between my lips; a groan rumbles up my throat. She makes a noise deep in her throat, then flattens her breasts against my chest. She feels lush and feminine.

Her curves cling like silk to the angles of my body. And when she twines her hands around my neck and slides her fingers through the hair at the nape of my neck, a primal thrill spirals under my skin. *Jesus Christ.*

This obsession with her is turning into a passion burrowing deep into my bones and hooking its claws into my soul.

I want to squeeze her tits, grab at the fleshy globes of her butt, and grind her core against my aching cock. I want to kiss her deeply and ravage her mouth. I want to throw her down on the carpet, tear off her clothes and rut into her until she comes.

I want to make her orgasm, until she's as high on endorphins as this balloon we're sailing in. Higher, even. I want to... Cuddle her after and take care of her. The feelings she elicits in me eddy through my body and pound against my mind. When she breaks away, we're both panting.

"Fuck," I say softly.

Her lips tremble. "Yeah." She cups my cheek. "Thank you for doing this." She looks around us again, then back at me. "I'll never forget this day."

"There will be more like these."

"Oh?" Her face doesn't mirror my conviction.

"There will," I say with finality. "I found you, and I'm not letting go of you."

"I haven't agreed to marry you," she waggles a finger at me.

"Not yet..." *But you will.*

She frowns. "I don't mean to lead you on. I'm not good marriage material. I can barely take care of myself."

"Let *me* take care of you instead."

She swallows.

"I have more than enough mind space for both of us."

She looks at me from under her eyelashes. "What makes you say that?"

"I'm perceptive enough to realize that something from your past is holding you back."

She pales.

"I'm not going to probe. I don't want you to feel uncomfortable. And I don't want to coerce you into deciding— Well, maybe not the last—" I shrug. "But I'm patient. I can wait."

She bites down on her lower lip. Distress is evident on her face, but I'm distracted by how her teeth worry her lower lip. How the creamy expanse of her neck makes me want to place my nose in the hollow of her throat and breathe in her essence deeply. I bring my fingers to my nose and sniff.

She stills. "Did you... Are you —"

"Smelling the remnants of your cum?" I nod.

She draws in a sharp breath. "That's...filthy."

"And you love it."

She blinks rapidly, then dips her chin. "I do."

"Good girl," I rumble.

She flushes. "I don't know what's happening to me." She lets out a breath and shakes her head. "Growing up, I was the rule-follower. Well, other than holding firm that I wanted to become a doctor and that I wanted to do it on my own strength." She chuckles. "My mother didn't approve, but I knew it was right for me. And perhaps, I wanted to prove her wrong. And I wanted to make her proud. So, I focused. No partying. No distractions. No staying out late."

A humorless laugh escapes her.

"Even when I graduated med school, when the others were out getting drunk and letting loose, I stayed home and celebrated by buying a stack of books. That was my idea of a wild night."

Her voice softens.

"But then I met you... And something shifted. Like I've uncorked some part of myself I didn't even know existed. This deep, aching hunger. For sensation. For danger. For things I've never let myself want."

She looks up at me, eyes dark and turbulent, brimming with something raw and uncertain.

"It makes me question if I ever really knew who I was... Or if I've just been living a version of myself built to win my mother's approval."

I lean in, my voice low. "That's a hell of an insight. How does it feel, realizing that?"

Her gaze flickers away, the muscles in her jaw shifting as she thinks. "It makes me want to throw caution to the wind...and revel in the feelings you've helped uncork."

The honesty in her voice is unguarded, almost fragile. She's laying herself bare, and she's choosing to do it with me.

Her trust humbles me. Her vulnerability arouses me. And the knowledge that I'm the one she's opening up to? That's a heady, dangerous thing. Warmth squeezes my chest. The need to take care of her overwhelms me.

I pick up a strawberry and hold it to her mouth. She bites around the plump fruit, the juice dripping down her chin.

Instantly, I lean in and lick it up.

When I sit back, she's staring at me with wide eyes. "That's what I mean." She chews and swallows slowly. "There's an unabashed sensuality about you that blows my mind."

In response, I pick up a slice of cheese and trace her lips with it. Her pupils dilate. Holding my gaze, she obliges. I feed it to her, then spread some pâté on a cracker and coax her to eat it.

"Not the only thing I want to blow," I confess.

She stops chewing, coughs. I smirk, satisfied at her response, and hold her wineglass to her lips.

She takes a sip. "You didn't come earlier," she points out.

"This wasn't about me. This was about your pleasure. I wanted to help you relax. To help you clear your mind of stress and give you time off from daily life."

"Is that what the doctor ordered?" She tilts her head.

"That's what *I* ordered," I agree.

"It's not going to make me change my mind about marrying you," she warns again.

"We'll see about that." I kiss her, and she responds with such ardor, my skin begins to burn with renewed need.

She may not realize it, but her actions undermine her words. Not that I'm going to point that out to her. That would be the quickest way of shutting her down, and I don't want that. I'm going to charm her into agreeing to my proposal. And once I make up my mind about something, I won't stop until I've accomplished it.

Softening the kiss, I wind my arm about her shoulder and pull her close. We watch the ground come toward us as the balloonist brings us back to where we started.

I help her out, then lead her to my car.

"Thank you." She turns to me as we pull away. "That was incredible."

"You're welcome." All too soon, we pull up in front of her house. I turn off the ignition.

She wrings her fingers in her lap, look straight ahead. "I, uh, I would invite you home but — "

I reach over and squeeze her hands. "I understand."

"You do?" She looks at me strangely.

"You're not ready to share that part of you with me, yet. But you will. Soon."

She seems taken aback, then a wry look comes into her eyes. "Damn your confidence. It should piss me off but… Lucky for you, I find it a turn on."

"And *you* turn *me* on in ways which shake me to the core."

She looks into my eyes and realizes how serious I am.

"A filthy talker who's self-assured and romantic." Her features soften. "I don't stand a chance, do I?"

23

Phoenix

"None," he growls.

God. That voice—rough and low—drags across my skin like velvet laced with barbed wire.

He's so confident. His gaze—hot, unflinching—locks me in place, tells me I'm already his target, and he's not backing down until he claims me. There's no hesitation. Just the kind of certainty that makes my breath catch. That he'll win. That I'll give in. That I'll want to.

And the worst part?

I already do.

My insides liquefy. Heat pulses low in my belly, spreading out in waves I can't control. The air between us grows thick—electric—with something volatile, something wild. I don't dare name it. Not yet. Not while he's watching me with that razor-sharp focus, like he's already undressing the layers I've spent years building.

His throat works as he swallows. A subtle hitch in his composure. Proof that this connection, this pull—it's not just me. He feels it too. And God help me, that knowledge hits me harder than it should. It turns me on even more.

Then he leans over and kisses me.

Hard.

It's a no-warning, high-voltage kind of kiss. A surge of claim and command that hijacks my breath. His lips crush mine, and I melt into the heat of him. His mouth is urgent, his movements sure, and for a moment, I lose myself in the rawness of it. Then he pulls back, just enough to reach across me and push the passenger door open.

"Go on," he murmurs. "I'll wait until you're inside."

Reluctantly, I step out, the press of his kiss still buzzing across my lips. I don't look back, but I feel his eyes on me. Watching. Waiting. He doesn't drive off immediately. I make it to the door, fumble with my keys—my fingers trembling slightly—and only once I'm inside does he pull away.

The house is quiet. The living room lamp glows softly. Just like it always does. A small thing, but it anchors me. Drew never turns it off either. Yet in all these months, I've never replaced the bulb.

We used to joke it had a DNR order even death respected. Gallows humor. One of the few things Drew and I shared. It's how you survive in the ER. By laughing at the darkness.

I strip off my clothes slowly, every movement deliberate. There's the option of a shower. I ignore it.

Because I want to smell him on me.

I slide into bed, turn my face into the pillow and am out in seconds. No spiraling thoughts about Drew. No regrets. No guilt looping on repeat.

For the first time in months, I just…sleep.

That feeling lasts six days. Mostly because I avoid Drew like he's MRSA and I'm fresh out of PPE.

I set my alarm an hour early every morning. Sacrificing sleep is worth it if it means leaving before he gets off his shift. Maybe, it's cowardly. Maybe, I'm just not ready. And that's okay. Some wounds need distance before they can scar over.

I don't see Connor either. But every night, without fail, he messages me.

Just a simple check-in. *How was your day?*

No calls. No demands. Just a consistent, quiet presence. The opposite of pressure.

True to his word, I don't feel surveilled. I don't even spot the gray sedan he mentioned, though I check. I do. More often than I'd admit.

On the sixth night—last night—he messaged again.

> Connor: Be ready at 8 a.m. I'm taking you out.

It's my day off. I should've resisted. Instead, I spent an embarrassing amount of time figuring out what to wear, then settled on a dress. Not yoga pants. Not scrubs. *An actual dress.*

One I didn't even know I wanted to wear until I put it on and saw the woman staring back at me in the mirror. My cheeks are flushed with excitement. I'm looking forward to going out with him. He knows how to get to me, that's clear.

I may not have forgiven him for the surveillance stunt. But I'll give him this—he's using the intel well. He's trying. Hard.

I'm not ready to reward him for it. But it's clear, he's succeeding in getting me to thaw toward him.

I walk into the kitchen later than usual, and freeze.

Drew is there.

Seated at the breakfast nook, hunched over a cup of coffee. His hair's a mess, his T-shirt wrinkled, dark circles smudged under his eyes. He looks like he hasn't slept in days.

"Rough night?" I ask, careful to keep my tone neutral.

He grunts. Sips the coffee. Grimaces.

"You really shouldn't drink that before trying to sleep."

No reply. Typical. Drew prefers his guilt trips to be passive-aggressive. Silent in person, pointed via his text messages.

Just when I think I'm beginning to heal, he finds a way to drag me back down.

I sigh and walk around him, setting up my French press while he continues his silent sulk. My coffee method versus his percolator — a small, petty act of separation.

"Have you found a new place yet?" I ask, voice low.

He frowns. Pretends not to hear me.

"You said you'd move out within a month, and that was a week ago," I say, fingers knotting together. "You need to leave when the three weeks are up."

His jaw tightens. "Are you doubting that I won't? I don't want to stay on a minute more than is necessary. Things have been crazy in the ER. I haven't had the time to look for a new place."

When he glances at me, he looks so knackered, my heart softens.

"I know it's been crazy, more than usual, maybe. I'm sorry to push things — "

"Then don't," he snaps.

My stomach lurches. *No, no. I can't allow him run roughshod over me.* I gave him a month to find a place. That's more than enough time. But apartments in London are never easy to come by. I feel myself beginning to vacillate and clamp down on the feeling. *No. Stay firm. You have to. You need him gone so you can move on with your life. You can't let him dictate how you live. Not anymore.*

"We agreed." I set my jaw. "You have three weeks to leave."

His grip on the mug goes white-knuckled. He doesn't shout. Doesn't argue. Just drains the rest of his coffee and storms off without a word.

I sag against the counter. Only then, do I realize how tight my body is, braced for a fight that never came. My hands tremble as I reach for the kettle. I set it back down.

Forget the coffee. I'm done.

Purse in hand, I step outside, closing the door on that heaviness. On Drew.

And right on cue, the now-familiar Aston Martin eases to a stop by the curb.

My pulse spikes.

The moment I see Connor, everything inside me realigns. He's leaned back in the driver's seat, one hand on the wheel, sunglasses pushed up on his head. The slow, assessing sweep of his gaze over my body sends a thrill cascading through my bloodstream.

The look he gives me? Possessive. Proud. Like I belong to him, and the whole damn world should know it.

His smile curves—lazy, confident, dangerous. He jerks his chin toward the passenger seat. A silent command.

I obey.

Sliding into the car feels natural. Like slipping into something familiar but forbidden.

"Good morning." He nods toward the drink in the cupholder.

I pick it up and take a slow sip, savoring the warm, spiced sweetness. No surprise—another dirty chai latte, just how I like it.

"Thank you." I lift it in a small salute. "You're looking pleased with yourself."

His grin deepens. "I have a surprise for you."

24

Connor

"We're going shoe shopping?" She wrinkles her forehead.

"Don't misunderstand me. I have a particular affection for those borrowed clogs you wear to work, since they're the reason you fell into my arms the first time we met. But given the number of hours you are on your feet, I'll feel more comfortable if you're wearing shoes that don't cause you to lose your footing and hurt yourself."

"Oh." She considers my words, then nods. "Okay."

Huh, she's being unusually compliant. "You're not fighting me on this?"

"Why should I? I do need new shoes; I just haven't had the time to buy them."

This woman never ceases to surprise me.

The shop I've picked is in Marylebone. Not one of those soulless chain stores. This one specializes in custom-fit, orthotic-friendly footwear—stylish but functional. I've already had them pull options

based on Phoenix's height and weight—both of which I estimated—
and job demands. Of course, she doesn't know that yet.

As we arrive, I open the glass door and step aside, so she can
walk in first.

She takes in the shoes on display. "You really planned this, huh?"

"I don't do improvisation. Not where you're concerned."

She swivels her head in my direction. The look in her eyes is
pleased, and surprised, and something else—something soft.

I do believe I'm wearing her down.

I nod toward the rows of shoe-lined shelves. There's no loud
music. No gimmicky posters. Just comfort, and quiet, and the scent
of suede and beeswax polish. The owner, Amaya, gives me a nod.
She already knows who we're here for.

"You must be Phoenix," she says warmly.

Phoenix throws me a look. "You briefed her?"

"Of course, I did."

She presses her lips together—maybe to hold back a gasp of
surprise? Maybe to stop herself from saying what she's thinking.
Her pulse flutters at her throat, though. That little giveaway I've
come to recognize. She likes that I see her. That I pay attention to
her needs.

Amaya brings out three boxes.

"Specialized shoes with neutral soles. Cushioned arches. Reinforced heel cups. And handmade in Italy." She beams.

Phoenix sits gingerly on the lounge chair, her eyes wary.

I wave Amaya away, then go down on my knee in front of Phe. I
coax her to place her foot on my thigh.

She swallows. "What are you doing?"

I ease the ballet flat she's wearing today off one foot. When I
press my thumb into the ball of her big toe, she sighs. When I
massage her heel she groans. "That feels so good."

She works twelve-hour shifts, holds dying men's hands, saves
children in cardiac arrest… She's so busy saving others, she has no
time to save herself.

That's where I come in.

"Whoa." She sinks back in her seat. "That feels incredible."

I slip off one ballet pump then the other. I pull at her toes, massage the balls of her feet.

By the time I finish, she's sprawled in the seat, head lolling. "Anytime you want a second career as a masseuse, I guarantee, you'll have a long line of people queuing up for your services."

"I'm afraid my services are reserved."

"Oh?" she asks, interested. "For whom?"

"For the woman who deserves the best in everything."

She flushes. "Laying it on a little thick, aren't you?"

"It's the truth." I pull on her socks, then ease the new shoes onto her feet—black leather with a molded sole, discreet enough to pass with her ER uniform, yet solid enough to carry her through hell and back.

She stands. Walks a few steps. Pauses in front of a mirror.

"Oh, wow." Her voice barely raises above a whisper.

"They feel good?"

"It's like—like the ground isn't punching back anymore."

I chuckle.

She looks at her reflection with shining eyes. "And for the first time, I don't have to cringe when I look at my feet." She bursts out laughing.

I start to laugh with her, but my throat tightens unexpectedly. To see the delight in her eyes. To hear the lightness in her tone, that slight giddiness in her laugh, is the most incredible sensation in the world. More satisfying than all the biotech discoveries I led my team in. More fulfilling than the completion of any mission. I have to look away to rein in my emotions.

This… Feeling so moved, so exhilarated at fulfilling the needs of someone else is unfamiliar.

I swallow hard. "Try on the others."

Her gaze snaps to mine. "I don't need more than one pair."

I lean in, my voice dropping. "You take care of everyone else. Let someone else take care of you, for once."

She's quiet for a beat. Then she shakes her head. "You're intense, you know that?"

"*Only* about you."

And it's the truth. I would tear down every store in London if it meant she'd walk a little easier. Sleep a little deeper. Smile a little more.

She turns away, blinking fast. But not before I see the softness stealing into her expression. That unguarded warmth I crave more than oxygen.

And just like that, I know.

This woman is going to ruin me.

And I'll thank her for it.

Whatever she reads in my eyes has her giving in. She tries on and finally settles on three pairs.

I pay for the purchases. We walk out, me holding the packages. We get into the car, and before I can touch the start button my phone vibrates. I frown at the message.

"Everything okay?"

I begin to nod, then stop. "It's from the CEO of Save the Kids."

"That's the charity you want to fund?"

I nod. "Did a stint with them during my gap year, before I joined university, before I went undercover. And what I saw changed me forever. I know it's a cliché, but truly, children are our future. They're innocent of wrongdoings but pay the highest price for the faults of us adults. I knew then, I could use the resources at my disposal to help them." I type out a reply to the message. "Their situation is getting more urgent. They're going to run out of money, unless I arrange for a cash infusion in the next month." I rub the back of my neck.

In the silence that follows, I look up and notice the contrition on her face. *Uh-oh.* "I didn't mention that to make you feel bad." I set my phone aside.

"I know, you didn't."

"And I know, I brought it up as a reason for you to marry me, but you shouldn't let it influence you."

"I don't understand you." She furrows her eyebrows. "First, you propose a marriage of convenience to meet both our needs. Now, you tell me I shouldn't let it act as a motivator. Even though, if I marry you, you'll get access to your trust fund, and you plan to use it to improve the lives of children who desperately need help. Not to mention, it would save the jobs of so many of my colleagues who can't afford to miss a single monthly paycheck."

I drum my fingers on the steering wheel. "I don't want you to feel pressured into marrying me."

She shakes her head. "A little too late for that. I have the fates of these kids hanging on my conscience."

I turn to her. "I'm sorry to have put you in this position; I truly am."

"And now, you know exactly what to say to make me feel even worse." She throws up her hands. "Not only are you sexy, and charming, and rich, but you've paid close attention to my needs. So even though I'm upset that you followed me, I can't stay upset, because you're using the knowledge in a way that makes me feel appreciated. I should be pissed off that you tried to negotiate a marriage with me, but it turns out, you want to use the money it unlocks for a good cause." She scowls at me. "Also, you don't hesitate to apologize when you're wrong."

"And that's bad?" I ask slowly.

"Very bad. Because it makes you…" She points a finger at me. "It makes you incorrigible and irresistible."

My heart swells in my chest. A warmth courses through my veins. I feel like I've won a major battle… One I didn't realize I was fighting. I thought I'd been trying to woo her, but really, I was trying to show her that I'm good enough for her. That she needs me in her life. That she can trust me. That I am *the one* for her. And while my actions were aimed at making life easier for her, I'm selfish enough to hope it's made a difference in how she's coming to view my marriage proposal.

"If I could go back and change what I said, I would."

She tilts her head, a curious expression on her face.

"I'd do the wooing first and bring up the marriage proposal later." I purse my lips. "Except —"

"—except time's running out. You need to access your trust fund, and I need to find a way to save the ER."

"I wish it weren't so, but you're right."

My phone vibrates with another message.

I growl in annoyance. The entire world seems to need to reach me today. At this moment. When I'm spending time with the most important person in my life.

I don't look at the device.

It vibrates again.

"Maybe you should get it," she says softly.

"I'd much rather keep my eyes on your face."

She bites her lip, trying to stifle a smile. And damn, I'm chuffed that I made her feel good again.

My phone vibrates a third time.

I sigh.

"You really should get that." She reaches for the phone and hands it over to me without looking at the screen.

I take in the message, then wish I hadn't.

"Bad news?"

"Depends how you look at it." I look up at her. "How do you feel about meeting the family?"

Her gaze widens. "Your family?'

"That was Arthur, my grandfather. He's reminding me I'm expected at lunch for our weekly family get together." *One I'd hope to miss.* But Arthur's tone makes it clear I can't skip out on this.

"It's a family event. Why do you want me there?"

"Because"—I hold her gaze—"I want them to meet you."

Panic wells in her eyes. "I… I'm not sure that's wise."

"I think they'll love you," I say honestly.

"I'm not ready for this."

I allow my expression to turn pleading. "In all honesty, these weekly meetings are a torture. My grandfather can be rather presumptuous. And he won't take no for an answer. If I have you by my side, it might make the entire thing more bearable."

She scowls. "That's not fair. You know I can't say no to you, not after you've been so nice to me."

"I could drop you back home if that's what you want?"

A haunted look comes into her eyes. "I don't want to go home yet."

"So, you'll come with me?"

25

Connor

I can't believe she agreed. Everyone seems taken in by her. Including my least likely to be charmed brother.

"You and James' sister?" Brody eyes me as he takes a sip from his coffee cup.

Since when did my brother take such an interest in my personal life? Did something in my expression give me away? Do I look as shaken as I feel?

Has she undone me so thoroughly I can't hide how she's turned my world on its head?

Lunch was mercifully without event. Then, the family adjourned to the library. Those with kids, including my brother Nathan and my friend Sinclair, left.

"Didn't expect to see Toren and Viktor here." I glance toward where the two of them are deep in conversation with James. All three are sprawled in armchairs in the far corner of the plush room.

"All three are family friends. You know how Arthur loves stacking these 'family' occasions with people he thinks he can wrangle a deal out of." Brody lifts a brawny shoulder like none of this affects him.

But I'm not fooled.

No matter how much we Davenport brothers have carved our individual ways in this world, we've never managed to stay completely unaffected by Arthur's machinations. It's an unspoken worry that we've learned to watch out for, so we can deal with the fallout.

"What is he planning?" I scratch my jaw. Why does Arthur want to consolidate his relations with the Hamiltons, Whittingtons, and the Royal Family of Verenza? It makes business sense, of course. And the old man never misses a networking opportunity. But having these three men over, and at the same time? I'd love to get an inkling of what he's thinking.

"Arthur's not going to share anything." Brody sets his jaw. "He prefers his little reveals."

That, Gramps does. Normally, it has to do with getting us brothers married off. But given it's only me and Brody left now, I wonder if he's not looking at fresh pastures. "Maybe, he thinks the three of them need help with setting down?" I chuckle.

Brody shoots me a disbelieving look. "Like they want Arthur meddling in their personal lives?"

"Have any of us?"

The two of us exchange a smirk.

Brody's phone vibrates. He pulls it out, reads the message, and chuckles—low and deep. A sound I've never heard from him before. Then he taps out a quick reply, still grinning like he's got a secret, and leans back in his seat with a smirk tugging at the corner of his mouth.

"What was that all about?" I ask, narrowing my eyes.

His expression flickers, the smirk vanishing so fast, it's almost comical. He schools his features into bland neutrality, as if I've caught him with his hand in the proverbial cookie jar. "Just making sure my assistant's staying on her toes."

"You mean, making her life a living hell with enough work to drive three people into burnout?" I scoff.

He lifts a shoulder. "Actually"—a furrow appears between his brows— "she's the only one who hasn't quit on me. She's lasted the longest of any assistant I've had. That's saying something."

His tone is off. Curious. Like he's trying to puzzle something out and doesn't quite like how close he's getting to the answer.

"Maybe, instead of testing her endurance, you could try not weaponizing your to-do lists?"

"Where's the fun in that?" he murmurs, but there's a faraway look in his eyes now. "Her eyes spark when she's annoyed. And when she bites back—she's quick, wicked-smart. Challenges me. Doesn't flinch. It's…exhilarating."

I stare at him. My eternally grumpy brother, who scares interns with a single glance, sounds almost dreamy. Like he's replaying some particularly enjoyable verbal sparring match and wishing it weren't over.

"Careful," I say, voice low, "you sound like a man who's starting to enjoy the chase."

"It's not like that."

"Isn't it?" I tilt my head. "You've never noticed the color of your assistant's eyes before. Let alone, commented on how they spark."

"Don't be ridiculous," he gives a derisive chuckle.

But there's color rising on his neck. He wears the 'I'm too late to hide it, so I'll bury it under sarcasm' look.

Classic Brody.

"I'm just saying"—I lean back, let my words land—"watch out. You keep playing with fire, you might trip into it."

He snorts. "I've never lost control of a situation in my life."

And yet, from the way he glances at his phone again—like he's hoping for another message—I'm not so sure.

"What are you two cackling about?" James, who's broken away from his trio, approaches us. "You seem like you're up to no good."

"Not us." I nod in Arthur's direction. He's holding court on the comfortable settee which has been pulled up close to the fireplace. It's a balmy summer evening, yet he has the fire on inside the library.

Arthur beat the Big C recently. Still, he looks healthy, with glowing cheeks. And when he looks at his girlfriend Imelda, there's a look of contentment on his face. Right now, she's talking with a man I don't recognize.

"Who's that?" I nod in his direction.

"You don't know Adrian Sovrano?" James asks, surprised.

"He looks different, almost unrecognizable." Man must have been working out, for he's put on some serious muscle.

"He's been away, traveling. But with Michael having returned to Italy on a temporary basis to take care of his children, and the rest of the Sovranos busy with their families, they needed help running their family business." Brody shrugs.

Since having lost his wife, Michael has retreated from the business world. "What about these rumors that Karma is alive and that he faked her death to keep her safe from his enemies?"

I'm not one for conspiracy theories, but... Michael's the former capo of the Cosa Nostra, turned business tycoon. Everything he does is of interest to the business world—and the underworld—which puts him on my radar.

"I usually steer clear of gossip, except..." James pauses long enough for the silence to bite. "He never held a funeral for Karma. Which makes one wonder if there's some truth to these persistent rumors."

"Wonder why Arthur invited Adrian." I drag my thumb under my lip.

"He must be interested in Adrian's plans for the Sovrano's businesses," Brody offers.

"I'll wager; he wants to remedy Adrian's bachelor status." I purse my lips.

"You're referring to his machinations where he tries to marry off you lot?" James turns to me with a glint in his eyes.

"It's just Brody and me left. The rest of our brothers are married. I wouldn't be surprised if Arthur turns his attention to you and the single guys here. And find brides for the lot of you." I grin at him.

James pales. "And here I thought this was simply an afternoon with my quasi-family. Considering my parents are away, traveling at the moment."

Brody and I exchange another look.

"Arthur loves having his family around, simply so he can lord over them." Brody raises a hand. "Maybe I'm being a bit uncharitable. Arthur *does* care for his family. And he *does* believe that he's doing his best for them, but that translates into getting involved in our business and being confident that he knows what's best for us when, really, all he's doing is being intrusive."

"To give the old man his due, it's thanks, in part, to his schemes that our brothers and our uncle Quentin are now married to the loves of their life, so—"

"So, you're okay with him getting involved in getting you married off?"

It's my turn to stiffen. "He doesn't have a say in my personal life." I jut out my chin.

Brody's expression turns incredulous. "This is Arthur we're talking about. If he's not scheming to get one of us married, he's not happy."

And if it weren't for him, I wouldn't have proposed to Fever.

James narrows his gaze. "Is this why you asked my sister to marry you?"

"You asked Phoenix to marry you?" Brody bursts out. It just so happens, it's during a lull in the conversation, so his voice echoes around the room.

Every single face in the room turns toward us. I glare at him.

"Oops." He smirks, not looking very sorry.

Phe turns to us, her eyebrows twisted. She wears an expression of confusion.

"Remember what I told you?" James leans into my face. "If you hurt her, you'll have me to contend with."

"This has nothing to do with you," Phe snaps as she approaches us.

"On the contrary. I ask him to watch out for you, and he betrays me by coming onto you." James scowls.

"About that"—Phe glares at him—"I haven't forgotten you asked your friend to run surveillance on me," she whisper-shouts.

The others have gone back to their conversations, thank God. The last thing I need is the rest of my family weighing in with their opinions on the matter.

Fact is, we wouldn't have met if not for James' request to me.

I don't say that aloud. It's only going to piss off Phe further. For now, I enjoy watching her take down my friend.

James widens his eyes at his sister. "I understand it upset you, but I apologized. My intentions were only to make sure you were safe. I can't help but worry about you."

She makes a rude noise. "What you are is overly protective."

"It is one of my faults." His features soften. "And I truly apologize that it made you feel like I was intruding on your life. But Phe, you're our only sister. And it's natural for me... And for all our brothers to feel like we should take care of you."

She begins to speak, but he holds up his hand. "And before you can complain that they haven't been in touch because they're in different corners of the world, I promise you, they reach out to me for regular updates."

"You've become the central node for intra-family communication." She gives a theatrical shudder. "Trust me, I'm not envious at all."

"Does that mean you forgive me?" James asks, voice soft.

"I'm thinking about it." Phe tosses her head.

"That's all I ask of you, Little Sister." He holds out his hand. "At least let's shake on a temporary peace?"

"Don't be such a doofus." She rolls her eyes and smacks his shoulder then opens her arms.

James pulls her into a tight hug, the tension easing from his shoulders. "I really am sorry, Phe. You know, I love you."

"I know. I love you, too. Just... Try to give me some credit, will ya'? I'm an adult."

"You're right." He grimaces. "I overstepped."

"And just so you're aware"—he shoots me a sideways glance—"I give you permission to court her."

She opens her mouth to chew him out, then notices the teasing glint in James' eyes.

"Ugh, stop it." She scowls at him.

James laughs.

"You're courting her?" Arthur booms out.

I'm not surprised he's getting into the conversation. In fact, I wonder what took him so long. Also, it's *Arthur*. And I do want him far away from me and any discussions to do with my future.

"Come here, boy, and bring your woman with you."

26

Phoenix

So, this is what it feels like to be at the receiving end of Arthur's surgical stare.

Showing up at the luncheon on Connor's arm was both terrifying and thrilling. Everyone greeted me with the poise and decorum that befitted the famous Davenports. But there was no denying the way their eyes took everything in.

And now, several hours, and several glasses of brandy later, it seems Arthur is finally ready to stop staring and start talking.

I shift my weight from foot to foot and resist the urge to wring my fingers. Then, because I feel nervousness welling up inside, I tap my chest three times. A few slow breaths, and I start to relax.

On the rare occasions I rebelled, one sharp look from her—those laser eyes—and a quiet word of disappointment, was all it took to snap me back in line.

Later, when I started working as a resident, I found the same thing happened with my supervisors. Their disapproval hit hard. I wanted to impress them, to earn their praise. That's when I first began using the tapping. It gave me something to hold onto when I felt myself unraveling.

Except, Arthur's x-ray gaze seems to throw me off balance.

This, despite the fact I haven't done anything wrong.

Unless you count the fact that I haven't accepted Connor's proposal... *Yet.*

As if sensing my apprehension, Connor pulls me close. It doesn't occur to me to protest. Instead, I lean into his warmth. The feel of his hard body at my side makes me feel protected. Like I've reached a port in the storm and now, nothing can hurt me.

Arthur's shrewd gaze tracks between us. He nods. The look of satisfaction on his face makes me feel uncomfortable. Surely, it can't be a good sign that he leans back in his seat with a tiny smile tugging at his lips, like he knows a secret I don't.

"You going to marry her?" He nods at Connor, who stiffens.

The silence stretches. I hug myself tighter, reluctant to enter this conversation.

All I have to do is open my mouth and say no. *Do it.* I try to form the words, but they won't come out.

I can't stop thinking about the ER and my colleagues whose jobs depend upon it. And Connor needing to access the money in his trust to help the children... And...the fact that if Connor weren't in my life, I would miss him. The thought of him with someone else? It's inconceivable. That comes as a shock.

I'm not seriously considering Connor's proposal, am I?

The atmosphere in the room is so heavy, it presses down on my chest, making it difficult to breathe. Connor's grip on my shoulder grows stronger, almost to the point of hurting. The heavy weight is strangely reassuring. And grounding. My focus is anchored by his presence. I draw in a few deep breaths, willing the anxiety in the pit of my belly to dissolve.

Next to me, Connor's body seems to have turned into granite. Unmovable. Unshakeable. The pressure coiled under his skin makes the air around him vibrate. It pushes down on my shoulders, stretching the air between us until it crackles. My head spins with unspoken emotions.

On instinct, I slip my arm around his waist. For a few seconds, his body seems to grow even more still. Then, a ripple moves under his skin. His body relaxes. He slides his big palm down to wrap his fingers around my bicep. His thumb turns a slow circle. Even through the fabric of my dress, I can feel the warmth, like he's branding me.

Arthur tilts his head, a keen look infiltrating his eyes. He opens his mouth to speak. That's when the Great Dane slumbering at his feet yawns and rises to his feet.

He shakes his big head, pads over to us, and butts my thigh. His weight is enough for me to sink deeper into Connor, who pulls me flush against him. I feel the planes of his chest, the jut of his hip, the strong powerful column of his thigh. His scent seems to envelop me —soothing and arousing, at the same time. I relax a little more, unable to stop myself from melting into him.

"Guess that answers my question," Arthur drawls.

"What do you mean?" Connor growls from above me.

The Great Dane woofs, looking from me to Connor, then back at me. His jaw is open, and his tongue hangs out. He looks, for all the world, like he's laughing. "You're adorable, you know that?" I reach over and scratch him under his jaw. He chuckles.

No, really, this dog is halfway to being human. He's the most intelligent mutt I've come across. He nuzzles into my palm, then pads back to his place next to Arthur. He turns to face us, before sinking down to his haunches with a sigh.

"What Arthur means is that he would be a blind man not to see that the two of you are a couple, and that he's keen to find out when the two of you will be married. Isn't that right, dear?" Imelda fixes Arthur with a stern look.

Arthur's face grows ruddy. He looks like he's going to protest, but contents himself with nodding. He takes Imelda's hand in his and brings it to his mouth to kiss her fingertips. "You're right, my dear. Of course, if Connor wants to have access to his trust, he needs to get married. In fact..." he lowers her hand and looks at me. "If he wants to retain control of his patents, he'll have to tie the knot within the next month."

Every line of Connor's body pulls taut. His chest widens. Every muscle fiber in him goes into overdrive, like he's taken a cortisol hit to his bloodstream. I can feel the rigidity in his posture. If he were wound any tighter, he'd be pre-cardiac.

"Patents?" I frown.

Arthur nods. "Connor made one mistake. He trusted his team to patent his biotech work. I paid them to file the patents in my name. The revenue's been going to him through the company, but that stops now. Unless he gets married."

A whisper runs around the room. I'm aware that his friends and family are watching the unfolding of the drama. They grow restive, clearly not happy with what they're seeing. At the same time, they don't interrupt.

This is, strictly speaking, a family affair. From the corner of my eye, I see one of his brothers shift his weight from foot to foot.

He doesn't say anything, but the stiffness of his shoulders indicates he's not happy with Arthur's negotiating tactic. And that's what it is.

He's holding Connor's life's work over him. And the money that he could use to make a difference in the lives of so many children.

Connor's face is all hard edges, shadows, and sculpture that's unflinching. Only the nerve ticking at his temple tells me he's keeping his temper under control.

I touch his arm. "What are the patents for?"

He rolls his shoulders. "My team developed a seizure-reducing drug for pediatric epilepsy, a beta-cell regeneration therapy that could cure Type 1 Diabetes if caught early, and a treatment that's helping kids with Cystic Fibrosis live longer," he says quietly.

"That's incredible," I breathe.

He nods. "I had a good team."

I narrow my eyes. "A team that wouldn't have made it that far without your involvement, right?"

He exhales. "I was part of the first research group. We made early breakthroughs funded by money from my grandfather. I sold that IP to bankroll future trials. By then, I was already deep in the field on other assignments. It was…a lot."

Connor runs a hand through his hair.

"I left the day-to-day to the team my grandfather built. They handled the patents, the legal side. I didn't know he'd told them to file everything under his name."

His jaw tightens. A flicker of betrayal darkens his features.

"It's one of the few times I let my guard down," he mutters. "I trusted him." He aims an accusatory look toward his grandfather.

I can't help but feel sympathetic toward him. I would be really pissed off too if it turned out that my grandfather was holding my patents hostage until I got married.

I have two choices. Let the ER close and watch my colleagues—my second family—lose their jobs. Or marry Connor, and he'll use his influence to keep it open.

James tilts his head in my direction. I see the question in his eyes. He's watching me carefully. I only have to say the word, and he'll step in to help extricate me from this situation.

I shake my head. *No, I'm not taking any help from you,* I tell him silently. I need to figure this out on my own…

I could walk away. Start over somewhere else, but my conscience won't let me. This place matters too much.

Am I really going to marry a man I barely know? But can I say no to him? Could I watch him be with another woman—and wonder if he was the one?

And then there's Drew. I told him it's over, but marrying Connor so quickly? What will he think? *Is it fair for me to move on so quickly?* He asked me to marry him! I shouldn't be surprised he's not ready to let go.

As for telling Connor about him—I can't, yet. Not until we're married, and the ER is safe. Then, even if he's not happy with Drew staying under my roof, it won't affect my colleagues.

Perhaps, marrying Connor could be the impetus Drew needs to move on?

The truth is that, if I'm being honest with myself, I *do* want to marry Connor.

I'm attracted to him. He cares for me. And while he hasn't said that he loves me, my instinct says he's the man for me.

I glance at Arthur. A small thrill runs through me at the thought of proving him wrong. "You're right. We're getting married."

Arthur blinks slowly, a look of incomprehension on his face. Which changes to one of smugness. *Huh? Why do I feel like I've been manipulated?*

Connor whips his head around to glower at me. "What did you say?"

"I'll marry you."

27

Connor

I hustle her into the guest room on the first floor and shut the door behind us.

"What are you doing? I was going to woo you. I don't want you marrying me because you feel coerced."

My anger at my grandfather makes my words come out louder than I mean, but she just looks at me with her green and gold eyes.

"I haven't been coerced." She crosses her arms and tilts her chin in challenge.

That stubborn look I'm coming to recognize clings to the curves of her cheeks like honey on bread.

Everything about her is sweet and soft. She makes me want to sweep her up in my arms, protect her, and take care of her—only, I know she's tougher than she looks.

And she's a brilliant doctor, cool under pressure in a medical emergency.

She's a fiercely independent woman whose light shines bright, who thrives on helping others. Which is probably why she felt compelled to agree to my proposal. Which *is* what I wanted.

So why am I refusing to accept her agreement at face value? Why am I delving deeper into the reasons behind it?

Why do I want to come to her defense and make sure she doesn't feel coerced into agreeing? I'm the one who brought up this idea in the first place, after all.

"When I asked you to marry me, you said you weren't interested," I point out.

"Maybe, I changed my mind." Her tone is firm, but uncertainty lurks behind her eyes. "Maybe, all your courting has paid off."

"Firstly" — I raise a finger — "it's literally a couple of weeks since I started courting you. And secondly" — I scan her features — "did you really change your mind, or did being face-to-face with Arthur make you feel like you had to?"

"Are you saying I don't know my own mind?" Her gaze narrows. The stubbornness on her face turns to resoluteness.

I blow out a breath. "That's not what I mean. I simply think that, for someone who was so sure you didn't want to marry me, you've changed your mind rather quickly. And after you were so vehement in turning down my proposition, to now do an about turn—" I shake my head. "Well, it's unexpected. Not that I don't appreciate it — I do. But I want to make sure you're doing it for all the right reasons."

If she agrees to marry me out of duty, or guilt, or because she thinks it's the right thing to do—I'll have her name on paper, her body in my bed, but not *her*.

Not the fire in her eyes, the warmth of her laughter, the quiet trust when she finally lets someone in.

And that would be the worst kind of loss.

Because if she gives herself to me for the wrong reasons… I'll never know if she would've chosen me on her own. And I can't live with that. I need to know I *matter* to her. That she wants *me* — not just the solution I represent.

I've lived in shadows long enough. I won't start my future with a lie. What I want isn't just her yes. I want her heart. I want *all of her*.

"This is a matter of your life. Of your future. I want to be sure you've thought this through."

She stops a foot from me and plops her hands on her hips, her stance on the verge of being belligerent. "What does it matter what my reasons are? Besides, even if I wanted to walk you through my decision-making process, most of my decisions are amygdala-driven."

"You mean, you followed your instinct?" Good thing I'm well-read enough to follow along with her medical terminology-peppered style of conversation. It increases my respect for her. *It also turns me on, hugely.*

It makes me want to kiss her thoroughly, then throw her down and bury myself inside of her—but that will need to wait. I'll fuck her when she's completely on board with having me in her life, by her side—a decision I made subconsciously, but which I know is right.

She's special, unique. There's no one like her. She's the one for me, in so many ways. It won't be easy to hold back my desire, but I want to wait until she's a hundred percent sure that I'm the man for her. It's why I want to question the rationale behind her so abruptly agreeing to marrying me.

"Yes, exactly. A hypothalamic response. No cortex involvement, whatsoever. It's often what drives my actions. And many times, I can't explain it myself, but it mostly turns out to be right."

A shadow crosses her eyes.

"Well, ninety-nine percent of the time."

"And the one percent?" I lean forward on the balls of my feet, wanting to be as close to her as possible, without being too creepy about it.

She looks away. The shadow crossing her eyes seems to extend to her face.

It's as if a cloud is poised over her, and she's wrapped in her own microclimate. One in which I'm not allowed. The hair on the back of my neck rises. She's hiding something. The thought has occurred to me before, but now, I'm sure.

"Sometimes, my instinct leads me astray." When she turns back to me, her eyes are wet. "But that doesn't mean I trust it any less."

Her hazel eyes have turned green, and in their depths, a storm of hurt spills over the edges.

"I'll never hurt you… Not unless it's to cause you pleasure."

Her lips part.

"And if you trust me enough to put your faith in me, I'll never let you down. I'll be there to catch you in that one percent of the time when your instincts let you down."

A tear trails down her cheek, then another. Our gazes meet. The air between us crackles with emotions. The kind that can't be put into words, but which can be understood. Electricity crackles, lacing the molecules in the space with an energy that makes the hair on my forearms rise.

My heart skips, then slams into a gallop. A rush of blood roars in my ears. Something about this moment, about the rawness in her eyes, about how her gaze clings to mine like I'm her only mooring in a maelstrom that could sweep us both away, is etched into my memory.

I'm not conscious of taking another step, or of her moving, but she's in my arms. I grab her under her butt and lift her. She wraps her legs about my waist and presses herself into me, so her breasts are flattened against my chest. I hold her with my palms under her sweet fleshy butt and stare into her eyes, searching them like they have the answers to the questions I've had from the time I was a boy. Life. The heavens. The universe. *The number 42?*

Everything melds into a focus somewhere deep inside me, where I now carry her image. Then her gaze softens, her eyes growing luminous. She parts her lips, and my mouth meets hers.

I thrust my tongue over hers, dancing with hers, swiping it over her teeth, drinking from her. Absorbing her. Storing that heady taste of her in my taste buds, my cells, my bones. She twines her arms about my neck and kisses me right back. The hunger in her eyes fans the embers of need inside me that sparked the moment I saw her. I squeeze her butt as I pull her flush against my chest.

My feet seem to move of their own accord, until I have her up against the glass wall of the conservatory. I press into her, adjusting her until her core is fitted right over the throbbing tent in my pants. She must feel it, for she gasps.

I swallow the sound, tilt my head, and revel in the lushness of her lips, the expansiveness of being able to drink from her.

Her heart thuds against mine. The pulse at the base of her neck beats as fast as mine. Her curves tremble, her body shudders, and when she digs her fingernails into the base of my neck, the burn races straight to the base of my spine.

When we break apart, I'm breathing hard, like I've sprinted. My muscles are rigid, my cock stabbing into my pants and begging to be let out. I take in her swollen lips, her flushed features, her hair tossed about her beautiful face. And something inside me shifts.

I've changed since I first glimpsed her. But now, I've crossed a point of no return.

"Did you mean it when you said you'll marry me?"

She nods.

"And you're doing this of your own volition?"

She nods again.

I peruse her face, see the emotions swirling in her eyes, in her trembling lips, the way the pulse races at her throat. But I also see how aroused she is. How she clings to me like she can't let go. How she writhes against me, trying to rub up against the ridge of my cock.

I know she wants me. That she needs my body. That only I can satisfy the hunger I sense in her. But I want more than her body. I want her heart. Her soul. I want to understand her thoughts. Her innermost desires. I want to know her secret dreams. Her darkest yearnings, the ones she won't admit even to herself. I want to own her. Possess her. Make her mine. I want to stamp the mark of my possession on her, in her, so the world knows she's mine. So *she* knows she's mine.

It's what makes me pull back from the yawning abyss of my desire. Once I dive into it, there will be no looking back. And my instinct tells me, not yet. Right now, she's the focus.

I notch my knuckles under her chin and tilt her head up, so I can capture her gaze. I want to accept her acquiescence and rush her off to the altar, but I wouldn't be a man if I didn't reveal to her how much things have changed for me.

"You should realize that, while I told you this would be a marriage of convenience, I lied."

28

Phoenix

"You did?"

I wasn't expecting that. I knew he hoped I'd fall for him, that I'd want to marry him for more than his money or name—but to hear him say he wants more than a fake marriage? That catches me off guard.

It also makes me realize, I'm in dangerous waters. Despite my best efforts, I'm drawn to this man. And thanks to his actions, I've begun to develop feelings for him. At this rate, I, too, will want more than just a marriage of convenience. I'm halfway to being in love with him, in such a short period of time.

"You need to understand that this is real for me." His gaze grows intense. "Since I met you, I can't stop thinking about you. It would be wrong of me not to tell you how I feel. That this marriage, for me, would be for keeps."

Hearing his words blows my mind. A shockwave seems to detonate in my chest, like a million feet are stamping against my sternum.

"Why would you say that?" I force the words out through a throat that seems to have developed swollen tonsils.

"Surely, it hasn't escaped your attention that I'm more than a little obsessed with you." To punctuate the point, he pushes into my core.

The hard column of his shaft rubs up against my clit. He's so big, so well-endowed, I can feel each inch of his length through the clothes between us.

A shiver spirals up my spine. I can't stop myself from panting. I'm so turned on, my toes curl. Moisture drips out from between my legs. *It's only my sympathetic nervous system kicking into overdrive. Vasodilation of the blood vessels in my vagina.*

"My Bartholin glands are in good working order," I squeak before I can stop myself.

The skin around his eyes creases. But he doesn't smile or chuckle, which would make my mortification worse.

"Good to know," he remarks in a mild voice.

I clear my throat. "I often talk to myself, when I'm alone; it helps to, uh, understand my thoughts better."

"It helps with clarity." He nods, his expression very serious. "I like that you feel comfortable enough in my presence to do so."

"Uh, I wouldn't exactly call this being comfortable." I look between us. At how he has me pinned to the glass, with my legs still wrapped around his waist, and my fingertips entangled in the soft hair at the nape of his neck. I immediately withdraw them and place them on his shoulders. "You should let me down."

"Why? I'm enjoying the view." He continues to watch me intently. Those blue eyes of his burn with silver sparks.

Like fireballs floating on water. Like the skies lit up with sun rays on summer solstice, and the promise of the hours ahead stretches out in front. Truth is, I couldn't be happier than where I am. *Only thing better than this would be to have him inside of me and*—a buzzing sound infiltrates the room. I ignore it.

"And I...am agreeing to marry you because it's the only way you'll get access to your fortune, and to save the ER. We're both trying to do something good for the larger community. If I backed away from doing this, I wouldn't be able to live with myself."

What I'm *not* saying is that I can't stop thinking about him either. That every time he touches me—*even by accident*—my heart does this ridiculous flip like it's auditioning for a rom-com. That I, too, want this marriage to be real. And that scares the hell out of me.

So instead, I focus on the practical stuff. The noble reasons. The ER. His trust fund. Our shared sense of duty.

Because if I let myself admit how badly I want *him*—I'll unravel. And right now? Deflecting is the only defense I've got.

The buzzing sound is insistent. I ignore it.

"Of course. I wouldn't have expected anything less from you." He looks almost disappointed. "Just so we're clear"—he sets his jaw—"if you marry me, it will not be make-believe."

The buzzing fades away. Like the static between us has shifted, clarified. Some of the tension in my shoulders drains with it, but it's replaced by something heavier…weightier. The kind of awareness that settles low in my belly.

"So you said earlier." I keep my voice steady, even though my pulse is doing a slow, heady thrum. I think I know what he's alluding to. Or at least, I want to believe I do.

But a part of me—maybe the bravest part—wants to experience what he's alluding to. Because if we're doing this. If we're stepping into this fire together, I want to know exactly how hot it burns. I tilt my chin up and meet his gaze, holding it.

"But what does that really mean to you?"

He tucks a strand of hair behind my ear, his touch gentle, but his gaze intensifies. He's looking at me like I'm the antigen and he's the antibody, inescapably drawn to me, designed to lock in, mark me as his, with no escape.

"It means—" His cock throbs against my core. He bends and drags his nose up my jawline. It's all I can do to not purr loudly with delight. And when he follows up with little kisses following the same path, I lean my head back into the glass, giving him better access. "I'm addicted to your little cries, and your scent, and your heady taste—which I can't get enough of. It means that the chemistry between us can't be ignored. And I want to make love to you, but not until we're married."

I search his features and see the intent in his eyes. He's serious about this.

"I feel the same way," I say slowly.

"Good." His eyes flash with pleasure. "I want a real marriage. With no prenup. And no divorce."

"No divorce?" I should be surprised, but instead, I feel relieved. Apparently, this is what I've wanted all along. *Have I been lying to myself?* Was my refusal to marry him real—or just a way to protect myself from more disappointment?

"You'll be stuck with me for the rest of your days. How do you feel about that, Fever?"

My head spins. My heartbeat seems to infiltrate the rest of my body, so that blood thuds at my temples, between my legs, and at my wrists. It's a combination of disbelief and stark arousal that this man would want me so much. Suddenly, I wish I could trust him. I wish I could tell him everything.

Perhaps, he can look past what happened and still want me?

With reluctance I take my gaze off him and look over his shoulder to where my purse is placed on a coffee table. "I hear my phone going off."

"I don't hear anything." He pulls me even closer.

The heat of his body seeps into my skin like a drug, slow and potent, curling through my veins until I'm lightheaded. His nearness is a high—intoxicating and weightless—like I could float right out of myself. My limbs feel leaden and liquid, all at once, as if I'm sinking and soaring in the same breath. Somehow, I find the strength to peel myself away from him.

"I should get it. It might be the hospital."

He reluctantly steps back, and I lower my feet to the ground. He smooths down my dress.

I pull away from him, already knowing who it's going to be. I pick up the phone and head to the other side of the room, to reduce the chances of my husband-to-be listening to who I'm speaking with.

"Hey." I clear my throat. "How are you?"

"When are you coming home?"

I close my eyes against the pain in his words.

"Please, Phe, I miss you."

"You know it's over." I lower my voice. "You need to move on, Drew."

"It's not over for me, Phe. You tell me out of the blue that you're not in love with me anymore. That everything was a mistake. We've been together for over a year. You need to give me time to come to terms with what you're asking."

Why now? Why, when I finally feel like I can move on, is he calling me?

I grit my teeth.

Just as I am starting to let go of the guilt associated with him, he pops up. It's like he has a sixth sense of when I'm feeling good about myself and wants to mess up the moment.

I bite down on the rising frustration and force myself to take a breath.

"I'll be there," I blurt out, because it's the only thing I can say that will get him to stop.

I disconnect, drop the phone in my bag, then turn and gasp, for Connor's standing behind me.

"I have to go into work," I explain.

His expression relaxes. "As long as I don't have a competitor for your attentions."

My throat closes. My stomach bottoms out. I manage to keep the shock off my face. At least, I hope I do.

"And if you did?" I ask in a light tone. "What would you do about that Mr. Davenport?"

"You'd never be happy with anyone else."

A surprised chuckle wells up. "So arrogant."

He clamps his arm about my waist, then draws me up on my toes and into him.

"No one else can make you orgasm like me. No one else can satisfy you but me."

"Cool it, James Bond." I pat his massive chest. "It was only a colleague, and I really need to be getting to the hospital."

He scans my features, then nods. "You haven't answered my question."

"Which one?"

"How do you feel about our marriage being real? In every respect."

I like it too much. A flush steals over my cheeks. I want our marriage to be real. I want him. Want. Him. Need. Him. I ache to feel him inside of me. I have no doubt, when we make love, it's going to blow my mind. That he'll teach me just how much pleasure my body is capable of. That he'll bring to fruition those darker, most hidden parts of me that he's begun to awaken. My emotions must show on my face, for his eyes flash.

"Tell me," he demands. "I want to hear it from you."

"I want it." My breath hitches. "I want our marriage to be real, too."

29

Connor

I peer through the windshield of the car at the doors to the hospital. I parked a little way off, so she wouldn't notice my car.

After I dropped her, I wanted to wait for her and bring her home, but she said she didn't know how long she'd take in there. She told me it was best I leave and that she'd find her way back home. I agreed, but I couldn't bring myself to leave.

I can't stand to be away from her. But I also don't want to crowd her. I'll simply watch her from a distance. There's no telling how long she's going to be in there.

It might be midnight by the time she's done. But I'm fine to wait. I want to make sure that she gets home okay.

When I'm not with her, I think about her. And when I'm *with* her, it's all I can do to not keep touching her. To hear the cadence of her voice. Relish the touch of my fingers on her skin. To hold her close. To look into her eyes and track what brings her pleasure. To be inside her and feel her snug pussy squeezing down on my cock. I want it all. I want a future with her... And a part of me is sure she wants it, too. Only, she's conflicted about it, and I don't understand why.

On the other hand, when she confessed that she wanted our marriage to be real, I heard the sincerity in her voice. Felt the veracity of her intent. She wants this as much as me. But she's still marrying me primarily to get access to money to help her ER.

Perhaps, that's why it feels like she's holding something back from me? I felt sure the call she took wasn't from the hospital. But that must be my imagination working overtime. There's no need for her to lie to me, is there?

I could get my team looking into her background, question those she works with at the hospital. I could dig into her past and find out if there's anything she's keeping from me—but then I'd be doing exactly what she accused me of: prying into her life without her permission. So far, I've not crossed that line. I haven't intruded into her private life. And I intend to keep it that way. I plan to give her enough space and show her how much she means to me, so if she has anything to share, she'll do so of her own volition.

I crack my neck, roll my shoulders, then try to find that center of myself as I settle down to wait.

My phone buzzes. The screen shows: **Brody calling.**

I answer the FaceTime call. "What?"

"You still single?"

I groan. "The fuck do you want?"

His lips twitch, which is Brody speak for a chuckle. Man's sewn tighter than a switch on a ticking time bomb—holding together long enough to fool you.

"Is that a hint of frustration in your voice? Shouldn't this pre-wedding stage be when you're getting it on all the time?" he drawls.

And now, my normally more-silent-than-a-grave brother is making jokes. *What in the ever lovin' fuck is going on?*

I thump my forehead against the steering wheel. "If that's what you called me for, I'm going to hang up."

"Where are you parked?" He peers into the screen, taking in

what he can see of my surroundings. "Are you in the car? Are you waiting for someone?"

"Get to the point, will ya?"

"You're waiting for *her?*" His frown intensifies. "Are you *still* surveilling her?"

I stay quiet.

His jaw drops. "Oh, my buggering pisstard, you *are* still watching her. Does James know what you're up to? More to the point, does *she* know? Of course, not. If she did, she'd be upset with you. You do know that, right? Not that I'm finding fault with your caveman instincts. I'd be the same if she were mine—"

"She isn't."

He makes a disgusted noise. "Chill, mate. She's marrying *you*. She wouldn't have agreed if she didn't think of herself as yours. So why are you trying to screw things up in such a spectacular fashion?"

With a sigh I sit back in my seat. "How about *you* keep *your* bollocks away from mine."

"Don't like that picture, mate." He cringes. "But what-fucking-ever; it's your funeral."

"Fuck you too." I shift in the seat to find a more comfortable position. "Why did you call? Was it to find out when the wedding is going to be."

There's an uncomfortable silence. Then, "Gramps *is* on my case to get you to commit to a date." His voice is sheepish.

Knew it. "And since when do you do Arthur's bidding?"

"Since I'm the only Davenport bro left to marry, and since the old geezer won't let me access my trust fund or confirm me as the permanent CEO of a group company until I marry." He rolls his shoulders. "Ergo, it's in my interest to stay in his good books. With the rest of our brothers wanting to spend more time with their families, and you too busy setting up house, it's natural for me to take on the role of keeping Arthur abreast of news. Which reminds me, when is it?"

"When is what?" I keep an eye on the entrance.

Not that I expect her to come out anytime soon, but no harm being vigilant.

"The marriage, dumbass. Have you set a date yet?"

I stay silent.

"It's got to be within the month; Arthur specified that," he warns.

Which is true. "She just agreed to marry me. I'm not hustling her for a date."

"Bet she wants you to do just that."

"Huh?" I lower my chin. "How would you know that?"

"By keeping my eyes and ears open? This way, I know what to avoid. Trust me, women want you to commit to a wedding date. Makes them feel secure or some such shit."

"You've given this much thought, huh?" I frown.

"Only so I can do the exact opposite." He nods sagely. "And avoid any matrimonial traps."

"That's only until Arthur gets to you."

"Oh, I'm going in with no illusions. Love's a lie people tell themselves to feel less alone. I don't believe in it. And I won't pretend otherwise. I'll choose someone who understands the rules: clear terms, no expectations. We do what needs to be done, the marriage gets consummated, and she stays in the background. I get to continue with my life. That's how I keep control. That's how no one gets hurt."

"Sounds like a plan... If *you* want to screw up your life."

He grimaces. "And how's yours going so far, hmm? You ended up choosing someone under duress, and now you're embroiled in an affair-de-coeur. That's a surefire way to screw up your life."

I stare. "Having feelings for the woman you're going to marry would be considered normal, by most."

"And mess up your head and complicate your life? No, thank you." He sets his jaw. "I plan to steer clear of that malarkey. I'm never gonna fall in love, and I definitely will not have my emotions tied up with the woman I'm going to marry. My wife will be there purely to make Arthur happy. Which means, he'll allow me access to my money. It's a win for everyone."

Except for you. I'm not sure Brody understands the consequences of what he's thinking of doing.

For someone who was courageous enough to lead successful missions as a Marine, he sure can be a coward when it comes to emotional matters. I fear, in trying to avoid feeling too deeply, he's going to end up hurting himself. But that's something he's going to have to figure it out on his own.

"If you say so." I glance up and freeze. A second later, and I might have missed Fever leaving the hospital. I watch her disappear around the bend at the top of the road.

And this, after she told me she was called in to attend to an emergency. *That doesn't seem like an emergency.*

It's official; I must have walked into an alternate reality. That's the only explanation.

But seeing her very familiar back and swaying hips disappear around the corner tells me it's not. I'm here, parked in a car, spying on her, and she left the hospital—after telling me she wouldn't finish work until much later.

"I gotta go." I hang up, cutting off whatever he started to say, and ease the car forward.

I follow her at a distance, so as not to attract her attention. To my growing consternation she heads home.

I wait until she walks up the short garden path into her house. The door shuts behind her.

I park the car in the same parking spot I'd used to surveil her. I grip the wheel and watch the house. And watch, and watch. Around nine p.m. I message her:

Me: Are you home?

Fever: I am. Thank you for dropping me at the hospital.

Me: Hope you didn't work too late?

She doesn't reply.

I look up at the lights still shining in the windows on the upper level of the house. Anger squeezes my belly. My rib cage constricts.

Why would she not tell me the truth? Maybe, the emergency resolved itself and she decided to come home? But clearly, that's not what happened. For some reason, she chose not tell me the real reason she wanted to leave early. The more I think about it, the more the anger builds, until my muscles feel like they're going to split my skin. My jaw hurts from grinding my teeth. My fingers hurt from my unyielding grip on the steering wheel. I release it, shake out my fingers, and draw in a few breaths. Then, I push the door open and step out.

The cool night air should serve as a balm on my fevered skin. Instead, it exaggerates the contrast with the tectonic plates which seem to be re-calibrating themselves in my chest. On wooden legs, I walk up the garden path.

I reach the doorway to the house and ring the bell. I can hear the electronic chimes from inside, then footsteps sound. The door opens, and she's standing in the doorway.

She's taken down her hair and brushed it out, so it falls around her shoulders. She's in a fresh pair of yoga pants and T-shirt, and she's wearing her ballet flats. *Is she going somewhere?* Her features are a little flushed. Her gaze widens.

"Connor? What are you doing here? Is everything okay?"

I nod. "Everything is okay." *Not.* I lean in, until my nose is only a few millimeters from hers. I draw in her sweet scent, and instantly, some of the churning miasma of emotions in my chest subsides. "I missed you. I had to come see you."

Her face softens. "I missed you, too." She raises her lips.

I press my mouth to hers. She throws her arms about my neck and presses those gorgeous curves into my body. Any remaining tension fades away. Her taste, the way she clutches at me, the way she clings to me, the way she parts her lips to receive my tongue, and allows me to fuck her mouth like she belongs to me. She does belong to me. She's mine.

I frame her cheek. "You're mine," I growl. "Only mine."

She moans. I swallow down the sound.

"Say it," I order.

"Yours. I'm yours, Connor."

I begin to inch her inside the house. A few steps inside the doorway, she suddenly tears her mouth from mine. "Oh no, I need to get going."

"Now?" I glance at my watch. "It's almost 9:30 p.m."

"Skylar called me when I was at the hospital. Karma West Sovrano's atelier has agreed to do a private viewing so I can choose a wedding dress. This is the only availability they have within the month, so I agreed."

"Hmm." I look into her eyes, trying to gauge if she's lying to me again. Just because she did earlier doesn't mean she'll do it again. I'm sure there's a reason behind why she said she had an emergency and then came home. There must be an innocuous explanation for this. But something inside of me insists that I confirm her statement. I curve my lips into a smile.

"Why don't I come with you?"

30

Connor

"Traditionally it's seen as bad luck for the bridegroom to see the bride in her wedding dress before the wedding, but we believe this stems from the days of arranged marriages when the bridegroom may have backed out if he didn't like his first glimpse of the bride, which normally happened at the time of the wedding. And you guys, clearly, don't have that problem." The manager of the atelier beams at us. Apparently, she must be used to having customers drop in at all times of the day or night.

We're in the private fitting lounge of the boutique. There's a rolling rack of wedding dresses waiting to be tried on. Soft jazz plays through hidden speakers.

"I'm sorry, I wasn't thinking straight." I scan Phe's features. "I understand if you want me to wait outside?"

If that's what makes her comfortable, then of course, I'll do so.

She smiles slightly. "I very much want your input in choosing my wedding dress." She presses her fingers together and lowers her chin. "I like it when you watch me."

Her stance is that of a woman who likes to obey orders. It's one which pleases me greatly. The slight hesitation in the angles of her body adds to her innocence. I doubt she's aware of how submissive she appears.

The confusion from her earlier actions fades. They seem inconsequential in light of this connection between us.

The air between us heats. My cock twitches. My groin tightens. Unable to resist, I take a step in her direction.

The manager clears her throat. "I'll be in my office. Once you've made your selections, please call me and I'll help you try them on." With a discreet smile, she eases the door closed behind her.

I hold Phe's gaze. She closes the distance between us and comes to a stop in front of me.

"You like it when I watch you, hmm?"

She nods shyly.

"What else do you like, Fever?"

She swallows audibly. The fact that she's so affected by me triggers a tsunami somewhere deep within me. Those tectonic plates shift again. Something huge, something mind-blowing, a deluge of feelings too big to be contained inside of me, overpowers me.

I place my big hand on her head and apply gentle pressure. Instantly, she folds to the ground on her knees.

She looks up at me from under her eyelashes. Pupils blown. Color high. The moment between us sizzles, sparks, like a fuse lit from my eyes to hers, burning up the distance between us.

She licks her lips, lowers her chin, and fuck—the blood drains to my groin.

"I like bending to you." She swallows. "Is that…strange?"

"You're following your instinct. How can that be strange?"

"I want to ask you to use me for your pleasure. To give up my body to you to do with as you please. I want to trust you." A shudder spirals up her body. "I *can* trust you, can't I?"

"I'll do anything for you." The band around my chest tightens.

I'm so overcome by emotion; a trembling grips me. I squeeze my fingers into fists and try to regain control. "If I had to burn the world down to protect you, I would."

"Oh." Her chin trembles.

She locks her fingers together in front of her.

Seeing her submissive stance sends a surge of heat through my veins. My balls tighten. My cock lengthens. The need to be inside of her, to own her, possess her, mark her—so everyone will know who she belongs to—inundates me. I want to fuck her right here, but I resist. Instead, I force myself to unfurl my fingers. Then slide my hand into my pocket and deliberately keep my stance casual.

"And you, Fever, can *I* trust *you?*"

I know I can, but I want to hear it from her.

She nods. "Of course." Eyes clear, gaze steady, voice firm. She means it. Confusion boils in my throat. Her body language tells me I can trust her. The softness in her eyes shows she wants me. The compliant angles of her body scream that she's ready to be bent into any shape I want, that she'll give me anything I want, do as I command. *She won't betray me.* I'm confident of that. So, what the hell was going on earlier?

Unable to stop myself from touching her, I slide my palm around her neck. My fingers meet in the front of her throat. And when I squeeze, her eyes widen. Her pupils dilate. A mixture of fear and lust flares in her eyes.

"Good. You want me right now, don't you? You'd part your thighs and show me your pink cunt, wet and glistening and ready to be fucked by me. You'd have me in any orifice I ask you to bare to me, if I asked, wouldn't you?"

"Yesss," she hisses. Then seems to get herself together with difficulty. Her breath comes in little gasps that light a thousand tiny fires in my bloodstream.

"Can I?"

"Can I?" I arch an eyebrow.

She frowns. "Can I... Sir?"

I allow myself a small smile.

"Please. Sir?" she asks with more confidence.

"Have you earned it, though?" I angle my head. "I don't think so."

Disappointment flickers across her face.

I help her to her feet, but I don't release her right away. My hand stays wrapped around her wrist, anchoring her.

"Soon, Fever." I allow myself a small smile at the frustration etched into her features. "Soon, you'll know what it feels like to take your husband's cock inside that sweet, aching pussy. But first—" I lean in, breathing her in. "I want to give you the wedding dress you dreamed of. The one you couldn't stop staring at. The one you thought no one saw you fall in love with."

I finally let her go and stride to the rack of gowns. My fingers close around the one she paused at, her gaze lingering on it through the display window, when I followed her that morning. Before she even knew my name.

I turn and hold it up.

Her breath catches. Her pupils dilate.

"How did you—" Her gaze flicks from the dress to my face. Realization dawns. "You saw me... When I looked at it in the display, didn't you?"

I nod once. "I did more than see you. I watched you fall in love with this dress. You didn't even touch it, but it was written all over your face."

Emotion flickers in her eyes, soft and luminous.

I step closer, lower my voice. "I'm not sorry I followed you that day, Fever. And I won't apologize for giving you what you want. Because seeing you in this dress? That's the moment I've been waiting for."

I call the manager, and she comes back to help Phe in the fitting room.

I hear whispering and giggling then, I hear the manager exclaim, "This is unbelievable, the fit is perfect. No alterations needed. That's happened, maybe once, in my twenty-year career. This dress was made for you."

She exits the dressing room, still shaking her head, before retreating from the lounge and closing the door behind her.

Phe steps out and poses with one hand on her hip. "Is it too much?"

I can't look away. She looks like sin wrapped in silk. The dress hugs her like it was designed with only her in mind—no, like it was waiting for her.

The ivory satin sculpts her waist so perfectly, it looks poured on. The neckline dips low, a subtle challenge, drawing my eyes to the shadow between her breasts. Thin straps frame her shoulders like ribbons on a forbidden gift.

And then—Christ—the flare. Just below her knees, the gown explodes into a fan of layered tulle and lace, a cloud of decadence that swirls around her ankles with every movement. A mermaid silhouette, seductive and unapologetic. The train follows her like she's royalty.

My pulse rate kicks up. My breathing roughens. I try to open my mouth to tell her what a vision she is, but no words leave me. When I stay silent, a wrinkle creases her brow. She walks—no, glides—further into the room. As she inches closer, embers spark beneath my skin. They burn through my veins, and seem to incinerate my cells, until I'm but a husk of myself. The overwhelming need to claim her surges through me and turns my cock to stone.

I manage to get control of myself and growl, "Stop."

She pauses. The surprise on her face deepens. She stands, uncertain, self-conscious, while her curvy body wrapped in that dress screams that she's a temptress. She looks like desire and truth, stitched together in satin. Like she could burn a man down and rebuild him in the same breath. And she's mine—*except, she isn't*. Not yet. But she will be. I made the right decision in asking her to marry me. And I can't wait.

"Connor?" A visible tremor skates along her neck before she swallows. "What is it?"

I shake my head to clear it. "You're the most beautiful woman in the entire universe. I'm the luckiest man alive that you agreed to marry me. I'm consumed with jealousy for any other man who'll catch sight of you in that glorious dress."

I take a step in her direction, and another, until I'm suddenly in front of her.

"In fact"—I wrap my fingers about the column of her throat, and her pulse rate speeds up—"I can't wait any longer to make you mine."

A surprised look enters her eyes. Then she looks up at me from under her eyelashes. "I assume, you like the dress?"

"I fucking love it." I squeeze down gently on her throat, and her breathing grows choppy.

"I can't wait to bend you over and tear it off your sweet fleshy arse. Can't wait to hold you down while I take you from behind."

Her lips part.

"Would you like that, sweet Fever?"

She nods.

"I think we should get married, right now."

"What?" Her jaw drops. "You're kidding, right?"

"I never kid, especially when it concerns you."

Her expression melts. She slips her slim fingers around my wrist. "I can't wait to be yours, Connor." She shifts her weight from one foot to the other.

I'm so tuned into her; I notice the slight hesitation in her words. "But?" I lower my chin. "I'm sensing a but here."

She flushes a little. "I have a condition."

"A condition?" I massage my thumb into the pulse that kicks up at the base of her throat. My voice comes out sounding ominous. I won't apologize for that. *She's mine.* Doesn't she already know that? And she wants to be mine. I can see it in the way her body sways toward mine. The way her peaked nipples are highlighted against the satin of her dress, the way her fingers cling to my skin, and how she tilts her head, so her cheek brushes my wrist.

The core of me that's used to taking charge wonders why she feels compelled to hold back when she's so clearly turned on? When she so clearly relishes that I'm unable to take my gaze off her. But the protector in me understands her reservations and wants to resolve her doubts.

"What is it, Fever?" I increase the pressure around her throat, knowing it will ground her, and communicate my reassurance to her. "Tell me."

"I *do* want to marry you; you know that."

I nod, knowing she's working her way toward telling me what's on her mind and that I need to be patient about it.

"Go on," I say gently.

Something in my voice must buoy her confidence, for she tips up her chin and meets my gaze. "And it's going to be a real marriage. *I* want it to be a real marriage. Which means, we'll be sharing a bedroom."

I frown, wondering what she's getting at. I stay silent, knowing that's the best way to coax her into completing her train of thought.

"But you know how independent I am. It's why I left home and put myself through med school with the loans I took out and the money I made with the part-time jobs I picked up in the hospital." A crease forms between her brows. "It was my need to earn the money toward saving my ER that made me agree to your proposition."

"Your independence is one of the reasons I'm attracted to you." I hold her gaze. "You challenge me, Fever. You make me want to understand what makes you tick. What goes on behind your eyes and in that intelligent mind of yours. It's what makes me want to find a way to make you submit willingly."

She flushes. The color is so pretty on her cheeks and staining the column of her throat. I resist the urge to lick the line of pink and allow my stance to stay patient.

"But there's one thing I don't understand."

She tilts her head.

"Why do you feel responsible for finding the money to save the ER? Why are you so desperate to save this specific hospital, of the many in this city?"

Her expression turns inward like she's chasing a thought she hasn't quite caught. "I never realized how it might seem from the outside." She rubs at her forehead. "You're right, there's no reason for me to feel a moral obligation to save the ER—"

"But you do."

"I do." Her jaw locks. "I think, it's because I was born into privilege. My job—it's not just a career. It's how I prove I'm more than the circumstances I was handed. Yes, it pays my bills, and no, I'll never be on the streets—my family would never let that happen. But that's exactly the point. Most of my colleagues here don't have that safety net. They show up, day after day, giving everything they've got. And I've worked alongside them long enough to know their stories. Their struggles. Their quiet resilience. That's why I can't walk away. That's why I feel responsible."

Her voice drops. "I knew what was coming. I could've done something sooner. I didn't. So now, I have to fix it. Not just for the ER, but for them."

A shadow crosses her features.

"I've saved lives in this place. Countless lives. If the ER closes, people in this borough will die."

Her gaze turns inward, haunted. I know she's hurting, and damn, I'd do anything in my power to stop it.

"What is it, Fever?" I ask, low and urgent.

She doesn't respond, so I grip her chin and tilt her face up to mine. "Talk to me."

She blinks, comes back to herself. "Neurologically? I'm trapped in a feedback loop. My brain registers a failure—something I should've done but didn't. My body floods with cortisol, and I get stuck in fight-or-flight, without a real threat or a way out. So, I stay there. Spinning."

"You feel guilty for the advantages you had. And somewhere inside, you believe you haven't earned any of it. So, you overcompensate. You try to make it right by giving everything to the people who don't have what you do."

She draws in a sharp breath. "Am I that transparent?"

"Only to me." I curve my lips. "And only because I get it. That's why I'm donating my trust fund to Save the Kids. I need it to mean something."

Her eyes soften. "We're more alike than I thought."

"We are."

The seconds stretch, taut and silent. Our gazes lock. The air thickens, electric with the pulse of that constant chemistry. But beneath the heat, there's something deeper now. A sense of alliance. Like we're no longer just two people colliding but a single force, turned outward, facing the world together.

A team. A unit.

It hits me again—how lucky I am to have found her. How inevitable this is. Her and me. *Us.*

"Your condition?" I clear my throat.

"Eh?"

"You said you had a condition?"

She hesitates, then nods. "I want to keep my place after we get married."

Keep her place? That throws me. I blink. "You'll be moving in with me though?"

"I will." She looks away, then meets my eyes again. "I bought the house two years ago, with the money I earned as a junior doctor. It's the first place that felt truly mine. I don't want to give it up."

So, she'll live with me. Sleep beside me. Share my home. But keep a separate space… *Just in case?* I frown.

"You want to keep it… As… A backup?"

She shifts her weight, curling one foot behind the other. "I've been on my own since I was eighteen. Always had my own space. Always been independent. I can't let go of that part of me overnight. Moving in with someone and not having a place of my own...feels wrong.

"We're getting married so quickly. That's already a big change. Leaving home now would be to strip everything familiar from me, all at once.

"I'd like to keep my place until I adjust to my new life with you. I simply need to let go slowly, even as I jump into something exciting and new. It's not an escape but a way to transition without losing myself."

She swallows.

"There have been occasions in the past when I've moved quickly and regretted it."

Is she talking about an ex? Has to be. She hasn't told me about him. But she will. With my actions, I'll convince her to trust me enough to tell me all about him.

"I don't want to make that mistake again. I need time to adjust to the transition."

I stare at her. I shouldn't be thrown off by this. It's her strength, her independence that drew me to her in the first place. But still—

Fuck, I want her to be mine. Entirely.

Not part-time. Not one foot in and the other out.

"I'm a possessive man, Fever." My voice is low. "I want my wife in my bed every night. Under my roof. Wearing my ring, and knowing there's no out. I want her to feel at home in my space because it's hers too. I don't like the idea of you having one foot outside the door, even symbolically."

Her eyes search mine. "You're saying, no?"

I shake my head. "No. I'm saying I don't like it. But I get it. You're not asking for space. Just…a safety net. Something familiar while we build whatever this is."

I draw in a sharp breath. What I *really* want to say is that I hate it.

I hate that she's already planning an exit strategy—even after saying yes to marrying me. That she's still half-out the door while I'm already all the way in.

God, I want to tell her that once she moves in, she's mine. That I won't let her walk away. Ever.

But that would only make me come across as desperate and unreasonable, and it would put her on the defensive.

Better to agree to what she wants, because clearly, this is important to her. But once we're married, I'll convince her that she won't need that place. That she'll never want to go back.

Managing to keep my voice casual, I offer, "But if it offers you peace of mind, then keep it."

The tension drains from her face. Her shoulders drop. The tightness between her brows smoothens out. So, this is what was weighing on her.

"However—" I lean forward, narrowing my gaze. "It does make me wonder if you're unsure about moving in with me. Probably, because I haven't shown you what your new home looks like."

She blinks.

"What do you say we change that?"

31

Phoenix

I glance sideways at him as we drive back from the atelier. Connor wanted to pay for the dress, but I told him I wanted to do it. He didn't protest. Maybe, it was because of the conversation we had about my independence?

I tell myself I'm relieved Connor's okay with me keeping my place. That he didn't protest. Didn't push. But the truth is that a part of me wishes he had.

Wishes he insisted I don't need it anymore. That I belong with him—fully, completely. That there's no need for a fallback plan.

Maybe I wanted him to stake a claim. To tell me I'm his, and I don't need a place of my own because I belong with him.

Instead, he nodded, said he understood—and that hurt more than I expected.

And yet that very calmness, that quiet confidence, tells me this man isn't trying to control me. He respects my need for independence.

And that dissolves the last of my doubts about this marriage.

Yes, we met under the strangest of circumstances. Yes, he crossed lines watching me from afar. But the fact that he's secure enough to let me keep my place, the way he lets me choose. It makes me see him differently.

It makes me want to tell him the real reason behind my ask. That it's where Drew lives. He'll be gone without the month, so it's only fair to give him that time to find another place.

Besides, I'm mostly at the hospital. With our schedules, I won't be home at the same time as him. It's not as if I'm trying to punish him for falling in love with me. That's just cruel.

But I can't tell Connor that; it would piss him off. And then, the fact that I never mentioned Drew to him, at all. But then, he never asked about my past, either, so it's only lying by omission, really... Which isn't too bad. *Is it?*

Then again, he hasn't volunteered information about his past, either.

I never should have agreed to Drew moving in with me. I knew I wasn't in love with him... But also, I didn't have a concrete reason to say no.

I allowed myself to be swept up in the moment. And when we started drifting apart, I didn't have the courage to ask him to leave.

I knew, by then, that I didn't really love him. But I didn't have the heart to tell him that.

I didn't want to hurt Drew. So, I kept putting off having the conversation with him, even though we'd started leading separate lives while we lived under the same roof. And by the time I broached the topic with Drew, it was too late.

Connor eases the car into the parking bay next to a converted warehouse. I was so lost in my thoughts, I didn't realize we'd reached our destination.

I look around. "Where are we?"

"Shoreditch." He mentions the name of a very expensive, artsy and chaotic area of London which is a hotspot for creatives and entrepreneurs. It's gritty, edgy, and the street-art-meets-serious-money vibe suits him.

He gets out of the car, then walks around and opens the door for me. When I step out, he grabs the garment bag with my wedding dress from the back of the car.

He leads me to the doorway, presses his thumbprint, then scans his eye at the panel set into the side.

When the door swings open silently, I gape. That was unexpected. It's a lot of security, but I suppose, I shouldn't be surprised. He did say he's an international man of mystery.

He steps in, then glances at me over his shoulder. "I've registered your name in the system. Once you add your thumbprint and iris scan, you can come and go as you please."

I follow him to the reception desk with the porter and take care of the biometrics. "Welcome to Lion Mills, Miss." The balding, chubby-cheeked porter smiles. "I'm Alfred."

"Alfred?" I ask bemused.

He beams. "Just like Batman's valet, Miss Hamilton."

He's so friendly, I can't help smiling back. "No doubt, you're more distinguished."

Alfred's smile widens until his eyes seem to disappear. "Anything you need, feel free to call down to me, Miss."

"Soon to be Missus, actually," Connor interrupts.

"Oh!" Alfred's face breaks into a grin. "Congratulations, Miss. And sir. And if I may say so—about bloody time."

He tips his head toward Connor, eyes twinkling. "When you meet the woman of your dreams, you don't muck about."

Then, with a sincerity that softens his rough edges, he brings his fingers together in front of him—a quaint, almost reverent gesture that somehow suits him perfectly.

"Truly. I couldn't be happier for the both of you."

"Thank you." Connor wraps his arm about my waist and pulls me closer.

I shoot him a glance to find he's watching me with a possessive look in his eyes. One which makes my cheeks flush. Our gazes meet, and the air between us spikes with heat. Unsaid emotions tremble in the space between us, turning it into a living, breathing thing which connects us and snaps us closer. I find myself swaying toward him, when Alfred clears his throat.

I blink and turn to him. "Thank you for the warm welcome," I say softly.

"Of course, Miss." He guides us to the elevator.

"Call me Phoenix, please."

"Of course, Miss Hamilton." The expression on his face indicates he has no intention of calling me anything other than Miss, but that he's happy to humor me into thinking otherwise.

He reaches the elevator, stabs the button to summon the car, then turns to me.

"The Lion Mills building formerly housed cotton, silk, and wool manufacturing facilities. Now, the repurposed structure offers loft-like apartments that pay tribute to the site's storied past."

"It's gorgeous." I glance around the reception area with its arched ceilings and wooden floors, which I swear, must be original.

"We have a shared courtyard garden at the back, but there are also a number of nearby green spaces, including Haggerston Park, Victoria Park, and London Fields. The flat is also conveniently located less than a mile from Broadway Market, as well as the Columbia Road Flower Market."

"The flower market?" I clap my hands. "It's one of my favorite parts of London. Of course, I'll have to commute a little more to get to the hospital, but this building has so much character." I look around again. "I'm sure it will be worth it."

"Hospital, ma'am?" Alfred frowns. "Is everything okay?"

"Oh, yes, of course." I wave my hand in the air.

Before I can clarify further, Connor jumps in with, "My wife-to-be is a brilliant ER doctor. In fact, she saved my life."

"That might be an exaggeration." I flush a little more.

The pride in his voice is evident, and it does funny things to my insides.

"No exaggeration when I say you're simply in your element in the ER. I've never seen anything sexier than when you're in your scrubs, taking charge of the chaos, and taking care of patients." His eyes shine.

"Oh." My chest swells.

Could he be more perfect? The fact that he sees me as not just a woman who's malleable to his commands, but as someone who's a thinking human able to make decisions, and that he respects my calling, makes me wonder if he's real.

He's so different from Drew, who never lost an opportunity to rub in the fact that he was a more experienced medical professional than I was. I realize now, it was his insecurity that made him put me down in front of the hospital staff every chance he got.

Drew came from an impoverished background, went to medical school on a scholarship, and is brilliant at his job. In comparison, I felt I wasn't good enough at my job. He took full advantage of that. Especially since, I never told him off.

Connor, though... The way he speaks about me—with that quiet certainty, that unwavering confidence in my skills. It anchors me. His pride in the work I do, in who I am as a trauma specialist, seeps under my skin and settles somewhere deep. It makes me stand taller. It makes me believe I'm more than just capable—I'm exceptional. He makes me feel good about being me. He makes me feel complete.

I bite my lower lip. Connor's gaze drops there. His blue eyes turn silver. His arm around my waist tightens. I tip my chin up and sway toward him. The elevator car arrives, and the doors slide open. I look away, and with my head spinning from the intensity of our connection, follow him inside. He nods in Alfred's direction.

"Thanks, Al. Make sure you watch out for her."

He half bows. "Goes without saying, sir." His plummy tones imply he's outraged that Connor felt it necessary to remind him about this.

As soon as the doors slide shut, Connor places his thumb into the biometric sensor next to the panel of buttons. The P on the top of the panel lights up. Of course, he has the penthouse. Then, he pushes me into the wall and takes my mouth. I sigh, allowing him to thrust his tongue between my lips.

He fucks my mouth with his tongue, miming the way he'll take my pussy.

I have no doubt; he'll be as ruthless. As single-minded. So

focused, it'll seem like he's putting his entire body behind each plunge, each drive into my body. He'd wring pleasure from my pussy, my skin, and from deep within my cells.

When he tears his mouth from mine, my breath comes in pants. My face feels hot, my breasts swollen, and sweat beads my forehead. The heat of his body crowds me, making me feel like I've plunged into a dry sauna. My entire body feels boneless, and I'm holding onto his arms for support.

"Wow." I swallow. "That was...something."

His lips curl in a pleased smirk, then he steps back, hands the dress over to me, before sweeping me up into his arms.

"Whoa, what—" Before I can say anything more, the doors to the elevator slide open.

He steps out directly into his apartment and sets my feet on the floor. I look around and gasp in delight.

Under my feet is what seems to be original wood flooring, faded with age and dripping with character. A few steps take us directly into the heart of the loft, a seamless transition from steel-and-glass precision to carefully curated opulence.

He takes the dress from me and hangs it on the coat rack by the door as I take in my surroundings.

Everything about the place is deliberate. The air is crisp and carries that underlying dark, smoky scent that instantly evokes him. And beneath that are familiar notes of secondhand books. I sniff, try to place it—then suddenly, it clicks. "India Ink."

"You recognize it?" He angles his head.

"I wanted to buy it at the candle stall at Primrose Hill Farmer's Market... Oh—" I make the connection. "You followed me into the Farmer's Market that day?"

He nods. "Couldn't resist getting it. I lit it every time I was home —" He points to the jar of half burned candle wax on the coffee table. "It made me feel closer to you."

"Oh." A tremor sparks low in my belly and ripples outward, leaving goosebumps in its wake.

The thought of him watching me with that kind of single-minded focus—then going out of his way to buy something I liked—should send alarm bells blaring. But it doesn't. It coils heat through my veins, leaves me flushed, tingly, and dizzy with the rush of it.

I feel seen. Chosen. Like, in that moment, the world narrowed to just him and me—drawn together by something deeper than logic, something that shimmered with purpose before I ever laid eyes on him. It feels like fate.

He continues forward, and I follow him.

To the left, a vast living space stretches beneath double-height ceilings, framed by black steel beams and a wall of Crittall-style windows overlooking the city.

A low, brutalist, concrete fireplace anchors one wall—unlit, but commanding. Overhead, a cluster of matte black pendant lights hang like a constellation, casting soft shadows over the sleek, modular sofa —a deep gray monolith flanked by built-in shelves stacked with tech journals, notebooks, and the occasional dog-eared paperback.

He continues inside. The kitchen, to the right—all graphite cabinetry, quartzite counters, and industrial brass fixtures—is surgical in its cleanliness. No clutter. No mess. Not even a water glass left behind. I could use the space as an operating theatre.

The espresso machine gleams on the counter and a half-full bottle of Lagavulin 16 sits on the floating shelf above it, as if waiting for him to pour himself a tumbler.

A blackened-steel, spiral staircase rises to the mezzanine above, where I assume the bedrooms must be.

It feels like I'm stepping into a fortress—*his* fortress—one disguised as art. All calculated surfaces, all edges and power, yet pulsing with something visceral underneath. Masculine. Monastic. Dangerous. Just like the man watching my reaction.

"Well?" The word is casual, the tone is drawled, but behind his eyes, I sense a question. A nervousness?

Will he let me sully his space with my mishmash of belongings? My colorful cushions on his black leather chaise? My romance novel next to his book that talks about the inner workings of a Beretta? My silk eyepatch and phone on the nightstand next to my side of the bed? My yoga pants, T-shirts, and scrubs next to his jeans, leather jackets, and tailor-made suits?

My sneakers and arch-supported shoes next to his Italian loafers and heavy boots?

This space feels so *him*. Every detail—subtle, intentionally unintentional—says more about who he is than anything he's ever told me.

The clean lines, the order, the intensity humming beneath it all. It's a smorgasbord of power and restraint. Unapologetically male. Quietly revealing. Every millimeter touched by his commanding presence.

Could I be happy here, surrounded by his brutal elegance, his hard-earned calm?

The answer rings through me, clear and certain.

Yes.

This dominant, self-contained man would flip this place upside down if it meant making room for me. For *us*. I know it. My gut confirms it so completely, I'm almost startled by the force of it. No numbness. No hesitation. None of that distant unease I felt when Drew moved in with me. Just warmth. Rightness. That click from deep inside of my instinct, confirming what I already sense.

It blindsides me, the way my eyes suddenly sting.

I don't want him to see how much it moves me. So, I keep it casual. Raise a shoulder.

"It'll do, I suppose."

His gaze widens, then he smirks. "Sassy, hmm? I'll have to punish you for that."

My pussy clenches. I'm suddenly inexorably so very wet. It feels like there's a gaping hole in my center which has dug its claws in and will not go away until he fills it. I squeeze my thighs together.

He raises a knowing eyebrow. "Does that turn you on, Fever?"

I jerk my chin, unable to lie to him. Not when he's watching me so closely, like I'm an insect, and he's the spider who's luring me into his web.

The silver in his eyes glows until it seems almost gold in color. He pulls me into his arms. "You flay me, Phe. Knowing I lit that hunger in your eyes? It's a feeling a man could lose himself in."

And just like that, he hands me the power.

He could tell me to drop to my knees and I'd do it—gladly. Out there, I'm a trauma specialist. Calm under pressure. In control. But with him? One command, and something deep inside me surrenders.

To the world, I'm strong, independent. But behind closed doors, I ache to let go. To obey. To give myself over to a man who knows exactly what I need, even when I don't.

It took Connor to show me this part of myself. The flip side of projecting a strong façade is this secret, desperate need to yield to a will stronger than mine.

He's the spark, and I'm the electric response. Each time I give in, it's not instinct. It's choice. Pure, deliberate submission that lights up every nerve ending in my body.

Because he's earned it. Because everything he's done to me has brought me pleasure. He's affirmed I can trust him with his actions.

Without breaking eye contact, he sweeps me into his arms again and carries me up the staircase.

He holds me like I'm something precious, like if he blinked, I'd vanish. It turns my insides to putty, and my pussy to liquid heat. When we reach the main bedroom, the hush of the space wraps around us.

Moonlight spills through the skylight above, casting silver shadows across the deep blue covers of a super king-sized bed that looks like it was made for slow seduction.

Floor-to-ceiling sliding doors open onto a private patio which, in turn, overlooks a private courtyard. The soft glow of hidden lights paints the garden in quiet gold. It's an enchanted little world, carved out of the night.

A partial wall screens the bed from the en suite beyond, where a freestanding tub waits under another skylight. Stars gleam above it like scattered diamonds, while the subtle mood lighting softens every edge, turning the room into a dreamscape. An ethereal haven.

There's another door at the far end which must lead into a walk-in closet. I can't wait to explore it. To unearth more secrets about this man who's come to mean so much to me so quickly, despite my attempts to resist him.

He walks across the floor and to the bed, where he drops me, then follows me down, folding his body over mine.

"What do you think?"

"Of what?" My voice comes out squeaky, and I clear it.

He raises an eyebrow. "The bedroom, of course."

"I haven't seen much of it," I say coyly, looking at him from under my eyelashes.

"You have my bed at your back and me on you. You don't need to see anything else." His tone is arrogant. His gaze that of a conquering emperor.

The confidence with which his body envelops mine is the kiss of heavy clouds over the peak of a mountain range—inevitable, elemental, made to alchemize the other. The way a storm crowns a summit. The way mist claims the jagged edges until mountain and sky blur into one, indistinguishable.

He presses closer, and I feel it—how he's reshaping the terrain of my body, flooding into every hollow, filling every silence between my breaths. Like weather rewriting a landscape.

Oh God. He's changing me. With his commanding touch. His possessive growls. The way every angle of his body proclaims I'm his. I swallow around the emotion in my throat and manage to speak. "I should *not* find that hot, but I do."

"I'm aware." He leans more of his weight on me.

He's a big man, at least a foot taller than me, and much heavier, *and* larger. But having his bulk pin me down doesn't feel threatening or suffocate me. It makes me feel anchored. Grounded, like he's holding down my body, and stilling my mind so I'm more at peace. He makes me feel secure. And perhaps, I shouldn't be surprised by that realization.

It's why I'm here with him in his apartment, and why I agreed to marry him. I could fool myself and say it was to save the ER, but that's an excuse. Really, it's because I want him. Because I feel this connection with him—have felt it since he stalked into my ER.

I want to feel the bite of his command, the unwavering absorption of being at his center of attention. To have him pay attention to my every move, as he does when we're together. I want to feel his skin on mine, his fingers on me, his cock inside me, his voice ordering me.

I want to fold for him—slow, exact—shaped like a piece of clay in his hands.

I'm a blank page, waiting for him to create a story through me. *Our* story.

Tying my future to Connor's is like gripping a blazing rocket—its core aglow, trembling with power—on the brink of ignition, poised to ferry us both beyond the stratosphere. It feels electric. True. Organic. My pulse races with an exhilarating charge, as if every nerve is awake and alive.

The charge builds in my chest, races down my limbs, sets every nerve alight.

It's electric. Raw. Like my heart skipped a beat—then found a rhythm that only exists when he's near. My body knows it before my brain can catch up—this isn't just adrenaline.

This is resuscitation. This is breath.

This is us. Alive. Vital. Real.

Before Connor, I almost surrendered to the comfort of a safe lie. To the illusion that I was content, when I wasn't. Now I realize, I would have traded my own happiness for safety.

To think, unaware that meeting Connor was just around the corner, I might have settled down for half a life instead of something magnificent.

With Connor, my instinct tells me it will be different. There are hidden corners to this man which excite me and make me want to find out more. Make me want to tease his secrets out and find out everything about him.

He wants to own me... Yet he's confessed that he belongs to me, too. I didn't see *that* coming. The thought burns hot under my skin.

He runs his nose up the column of my neck. "You smell delicious. Roses, jasmine, and vanilla. It drives me crazy."

"A mix of my conditioner and my lotion," I say on a breathless note.

He licks the skin under my ear, and I shiver. Goosebumps pop on my skin. My nipples are so hard, they hurt.

"Connor." I dig my fingers into his wide shoulders, enjoying their breadth, the cut of the muscles there, stretching the jacket he wears. The leather is beaten and worn smooth, and its scent adds a distinctive note.

"Hmm?" He nibbles on my ear lobe, tugging on it, then sucking it. My core quivers. My belly seizes up. That yawning hole in my center just got bigger, spreading to my extremities. I'm a black hole of longing, wanting... Waiting for him to fill me up.

Tiny tendrils of need curl their tentacles around me, digging their claws into my skin, and opening pathways of sensations I didn't know I possessed. I'm burning up. And I have a feeling, if I don't get him to move, this is going to reach its logical conclusion, with him taking me right here on his bed. *And I want that.* I want him to possess me under his roof where I'm surrounded by the signs of his presence. But not yet.

Maybe I'm more traditional than I care to admit. Because if we're getting married, then shouldn't our first time be on our wedding night?

The thought sends a thrill down my spine.

What's strange is, I never felt that way with Drew. It never even crossed my mind to wait. I didn't care enough to make it meaningful.

That alone should've screamed that something was wrong. That I was settling for comfort over connection. For convenience over passion.

Besides, I want to see if Connor can hold out until then? Once he fucks me, I'm not going to be able to think straight. And I want to save that feeling. As if on cue, my stomach growls.

He stills. "You're hungry?"

I am, and not just for food. I want to feel him inside of me, but that sounds so corny, I don't say it aloud. Instead, I nod.

He pulls back, eyelids hooded, pupils blown wide, so the black swallows up everything but for a ring of electric blue around the irises. His eyes seem even more piercing. Like a solar eclipse edged in cold fire.

He rolls off me and to his feet. I instantly miss his warmth. His weight on me. His scent surrounding me. Then he holds out his hand, and when I take it, he pulls me to my feet. "Let's get some food into you."

32

Connor

"How did you find the time to learn to cook?" I pop the cork on the bottle of red I retrieved from my personal collection, then pour it into two glasses.

Since she's chopping up tomatoes, I hold a glass to her lips. She takes a sip of the wine, swirls it in her mouth, then swallows with a sound of appreciation. One which goes straight to my cock. I widen my stance, trying to find a more comfortable position, without having to adjust myself. My gaze is riveted to her plump, glistening lips.

She exhales. "It tastes so good."

Unable to stop myself, I lean in and lick up the drop of red that clings to the edge of her mouth.

"It does," I agree.

She blushes and drops her gaze to the chopping board. "James made sure we could all cook. He enjoyed eating, and when he became a teen, insisted on learning how to cook from our chef. Then, he insisted the rest of us, too, were independent in the kitchen. And when he moved out, he left instructions with the chef to continue teaching us."

I place her glass down and take a sip from my own. "And was he as dictatorial in the home kitchen?"

I've personally never seen James throw one of his tantrums, but given how detail-oriented he is, I could believe that, in his quest for excellence, he's very demanding on his staff. Then, he launched into one when a TV crew was filming in his kitchen. It resulted in a viral moment that launched his career. Knowing James, my guess is that he didn't give a shit that the crew was filming. It was clear, he was focused only on putting together the best dish possible for his diners. But the general populace hasn't been as understanding. It's resulted in a lot of criticism about his demands on his staff.

"He never got angry with us, if that's what you're asking. In fact, he was quite relaxed and fun to be around. He's far more exacting on his employees." She shoots me a glance. "Almost as much as you are —" She hesitates.

I complete the sentence for her. "—in the bedroom?"

Her flush extends to her décolletage.

"Yes, that's what I was trying to say," she says in a prim voice.

She chops the garlic, her movements precise, yet also graceful. Her fingers are long and tapered. There's a confidence about her which calls back to the fluidity I noticed about her the first time we met.

"What about you?" She moves on to the tomatoes, pausing to offer me a slice.

I take it from her, making sure to wrap my tongue around her fingers.

Her lips part. "You're a scoundrel."

I smirk.

"Don't look so pleased." She turns to the pan I placed on the range for her and lights the flame below it. Then adds the olive oil and garlic, followed by the chopped tomatoes.

Separately, she sets a pot of water on the other burner and adds a dash of salt. When it starts boiling, she slides the pasta in.

"Why shouldn't I be? I have the most beautiful woman in the

world cooking for me." And then, because I can't keep my thoughts to myself when I'm with her, I add, "When I'm with you, the world makes more sense. When I hear you speak, it's like the rhythm that calms the restlessness in me. When I'm surrounded by your scent, I feel like I'm home. The sound of your breathing rewrites every broken piece of my past. You don't just fill the silences inside of me. You own them." I take a step in her direction. "Just like you own me."

I've never told anyone this. Never even believed I could. But with her, the words don't feel like confessions—they feel inevitable. Like she reaches into the places I've buried and breathes life back into them.

She finishes stirring, then shoots me a sideways glance. "Are you being sarcastic?"

"Of course, not." I frown. "Why would you think that?"

"You have to admit, that was over-the-top."

"I've never said anything like this to another person," I confess.

I've never let anyone in this deep. But she tears through my armor like it's made of paper, and leaves me standing there—bare, aching, and hers.

She scans my features. Whatever she sees there makes her eyes shine. A pleased look comes into her expression, which she bats away as quickly. "You don't have to woo me. I already agreed to marry you." She drains the pasta and sets it aside.

"Wooing you isn't a means to an end." I try to inject what I'm feeling into my words.

Her forehead furrows. "Didn't you suggest I marry you as part of a proposition?"

"It started out that way, but somewhere along the way, it became more." I speak slowly, taking care with how I phrase my thoughts. "I enjoy taking care of you. Satisfying your needs fulfills something deep inside. It makes me feel like the luckiest man in the entire world, and I never want to stop."

She stiffens.

I realize the words might sound trite, but I hope she understands that I mean them.

Then she drains the pasta, switches off the flame under the sauce, and plates it out, finishing it off with a touch of parsley. Turning, she hands one over to me, then walks past me with the other. Her thick lustrous hair has fallen over her cheek so I can't see her face.

She reaches the island and places her plate on it before sliding onto a stool.

"Could you get the cutlery?" Her voice is low.

I'm still unable to see her features. I grab the cutlery, walk back and place hers next to her plate.

"You, okay?"

She nods. And sniffles.

"Hey"—I cup her cheek—"what's wrong?"

"Nothing." The sheen in her eyes says the opposite.

"Is it something I said?"

She nods.

I peer into her hazel eyes, which appear almost green, cast my mind back over my words, and come up empty. She must see the confusion on my face for she half smiles.

"What you said... It was unexpected."

"Why?" I incline my head.

"I don't expect someone like *you* to articulate your feelings."

I allow my lips to curve in a half-smile. "You mean, because I'm a man, I have a low emotional quotient, so I won't be able to share what I'm feeling?" I say, only half-joking.

She chews on her lower lip, a thoughtful look on her face. "Women, score higher than men on certain aspects of emotional maturity, especially in empathy and interpersonal relationships. Of course, these differences are largely attributed to cultural and social conditioning, not biology. So—" She flushes at the knowing look on my face. "Sorry, that's the nerdy side of me."

"You can nerd out any time you want," I murmur.

She holds my gaze for a second more. That chemistry always thrumming under the surface between us blooms further. She clears her throat, then glances away.

"In my experience, when you come from money, you don't always appreciate what you have."

"You come from money and look how *you* turned out." I sit on the stool tucked around the corner of the island, at a right angle to hers.

She picks up her fork and begins to eat. "You're right. I was talking about men who are good-looking *and* built *and* have the wealth to indulge their whims. Not to mention, are as arrogant and as dominant as you—" She lowers her chin. "In my humble opinion, the masculine of the species, when they're entitled, act like complete twats."

I bark out a laugh. "Hearing you speak a quintessentially British cuss word in your American-accented voice gives me a real kick."

"Annoyingly I can't rid myself of the accent." She wrinkles her nose, looking disgusted with herself.

"Just to be clear"—I hold up a finger—"you did call me good-looking and built. Also arrogant. And dominant. Which, for the record, I'm taking as a compliment."

I can't help the note of satisfaction in my voice.

She rolls her eyes. "Don't stop hyping yourself up, will ya?"

God, she's cute. My chest softens, the edges of me turning to mush.

"I'm glad I surprised you...in a good way. I plan to keep doing that. Even after we're married."

Her lips part, and for a second, I see it—that flicker of surprise in her eyes.

"Is it only just sinking in?"

She looks away, her gaze thoughtful. Then, instead of answering, she gestures toward the food. "How is it?"

I let her pivot, pick up my fork, and take a bite. "It's really good."

"Thanks." She brings another forkful of pasta to her mouth and chews. "I've only begun to accept that we're getting hitched." She tilts her head. "Of course, I'm doing it because it's the best way to save the ER."

I'm disappointed that she's still using the ER to justify agreeing to marry me. Surely, there's some part of her beginning to thaw toward me? Surely, the light I see in her eyes every time she looks at me, is because she wants me, too?

"And here I thought, it was because you've developed feelings for me," I say, only half in jest.

Something flashes across her face, then she lowers her chin. "I'd be lying if I said you haven't made an impression on me. And it's clear, we're physically attracted to each other—" She swallows. "As for anything else, it's too soon."

I sense her distress, and my heart jumps in my chest. "I don't mean to put pressure on you." I squeeze her shoulder, wanting to comfort her.

"Thanks." She looks at me from under her eyelashes. "I really do appreciate that you have the connections to stop the ER from closing."

"The Prime Minister and I are alumni of the same school." It might be a cliché, but the *old boy's network* has its uses on occasions like this. "There must be some use of being a Davenport. Having access to people in power, who can make a difference, is the least of it. In fact, I believe you can help me craft the argument that should help convince him."

She gapes at me. "You want me involved in building the case to keep Archway Hospital's ER open?"

"You're the doctor. You work there. You have firsthand knowledge of how important its services are to the community. So absolutely, I want you to draw up the proposal making the case why the ER needs to stay open. Why don't you send it to me in the next few days, and I'll make sure it gets to the PM.

She places her fork down on the plate and pats her mouth with her paper napkin. Then she slides off the stool, moves around the breakfast counter, and throws herself into my arms.

I catch her, haul her into my lap, and she straddles me. She locks her fingers around my neck and looks up into my face.

"Remember what I said earlier about you being handsome, and built, and arrogant?"

"Yes?" I offer warily.

"Add sensitive, empathetic and caring."

I hitch up the left side of my mouth. "I take it, that's good?"

She swallows, a myriad of different emotions flitting across her features. "It's very good," she confirms. "And so sexy."

Her lashes dip, a sensual tension gathering around her eyes.

"That you're confident and so self-assured is a turn on. But add on that you're not an asshole. That"—she licks her lips, her gaze on mine—"you're perceptive enough to include me in this initiative.

You have no reason to do so. In fact, you don't need me. You could reach out to the Prime Minister and use the influence in your network to deliver on this for me. You could use this as negotiating tool, but instead you've decided to give me agency in this."

"There is no way I would not involve you in this bid to save the ER."

Her lips curve, admiration softening her gaze. "You're that rare mix—a commanding, confident man who's also emotionally open."

"Only with you," I say, my voice low. "When I'm undercover, I'm never really myself. I'm always playing a part. I might feel things. But it's the character who feels them, not me. My real emotions, my preferences—they stay locked away."

I rake a hand through my hair, tension settling across my shoulders. "When I'm in that world, I suppress everything real. It's the only way to survive. To get the job done."

I widen my stance and plant my feet, like I need the reminder I'm here. With her.

"But with you, it's different. I can feel. Really feel. You bring out parts of me I buried a long time ago. With you, I don't have to pretend. I don't have to hide. I can just…be."

"I feel that too," she murmurs. "You know me in ways no one else does. Sometimes, it blows my mind how much."

I do have prior knowledge of her preferences from stalking her. Guilt pricks at my subconscious mind. I push it aside. *If it helped to get her to stay with me, then surely, it was worth it?*

To distract myself—and her—I drawl, "Of course, there are other parts of me which I would love for you to blow them, too."

She rolls her eyes. "And I was just beginning to think I made the right choice in marrying a man who's a virtual stranger. You don't have to be a bossy bastard just for the sake of being one."

"Oh?" I slide my hands down to cover her arse cheeks and squeeze. "You don't tell me what to do."

Her eyes widen, the color of her pupils leaching out to indicate her arousal.

"And there he is," she says breathlessly.

"I was always here, baby. I simply had to show you there's more than one side to me. Don't try to categorize me; you can't." I position her over the bulge in my crotch and am rewarded by a subtle shiver that travels up her spine.

"Connor," she says on that tiny whimper that makes me want to throw her down and fuck into her.

"Damn." I survey her features, including those rosy lips I haven't been able to resist since I first saw them. "You turn me into a walking hard-on."

"Oh?" She draws her gaze from my mouth, up over the contours of my face. "Physiologically, arousal in men is a cascade triggered by visual, tactile, or psychological stimuli. The hypothalamus activates the sympathetic nervous system, increasing heart rate, dilating blood vessels, and redirecting blood flow—specifically to the corpus cavernosum of the penis. It's not subtle. Increased oxygenated blood causes an erection."

She grinds down on said part of my body, which exhibits the reaction she outlined.

"Pulse rate spikes. Skin flushes. Pupils dilate. Voice deepens. Testosterone may surge. All very textbook." She bites down on her lower lip. "But sometimes, it's not about biology, at all. Sometimes it's… Proximity. Eye contact." She tips up her chin and looks me in the eye. "A whisper." She lowers her voice until it reflects that breathy inflection which drives me crazy. "And sometimes, it's because a woman says the word penis in a clinical tone, and a man still reacts." She winks.

The blood drains to my groin. My balls are so hard, it feels like they've been replaced by Colt Pythons.

"Fuck," I swear against her lips. "When you talk dirty in your medical jargon, you kill me."

She smiles a tiny, secret smile.

"But you should know"—I increase my pressure on her luscious butt cheeks—"I have no intention of consummating our relationship until we're married."

I position her core over the tent at my crotch, then push down on her hips so she's grinding down on it.

She sucks in a breath, a darker color blooming across her cheeks.

It isn't until I say it aloud that I realize how much I mean it. When I first held back from making love to her, it was unintentional. But once it became clear I wanted to marry her... There's a particular satisfaction in knowing that the first time I'll be inside of her is when we're husband and wife.

Her gaze widens. "Didn't take you to be traditional."

"Didn't think I was." I twist my lips. "You, my beauty, bring out a primal part of me I didn't know existed. I want to own you, in every way possible, before I have my wicked way with you."

A part of me hopes this will make her agree to get married sooner than later. I know she wants me. I can feel it. When I run my nose up the curve where her shoulder meets her throat, she quivers. When I bury my nose in the hollow at the base of her throat, the aroma of her arousal blooms in the air. Which only turns me on further.

She whimpers; her chest rises and falls. She begins to hump her fabric-covered core over my rock-hard crotch. She locks her arms firmly around my neck, curves her spine, and arches her neck. I take what's offered and drag my whiskered chin down her décolletage, to the valley between her breasts.

"Connor." Her voice is husky and filled with so much need.

My name on her lips turns me on, sets my skin on fire. The blood begins to pound at my temples. "What do you need, Fever?"

"You, I need you."

"Hmm, show me how much." I wrap my fingers around her hair and tug just enough, knowing it will spark off pinpricks of sensation under her scalp.

Sure enough, she shudders and begins to squirm in my hold. She locks her knees around my waist and squeezes down, grinding the hard nub of her clit against the outline of my cock.

"Oh my God." She groans and shudders, then tightens her hold around my neck. Her thigh muscles quiver, and her movements get more frantic. "I'm so close. So very close."

I wrap my other hand around her throat and squeeze, just enough to slow down the air through her lungs. She opens her heavy lids, and in her eyes is a mixture of lust and curiosity.

When her body bucks of its own accord, she opens her mouth and pants. "Asphyxiation. Meaning, oxygen deprivation used to amplify arousal. By restricting airflow, you stimulate the release of adrenaline and dopamine—intensifying sensation, blood flow, and emotional high. Risky, if mishandled."

She licks her lips, her cheeks stained red, the hazel of her eyes a shining emerald signaling just how turned on she is.

"But when done with trust and precision?" Her throat moves as she swallows. "It's like hacking the brain's pleasure circuitry."

A bloom of satisfaction bursts in my chest and extends to my extremities. Every part of my body is honed in on her, the mission clear now in my mind. Make her come, like she never has before, in her life. Give her so much pleasure, she'll be high on endorphins and will agree to what I want. *Manipulative?* Maybe.

But when it's an honest byproduct of how much she's going to love what I do to her, surely, it can't be that bad.

"Good answer. I do believe you've earned this ride." I grasp her hip with my free hand. "Hold on."

33

Phoenix

"What?" I've barely registered what he means when he pins me in place and thrusts up and into my pussy.

It doesn't matter that I'm in my yoga pants and he's wearing his clothes. That rod he wields between his thighs like a weapon is so unyielding, I can feel its inherent strength, and when it connects with the swollen button between my pussy lips, sensations zip up my spine. It's as if I've been electrified, shockwaves of pleasure-pain pouring through my capillaries.

I open my mouth to cry out, but no words spill out. He looks into my eyes, the winter blaze in his like a clinical cautery tool. Cold on contact but designed to burn.

He begins to pound into me. Dry fucking me through our clothes, he pulls me in and thrusts up and into me. The impact sends more shockwaves through my system. My nerve cells seem to fire all at once. My own personal meteor shower flames across the sky of my chest.

The way my body reacts to him is almost too much to handle. He knows exactly where to touch me, how to hold me, how to maneuver my body so I feel the most pleasure. I have never felt this... Out of control.

I pant and groan, trying to pull away as the pleasure becomes too much. At the same time, I tilt my hips forward at an angle to increase the impact.

My body has a mind of its own, one divorced from my brain, my sense of survival. Flush with the desire of the impending orgasm knocking at the tailgate of my subconscious, I'm drowning in the phantom wave of pleasure that's approaching, that's towering over me, coming closer, closer.

"Connor, please, please," I moan.

"What do you want?" he growls against my mouth. His gaze holds mine captive as firmly as he has me captured between his hands.

"Make me come, please, please, make me co—" I cry out, for he rocks against me slowly, agonizingly firmly, circling his pelvis into my swollen cunt, just so.

Rolling, thrusting, bucking into me, against me, igniting a perverse rodeo of pleasure that roars up my spine and crashes behind my eyes. I throw my head back, cry out, and hear his gritted command to, "Come."

That's when he releases his hold on my throat. The oxygen rushes into my lungs. My insides seem to catch fire. Flames streak out from my core, searing my stomach, my chest... I climax.

The white-hot sparks of ecstasy streak across my vision, fountains of fire raining in their wake. Strands of rapture dig their claws into my skin and tug. I feel suspended on a flywheel of euphoria, spinning out into space at a dizzying pace. Faster and faster, out over the horizon, until I burn out completely.

Peace. White. Silence. I float down to earth.

Holy hypothalamic meltdown. I think I had an out-of-body experience. If he touches me, I'm putty in his hands. If he demands, I'll share not just my body, but my mind, my emotions...my soul with him. *And your secrets? Do you trust him with them?*

When I open my eyes, I'm cradled in his lap. He must have pulled me into that position. I'm aware of the still throbbing cock in his pants stabbing heavily into my side.

"You didn't come?" I clear my throat and peer up at him.

"*You* came," he states with satisfaction, voice gravelly, blue eyes a deep indigo, reflecting a smugness that makes me flush.

"What?" I mean it to come out on a snap, but it's more like a breathy sound, betraying just how relaxed I am.

"That looks good on you, Fever."

"What does?"

"That languid laziness that comes from being almost fucked." He smirks. "Imagine how it's going to be when I do."

"I'll probably be comatose for a few hours after." Because credit where credit is due. I slide off his lap, straighten my top, then yelp when he slaps my butt sharply.

"Hey!" I scowl over my shoulder. "Stop that."

"This luscious peach of an arse is mine. Did you forget?" To mark his words, he places his palms on my butt and squeezes hard.

I jump, more from the cortical stimulation than shock, which turns my already wet pussy into even more of a puddle.

He must notice my consternation because his eyes light up with interest. "Does that turn you on? You like being slapped and squeezed, eh?"

Yes. Yes. I shake my head. "You surprised me, that's all."

A knowing smile curves his lips. Before he can call me out on my blatant lie, I round the island and plonk myself back in my seat.

"If you think you're torturing me with these orgasms, you're wrong. It's gratifying, actually."

"But for how long?" He twirls some of the pasta and holds it to his mouth. Then, the showoff slides it between his teeth and sucks the strands off the tines. *Oh my God.*

Despite just orgasming, I'm instantly horny. Again. My clit throbs. My heart descends to between my legs. My own food forgotten, I watch, fascinated at the deeply erotic tableau of Connor Davenport licking the fork with his tongue before going right back in to repeat the action. This time, when he sucks off the pasta, it's as if he's drawn my clit between his lips. I squeeze my thighs together, trying to stop the emptiness that dawns between my legs. Is it possible for him to turn me on by the simple act of eating?

He arches an eyebrow at me, all indolence and superior attitude. I blow out a breath and reach for my food.

"Want me to eat your pussy instead?" he asks casually.

My fork clatters onto the plate. "Jesus Christ, cut me a break, will ya?"

He chuckles. "I was only offering to ease your discomfort, Doc. Don't like to see you unfulfilled."

I tip up my chin. "I'm fine."

"You don't look fine. In fact, I'd say"—he scans my features with a pointed look—"elevated heartbeat, erratic pulse rate, temperature surge. All the signs of autonomous nervous system activation. You look like you could do with another orgasm."

"I'm aware of what you said. Also"—I knit my brows—"where did you pick up the medical terminology?"

"I read up on it."

"You did?" I'm strangely pleased by the fact that he cared enough to research medical terms, and then used them in his daily parlance in a way that makes sense. But I'm also disconcerted. I already told him I'll marry him, so there's no need to put himself out like this.

I'd called him a unicorn, but he's even more rare. Like a sterile surface in a trauma bay, which has never ever happened.

"Why would you do that?"

He shoots me a look from under those very masculine brows. There's no mistaking the heat in his eyes. But there's also reproach. He slowly places his fork in his plate, then takes my hand in his. "Because… I love your nerdy references, and how you tend to use doctor speak whenever you want to be more eloquent, and also, when you want to hide your feelings."

Holy myocardial infarction. He used the L word. In a different context but still. He. Used. The. L. Word. My heart starts galloping like it's being chased down a dark alley by a pack of wild adrenaline molecules.

I swear, he did it on purpose. Like a slip that wasn't a slip at all. Like maybe, his feelings already run deeper than he's letting on.

And suddenly, I'm breathless. Excited. Lightheaded, like I've stood up too fast after a night on call.

I have a feeling; I'm on the verge of something momentous with him. The kind of moment you only recognize after it's cracked your world wide open.

"I don't hide my feelings," I manage to reply to his earlier comment.

When his cerulean gaze slices through me like the beam of a submarine cutting through the murky dark in deep sea, heat flushes my cheeks.

"Okay, maybe I do. Sometimes." I dip my chin.

"Only sometimes?" he asks gently.

My heart squeezes. The soft reproach in his voice somehow affects me more than his de facto dominant nature. *Life with this man will never be boring.* It'll be more intense than being paged into a crash call in the middle of a double shift, and I'll love every moment of it.

"Hey, look at me." His voice grows even more tender, if that were possible.

I swallow around the ball of emotion in my throat.

"Take it easy. It's understandable to not want to be vulnerable." He hesitates. "I mean, it's not like I can talk about being open with my feelings, right?"

That makes me turn in his direction. "I think you've been awfully open... For a man."

He chuckles. "I think it's you."

"Me?"

"I've never been so forward with sharing my emotions as I am with you," he admits.

The intent turns his eyes into frost fire. "I wish you'd be as open with me. You say you trust me, you agreed to marry me, but you're not committed fully. There's something stopping you, and I wish I knew what it was. You say you trust me, Fever..." He tucks a strand of hair behind my ear. "I wish you really meant it."

Me too. I wish I really did trust him. If I did, I'd share my secret with him. The fact I haven't tells me I'm not there yet.

"You're very perceptive." I swallow.

He nods. "Comes from spending so much time undercover. Often it was only my instincts preventing me from being killed. I wish I could switch them off, but they're a part of me." The light in his eyes burns so brightly, it feels like he has me trapped in their glacial beam. "Whatever it is you're facing, you can tell me. I can help you, Fever."

A tremor runs through me. His words are so real, his gaze so open, it makes me want to tell him everything. About Drew. About why my ex still shares my home. About why I couldn't ask him to leave right away, despite our breaking up.

But would he understand?

Connor is a deeply possessive man—territorial down to his marrow. Finding out now could push him too far. He might walk away. Not just from the wedding, but from me. And that would mean, no lifeline for the ER. It would likely mean a life without the man who's come to mean so much to me already.

I can't risk that.

Not yet.

Once we're married—once he's pulled the strings only a Davenport can, once the ER is safe—then, maybe.

Maybe, we'll have built something real by then. Maybe he'll love me enough to understand why I haven't been upfront with him. Maybe I'll trust *myself* enough to tell him.

When I stay silent, his forehead furrows. "I realize, I had a head start on our relationship. And though I've tried my best for you to get to know me, perhaps, it hasn't been enough. Perhaps, it's unfair to ask you to share things with me, but..." A small smile curves his lips. "I'm patient, Fever."

Something hot punches through my chest—sharp and blinding. This man floors me. Completely undoes me.

Every word, every look, every instinct in me screams that I was right to say yes to him. Right to agree to marry him. Right to take a risk on him. Now, I just want more. More time. More closeness. *More of him.*

I need to accelerate this—get the wedding done, seal the deal—so I can finally breathe beside him without holding anything back.

So, I can tell him everything...before the lie festers between us.

I look into his eyes. "Patience. It's the waiting for the body to stabilize after trauma. You can't rush it. You monitor vitals, you watch for signs of deterioration, but mostly you hold. You resist the urge to intervene too soon, because premature action can do more harm than good. It's controlled restraint. Knowing when to act, and when to wait. And right now, I can't wait."

The lines around his eyes deepen. "I'm not following."

I allow myself a small smile. "I'm trying to say that I'm not patient, by nature. Hence, I'm a trauma doctor. I thrive on the adrenaline and the pace of the ER, you see."

"O-k-a-y." He chuckles. "If there's a puzzle somewhere in this—"

"I mean, let's elope."

34

Phoenix

I always imagined my wedding as some distant, dreamy event. The only certainty? I'd marry someone who loved and respected me. Connor may not love me—yet—but he respects me, deeply. And he *feels* for me.

When I suggested we elope, he didn't blink. Just pulled me in for a kiss, then reached for his phone to make arrangements. We stopped at my place for my passport—he wouldn't let me pack. "I'll get you everything," he said.

I already had my wedding dress with me.

Now, on a private jet he summoned with a single call, I wonder if he hoped I'd suggest this. He was ready. Waiting.

Maybe, I've unleashed something I can't rein in. Because beneath his charm and care, Connor is a predator. A man who claims what he wants. And now, that's me.

Maybe, this is the coward's way out, but I didn't want a London wedding. I don't want my family—or Drew—there. If he found out before I could speak to him, it would only make things worse.

I'll tell him. Just not yet. I pull out my phone and message him.

> Me: Will be away a couple of days.
> Something urgent came up.

I send it off, but it stays unread. A few more minutes pass without any change in status. Guess he must be busy?

I start to message my mom, then stop. Because if I message her, she'll call. And once she calls, I'll have to explain everything—how I met Connor, why I agreed to marry someone I barely know.

She'll worry.

Of course, that's a bit late to consider now... I'm already on the flight.

I should've told her when I first started thinking about it. Or maybe, years ago, when I met Drew.

Better yet, I should've called her more often after I left home.

I remember being close to her when I was younger.

But after I hit puberty, she became stricter, less forgiving. One set of expectations for my brothers... And another for me.

So, I left for a life that didn't require her permission or approval.

But deep down, under all that defiance... I'm still reaching for her approval.

Because if I can just pull this off—if I can fix something, save something, protect something that matters—maybe then, I'll finally be enough.

Now, the distance between us feels like too much to surmount.

Instead of my mum, I message James and let him know that I'm eloping with Connor. I tell him not to be pissed off, that this was my decision, and that I'm happy.

Then, I message my friends' group chat.

> Me: I'm on a plane. To Gibraltar.

Instantly, the dots jump around.

> Harper: Gibraltar? What's in Gibraltar?
>
> Grace: Read the room Harp. Why does one go to Vegas? Hint: it's not for the gambling.
>
> Harper: Wh-a-a-a-t? No way 😆 Phe! Is that why you're headed to Gibraltar?
>
> Zoey: Are you sure?

It's my turn to pause. My thoughts run pell-mell through my mind, then I type out:

> Me: I'm not. But also, I kind of am. It's complicated.
>
> Zoey: Considering the off-the-charts chemistry I saw between you two... Can I just ask—are you marrying Connor?
>
> Me: No, I met someone else.

I watch in amusement as the dots on my screen flash, then disappear, as if everyone is trying to figure out how to respond.

> Harper: 😮
>
> Grace: 😬
>
> Zoey: 😶

Deciding to put them out of their misery, I type another message.

> Me: 😳 Of course it's Connor. Who else could it be?
>
> Zoey: As long as this is what you want?
>
> Me: I think it IS. I'm so sorry I'm eloping. Can you forgive me for doing this?
>
> Harper: Woman please. We're just happy that you're happy. You deserve it.

I bite my lower lip. Harper's response gives me the courage to ask the question I've been wondering about.

> Me: You don't think it's too soon?
>
> Harper: Of course not. When you know, you know.

Harper's a romantic. She thinks Connor and I fell in love very quickly and decided to get married. She doesn't know the main reason why. And I'll tell them, once the ER is safe.

> Grace: Listen bish it's called eloping because you don't tell anyone about it and just go ahead and do it. Personally I think it's the fastest most efficient way to do it.

I chuckle. I bet Grace is thinking it's the only way she could get married without missing her morning show. I'm doing it this way because I'm a coward. Because I don't want to explain myself to anyone.

Why can't I simply be open to my friends and my family? Why do I have this awful worry that I'll be judged by everyone for my actions? Why can't I stop worrying about what others think about me and simply allow myself to be? *External locus of evaluation: Basing self-worth on others' opinions rather than internal validation.*

Or in this case, it's one person's opinion. My mother. I'll face her when I'm back.

> Zoey: I'm guessing, the sex is phenomenal. You do realize you don't have to marry him for that, right?

Uh, am I going to tell them I haven't slept with him? Not in the strictest sense, anyway. *Probably not.*

> Me: That's not the reason I'm marrying him. Not only 😉

> Harper: Spill the tea woman! Let me at least live vicariously.

> Me: When I'm back.

> Grace: Take pics. Lots of pics.

> Zoey: As long as this makes you happy go for it.

It *does* make me happy. I'm so glad I shared this with my friends. I'll tell Drew when I return. He's not going to be happy, but perhaps, it'll be the sign he needs to move on.

My phone vibrates again. As if thoughts of him have conjured him up, there's a message from him.

> **Drew:** I wish you'd change your mind, Phe. You know I still love you. I'll always love you. We belong together.

My stomach twists. My chest pulls tight, like a rubber band stretched to snapping.

The jet hits an air pocket — sudden, jarring. I lurch in my seat as the phone slips from my hand and lands on the carpet with a dull thud, skidding to a stop beside Connor's feet.

Before I can reach for it, he bends down, picks it up, and — Shit. He glances at the screen before handing it back to me. I take it from him, fingers stiff. The message from Drew is still there.

A flush creeps up my neck. Did he see it? Did he read enough to know? Maybe, this is it—the moment the secret cracks open and I finally get to tell him. Maybe, I don't have to hide anymore.

But when I glance at him, he's already looking down at his own phone. Calm. Blank-faced. Like nothing happened.

No reaction. No sign he noticed anything. Guess he didn't see it. Or if he did, he's not letting on. Either way, the moment passes.

The band around my chest cinches tighter. There's no easy way out of this, is there? God, I hate that I'm still holding something back from him. And worse—how much that makes me hate myself.

I slip the phone back in my bag, which I've placed in the space between my seat and the window.

The pilot's voice comes on over the loudspeaker. "Sorry folks. That was a brief patch of bad weather. But we're through it now. The rest of the journey should be smooth."

"Hey, you look serious." Connor touches my shoulder.

I startle out of the reverie I'd fallen into and turn to him. "Just feeling apprehensive." I try to smile, but my lips feel frozen. "My stress hormones are running a marathon, I'm afraid."

His lip quirks slightly, enough to reveal that slight dent in his cheek, which instantly puts me a little more at ease.

"Having second thoughts?" he murmurs, weaving his fingers through mine. "Say the word, and I'll turn the jet around. We don't have to go to Gibraltar today. We'll wait until you're ready."

"You'd really do that?" I whisper, stunned.

"Of course." There's no hesitation on his features. Just steady, quiet certainty.

"But...what about the officials? The appointments you've arranged?" I falter, clinging to the excuse even as I test him.

He raises a shoulder, the arrogance on his face the hallmark of someone used to being obeyed. "It's their job."

I lock my fingers in my lap. "You'd lose the money involved in chartering the flight and—"

"The plane belongs to the Davenports."

I open my mouth, but he shakes his head. "And before you bring it up, we donate to environmental charities to offset our carbon footprint, and the jet is used only in times of emergency, which is what this is."

"Oh."

He called this an emergency. I told him I wanted to elope and he chartered a jet. Scheduled officials. Pulled strings I don't even understand, all at what must be a staggering cost to him.

And now... He'd scrap it all in a heartbeat. Just because I looked uncertain.

The weight of that hits me like a punch to the chest.

He's not just doing this for show. He's doing it for me. And I'm completely, utterly undone.

He leans in then and peers into my eyes, so all I can see is the sea of frozen blue, the silver sparks in them like flares have been set off from deep within. The dark pupils, a black layered with resolve.

"You come first. Your needs take precedence. I want you to be comfortable with what we're doing. I want you to feel you have the agency to stop it. We will not do anything that makes you feel helpless. You're my wife-to-be. My partner-to-be. The one I chose. You have the power in this relationship. You hold the claim on me. The reign over my life. The chokehold on my senses. Never forget that."

My brain cells feel like they are fried. *He's committed to this relationship.* While I? I'm still afraid he'll reject me if I share my past with him. I'm a terrible person. I'm more flawed than I realized. But maybe I can make up for my mistakes by showing him that I, too, care...in my own way. Even if I'm unable to profess it in words?

"You have no idea how much what you said means to me."

He tilts his head.

"In fact, I'm going to *show you* how much it means to me." I unhook my seat belt, glad that the carpet is thick enough to cushion the impact as I slide to my knees in front of him.

35

Connor

I know she's delaying, but it's impossible to chastise her for it when I see the intent in her eyes. When she reaches for my zipper, the light whisper of her fingertips against my crotch drains the blood to my groin. I know, then, she's succeeding in distracting me.

She lowers the zipper and stares at the tent in my boxers, and all thoughts drain from my mind.

I feel myself grow thicker, longer, harder under her perusal. I lean back in my seat and slide my thighs apart. She moves forward on her knees until she's positioned between them, still watching my crotch with big eyes.

"Take it out," I growl.

Instantly, she reaches inside my boxers and closes her fingers around the hard column. Goosebumps pepper my skin. My thigh muscles burn with need. Every muscle in my body seems to lock in. I'm a quivering mass of tension, lava building up at the base of a long dormant volcano, pushing at the seams and ready to explode. She pulls me out over the waistband of my briefs.

Without looking down at myself, I know the head will be swollen, the crown engorged and almost purple with need. And when she licks her lips, I'm sure there's precum oozing from the slit.

"Lick it off," I command.

Instantly, she dips her chin and licks up the column, curling her tongue around the head of my shaft.

"Fuck," I bark out. My thigh muscles bunch. I can't stop my hips from lifting off the seat, so my dick slides over her tongue.

A small smile curves her lips. A knowing smile filled with feminine delight. My Fever's discovering her power over me. She's realizing I wasn't lying when I said she holds my future in her hands. Certainly, the most important part of me at the moment, too. Though, I could argue that the most important part of me is now outside of my body.

I stare down at her bent head. As she opens her mouth wide, she, unprompted, takes me down her throat.

"Jesus Christ." I hold the hair back from her face so I can watch my cock disappear inside her mouth.

To call it erotic would be doing her and me a disservice. It's almost sublime to see her close her eyes and feel her gag around my girth. To watch the tears squeeze out from the corners of her eyes and the spit drool from the edges of her mouth. I ease her back until my length is poised at the rim of her mouth.

She looks up at me from under her heavy eyelids, her hazel eyes shimmering like forest leaves dotted with early spring rain. The golden flecks in them allude to how aroused she is.

"If I touch you between your legs, will I find you wet, my Fever?"

A breathy whimper emerges from her lips. The black of her pupils encroaches further into her irises.

"Does using your mouth to bring me pleasure turn you on?"

She jerks her chin.

"And does the thought of my taking your other holes in the same way turn your cunt into a raging river of need?"

Her chin trembles. The tendons of her throat flutter, the pulse at the base like a caterpillar struggling to be released from its cocoon. She seems caught in the midpoint between pleasure and pain, that perfect knife's edge where she could shoot out into the stratosphere or enjoy the security of staying tethered within the sweet bonds of torment.

"Want me to bring you some relief, baby?"

She nods eagerly.

"Then put your hands behind your back and keep your mouth open."

She instantly complies, her pulse beating faster, her chest rising and falling with anticipation. "Breathe through your nose." That's all the warning she gets before I ease her forward.

My cock slides down the slim column of her throat. The walls press down on my shaft, kindling a thousand little sparks in my bloodstream. She gags, and the sensation goes straight to my head.

"Woman, you're killing me." I ease her back again. Anchor her with my gaze, even as her knees tremble.

"Hold on." I begin to fuck her mouth in earnest. Each time I slip down her throat, she moans, her torso undulating like a reed in the currents at the bottom of the sea. Slim but curved in the right places, she's a thing of beauty. An object of desire. The most intriguing secret that I've stumbled across. One I intend to keep, and own, and make mine in every way that counts. I intend to coax her to bare her burdens, so there are no shadows between us.

Sweat beads her forehead, and she squeezes her thighs together. The sugary scent of her arousal is heavy in the air, fanning those sparks into infernos of desire.

I slip the top of my shoe between her thighs, coaxing them apart. Instantly, she begins to hump onto the curved surface, her actions desperate, saliva hanging in threads from her chin, mascara running freely down her cheeks. She looks like a goddess. Like she's consumed from within. Like she's lost her mind, all coherent thought vanished from her head. *Like me.* Her eyes are big, feverish with need, and that, strangely, makes her feel innocent. A butterfly pinned to a table by the knife of longing.

I increase the pace of my actions, fucking her throat as gently as possible, wanting to extend the pleasure, wanting to make sure she comes along on this ride with me.

"Get yourself close to the edge," I direct her.

Her eyelids flutter. She sinks down further onto my foot. Through the leather of my shoe, and the fabric of her yoga pants, I sense the throbbing bud of her clit. Sense the moisture drenching her panties and dripping down her inner thigh. And when she arches her spine and every nerve in her body draws tight, I know she's almost there.

I pull out of her mouth, then bend and close my lips over hers. I kiss her deeply, savoring the briny taste of my precum combined with the sweetness of her tongue. I reach under the waistband of her yoga pants and find her melting center. I stuff three fingers inside of her, capturing the cry that erupts from her. I hold her in place with my other hand on her shoulder and fuck her with my fingers.

I trace the swollen nub between her pussy lips, and her spine snaps straight. As if every fiber in her body is braced for impact. And when I curl my fingers inside her to touch the spongy bead behind her clit, she explodes.

Her lips lock, her muscles twitch and she throws her head back as she lets out a keening cry. Her eyelids flutter down as the climax has her in a chokehold. Her pussy clamps down on my fingers, and her orgasm goes on and on. I hold her in place, continuing to fuck her with my hand, until she slumps. Then I urge her to sit back on the balls of her feet. "Open your mouth."

She does.

I squeeze my swollen, painful cock and swipe my hand from base to crown in a hard twist, again and again. Now that I'm confident there's no turning back, now that I know we're on our way to get married, it feels like it's inevitable that she become my wife. Something knotted inside of me loosens.

Here on *my* turf, on a flight which feels like a metaphorical midpoint between where we started and where we're emotionally headed, I give in to the feelings I have for her. I accept what my subconscious has always known: that this arrangement was never fake.

But for someone whose survival hinged on unwavering control —
on camouflage, detachment, discipline — this is the first time I allow
myself to *relax*. To *let go*.

The pressure at the base of my spine breaks through the barriers
I imposed on it, and I let myself come. My orgasm crashes out from
my tailbone and up my spine and radiates out to my extremities.
Strings of my cum paint her mouth, her neck, across her cheeks.

She licks them up, still spasming with the aftermath of her own
release. I come and come, and she swallows everything she catches in
her mouth. When I'm done, I scoop the mess off her face and into
her mouth. She swallows, opens her eyes, and I witness a thunder-
struck expression in them like she's seen something holy. It certainly
felt that way to me.

When she begins to slump, I put myself to rights then scoop her
up and into my lap and cradle her.

I hold her until she finally opens her eyes and looks up at me.
"You finally came." She yawns.

"And you're wrecked."

36

Connor

"Long day. Long week." A furrow forms between her brows. "Long months," she says on another yawn.

Long *months?* What does that mean? Those shadows drag down those beautiful hazel eyes of hers. Or perhaps, it's the specter of sleep which turns them a dark green.

I tuck myself back into my boxers, then cuddle her close. "Sleep, I'll wake you when we land."

I kiss the top of her head, lift her in my arms and walk toward the bedroom at the back of the plane.

The ability to be horizontal on a flight is not something I'll ever take for granted. Not after being undercover and having to fold my six-foot-four-inches height into economy class seating.

Or curling my length into spaces where I needed to stay hidden as I conducted surveillance. It's made me appreciate the Davenport name, and the wealth that comes with it, anew.

It's why, when I realized I could help children in war-torn countries by supplying food and medicine, I knew I had to find a way to access my trust fund.

How can I sit on my hands when the means to save lives is within reach?

I tighten my hold around the woman I know is responsible for that. The trained part of me tells me it's healthy to feel these emotions. It confirms to me I'm alive, that I'm not living a lie.

That I'm in my skin... Living a double life means, I'm mostly closed off to emotions that normal humans face. It's the only way to survive living in another character's skin. This freedom to allow my thoughts and feelings to lead is refreshing and scary. And I'm not prepared for it. Which is why meeting Phoenix has hit so hard. I'm like a child learning to self-regulate all over again.

I walk into the suite and lower her sleeping form to the bed. Wanting her to be more comfortable I decide to undress her. I slip off her ballet pumps and strip off her yoga pants.

Unable to resist, I lean down and sniff her the triangle between her legs. The sweet scent of her arousal makes my mouth water.

I really shouldn't... but if I pulled off her underwear, I could make her come properly. I could give her relief.

As if reading my thoughts. She rubs her thighs together. Then parts them on a moan.

I glance up to find her lips parted, her cheeks flushed. Her eyelids flutter open.

"Connor, please," she whispers.

Instantly, I slide her panties down her gorgeous legs. When I glance down at the flesh between her thick thighs, I take in the moisture coating her lower lips. My heart rate escalates. My blood pounds at my temples. I need to taste her. *Right now.*

I sink down to my knees beside the bed and lick it off. A low groan emerges from her lips.

Unable to stop myself, I lick up the crease between her legs, around her already engorged nub. I slide my fingers inside her, gently weaving them in and out of her while I nibble on her clit.

She writhes. A fully body shudder grips her. She's so close.

I go to work, licking her pussy, curving my fingers inside her, biting down gently on the irresistible button of her cunt until, with a sigh, her hips twist, her back arches and the moisture of her cum coats my mouth and runs down my chin. Her orgasm is like a gentle summer shower sweeping over the English countryside, coating the greenery with pearls of reflected light, and turning the earth into a fertile life-giving organism.

When she's still, I raise my head, and move up her body, making sure not to touch her until I kiss her lips. I share her breath, and when I pull back, her lips cling to mine briefly.

Then she turns over on her side and lapses into slumber. I pull the cover over her, watching her sleep for a few minutes, before I straighten, then leave the room. Walking into the main cabin, I take my seat and pull out my phone.

The steward, who magically disappeared while we were occupied, comes by to check on me. I tell him I don't need anything before I dial Brody's number.

It rings twice then, "Wassup?" Brody's voice is alert.

"What are you doing up so early?"

I hear the creak of a chair, then the shuffle of papers. He must check the time, for he exclaims, "I lost track of time."

"You've been working all night?"

"It would seem that way." I hear him crack his neck. "But since you've interrupted my flow, this is a good time to go home." I sense him rising to his feet, the rustle of fabric indicating he must be pulling on his coat. "Which begs the question, what are *you* doing up at four in the morning?"

"I'm on the jet."

"Okay."

"With Phoenix.

"*O-k-a-y?*" A note of caution sweeps into his voice.

"A couple of hours from Gibraltar."

Silence. "Did you say Gibraltar?"

I nod, though he can't see it, but he must sense it because the air over the phone waves grows heavy. Then he whistles. "Holy shit, you're doing it?"

He makes the connection right away, since Gibraltar is one of the few places where couples can marry quickly without needing a lengthy residency—much like Vegas.

"It would seem that way, yes." Unable to sit still, I rise to my feet and begin to pace the aisle between the seats. I take in the plush leather of the chairs, the darkness outside, interrupted by occasional far-off lights of a city we're flying over.

"You sure?" His voice is steady, but there's doubt bleeding into his words.

"No. Yes. I don't know."

"So... You're not sure if you want to marry her?"

"Oh, I'm sure about that." I hesitate.

The silence stretches. When he speaks next, his tone is softer. "It's not like you to be this indecisive. Of all of us, you were very clear about not wanting to be a Marine. You were the only one who could stand up to Arthur and tell him that life wasn't for you. You convinced him there were other ways you could be of service to the country. You argued with him and refused to give in. And when he still didn't listen you—"

"I went off food and water for almost a week until he gave in." Yeah. That was me. Stubborn bastard. Even more stubborn as a child, when life's experiences hadn't yet chipped away at my determination. One could argue, at my core, I'm the same. More cautious, perhaps, since getting in the Secret Service. More patient, since I've learned to channel my brain power into biotech advances.

At heart, though, I'm still that child. Idealistic. Wanting to make the world a better place.

Getting bored easily was the bane of my existence. Until I understood that there's a bigger picture—a reason for our living.

It was my mother's devoutness that helped me find a focus. Going to church with her, realizing there was a higher power... Then discovering that didn't explain many of the phenomena in daily life. Like why the sun rose in the east. Or why the sky was blue. Or why water never flowed uphill.

It was the laws of science that helped me understand the world around me better. It helped me understand myself better. I'd found my calling: explaining the hidden, finding solutions to what people had deemed unsolvable. And then, needing to have more than one obsession, and perhaps, because all of those arguments with Arthur had stuck in my head, I also applied to be in the British Secret Service. And was accepted.

No one was prouder than Arthur that I worked for the government. It did mean having to spend long lengths of time away from home on undercover missions, while building up my own company within the Davenport Group to drive biotech breakthroughs.

And then, the shock that Arthur owns my patents. I was pissed off at myself. I left the process of patent registration to my team.

A team which, I now realize, Arthur bribed to register the patents in his name. A team I've since let go.

The anger I felt at the betrayal gave way to resignation.

I should have been more vigilant.

The crafty bugger found a way to hold something over me. A route to coercing me into settling down.

Of course, it resulted in finding Phoenix. I might have met her anyway, but to think of marrying her so quickly after meeting her— that's due to Arthur putting that thought in my head, I must concede.

Maybe, that son of a gun's methods work, after all?

"So, what I'm saying is that you always knew what you wanted and went after it. To find you vacillating is unusual."

"I'm not vacillating," I protest.

"No?"

"I've never been as sure of anything as I am about wanting Phoenix as my life partner. However—" I hesitate. "There's the fact that she doesn't feel the same."

Another silence, this time filled with surprise, and more than a little disbelief. Then he barks out a laugh. "Mr. Bachelor-for-Life finds someone, only the woman doesn't have feelings for him. Who'd have thought?"

"I'm going to disconnect now."

"No, hold on. I didn't mean it to come out like that. Or maybe, I did. You have to admit, it's a surprise. It's not like any of us Davenports have a problem finding women."

It's true. Thanks to the money and prestige that come with the

Davenport name, women have been throwing themselves at us since each of us hit puberty. I see the truth in what he's saying. But it doesn't make it any easier to hear it.

"I gotta say, I have no idea what it's like to be in your shoes, except, ouch, that must hurt."

I wave at the steward who's hovering in the doorway to the galley. He snaps to attention and disappears inside the sleek space.

"I'm sure I can change her mind," I say with confidence. "Only —" I hesitate. "Only, she has something on her mind. Something she's promised she'll share with me... Just not yet."

"Okay."

I hear him thinking.

"She's been upfront with you about it, so there's that."

"It's the one thing giving me hope that she'll eventually tell me about whatever it is that's bothering her, but damn, if I don't want her to tell me about it right away."

"It's bothering you, huh?"

"Of course, it is."

The steward walks over with a snifter of whiskey and places it in the holder built into the armrest.

Yes, it's almost dawn and I have a big day ahead, but I need the crutch of something a little more substantial to keep me going. I nod my thanks, and he leaves, sliding the doors to the galley shut behind him.

I cup my fingers around the tumbler. "We're getting married. Surely, she should trust me with her secrets?"

"And have you told her *all* of your secrets?"

"I don't have any... Not the kind she's hinting at."

"Have you told her about your undercover missions?"

I pause. "You know, I can't. That shit's classified."

I sense Brody nodding.

"I'm not saying she's right to shut you out. But you both have secrets. And you've known each other — what? A month?"

He has a point.

"That's the deal with marriages of convenience, right? You commit first. Then you unpack the rest...later. If you're smart."

I sip my whiskey, letting the burn remind me I'm still in control. I've known Phoenix for just over thirty days. Many people don't reveal their real selves in thirty years.

I watched her before I ever spoke to her. I mapped her routines, her tells, her moods. I learned what makes her laugh, what grates on her nerves, what pulls her attention when she's pretending not to care.

But knowing her preferences and her patterns isn't the same as knowing her soul.

And I want that. I want her—entirely.

To get under her skin and stay there, I have to earn more than the right to her body. I need her trust. Her truth. Her past. Her fears. Her fire. Her secrets. The parts she doesn't even show herself.

I know she feels the pull too—the gravity between us. It's not just physical. It's cellular. Atomic.

My pulse spikes every time she walks into the room. My brain generates white noise when she looks at me like she might let me in. It's not want. It's need.

And I know she feels it. She just doesn't trust it yet.

Brody's right.

I should stop expecting full surrender from someone still bracing for impact.

I need to give her room to breathe. Need to give her enough space to choose me on her own. Then, when she does... She won't just open up. She'll fall for me.

"When did you get this wise about relationships?" I scowl.

"Might have to do with watching each of you fall for your women and tie yourselves up in knots."

I hear the smirk in his voice.

"But seriously"—his tone turns serious—"give it time, eh?"

"Yeah." I lean back in my seat. "Thanks for the reminder."

"I assume Arthur doesn't know about this sudden little trip of yours?"

"Of course, not."

He blows out a breath. "You realize, I'll need to let him know?"

37

Phoenix

I open my eyes and glance around the space. Where am I? I sit up, and when the cover falls to my waist, I realize, I'm not wearing my yoga pants and my panties. It's that and the sense of well-being I wear about me like a made-to-measure bodysuit which brings the memories tumbling back. Connor making me come, then carrying me to bed.

I have a vague recollection of him making me come again before I fell asleep.

I glance at the closed door to the suite. I wonder what he's doing in the main cabin. A shiver of anticipation squeezes my lower belly. Thinking of him makes my clit throb and my toes curl. That was one helluva orgasm. My limbs still feel limber from the endorphins which are probably still circulating through my bloodstream. Man knows how to use his fingers, his tongue, and his cock.

The slight soreness in my throat reminds me of how thoroughly he used my mouth. And he hasn't even fucked me yet. The thought of that beautiful, monster cock inside me makes moisture pool between my thighs. *I swear, my pituitary gland just moaned.* He's making me sex-obsessed.

I glance around for my clothes and spot a few boxes laid on the loveseat below the window of the cabin.

It includes one I recognize. We brought my wedding dress, and it seems, he kept it out for me. I walk over to it and spot the note on top.

Shower first. Then wear these.

I hear his dark voice command me in my head. I run my finger over the strong strokes of his handwriting. It's the first time I'm seeing it. And it feels, somehow, personal. Like he wrote this into my skin. Goosebumps pop on my flesh. I set the note aside and pick up the smaller of the boxes. It has the name of a well-known shoe brand, and when I open it, a small cry escapes my lips.

Kitten heels, but with the familiar red soles indicating they belong to a very famous brand. One with a reputation for making very comfortable to wear footwear. A burst of joy squeezes my chest.

Did he realize that I don't often wear heels so I wouldn't be comfortable in anything over two inches? These are cute and sexy, but also, practical. The man thinks of everything.

I stare at the smallest box. When I open it, I find a beautiful bouquet. Made of white anemones nestled amongst dusky mauve freesia, twined with baby's breath and sliver eucalyptus leaves, it's bound in a blush silk ribbon. It feels like hope, and resilience, and joy, and a promise, all rolled into one.

Not sure when he did so, but I'm sure, he chose it personally. He also managed to have it delivered before we took off.

I'm strangely moved by it, even more than the shoes. Impatience grips me. I can't wait to wear these and show myself to my bride-groom. I head for the attached bath and step into the shower.

When I walk out, I find him seated by the window, head bowed as he peruses a newspaper.

He likes to read an actual, honest-to-God, real-life newspaper? Not the digital version? Another thing I only just found out about my bridegroom. Along with the fact that the early morning rays pick out the almost blue strands in his jet-black hair.

There is so much about him that I don't know. And I'm going to marry him. *Oh God!*

The repercussions of what I'm about to do dawn on me. Maybe, it's the slither of the silk of my dress against my curves, or the way my feet feel so very comfortable in my perfectly fitted heels, or the scent of the flowers from my corsage permeating the air around me, creating my very own bubble within which to glide forward toward him. Only... My steps falter.

What am I doing? Am I insane to agree to marry him?

I'm doing it for a good cause, of course. It's going to help everyone. And it's going to help me keep my job.

So why does my heart skip a beat? And my knees begin to knock together the moment I lay eyes on him? Is it because the marriage is real for him? *For me?* No matter how we met, or why I claim to be marrying him, my feelings for him have only grown since.

Enough that I can't stand the thought of him being with anyone else. It was another reason to go through with the wedding.

He keeps reading the newspaper, unaware of my scrutiny.

I drink in the aristocratic lines of his profile. High cheekbones, a patrician nose, a full lower lip, the uncompromising jut of his chin, the sinewed column of his throat. He doesn't just sit in the chair. He dominates it.

The space seems to bend toward him, drawn by the gravity of his presence.

I slowly complete the rest of my scan down his powerful thighs, the crisp fold of his pants, the pointed tips of his custom-made shoes. Even sitting down, with his attention else-where, the hum of awareness clings to him. Like he's the sun, and I'm a star that orbits around him. Caught in his gravitational field, no matter how far I go, I'll always find my way back to him.

It was only a matter of time until I crossed paths with him. Even if James hadn't asked him to watch out for me, I have a feeling, I'd have met him.

This thing between us is so elemental, it makes me forget to be careful. Makes me want to throw caution to the wind and follow my heart. *Which is what brought me here.* And I owe it to him to, at least, tell him a little more about my situation.

As if he senses my perusal, he glances up from his newspaper. His gaze fixes on me. His eyes widen. I have the satisfaction of seeing the newspaper flutter to the ground from his nerveless fingers. He rises to his feet, steps over it, and walks toward me.

He comes to a stop in front of me and, just as I had surveyed him previously, he gives me his complete attention. From the top of my head, to where my full breasts cause the bodice of my dress to jut out to where it's pinched in at my waist; then down the skirt, which flares out, with my toes peeping out underneath it.

When he raises his gaze to mine, his is lit with admiration, worship, and a touch of another emotion which has to be lust... Right?

He holds out his hand, and when I place my palm in it, he brings it to his mouth and kisses my knuckles. "You look beautiful." His voice is reverential. There seems to be a hidden meaning between the words which I'm not ready to tease out yet.

"Connor, I — We need to talk."

He searches my features. "Are you nervous?"

I nod.

"I'm nervous, too." His lip quirks.

"You don't look nervous."

"I'm good at hiding it. I've had a lifetime of learning, with having to hide any weakness from Arthur."

"Oh." I digest that. Another piece of something personal to go into creating the tapestry of Connor in my head.

"But it's not just that, it's —" I look for words. *How do I say this?*

"I... You..." I can't seem to form them. The connection between my tongue and my brain seems to be temporarily frozen.

"Hey, it's okay." He places his hand on the small of my back. "Come. Let's sit down." He guides me to the seat across from where he was seated and urges me to sit.

Then, he picks up the newspaper, folds it, and sets it aside, before sitting opposite me. Our knees knock together, and when I would have pulled away, he squeezes the sides of my legs. Once he's sure I'm not moving away, he raises his hands, and once more, captures mine between his much bigger ones.

"Let me look at you." That frost-and-fire of his gaze captures mine. Instantly, I still. The weight of his attention pins me down, but it also grounds me. An anchor of certainty in a sea of confusion—it causes all thoughts to slip from my mind, leaving it curiously empty. I draw in a breath, and my lungs fill with oxygen.

"That's it." He nods. "Allow your mind to relax. Allow your body to fall into your skin. Feel every part of yourself completely. You're here, with me. Just allow yourself to enjoy this moment in time when you're alive."

His voice has a hypnotic cadence that soothes my frayed nerve endings. I feel my muscles relax by degrees, allow my shoulders to lower, and lean back in my seat.

He releases his hold on my hand. "How are you feeling?"

"Better." I tilt my head. "I didn't realize how close to hyperventilating I was."

"It's going to be okay, I promise."

The sincerity in his voice causes my stomach to flip and my pussy to flutter. Also, a heaviness squeezes my chest. "Connor, I have something to tell you."

38

Connor

From the moment I saw her looking like a vision in her wedding dress, to seeing the panic in her eyes, and now, the sense of inevitability coloring her words, I know every encounter we've had has been building up to this. Is this when she finally tells me what's bothering her?

The fact that she's brought it up on her own is a good sign. I know better than to interrupt her train of thought, so I stay quiet.

The silence stretches, not particularly uncomfortable. More like a holding pattern, much like our position in the air at the moment.

"I... I haven't told you much about my past."

"What is it, Fever?" I take her hand, "You can tell me anything."

She blows out a gust of breath. "My ex-boyfriend... He worked —*works*—at the same hospital. We were together for almost a year. But then, things began to deteriorate. It was so difficult to find time together because of our schedules."

She raises a shoulder.

"We drifted apart. I knew our relationship was over, but it felt much easier to let things continue as is. That was a mistake I made. By the time I got around to telling him that things couldn't continue in this fashion, it was too late."

I was right. She has an ex. The thought of her with anyone else flashes hot and ugly in my head. Jealousy claws at my insides.

I force it aside, lock it down, and pin my focus on her. "What do you mean?"

She blinks the tears out of her eyes. Jealousy squeezes my guts. The fact that she was with someone else is to be expected. She's gorgeous and bright. Of course, she's been with men before me. Nevertheless, I want to wipe their memories from her head. I will make sure she forgets them once we're married. She's mine to claim. Mine to keep. *Mine.*

And I'll make sure no other man will ever look at her in any other way than respectfully. No other man will look at her and not know she's taken.

I manage to keep my caveman tendencies out of my facial expression, though maybe not completely, for she narrows her gaze on me. She must sense some of my thoughts, but I make sure to keep my expression clear of them.

"By the time I told him, he'd begun to think of our future together. He'd made plans. Wanted to introduce me to his family. He was very upset."

She bows her head.

"I should have broken up with him sooner. I shouldn't have let things develop between us until he thought we had a chance to stay together."

"It's not your fault. He should have sensed you were growing apart. If he'd been more focused, don't you think he'd have noticed that things weren't the way they should be?"

Her lips curve. "Thanks for being in my corner. But the truth is, both of us had equal responsibility to end the relationship before it got to the stage it did. I should have ended it earlier."

"So, when did you have this…conversation with him."

"The morning before I met you in the ER." She watches me closely.

"Ah, I see." I lean back. "So, it's a recent breakup."

She nods. "You have to understand, I wasn't looking for a relationship. In fact, I was sure I would not be in another relationship for a while. I had internally sworn off men, and then you walked into my ER." She wrings her hands. "I sensed the attraction with you right away, of course. I tried to resist. I didn't want anything to do with you. I didn't think it would come to anything, until — "

"I told you James sent me to watch out for you because he was worried about you," I finish her sentence.

"With good reason, as it turns out." Her lips twist. "My oldest brother's protective instincts, led him to suspect something wasn't right. And as it turns out, him sending you was going to help me move on." She gestures to the space between us. "Maybe not quite in the way I expected — or he did, for that matter — but it's certainly put things in perspective."

"Why didn't you tell James about your ex?"

She tries to pull her hand from mine, but I hold onto it. After a few seconds she gives in and lets me weave my fingers through hers.

"Mainly, because I was so overwhelmed in the ER. Between managing my job and a relationship I wasn't sure about, I didn't have the time to speak to James or the rest of my family."

She looks out the window and sighs. "That sounds like the excuse it is." She rubs at her temple. "I think I, subconsciously, knew this relationship wasn't going to last, so I didn't introduce him to my family."

She swallows.

"I wanted to avoid questions from both my family and my work colleagues about a possible relationship, especially since we never even said anything to HR. I never mentioned Drew to my family or to my work colleagues. I'm getting married without inviting any of them." She lowers her chin to her chest. "I'm a terrible daughter, and sister. And a coward. I don't want to explain myself to them, and I don't want to face the fact that I didn't tell them about having come close to marrying Drew, so — "

"Hold on, you came close to marrying him?" Anger snaps its jaws into my chest. I feel like I've been hit by a windmill.

"Not me. But *he* thought we would get married." She hunches her shoulders. "I misjudged our relationship. When we broke up, he didn't take it well." Her breath hitches. "It was very difficult."

"I'm sorry." I swallow down the animalistic instinct to grab her and hold her close, insisting that she never take any other man's name on her lips. This is part of her past. I can't take that away from her. And she's confiding in me; that's good. That's healthy.

I need to keep my possessiveness in check. The best way to help her is to let her speak and get this off her chest. And I do want to know about her past. As much as it might cause me to resent this man who spent any part of her life with her, it's part of her story. Her experience. What made her the woman she is today. The kind of woman I respect and have developed feelings for.

I must give her the space she needs to share this part of herself with me, as well. "I truly am. The end of any relationship is like death of an entire future you built in your head. A kind of mourning."

She jerks her chin my direction. "A cascade of physiological responses—elevated cortisol, disrupted REM cycles, appetite suppression."

"Yeah, that's grief." I'm glad I'm holding her hand in mine. Glad I can support her through the emotions she's going through.

A tear slides down her cheek. I instantly brush it aside. My heart squeezes. It feels like someone stuck a burning knife in my chest.

"Don't, Fever."

"Sorry," she chokes out, "I haven't mentioned this to anyone else before."

Her confiding in me is a start—a sign I'm earning her trust. But the suspicion she's still hiding something gnaws at me.

I lift our joined hands and brush my lips over her fingertips.

In time, when she's ready, she'll tell me the rest. Until then, I'll be here for her, steady and unshakable.

"It means everything that you let me in like this." I run my thumb over her wrist.

She shivers. Her gaze grows heavy. "You must think I'm crazy to cry over...something like this."

"Not at all. Your feelings matter. Never let anyone tell you otherwise or make you doubt their weight."

Some of the tension slips from her shoulders. "You're pretty amazing, you know that?"

"I do, actually." I smirk, knowing full well that will break the tension that's gripped the air between us, and it does.

She rolls her eyes. "And just as I was thinking you're a real, genuine person, despite your ego."

"I am real. And genuine. And I'm your person." I cringe hearing my words. That was corny. But it seems to have done the trick, for she smiles widely.

"I'm glad you're my person."

"Speaking of..." I pull a long rectangular box from my pocket. When I snap the lid open, the sunlight draws sparks of green from the stones in the platinum setting.

"Wow!" She stares at them. "Are those real?"

"What do you think?" I ask, amused.

"I mean, of course, they're not imitation. But I've never seen anything this beautiful."

As if in a dream, she reaches out to touch them.

I snap the lid forward, so it traps her fingers.

"Ow!" She pulls her hand back, surprise flashing across her face —then she bursts out laughing.

"That was a bona fide *Pretty Woman* moment."

I've never seen the movie. I did it to hear her laugh. *Jesus.* It's like the pattering of raindrops on a windowpane. Like water bouncing off pebbles on its way downstream. I'd give anything to hear her laugh like that every day.

I flip open the lid. "Go on; touch it."

She reaches for it.

Once again, I shut the lid.

This time, she pulls her hand back before I can trap her fingers. "Connor!" She smacks my hand and giggles.

I burst out laughing. "Sorry, couldn't resist. This time, I won't stop you. In fact"—I place the box in her lap—"it's yours."

She runs her fingers over the choker, and I watch as the stones react to her touch—warming, responding.

She lifts it to her throat, and something primitive uncoils inside me.

"Let me," I say, rising before she can fasten it.

I walk around to stand behind her, carefully shifting her hair to the side. My fingertips graze the back of her neck and I feel it. The jolt. The way her breath hitches, the way her skin draws heat from mine.

I fasten the clasp. "There. All done."

I return to my seat, but my gaze stays locked on her.

"How does it look?" she asks, tilting her chin, fingers skimming the line of the necklace.

It hugs her neck perfectly. They way it clings to her makes it resemble a collar. It looks like a mark. *My* mark.

It looks like possession. Like promise. Like the ghost of my hand resting there, claiming her in every unspoken way.

"You look…" My voice roughens. "Incredible."

I lean forward, until one of my knees slides between hers. I want to get closer. Always closer.

She swallows hard. I can see the shift in her breathing, the way her pupils dilate. Her heartbeat's spiking—beautifully, uncontrollably. She's fighting it, but it's there. The draw. The hunger. The surrender.

"Do I?" she asks, voice low, turned thick with desire.

I'm immeasurably moved by her beauty. "You're a vision. A goddess. A dream come to life."

Sitting there with that necklace at her throat, eyes wide and shining like she doesn't know how powerful she is. She's everything I never dared want. And now that she's mine, I'd burn the world to keep her safe.

"You chose me. You'll never regret that."

As if the universe agrees, the captain's voice crackles overhead.

"Ten minutes to landing."

39

Phoenix

"You may kiss the bride." Edward Chase, the former priest and Connor's half-brother flashes us a big smile.

He flew in to conduct the wedding at the Gibraltar Registry Office.

It's an elegant, whitewashed building that lets in the Mediterranean light through the many windows flanking its sides. We're in what's called the Marriage Room, standing in front of an ornate mahogany desk, behind which Edward stands. The registrar read out his words, then stepped aside for Edward to conduct the ceremony.

A gilded mirror hangs above the table, reflecting a handsome couple standing shoulder-to-shoulder.

The man towers over the woman; he's at least a foot taller. In his dark suit, hair styled back from his face, and the serious cut of his features, he looks intent. The green of his shirt compliments the emeralds the woman is wearing. Her hazel eyes have turned almost as green as the choker she's wearing. It brings out the golden specks in her eyes.

I meet his gaze in our reflection and am unable to look away.

The seriousness on his face reminds me that this is very real. I'm getting married. To this man. To this very handsome, charismatic, gorgeous, dominant man who, so far, has shown he can also be tender and genuine. And who wants access to his trust fund so he can literally save children. And who I felt compelled to help.

The fact that his influence will save the ER where I work from shutting down is a bonus—but really, it was his genuine desire to help children that compelled me to say yes, then accelerate the wedding by suggesting we elope.

I turn to him, lift my chin and hold his gaze as he dips his mouth closer. He places his left hand, the one where I placed a simple wedding band on his finger, on my hip. The other on my shoulder.

He lures me to my tiptoes and slants his mouth across mine. It's an explosion of sensations. I imagine this is how it might be to get tasered. To feel the lightning strikes of electricity ignite my synapses and trigger a cascade of sensations to my extremities.

It all emanates from where his lips tease mine and our tongues tangle. It's a kiss that feels like sealing a deal, like the start of something new and different and exciting—that's what the roller coaster of emotions bottoming out my stomach signals to my brain.

By the time he steps back, my head is spinning, my bones feel like they've dissolved, and moisture pools between my legs.

"Whoa," I say hoarsely.

He smiles in satisfaction and keeps his arm about my waist, probably realizing I've already lost my ability to stay upright.

"Thank you for coming out at such short notice." He shakes Edward's hand.

"You're lucky I was in Spain for work." Edward turns to me. "Congratulations, Mrs. Davenport."

That's…me? That's me. I take his proffered hand. "Thank you," I echo Connor.

"I'm sure there will be time for us to meet properly, but I believe you have a yacht waiting?" He smiles at Connor.

"A yacht?"

"You didn't think I was going to let us return without a honeymoon, did you?"

Our gazes meet, that chemistry between us roaring to the surface.

Edward clears his throat. "I need to be getting back."

Connor shakes his hand for a second time. "Thanks again, Ed. Appreciate it."

"You two have a wonderful honeymoon." Another nod in my direction, and he leaves.

And then it strikes me. A sharp jolt of realization. "I need to get back to the ER." I whirl toward Connor, my chest tightening. "I can't just disappear. What if they need me?"

"You have leave saved up," he says gently. "And I promise, I'll have you back in three days."

I hesitate. He's right. I do have holidays I've never taken. "But—"

"I called Arthur while you were asleep," he says, his tone deceptively casual, "and told him we were eloping. He was so relieved that I was getting married, he agreed to give me access to the money in my trust right away. I've arranged to donate part of it to Archway Hospital."

I blink. "You—what?" My voice trembles. My heart beats so hard and so fast, I feel dizzy. "You did *that*?"

A tide of emotion crashes over me. My lungs feel too tight to breathe. *He did that—for me?* For the ER. For the hospital. I can almost see the beds filled, the monitors blinking, the staff I love so much able to keep doing what they do best. *Hope.* It floods me, dizzying and golden. I feel like I'm flying, and somehow, drowning, all at once.

"Of course," there's a cautious edge to his voice. "I also spoke to James to let him know we were eloping. He's one of my best friends. We met because of him. It felt right to inform him."

I swallow past the lump in my throat. "I messaged him too."

"Good," he lowers his chin, almost sheepish. "I hope you don't mind that I took the liberty of informing the hospital management that we were getting married and…that you wouldn't be back at work for the rest of the week."

For a second, I'm too stunned to speak.

Then, softly, "Okay."

He blinks. "You're not upset?"

I shake my head, a slow smile curving my lips. "Maybe a little surprised at how quickly you got everything done. And yeah, part of me wishes I'd been the one to tell them myself—but honestly?" I exhale. "You thought of everything. You handled it all, so I don't have to worry. Not once did you make me feel small or sidelined. So no, Connor. I'm not upset. I'm…" My voice thickens. "I'm in awe of you."

He jerks his chin, a muscle flickering along his jaw. "I didn't want to wake you. And I wanted to make sure they had time to arrange cover." He looks almost boyish now. Uncertain. "I promise, I'll do better next time."

I step closer, pressing my palm to his chest, right over that steady, solid heartbeat.

"You're incredible. You know that?"

I'm still coming to terms with the fact that the ER is probably going to be safe. That my colleagues will, hopefully, keep their jobs. *And* the hospital is going to get the funding it needs too.

I'm also so overwhelmed, my thoughts race around in my head.

"And you weren't kidding when you said you Davenports have clout." I half-laugh.

He looks at me warily. "Does that make us less in your eyes?"

I'm about to protest, then sigh. "I guess, I'm more cynical of wealth and influence since I grew up with it. But being out in the world, without the benefit of my parents' money, has taught me to be more appreciative of it. And the kind of influence it can buy, too," I add as a grudging afterthought.

Which is not being charitable, because it's thanks to the Davenports' reach that the issue with the ER was brought to the attention of the most powerful man in the country.

"Or maybe, like most people, I value what I work for more than what's handed to me?" I raise a hand.

He tilts his head. "I don't disagree. I prefer to think about how best to use the wealth I already have—for something greater than myself."

He says it slowly, carefully. And I believe him.

"It's what I admire about you. It's why I said yes to marrying you," I murmur, because it's safer than admitting I'm developing feelings for him.

Something flickers in his gaze—not quite surprise, but something sharper. Like my words struck a nerve he wasn't ready to expose.

Then he nods.

A sharp action, that makes me wish I could be honest with him. That I could tell him that, perhaps, this marriage is real for me too.

But that doesn't change the fact that I walked into it with strategy first and emotion second.

Or... Is that a lie I'm telling myself?

A shield I've trained myself to raise.

Because admitting I feel more would mean letting him in.

And if I do that—if I let him matter, if I tell him all my secrets—then he could break me in ways I swore I'd never let happen.

The insight confuses me.

He thanks the wedding official, then the two silent witnesses he provided, before leading me out of the room.

He doesn't say anything, but I feel it—the anger, the disappointment. Radiating off him like static. A quiet, invisible wall I don't know how to breach.

I stay quiet as he walks me down the stairs of the heritage building and down the promenade that lines the waterfront. The newly signed marriage certificate, tucked into an envelope, still warm from the registrar's desk, is in the inner pocket of his jacket.

The sun hangs high over the Rock, lighting up the stone buildings that line one side of the street with a golden glow. We pass a farmer's market in progress; the smell of freshly baked bread and cheese, mixed with herbs and flowers, washes over us. A mix of locals and tourists, marked by their uniform of straw hats and Hawaiian shirts, walk in between the shops.

An older couple stops to admire us. The woman smiles and says, "Congratulations," as we pass.

"Thank you." I smile back.

Connor, however, stays focused on wherever he's taking me, which I assume is to the yacht. Palm trees sway above us, the market giving way to a stretch of quaint boutiques and wine bars which function as coffee shops by day.

More admiring eyes follow us, and a couple of teenagers glide by on their skateboards. One of them catcalls. When I look in his direction, he throws me a cheeky look, followed by an admiring glance. I laugh and wave at him. He throws me a kiss.

Before I can respond, Connor grabs me around my waist and hauls me closer. I look up to find him glaring at the boy, who laughs, then faces forward and pushes off, following his friend.

"He was a kid," I point out.

Connor doesn't reply.

"He was merely being flirtatious."

Connor grunts back.

My steps slow, forcing him to adjust his speed, else he'd have to drag me around. He glances down his patrician nose, a look of bored inquisitiveness on his features.

"Oh, stop that."

"Stop what?" He lets go of my hand, and instead, jams both of his in his pockets.

"That." I wave my fingers toward his face. "You're trying to be all cool and casual when really, you're being all grumpy and growly inside."

"I'm not grumpy and growly," he growls back.

"See." I jut out my chin. "You're growling at me."

He opens his mouth to speak, but a growl emerges again.

"Definitely growling." My lips twitch, but I manage to keep my mirth at bay.

He slams his lips together and takes a few deep breaths, which results in those perfect teardrop shaped nostrils of his flaring in and out—I hope he never finds out that I think his nostrils are perfect—then seems to get a hold of himself.

"I was growling, but now, I'm not." The hard line between his brows relaxes.

"Okay." I draw in a breath.

"Okay." He rolls his shoulders, seemingly calmer now.

"Better?" I ask cautiously.

He nods back, just as cautiously.

"Can you tell me why you're so upset?"

To his credit, he doesn't pretend he doesn't know what I'm talking about. "I'm jealous of anyone else who sets eyes on my beautiful bride," he bites out.

Something hot and melting coils in my chest and drips through my veins, like honey spilling from an overfull honeycomb. Rich, thick, and sticky, and flooding my bloodstream with too many feelings. "Oh." I bite my lower lip.

Instantly, his eyes fasten on my mouth, his gaze sharpening. That not very well-hidden beast inside of him peeks out from behind his eyes. I swear, his entire demeanor changes. That dark, primal part of him I've sensed from the moment I met him seems to saturate his personality.

"But that's not the real reason you're upset, is it?" I venture, wondering how far I can prod this lethal version of him. There's the Connor who's tender and understanding. Who respected me enough not to overstep the line in invading my privacy by placing cameras in my house or investigating my past.

Then there's this version—animalistic, visceral, and so very sexy. Both sides of him are appealing. Together, they constitute the best possible combination I could ask for in a man. But I want more. I want to unleash that part of him he keeps under control. That carnal side he's hinted at and never fully revealed.

Can I get him to show me what would happen if he fully let go of the boundaries he's laid down between us.

He must sense my thoughts, for his jaw clenches, and a fierceness sweeps over his face. "You want to know the real reason I was upset?"

His voice has turned gravelly, with an underlying menace curling around my waist and keeping me rooted to the spot. It's like there's this heaviness in the air, a static electricity lighting up my nerve endings and causing the hair on my forearms to rise.

"Yes," I manage to whisper, "I do."

"I was upset because"—he bends his knees and peers into my eyes—"I want more from you."

"More?" Anticipation runs down my spine. I have a sense I know what this man is talking about. This man who is now my husband, who I sensed could surprise me in ways I couldn't imagine, who I instinctively sensed could show me the kind of pleasure I've never experienced before. He would, surely, want something in return.

He nods slowly.

"I want you to give yourself up to me fully. I don't want you to hold back anything from me. I will not let you hold anything back. I want to know your innermost thoughts, your fears, your deepest insecurities. I want you to give yourself up to me completely. Can you do that?"

40

Connor

She hesitates. A myriad of emotions cross her face. Eagerness, lust, then a flash of apprehension. A part of me is disappointed that she didn't say yes right away. That my wife...had to think before answering whether she could give herself to me completely. It's up to me to change that. It's up to me to coax that level of surrender from her. If she doesn't feel comfortable accepting me completely, if she's unable to trust me fully, then *I* haven't done a very good job of giving her the reason to do so. Conviction tightens my chest. A surge of determination turns my insides into a river of need.

"I want to say yes," she whispers.

"Say yes," I coax her.

Her eyelids flutter, a sheen of awareness of exactly what that means gleaming at the bottom of those almost completely green mirrors to her soul.

Then she lowers her chin. "Yes," she says on a breath.

"I didn't hear you, Fever."

She tips up her chin. "Yes."

"Yes what?"

A flash of defiance turns the green into sparkling silver. "Yes, I won't hold back. Are you satisfied now?"

Not likely. Not until you say it without hesitation. Not until you show me with your body. Not until you mean it with your mind.

Outwardly, I nod. Then I lift her in my arms.

"Hey." She clutches at my shoulders. "What are you doing?"

"Carrying you to the yacht."

"I can walk."

"Not bloody likely in those heels."

"They're kitten heels. And low ones, at that," she protests.

"The ground is uneven. And by the way, I do love you in them and I want you to have them on when I fuck you."

"Oh."

I glance down to find her features flushed and her looking at me with stunned amazement and eyelids weighed down with lust.

"If you keep staring like that, I'll have to pull down your panties and take you right here, and I don't want to be picked up for indecent exposure."

She clears her throat, then presses her palm to my chest. "Your heart's racing. I don't think you're up for such strenuous exercise."

I spot the humor in her voice and make a growling sound.

"Definitely growling. And grumpier than when I first met you. All that—holding yourself back—is telling on you," she says in that sweet voice which seems designed to edge my desire.

I increase the pace of my steps. Not far now to the yacht. I can see it anchored off the jetty.

"You underestimate my self-control," I say in a steely tone.

I need to simply get to the yacht, dismiss the captain so we can have privacy, and then get it out into the harbor and to my favorite cove, not twenty minutes away, where I can drop anchor and—

"It starts slowly. Subtly." Her voice dips in tenor. "A flicker of blood flow, a shift in pressure. The parasympathetic nervous system kicks in—heart rate elevates, pupils dilate, blood rushes to the pelvic floor, muscles tense in anticipation."

My steps falter. My groin tightens. I squeeze her closer to my chest, and a gust of air leaves her lips.

"Everything heightens—sensation, sensitivity, breath." She swallows. "It's not just physical, though. The brain is in on it, too. Dopamine floods the system, ramping up desire. Oxytocin stirs, priming you for connection."

"I take it you're describing the sensations you're going to feel when I lick your pussy?"

She shudders. To my intense satisfaction, she squeezes her thighs together, and I swear, the caramel-laced scent of her arousal fills the air.

"Touch becomes magnified..." Her voice falters. "Th-thought narrows. The body starts chasing a single point of release—like every nerve ending is being drawn forward, pulled taut, until it's almost unbearable. Until it has to snap."

I keep going. Keep my eyes on the yacht, now less than a five-minute walk away.

"And when it does? Every muscle contracts. The pelvic floor spasms. The abdominal wall quivers. A full-body seizure of pleasure. And then... A collapse."

"This must be how you're going to feel when I lick into your cunt and the cleavage between your butt cheeks."

A moan spills from her lips. She digs her fingers into the lapel of my jacket, and a trembling grips her.

Reaching the jetty, I turn in. I'm almost running now. Not far... Twenty steps. Ten...

"A wash of serotonin. A flood of calm. It's the most controlled loss of control the body allows. And it leaves you wrecked." She raises her head to press her nose to the underside of my chin and breathes deeply. That viselike grip at the base of my spine tightens.

Desire is a demanding mistress, urging me to reach the yacht and climb aboard.

"Rewired. Sometimes, wrecked for good." She presses her breasts into my chest, whimpering with need.

That's it. Something inside me snaps. I stop at the edge of the gangway which leads to the yacht.

I lower my head as she raises hers, and our lips clash. Our mouths fuse. Our tongues tangle. Teeth, breath, a mingling of our saliva, of that sweet essence of hers which goes straight to my head. I kiss her deeply, and she holds onto me and kisses me right back. I'm drowning in her.

Losing sight of my surroundings, wanting to take her below deck, but also wanting the evening to unfold as I planned.

Knowing I need to stop before we're spotted, when the sound of someone clearing their throat reaches me.

She must hear it at the same time as me because she freezes. We stare into each other's eyes. Hers gone dark with desire. No doubt, mine must show my frustration and my crazed desire, which I'm fighting hard to bring under control.

"Mr. Davenport, the yacht is prepped as per your specifications. You have everything you need for your trip," the crew member who readied the craft says. There's a hint of apology in his voice.

Without taking my gaze off my wife, I nod in his direction. "Thank you, Simon."

"I've made the final checks, so with your permission, my team and I will leave. If you need anything at any time —"

"I'll radio you."

Simon leaves, accompanied by another man and a woman. His footsteps fade away.

"We're taking a trip?" Fever's voice is more composed, but her eyes hold the lingering effects of our earlier kiss.

"We are."

She glances toward the sleek craft moored on the other side of the gangway. "That one's yours?"

I nod. Then walk with her in my arms, across the gangway, and onto the side deck.

"Carrying me over the threshold?" Her voice is soft, almost shy.

I glance down at her flushed cheeks. "You didn't think I'd pass up the chance, did you?"

She nuzzles into my chest. "You are the most romantic man on the planet."

"And this"—I brush a kiss to her temple—"is only the beginning, baby."

I step inside the main salon. It's a sunken living space with rich walnut flooring, oversized, cream, modular sofas, and a glass ceiling strip to let in sunlight. Floor-to-ceiling windows on both sides frame the ocean. Sunlight bounces off the waves, and in the distance is the outline of islands, with the occasional sail from other boats billowing at intervals.

"Breathtaking," she breathes.

"It is." I watch her take in the surroundings.

She looks up to catch me watching her and blushes further. "I was talking about the view."

"So was I."

She chuckles. "Charmer."

"Only because I can't stop myself from appreciating my good fortune."

She looks taken aback, then something like sadness filters into her eyes, before it's replaced by a determination. She locks her arm about my neck and juts out her chin. "Are you going to show me the yacht?"

I want to ask her what brought about that wistful expression on her features but decide to save it for later.

"Your wish is my command, milady," I say lightly, drawing a giggle from her. Glad I lightened her mood; I nod toward the space we're in. "This is the main salon, or the main deck, as it's called." I head toward the adjacent kitchen. A steel island separates the prep area from the living space. "This is the galley." I jerk my chin in the direction of the gleaming appliances. Then I carry her up a short flight of steps and into the wheelhouse.

"This is the pilot's cabin." She takes in the curved console which constitutes the helm, the twin leather captain's chairs, the holographic navigational maps glowing softly on the dash. "Every dial and screen is voice activated, or fingerprint activated."

"Very modern." She nods.

"I had it updated recently." I demonstrate with a voice command that turns the floor-to-ceiling window that offers a view of the horizon opaque; then use another command to turn it transparent again.

"Wow."

For some reason, I feel like I'm a teenager showing off my first car to my girlfriend. Strange, how being with her makes me want to impress her, and take care of her, and own her, simultaneously.

"Aren't you tired of carrying me?" She looks up at me from under her eyelashes.

"I'll never get tired of carrying you."

A pleased look lights up her features.

"Besides, I haven't shown you the living quarters yet." Turning, I make my way past the galley, then the living space, down the steps to the lower deck, and into the master suite.

When I put her down, her heels sink into the luxurious carpeting.

She makes a slow turn, taking in the king-sized bed, fitted with crisp linen, a black silk throw, and pillows. The walls are paneled in warm-toned teak. A curved leather chaise lounges by the oversized porthole.

She peeks into the private en-suite bathroom which features his-and-hers sinks, and a rain shower with a skylight above.

"Whoa, that's some tub." She stares at the deep Japanese soaking tub set in the middle of the room. It faces a view of the ocean through a one-way window. Plush towels are folded, along with other essentials, on a shelf built into the wall. "The floors are heated, too," she exclaims, looking at me over her shoulder.

"I don't skimp when it comes to my comfort, or yours."

"Hmm…" She walks over and slips her arm about my waist.

The gesture is natural, and the sheer normalcy of it makes my heart stutter. Which is a first. I'm not one to be moved by casual gestures of affection. And that's what this is. I wonder if she realizes it's a sign that she trusts me, whether she admits to it or not.

I place my hands on her hips, stopping myself from pulling her up against me with difficultly. Instead, I content myself with a kiss on her forehead. "Why don't you change into something more comfortable and meet me up on the bridge?"

"How did you manage to get my clothes in there and unpacked so quickly?"

I turn to find her walking up the steps to the pilot's cabin. She's wearing a simple white cotton dress that leaves her shoulders bare and dips toward her cleavage, while showing off the shape of her legs. She's wearing the kitten heels from earlier, and my groin hardens in response.

I remember my promise of fucking her in them and barely hold onto my patience. I can't wait to feel her pussy clamp down on my cock.

"Would it be too creepy if I admitted I began assembling a wardrobe for you before I even proposed?" I drawl.

She freezes at the top of the steps. "You were *that* sure I'd say yes?"

I nod, slow and unapologetic. "Maybe not immediately; but I was confident I'd do everything in my power to make you *want* to."

"It *is* a little creepy." She takes a step forward, graceful and deliberate, eyes scanning my face like she's trying to read between the lines. "But it also makes me feel…wanted. Like I've had your full attention all along. It's unsettling—but kind of intoxicating."

"You'll always have my full attention"—I drag my gaze down her body—"especially when you look like *that*."

Heat curls low in my gut. I step closer, lowering my voice.

"I had Simon's team unpack our clothes." Making sure it was the woman who handled her clothes. I'd never allow a man to touch them. "Hope you don't mind."

"I don't." Her gaze softens.

All the desire I thought I'd managed to curtail comes roaring to the forefront. My groin hardens, and I widen my stance to accommodate my erection. I've taken off my linen jacket and pulled out the tails of my shirt, so it should, hopefully, hide the evidence of my desire… For now.

"For the record you have impeccable taste." She gestures to herself. "And they fit."

"Of course, they do."

"There he is." She laughs. "When your arrogance makes an appearance, it's a reminder that underneath that tenderness and gentlemanly image is a man who gets what he wants."

"Does that bother you?" I ask, genuinely curious.

Because I've made peace with who I am. I stopped apologizing for it a long time ago. That instinct to hide myself to make others more comfortable? I unlearned it.

Yes, I grew up with privilege. For a long time, I flinched at the word—*privilege*—like it exposed something rotten in me. Something I had to overcompensate for.

But I know better now. It's not the money or the name that defines me—it's what I do with them. And I've done my best to use them for good.

Still, I won't lie. That silver-spoon upbringing left its mark.

I like control. I crave efficiency. I want things done right—and that usually means being done my way.

I can be possessive. Demanding. Unapologetically focused when I want something—and when it matters, I don't back down.

But none of that makes me cruel. Or blind.

Life—and my time undercover—taught me how to temper those instincts. How to command without bulldozing. How to lead without shouting.

I've learned the power of staying silent when needed, of letting others speak first. Of reading a room before I take it over.

Because logic gets me farther than force. And empathy? That's not weakness. That's leverage.

I'm used to getting my way. But I've earned that. Not with arrogance, but with precision. Not through status, but by listening. By trusting my instincts. And right now, every instinct in me is tuned to her.

She starts to shake her head, then pauses, her expression caught between exasperation and desire.

"Maybe it does bother me, a little," she admits. "But I also find it hot and that confounds me." A low laugh bubbles out of her. "There's something ridiculously sexy about a man who knows what he wants.

Who takes charge — but only when it counts. And knows when to let things take their course. Of course" — she waves a hand in the air — "if you'd given me the chance to pick up some clothes — "

"But then I wouldn't have been able to surprise you."

"And was it important? To surprise me?" She closes the distance between us.

"It was worth it to see the pleasure on your face," I say honestly.

She comes to a stop in front of me. Her thick auburn hair hangs down her back. The pale pink of her dress picks up the flush in her cheeks. Likely, a result of the heat, but I'd like to think my nearness has something to do with it, too. And when she tucks a strand of hair behind her ear in what I know is a nervous gesture, the ring on her finger sparkles in the light slanting through the windows.

I reach for her hand and, bringing it to my mouth, kiss the ring. "You look beautiful, Wife."

"Thank you." She swallows, her blush deepening, and pulls her hand back.

I release it, then reach for the bottle of the Bollinger La Grande Année I've chosen especially for this occasion. I pop the cork and, pouring the frothy liquid into both of our flutes, I offer one to her, then raise my glass. "To new beginnings."

Something dulls in her eyes. *Damn.* I need to find out what's behind that. *What's bothering her?*

But I know better than to ask the question outright. I'm going to have to bide my time, until she volunteers the information on her own. And she will, I promise myself.

She pushes aside whatever was on her mind, and when she smiles, it's genuine. "To new beginnings."

We clink our glasses. Then she raises her glass to her mouth and takes a sip. She makes a 'mmm' sound which turns my already-thickening cock into a column of steel.

"Do you like it?" I clear my throat, trying to rein in my desire.

I must succeed, for she smiles. "I love it. The taste is elegant, powerful, and commanding..." She frowns. "Quite like you."

"Thank you." I dip my chin.

"How did you get everything here?" She shakes her head. "I was already taken aback when you had the paperwork for the wedding organized overnight, and now this—" She shakes her head. "I'm still finding it difficult to believe."

"I asked my team to do the grunt work. They knew it was important to me. Besides, I did compensate them for their time."

She takes another sip from her champagne and rolls it around in her mouth before swallowing it. The movement of her throat, the way she licks her lips... All of it sends my pulse skyrocketing. I take a sip from my own flute and set it aside, then touch the screen to start the engines of the yacht.

She places her own flute aside and turns to me. "Where are you taking us?"

41

Phoenix

Turns out, he was taking us to Playa de Levante, to the northwest of Gibraltar. Half an hour after easing out of the harbor, he drops anchor in the calm waters of a bay. The sun is high in the sky, the white sands of the beach stretched out behind us. In front of us is a view of the Rock soaring into the sky. In the distance, the coastline shimmers in the sunlight. We're not that far from the city, but when he switches off the engine, the silence makes it seem like we're the only two people on earth.

He hands me my flute of champagne and, carrying his own, he leads me out to the foredeck, and then onto the bow of the yacht. A gust of wind blows the hair from my face. I lean my head back and drink in the sight of the Rock.

"I've always wanted to see it." I take in the upper ridge rising high above us.

"It's supposed to be one of the pillars of Hercules in the ancient world. Thought to mark the edge of the known world, beyond which are gods and monsters." His voice is soft, seeming to echo the ancient, silent sentinel before us.

I have a strange sensation that I'm standing on sacred, mythic ground, confronting my own fears. Perhaps, sealing my fate. Perhaps, I always knew it would lead to this when he walked into my ER. Perhaps, I let him into my life, knowing it was the only way to move forward. Perhaps, I wanted to put myself into a situation where I'd be forced to share my secrets with someone. And I picked Connor, knowing... He won't rest until he finds out. And I want him to. I so want to tell him everything. I sigh.

"That was a heartfelt sigh." His lips graze my ear.

The warmth of his breath raises the hair at the back of my neck. I can feel his body, big and solid at my back. Almost as immovable as the Rock we're facing.

I place my glass on the cap rail, then turn to face him. "Thank you for bringing me here; it's beautiful."

He places his glass next to mine, then wraps his arm about my waist. He pulls me to my tiptoes and bends, capturing my lips. Where the previous kisses have been urgent and demanding, this one is slow, sensuous, and seductive.

I melt into him, and his grasp on my hips tightens. He hauls me closer, fitting me over the hard column at his crotch. A gasp leaves me. He swallows it, sharing my breath, bending me over his arm so I feel like I'm floating. He licks into my lower lip, and I feel his touch all the way to my toes. And when he nibbles gently on my mouth, my pussy clenches. I groan into his mouth, holding onto his shoulders. If I let go, I fear my knees aren't strong enough to hold me up. His kiss is so potent, I feel like I'm levitating. Something makes me open my eyes, and I find I really am levitating, for he's carrying me in his arms.

"Oh." I blink. "You're making a habit of this."

"I could get used to it, too." He smiles, then presses another kiss to my forehead, before carrying me to the table and chairs on the main deck.

Covered by an overhang, it's shielded from the sun. It's already laid out for two people, complete with a white cloth, plates, and cutlery, as well as a bucket of ice. Clearly, he has a very thorough team.

He lowers me to the ground, making sure every part of me comes into contact with him on the way down. Heat sizzles under my skin. The pulse between my legs grows insistent. Even though I'm wearing only a simple cotton sheath, I feel too warm. Like there's a volcano inside me which has come to life, and the lava runs through my veins.

He must be aware of how turned on I am, for his lips twist into a knowing smile. He kisses me hard, then urges me to take a seat. "I'll be right back."

He heads to where we placed our glasses and carries them back before pressing one into my hand. Then, he kisses my forehead again and walks inside, emerging a few seconds later with the bottle of champagne, which he slides into the ice bucket.

When he leaves the table to get the food, my phone vibrates. I glance at the message on the screen.

Drew: When are you back?

I type out a quick reply.

Me: In a couple of days.

Drew: I miss you.

I frown. That knot of tension at the base of my neck throbs.

Of course, he's messaging me when I'm feeling light for the first time in ages.

It's always the same pattern. He seems to pop up just when I'm reclaiming a little happiness. Like he knows I might finally be okay without him and can't stand it.

I'm not going to feel guilty about breaking up with him. I'm not going to give in to his bullshit tactics of making me feel responsible for what happened between us.

I clench my jaw. Well, tough.

I'm not going to spiral into guilt. Not this time. I'm not going to let him manipulate me into thinking I owe him something.

I grit my teeth, force my hands to stay steady, and type back a reply intended to convey that he can't take any more of my peace.

. . .

Me: You know we don't have that kind of relationship anymore. You really should move out.

Drew: Just give me a little more time to get to grips with everything.

"Who're you messaging?"

"What?" I press the side of the phone, so the screen goes dark, then turn it upside down.

He gives me a strange look, then walks over to the table. He sets a domed plate in front of me, and one in front of his seat. He reaches for my phone, and before I can react, he's picked it up. "I'm going to put this aside, along with my device. I want us to have this time uninterrupted by the outside world."

His tone brooks no argument. If I say I want to keep my phone, it's going to seem strange, so I nod. "I'm going to charge it along with mine." He turns and heads inside—presumably to the galley—since he returns in seconds.

Removing the dome from my plate, he announces, "Pan-roasted sea bass on pea purée with grilled asparagus and a poached egg." He takes the seat next to me.

My mouth waters. Only then, do I realize how hungry I am. "You didn't cook this, did you?"

He snorts. "I can cook, but not this fancy. Nope. James recommended a local chef who had this cooked and delivered to us for brunch."

"You planned for this, too?" A soft sensation squeezes my chest. To think, this man thought through all of this, then made it happen— overnight. "That's a lot of scheduling and organizing."

"I wanted it to be perfect." He places his hand over mine. "We're only going to be married once. I wanted it to be everything you could hope for."

"It is." I turn my hand over so I can entwine my fingers through his. I'm deeply attracted to him. And my body craves him. And I have no doubt, he's going to make sure I enjoy every moment when we first make love. I'm sure, it's going to be far more passionate and erotic than just 'making love' but... Somehow, these thoughtful things he's done for me feel even more intimate. "Thank you."

"You're welcome." He brings my hand to his mouth and kisses my fingertips. "Eat now. I want to make sure you keep your strength up." He winks.

That ever-present chemistry between us leaps to the surface. I feel my cheeks flush. To distract myself, I cut into the sea bass. It's so soft, it melts on my tongue.

"This is so good."

"I'll pass your compliments on to the chef." He digs into his own food.

For a few seconds the only sounds are the clinking of our cutlery as we polish off the food. When I'm done, I sit back. "That was delicious."

He takes a sip of his champagne and tops me off before relaxing in his chair.

I take in his gorgeous face, his hair ruffled by the breeze. The shirtsleeves, which he's rolled up to reveal his veiny forearms—*oh God, those forearms*. The pulse between my legs turns more insistent.

He notices me staring and his lips curl into a smirk. "What're you thinking about?"

My cheeks grow warm. "You're very handsome, Husband," I say truthfully.

"You think so?" He smirks and I roll my eyes. Then, his mouth curves in a genuine smile. "Thank you."

His features light up with pleasure and, damn, it only makes him so much more appealing. That familiar chemistry crackles between us, turning my blood into a river of desire. I clear my throat and try to find some composure. I decide to ask him a question that's been on my mind.

"A biochemist *and* an undercover agent? Strikes me as a strange combination."

"Is it?" he asks, a hint of humor in his eyes.

"Being a biochemist feels so very scientific. And nerdy. While an undercover agent brings to mind a dashing, alluring figure."

"I can't be both?" His eyes gleam.

"I guess?" I tilt my head. "Why biochemistry?"

"Came across the model of DNA in high school. Found out the

genetic coding for the entire human body is contained in it. The thought blew me away. And I was hooked. But I also loved sports."

"Let me guess, captain of the school cricket team?" It's my turn to scoff.

"Also played in the national football league. And won a few university level Jiu-Jitsu championships." He raises his shoulder.

"Wow, an all-rounder?" I ask impressed.

"Helped me get a scholarship to Oxford to study biochemistry. And while I was there, the MI5 recruited me. Turns out, being able to work as a biochemist made for a great front when I was on an undercover mission."

When he puts it like that, it begins to make sense.

"Were these assignments dangerous?"

He hesitates. "Most of what I did meant I had to be in enemy countries, playing a role. So if I were discovered"—he taps his knuckles on the table—"let's just say, it would not have done me any favors."

My chest seizes up. The thought of this vital man hurt in any way makes me feel like I'm choking.

He must notice the anxiety on my features for his soften. "Not that there was any danger of that. I am very good at my job."

The quiet confidence in his words abates my worry somewhat.

He flashes me a smile. "Besides, I know how to maneuver my way out of difficult situations."

He rises to his feet, takes our now empty plates inside to the galley, and returns with one plate, which he places on the table in front of him.

"Dark chocolate délice with a blood orange sorbet," he announces.

"It's almost too pretty to eat." I stare at the beautifully arranged dessert. "But why is there only one plate?"

"Because you know what I'd really like to do?" he asks in a voice so dark it pulses liquid honey through my veins.

"What?" I clear my throat.

"I'd like to eat it off you"—he licks his lips—"if you'll let me?"

That pulse in my lower belly catches fire. It's as if the honey in my veins turns to gasoline, and the fire zips out to my extremities. My scalp tingles. My nipples turn into pebbles of need.

"Will you, Fever?"

I nod. The images he paints in my head are so striking, so erotic, I need to find out how it'll be to live them.

"Good." He pats the table. "Climb on."

42

Connor

She stands and eases herself onto the table.

"Lay back."

She gulps, then does as she's told, and her spine touches the table. Her obedience pleases me and turns my cock into a column of stone. It also tells me that she trusts me to pleasure her. And I intend to deliver on it.

I slide the skirt of her dress up her thighs. She shivers. And when I pull her legs apart, she gasps. I step in between them, and when she reaches up for me, I take her hand and fold it over her head, then the other. I lock my fingers around her wrists and hold them there.

She wriggles, testing my hold, and realizes I'm serious. Her eyes widen, but the look in them turns heavy with lust. I nod. "That turns you on, Fever?"

She swallows, then slowly nods.

"And this?" I bend and fix my mouth around the jut of her nipple through the fabric of her dress.

Her entire body bows off the table. "Connor!" she yells.

She's primed for me, the awareness between us has been building since the day we met. And every time I've held her in my arms, I've wanted her so much, but I've held back. I've focused on her pleasure, but I've also been edging her and myself.

I've allowed her to come, but those have only been previews of how amazing it's going to be when I'm finally inside of her. "What do you want?"

I turn my attention to her other nipple, and when I pull down the neckline of her dress to expose it, she moans, then pushes her breast further into my mouth. I pull back. "Use your words."

"I…" She groans. "I want you."

"How do you want me? Should I use my fingers, my tongue, or my cock?" I raise my head until I hover over hers, only a sliver of space separating the two of us. "Or should I use all three?"

Another moan crawls up her throat. "All three," she pants.

"Good girl." I rub up against the wet triangle on her panties.

She expels a breath. "That feels so good."

"I use shallow strokes, grinding down on her, making sure she feels every millimeter of my swollen column through my pants. She locks her ankles around my waist, trying to pull me closer.

I chuckle. "Only I get to decide how to satisfy you. I get to decide how I'm going to fuck you, you hear me?"

She nods.

"How hungry are you for my cock, baby?"

"Very—" She swallows. "I… I need you, Connor. Please."

"Goddamn, when you beg me so prettily, it turns me on even more."

I lean more of my weight on her, and a trembling grips her. She begins to push up and against the thick pillar of my shaft. Each time she rubs up against me, her eyelids flutter. Her lips part. Her heart is beating so fast, it feels like it's going to bust out of her rib cage. Just like mine.

I allow her to hump herself against my crotch until her entire body shudders. Her breathing grows choppy, her eyebrows wrinkle.

Her hands tremble in mine, and I know she's so close to coming. That's when I step back.

She's so caught up in the impending climax, that it takes her a few seconds to realize I'm no longer dry fucking her. That's when her gaze widens. She tips up her chin.

"What are you doing?"

In reply, I grab the knife, turn it around so I'm holding it parallel to my arm, under my wrist, but with the blade pointing at me. Her eyes grow so huge they seem to fill her face. "Wh-what's happening?'

I slip the blade between her neckline and skin and, without touching her skin, I tug. The cloth tears. I slice through the fabric some more, until the slit exposes her cleavage, then I set the knife aside. I release my hold on her wrists completely, only to grip the gaping ends of her torn neckline and tearing the dress down the middle.

"Whoa." She blinks. "That's impressive."

"Right?" I concede. I slide my palms under her heavy breasts and weigh them. "Your tits are fucking gorgeous."

"They are, right?"

I look up to find a small smile curving her lips, her eyes twinkling with laughter. I push her breasts together and squeeze. She gasps. I bend down and lick my way up her cleavage. Then press tiny kisses up her throat until I reach her mouth. Then, reaching for a spoonful of the chocolate, I lick it off before I kiss her deeply.

She instantly melts into me, opening her mouth, allowing me entry. I bite down on her lower lip, and she moans. The chocolate, combined with her unique taste, is like an aphrodisiac. My thigh muscles harden. My cock lengthens further.

The kiss goes on and on, I swipe my tongue over her teeth. I suck on her tongue, until her essence fills me. When I finally lift my head, we're both panting.

I reach for the plate of dessert, scoop up the chocolate délice, and smear it over her nipples.

"Connor," she gasps in surprise.

I proceed to bite one of her nipples before I suck the chocolate off it. Then do the same to the other. "So fucking delicious."

She pants loudly, then grabs my hair and gives it a sharp tug. The pulse at the base of her throat flutters like a butterfly caught in a spider's web. *Like she's caught in my life.* I'm never letting her go. Never.

I reach down between us, slide my fingers into her panties and cup her pussy. "You're so wet for me, baby."

She huffs out a breath, then angles her body so she's humping my fingers.

"Not yet." I pull back, forcing her to lower her legs.

She whines.

I ease her panties down her legs. Then reach for the chocolate and paint it over her pussy lips. Little jolts of anticipation spiral up her body. Laid out on the table, with my saliva glistening on her breasts, and the chocolate smeared on her pussy, she looks like a feast.

Unable to stop myself, I sink to my knees between her thighs and throw them over my shoulders. Then I stare at the moist quivering flesh between her thighs.

I lean in and blow on her pussy. She shudders and tries to squeeze her legs shut. I stop her with my hands on her inner thighs. Then I lean in and sniff her deeply.

That draws another moan from her. And when I lick her from the knot of flesh between her butt cheeks, up the valley between her pussy lips, to her swollen clit, she cries out. Once again, her body rises off the table. But I hold her down.

The bitterness of the chocolate combined with the sweetness of her cum tastes like liquid desire.

I lick up her pussy, curling my tongue around her pulsing clit, and she digs her fingertips into my scalp.

The pinpricks of pain cascade down my spine, tightening the knot at the base. I slide two fingers inside her cunt, and she huffs. I begin to saw my fingers in and out of her while also slurping on her pussy.

A low, broken sound emerges from her throat.

It's animalistic and needy, and it calls to me in a way I can't ignore. I curl my fingers inside her, and bite down on her swollen bud.

Instantly, she begins to shudder. Moisture drips down her inner thighs.

"Ohmigod, Connor, I'm coming."

"Not yet." I move up her body and stare into her eyes. "You won't come until I allow it."

She nods.

Her instant agreement ratchets up my desire, until I can't hold back anymore. Reaching down between us, I undo the button at my waistband then lower my zipper.

Reaching into the pocket of my pants, I grab a condom before I allow them to drop, then push down my boxers. I sheath my swollen cock and fit it against her weeping slit.

Her gaze widens; she swallows. I stay poised at her opening, holding her gaze until the panic I saw in them subsides. It's replaced, once more, by lust. Then I punch my hips forward, and in one smooth move, bury myself inside her.

43

Phoenix

One second, I'm empty; the next, he's inside me. Big, long, thick and so full. He pushes down on the walls of my pussy, his fat cock ensconced in my cunt. He slaps his hand on the table next to me and holds most of his weight off me, except for the fact he has me pinned down with his shaft.

He stays there, looking deeply into my eyes, giving me the chance to adjust to his girth. His jaw muscles flex, the nerves on his temple standing out in relief.

With his bunched shoulders and his biceps taking the strain of holding him up, it's clear he's holding back.

"I don't want to hurt you," he says through gritted teeth.

In response, I squeeze my inner muscles around him. A groan spirals up his chest. Something like pain clings to the skin around his eyes. In that moment, the realization of just how much power I have over him sinks into my blood.

This man wants me. He's made it clear he's attracted to me. He may have married me so he could access his trust fund, but he cares for me.

The way he planned the elopement, including the actual wedding and honeymoon, as well as buying clothes for me, so I'd have the appropriate clothing, proves that. His attention to detail when it comes to me blows my mind.

I've never had any man so devoted to my needs. And the way he waits for me to adjust to his size before he finally pulls out, only to thrust back into me, takes my breath away.

He continues to hold my gaze throughout, and it's so intimate, it makes me feel connected to him in a way I haven't been to anyone else. *Ever*. He hooks his arms beneath my knees and lifts, sliding my ankles over his shoulders.

With him standing, I'm almost folded in half—completely exposed, held wide open for him.

A bead of sweat slides down his temple and plops on my forehead. It breaks this strange unspoken dialogue I'm trapped in with him. It must affect him, too, for he begins to move. He pulls back, then thrusts into me with so much force, the entire table moves. Some of the cutlery jumps off and falls to the floor with a clatter.

It sounds like it's coming from a long distance away, though; that's how wrapped up in him I am. It doesn't seem to bother him, either, for without losing momentum, he plunges back inside me. This time, he angles himself, so the ridge of his pelvic bone rubs up against my clit. Lightning-laced pleasure climbs my spine, stealing my breath.

The next time he thrusts into me, he seems to tunnel even deeper, brushing up against my cervix.

More sensations lick up my backbone like wildfire on dry earth. He stays there, pressing down, as if completing that circuit sparking my pleasure. I begin to shiver, like I'm running a temperature, but I know it's the first signs of my orgasm.

"Involuntary pelvic contractions…beginning now," I whisper.

His lip curls. My words seem to please him enormously, for his eyes glint. He picks up his pace and begins to fuck into me. Over and over again. With enough force that his balls slap against my butt.

Tension radiates off him, the heat from his body bathing me like I'm facing an impending sandstorm. Or maybe, that's my climax?

I lose all sense of time and place as he plunges deep into me again, burying himself to the hilt.

Once again, he presses against the anterior vaginal wall, applying just the right pressure to the periurethral zone—right where the Skene's glands are nestled. The friction sends a neural cascade through the pelvic plexus, short-circuiting my ability to think.

Flashes of heat arc up my spine, stealing my breath. My spine arches under the weight of a rising, electric hunger, rushing toward me like a sandstorm about to sweep me away. That's when he thrusts his face into mine, his nose bumping mine, his eyelashes twining with mine.

He grabs one of my arms and forces it above my head, then quickly does the same with the other. He wraps his fingers tightly around both my wrists, pinning them to the table.

His other hand comes down to squeeze my butt cheek before he slides his thumb into my forbidden hole.

The shock of that very taboo touch makes my toes curl and my scalp tingle. It's strange how the very fact that it's out of my comfort zone ramps up my need, pushing it past a boundary I hadn't been aware of drawing.

And when he growls, "Come." I shatter.

I open my mouth to scream but he's there, absorbing every single sound I make. His cock claims every inch of space inside me. He leans more of his body weight on me, so I'm pinned in place. And that gives me permission to let go completely, knowing he's there to catch me.

I can't breathe. Can't think. Just tremble—my sympathetic nervous system hijacked, heart rate hammering, skin prickling, pupils, no doubt, blown wide. It's the kind of full-body cascade I'm trained to associate with acute stress. Or raw, unfiltered arousal.

My limbs go slack; my core liquefies. Every nerve fires at once, overloading my brain, drowning out thought, leaving only sensation.

Heat.

Pressure.

A blooming pleasure that's thick and golden—and already laced with a craving for more.

I give over to the waves of pleasure rolling over me, cocooning me, folding me in a heated embrace promising more. More. *More.*

He continues to fuck into me, slamming into me, joining me, melding with me as he slides deep inside. And then, I'm dimly aware of him shouting his release.

I float for what seems like hours but must be seconds. Adrift on a silence which is pleasing and filled with a sensation I identify as satisfaction. I drift to earth, and when I open my eyes, it's to find him watching me.

"You, okay?"

I nod.

"You definitely, okay?"

I nod again. He searches my features, nods, then lowers his head and kisses me soundly. Instantly, I feel him thicken inside me.

He smiles against my mouth. "I'd better get you inside first."

He pulls out of me, reaches down and ties off the condom, before disposing off it. Then he straightens his clothes.

I begin to rise, but he scoops me up in his arms.

"The table—" I glance at the remnants of our meal.

"I'll clear it later." He takes me inside the yacht and down to the master suite. He bypasses the bed and heads inside the en suite.

Setting me down on the counter next to the sink, he runs the taps to fill the massive bathtub, drops in bath bombs, and dims the lights so the sunlight pouring in from the massive windows overlooking the bay caresses everything in a golden light.

When the tub is half full, he turns off the taps, then scoops me up in his arms and sets me down next to the tub. He kisses my forehead tenderly and pushes the remnants of my dress off my shoulders. Kicking it aside, he urges me to get into the tub.

I sigh as I sink into the bubbles. He folds a towel and places it under my neck.

"Comfy?"

I nod. "You're spoiling me."

"You're worth it." He takes my hand and kisses my fingertips. "Rest up. I'll be right back."

He rises to his feet and is gone, leaving me to close my eyes and savor the warmth of the water. My muscles, already relaxed from that orgasm, unwind further. Any tension I carried begins to slip away. I sigh, spread my legs and allow the warm water to soothe the ache between my thighs. It reminds me of how it felt to have him inside of me.

How he took me, how he zeroed in on that deep pelvic zone—where nerves, pressure, and arousal converge—like he mapped the exact coordinates of my release.

I close my eyes and when I open them again, I find him placing a bottle of champagne at the head of the tub. "Scoot forward."

I do.

He hands me a flute of champagne. Placing his own down next to the bottle, he strips off his clothes, then slides into the bath behind me.

He stretches his legs out on either side of me, then coaxes me to lay back against him. The feel of the hard planes of his chest at my back and the warm water lapping around me draws me into a cocoon of comfort. "Thank you."

"You're welcome." There's a soft touch on my hair, and I know he must have kissed me. I sense him taking a sip of his champagne, feel the vibrations in his chest as he swallows, then the clink as he places his flute down.

"Take another sip." He brings my flute to my mouth, and I oblige. Then he takes the glass from me and sets it aside. He cups my breasts in the water and runs his thumbs over my nipples. I shudder.

Goosebumps pop on my skin. And when he slides his hand down to toy with my navel, I whimper. I turn my head in his direction, and he lowers his, so our lips meet. It's a sweet, long kiss, filled with tenderness, but when he nips at my lower lip, a fountain of heat bursts to life in my lower belly. I wrap my arm about his neck, hold on, and when his fingers find my melting pussy, I arch up my aching breasts. He squeezes one, then the other, all the while thrusting three of his fingers inside me.

"It's not too soon, is it?" he whispers.

I shake my head. "I want you, I—"

He closes his mouth over mine, swallowing my other words. Then, he saws his fingers in and out of me, increasing the speed, so the heat in my belly becomes a wall of flames spreading to my feet and ebbing up my spine.

I moan into his mouth and begin to hump his fingers in earnest. At my back, I feel his cock thicken and lengthen, signaling how turned on he is, too. I begin to rub up against his shaft, upping his level of desire. He makes a guttural sound at the back of his throat. So quintessentially male. So erotic. Hinting how close he is to losing control. It excites me that he's feeling the intensity, the need for me as much as I am for him.

All the while, he continues to thrust his fingers in and out of me with practiced precision. He repeatedly strokes that sensitive zone just behind my pubic bone, where dense vascular tissue and nerve endings converge. It's as if he's learned the contours of my pelvic floor by touch alone.

My thighs tremble. My pelvic muscles clench instinctively around his fingers, as if my body's trying to pull him deeper, hold him there.

Pressure builds—sharp and urgent—behind my pubic bone, radiating outward in ripples I can't contain. Every glide of his fingers sends another burst of sensation ricocheting through my visceral nerve network, overriding cognition. I'm reduced to reflex and instinct, trapped somewhere between the clinical understanding of what's happening…and the primal need to surrender to it.

Then, just when I think I can't stand it, he tears his mouth from mine. He flips me around so I'm straddling his thighs. His big hands on my waist make me feel impossibly tiny.

I love that he's able to maneuver my body like I weigh nothing. That even with my plus-size figure, I feel petite next to his big body. He makes me feel cared for, and protected, and worshipped. And also, dominated.

How is it possible that all of these emotions can be woven into the same moment? How is he able to elicit so many different feelings from me at the same time? I glance down to where his cock stands erect, the crown purple and engorged. I wrap my fingers around his girth and am not surprised when my fingers barely meet.

"When I felt you inside me, I knew you were large, but now—" I stare at his cock pointedly. "Now, I wonder how you fit inside."

"The trick was to make sure you were both aroused and relaxed." He smirks.

Oh, that ego. It's sexy as hell, but it makes me want to chip away at it, just to watch the cracks form.

And I know exactly how.

I slide back, settling myself on his knees, then reach for the lever on the side of the tub. One flick, and the water starts to drain.

He arches a brow, silently questioning.

I hold his gaze. And wait.

The waterline drops, inch by inch, until it's where I want it. Then I hit the lever again, stopping the flow.

He dips his chin, understanding.

I glance down—his cock, now exposed, proud and gleaming. I lower my head and take him down my throat.

44

Connor

She swallows around my cock, and it feels like my entire body is going to burst into flames. My balls tighten. My heart pounds against my rib cage. I'd say it's a predictable reaction when any gorgeous woman has her mouth wrapped around my dick. But it's not *any* woman, it's *my wife*. And there's something very intimate, and very erotic in having Phe deep-throat me. There's something very personal, knowing there won't be anyone else but me who'll see her in this position. I'm the only person she'll ever be giving a blow job to. The only man whose cock and fingers and mouth she'll have on her body.

Possessiveness tightens my belly. The feeling in my chest turns viselike. I want to position her over my cock and fuck into that tight, hot pussy. I want to squeeze her butt, and her thighs, and then her breasts. I want to bite down on the curve of where her shoulder curves into her throat and leave a mark, so the entire world knows that she's mine. Only mine. I curl my fingers into fists and force myself to take deep, calming breaths. Then I fold my arms behind my neck and lean back.

"Curl your fingers around the base," I direct.

She does so.

"Lick up the length to the crown."

She swirls her pink tongue as instructed, hazel eyes shining with lust, long eyelashes spiky with moisture. She licks around the head, then once again, curls her mouth around the crown. Her cheeks hollow, and it feels like she's sucking my soul through my cock.

"Fuck," I grunt, unable to stop myself from surging forward. My shaft slides down her throat, once more ensconced in that tight column. She gags, and the suction shivers up my length. It tugs on the tightening knot of need at the base of my spine.

"Squeeze harder."

She instantly obliges by tightening her hold on me. She pulls back until I'm balanced at the rim of her mouth. Then angles her head so I slip down her tongue. She bites down gently so her teeth graze the delicate skin of my shaft. The tension at the base of my belly roars into something primal. I feel myself grow harder, thicker, pushing against the column of her throat. Her chest rises and falls, and a quiver runs up her body. Drool drips from the corners of her mouth.

She looks elemental, and naked, and so fucking sexy. When she swallows around my shaft, my entire body turns into one long, needy gasp. I can't hold back. I hoped to tease her a little, taunt her with the feel of my cock thrusting into her mouth, an imitation of how it feels to have me plunge into her wet pussy.

I hoped to arouse her, take her to the edge of wanting, and drive her need sky-high, but really, it's me who's feeling the effect of drawing out the agony of anticipation. It's short-circuited my brain cells, turned my heart to glass, and my groin into a titanium shield which feels too heavy for the rest of my body.

I manage to hold onto my control for a few seconds more. That's until a wicked gleam enters her eyes. She reaches down to cradle my balls and massages gently. A thick, broken sound emerges from my throat. An audible snapping sensation whips through my body. In a move so quick it feels like my arms blur, I reach down and, digging my fingers into her hair, I haul her up and toward me.

She opens her mouth. "What —"

I lock my lips to hers, absorbing the sound, keeping my eyes open to take in the drugged look that seeps into her gaze when I deepen the kiss. I angle my head, sliding my tongue over hers, tasting myself on her sweet palate. And the combination of our tastes, the tiny whining sounds she makes, the way she quivers against my chest... She feels tiny and delicate, and yet, vibrates with so much desire, it feels like her body can't contain it... All of it pumps up my blood pressure and floods my senses.

I slide my hands down to the fleshy globes of her arse cheeks. I squeeze, and a fully body shudder grips her. I position her over my cock, and just as I imagined, her slit is wet and juicy, and not just from the bath water. I tease her opening, and she moans into my mouth. She holds onto my shoulders and wriggles her tush so I slide in deeper. So hot. So moist. So fucking perfect and receptive.

My heart swells in my chest, as if unable to be contained by my rib cage. My pulse rate kicks up. The blood slams at my temples, my wrists, even in my fucking balls. Sweat breaks out on my forehead.

This is it. This intense connection where it feels like my heart beats in sync with hers, where holding her in my arms seems to fill the hole in my soul I didn't realize I had, where being inside her feels...like I've come home.

This...is what I've been searching for. In every mission. In every race to a far-off country on an assignment.

Every time I slipped into another character's skin. Each time I ran away from the emptiness in my life. I was searching for something... Someone.

Her.

She's here. With me. I'm holding her. My life. My heart. My soul. My everything. I tighten my grasp on her and sense the instant reaction of her body when she squeezes her thighs around my waist and digs her nails deeper into my neck.

She opens her mouth, her hips, her body, and slides down my shaft until I'm lodged deep inside her. My favorite place. The only place where I feel both relaxed and turned on, at the same time. Which is a contradiction, but also a culmination of my entire life which has brought me to this juncture. This moment, when I'm looking into my wife's beautiful eyes and watching them cloud with rapture, when I propel my hips up and thrust into her.

Her body jolts. Her spine arches. Her breasts seem to swell with erotic longing. I hold her in place, and my cock thickens inside her. Her snug pussy has me in a viselike hold. I angle my hips and work myself further inside of her. I brush up against that spot deep inside her. Instantly, her mouth falls open, and a low, keening sound emerges from her. I begin to fuck into her.

Every time I thrust up and into her, her entire body shudders. She bounces on me, her full tits jiggling in a way that feeds the burn in my lower belly, which in turn, pushes me to kick into higher gear. The next time I power into her, she cries out, throws her head back, and grabs hold of my forearms. She squeezes her knees into either side of my hips and slides down further on my cock, impaling herself.

A bead of sweat slides down the valley between her breasts. She's glorious. The frantic pulse at the base of her throat, and the rhythmic rise and fall of her chest tell me she's close. I release my hold on her waist, only to rub on her clit. Her eyelids fly open, that hazel gaze now green with flashes of gold.

"Come with me," I command and slide my other hand between her arse cheeks. I play with the knot of flesh there, and she instantly orgasms. Her inner walls contract and milk my shaft. I feel the suction all the way up my spine. *Goddamn.*

My balls draw up. My cock lengthens. Another thrust into her, and I come, emptying myself inside her. I hold her as the aftermath rocks through her. As my body jolts with the pleasure of my orgasm. Goosebumps dot my skin. My scalp tingles with the intensity. Light flashes at the corners of my eyes as I fill her up with my cum. When she slumps in my arms, I hold her close. Tuck her damp hair behind her ears. Only then, do I remember. "I didn't wear a condom."

"I'm on birth control," she murmurs into my chest. "You don't need to wear a condom."

"We should have discussed it earlier—" I cradle her, savoring the feel of her curves against me. "I blame wanting to be inside your luscious body for having distracted me." I notch my knuckles under her chin and lift it. She raises her gaze. "Are you sure?"

Her lips smile. "After that orgasm? You bet, I am."

I chuckle and cradle her closer. "I'm just getting started."

"Oh?" She frowns.

I rise to my feet, carrying her with me, then step out of the tub. "First, I'm going to dry you. Then, I'm going to get you wet all over again—from the inside. Then, I'm going to fuck you again, then feed you, in that order. Is that okay with you?"

"I can't remember the last time I was this relaxed." She places the tablet she borrowed from me aside and leans back with a sigh.

"Only *you'd* spend the last hour working on the proposal to send to the Prime Minister and say you're relaxed." I chuckle.

"Listing out the reasons why the ER needs to be kept open was a labor of love. And I wanted to make sure you have it so you can send it off to the PM right away."

I pick up the device, log into my email account and, attaching her proposal to my email, send it off with a note outlining why the PM needs to give his attention to this specific issue of keeping Archway Hospital's ER open.

Then I lean back on the sun lounger.

We're on the main deck, having decided to come up to get some sun, after I made good on my promise to fuck her and get more food into her.

"That feels so good." She closes her eyes and tips her chin to soak up the sun's rays. "I don't think I've ever felt this content in my life." She places her cheek on her hands folded under her head and looks at me through her sunglasses.

She's wearing a bikini, whose bottoms are cut high enough to show off her fleshy thighs, and a triangle top tied in a knot at her back, which I can attest, does not do much to hold in her D cups.

"Might have something to do with the fifth orgasm you had earlier." I smirk.

Her cheeks turn pink. Those dark circles she sported under her eyes are on their way out. Even her hair seems thicker and shinier. A day away from her ER and her duties, and she already looks so much healthier.

"I'm not keeping track." She shoots me a sideways glance. "Besides, an orgasm is a normal bodily function. It's only a crescendo of autonomic nervous system activation."

"Hmm." I tap my chin. "That was some crescendo your voice rose to earlier when I fucked you against the window of our cabin."

The pink in her cheeks turns a fiery red. "A gentleman wouldn't point that out, after the fact."

"As I recall, you loved that I didn't behave like a gentleman. As the print of my palm on your left butt cheek will attest to."

"Wha-a-t? I don't have a print on my bum."

"What's this then?" I lean over and place my right hand on the print over her left arse cheek.

She huffs out her breath. Her throat moves as she swallows. "That... That's because you put me down heavily on the galley counter." She pouts.

"Only because I needed to feel your legs around my waist and fill up your pussy with my already engorged cock."

She draws in a sharp breath, then manages to school her features into one of boredom, which I don't buy, *at all*. "As I recall, you've done so a few times today already." She sniffs.

"As I'm finding out, it's not enough." I slide my hand down to cup her core through her bikini bottoms.

"Oh." She twists her mouth into a delicate pout, but her hazel eyes go green, revealing how turned on she is.

I slide my fingers inside the gusset of her bottoms, and she gasps.

"So fucking wet for me," I growl.

She shivers. I run my fingers down her slit, and she whimpers, "Connor, I can't possibly come again." She's gripping the sides of the sun lounger, the skin across her knuckles stretched white.

"Are you sore?" I pause, looking into her face.

She hesitates, then nods slowly. "A little."

I pull my fingers back and bring them to her mouth instead. She takes in my fingers, down to the knuckles, and licks them clean.

"Good girl." I trail my fingers down the curve of her shoulders and to her back. "You don't need this." I flick the knot at the top of her bikini.

"But—" she begins to protest but I've already undone her bikini top. It falls to the side. I reach for the sunscreen and pour a liberal amount onto my palm. Placing a knee on one side of the lounge, I straddle her hips without leaning my weight on her. I begin to massage the sunscreen into her back.

She groans. "That feels amazing."

"You work too hard." I dig my knuckles into the muscles in her back and feel the tension drain out. "You need to take more time off."

"When you specialize in trauma, it means you're dealing with accidents, which means, it's mainly periods of high stress and high adrenaline. And when there's an emergency, I can't say no to coming in." She looks up at me from the corner of her eye. "I imagine, it's the same for you?"

I pause, then dig my knuckles into the muscles on either side of her spine.

It draws another groan from her throat. "You're so good at this."

"Learned it from going undercover as a masseuse."

It's her turn to go quiet. "You went undercover as a masseuse?" She clears her throat.

"I did. Being good at giving a massage is a useful skill in impressing women, as it turns out."

"Hmph. You had a lot of women to impress in your undercover assignments, huh?"

I allow myself a small chuckle. "You sound jealous."

"I'm not."

"If you insist."

"Are you allowed to tell me all this?" She scowls.

"All what?"

"About your assignments."

"I'm not giving away anything."

"Well, I don't want to know any details, especially of how you impressed women," she says in an irritated voice.

"Definitely jealous." I knead the muscles of her shoulders, and she makes a whimpering sound. My already alert cock does an imitation of being a loaded gun ready to go off. I reach down to adjust myself, then continue to work gentle pressure down the length of her spine. I reach the small of her back and trace the flare of her hips with rhythmic strokes. She shifts restlessly. "Umm, I think that's enough."

"Am I turning you on?"

She blows out a breath. "You know you are. Just like you're also getting turned on."

"Touching you is the most erotic, most satisfying experience of my life. Smoothing the stress from your body is more gratifying than any assignment I've undertaken."

She cracks her eyes open and stares at me over her shoulder. "You mean it." She sounds surprised.

I hold her gaze. "I have never told you something I didn't mean, and I never will."

Her lips part. Her eyes shine. She turns over. Her bare breasts are revealed to me. Perfectly crafted. Just right to fill my big palms to overflowing. Her pink areolae are puckered tightly, begging for my mouth. My teeth. To bite down into the nipples topping them like buds made of candy.

Without breaking the connection, I lower my chin and close my lips around one of them. I tug on it, and she whimpers. She throws her arms over her head, pushing them further into my mouth, while arching her spine. I nip and suck and curl my tongue around her nipple, biting into it, then licking away the hurt. She squeezes her thighs together and writhes around, raising her hips until her core brushes against the column in my swim shorts.

"No cheating." I press my hand into the center of her chest, holding her down, which only makes her squirm further.

"Connor," she protests.

"Hold still." I grab her bathing suit top.

I tie it around her wrists, then anchor it to the horizontal bar just behind the headrest — at the top of the sun lounger's frame.

"What are you doing?" She tugs at her wrists.

I make sure the knots are loose enough to not chafe at her skin.

"You'll see." I slide her bikini bottoms down her legs and toss them aside. Rising to my feet, I shrug out of my swim trunks, then look up to find her watching me with lust in her eyes. Her gaze slides down my chest to where my cock stands at attention.

I grab one of the towels, then use it to tie her ankle to the metal bar at the base of the lounger, near where her feet rest.

Then do the same to the other. When I stand at the bottom of the sun lounger, I look at my handiwork.

She's tied spread-eagle with the sun's rays gleaming over her. A trembling grips her. The sweet scent of her arousal mixes with the nutty one of the sunscreen. A powerful aphrodisiac. I walk around to stand behind her. She looks up at me with curiosity.

I pour out more of the sunscreen into my palms before placing my knees on either side of her head. I massage her breasts in ever widening circles. Breathless cries of need whisper from her as she undulates her hips with need.

I move down to her stomach, circling the flesh and dipping into her belly button.

She whimpers and jerks.

When she opens her mouth again to gasp, I position my cock at her lips. "Swallow it," I order.

She instantly closes her mouth around my cock and begins to lick around the crown. Sensations light up my nerve endings. It's as if I've stuck my fingers into a source of electricity; it buzzes through my veins. I squirt some of the sunscreen across her thighs. Then I begin to stroke it in.

45

Phoenix

Each time his hand comes close to my pussy, he stops. He brushes up against my pussy lips again and again, but doesn't touch my clit.

My body feels like it's on fire. Every pore in my body feels like it's open and thirsty for his touch. For more of him. He circles my core, grazing the inside of my thighs like the wings of a butterfly. I buck under his touch, the sounds I make muffled around his cock. The salty taste of the precum leaking from the crown coats my tongue and slides down my throat.

The wiry hair at the base of his shaft is a rough scrape of delight against my skin. The sensations, the smells, the tastes, his powerful thighs on either side of my face... All of it adds to the feeling that I'm not in control which, strangely, adds to my arousal.

Then, the fact that I can't touch him, except with my mouth, focuses all of my attention on where we're joined—at my mouth and at my pussy. The knowledge is so carnal, so sensual, so animalistic, it ratchets up the need inside me to heights I've never felt before. It's intense and feels like a thousand dragonflies are beating their wings under my skin. My core clenches, and my thighs hurt. Every part of my body feels like it's turned into an erogenous zone.

I continue to lick and suck on his shaft, and the weight of his dick on my tongue makes me squirm further. It simulates the weight I want to feel between my legs, which he refuses to give to me.

He replaces his finger with his tongue, skimming it around my weeping slit, coming closer and closer to my clit, but never touching it. I make a frustrated sound at the back of my throat which vibrates around his cock. It seems to turn him on further, for his thickness presses into the sides of my mouth. I sense him chuckle, the heated breath rippling over my leaking pussy and turning my clit into a hard nub of desire. I try to push my core up toward his mouth, and he holds me down with his hands on my hips.

"Not fair," I try to say but it comes out garbled.

Of course, when my teeth scrape against the underside of his cock, it draws a growl from him. He slaps my pussy in retribution, and I cry out.

"Don't stop sucking," he growls.

Hearing that from his mouth is filthy, and it turns me on further. And when he finally, finally licks around my throbbing clit, a full body shudder spirals through me. Distracted, I allow his cock to slip to the rim of my mouth. Once more, he spanks my pussy.

Shockwaves shudder through my bloodstream. But it also spurs me on to take his cock inside my mouth and curl my tongue around the crown. I hollow my cheeks and suck and am rewarded by his thighs trembling.

The salty taste of his precum coats my palate. When I swallow, his hold on my hips tightens. He begins to lick around my clit and down my slit. He releases his hold on my hip to play with the knot of flesh between my arse cheeks. This time, he thrusts his finger through the ring of muscle, and I freeze. It feels like we've crossed into uncharted territory.

Then he sucks on my pussy lips, and a burst of heat caresses the wall behind my clit. Instantly, I relax.

Enough for his finger to slip further into my back channel. A burn flares and races up my vertebrae like a fuse lit from within. And when he begins to move his finger in and out of that forbidden space, the burn morphs to pleasure.

A molten ribbon of heat crackles through my nerves and erupts at the base of my neck, making me pant and slurp on his cock with renewed vigor. *Oh God!* My belly trembles. My womb contracts. Sweat slides down my back with the force of the impending climax. I know I'm close. And that's without him having licked my clit.

Whatever he's doing to that most forbidden part of me is turning me on in a most unexpected fashion. Who'd have thought that part of me is so erogenous?

He continues to lick around my clit, making sure never to touch it, but swiping his tongue to come very close. Then, he curls his fingers inside my back channel and touches a part which sends something raw and electric lashing up my back. A whip of sensations. A blaze licking up my spine, fierce and unrelenting. With the last moments of clear headedness, I manage to take him down my throat, which draws a guttural sound from him.

That's when he closes his mouth around my clit and bites down gently. But the rough edge of his teeth on my sensitive nub fuels my desire. It's like a match to my bloodstream which has turned into rocket fuel. It ignites sparks that zip through my body, catching momentum, growing bigger and bigger, growing in size, until it's a fireball engulfing my consciousness, and shoots me into space.

I'm conscious of my pussy vibrating like it's wired to a high voltage paddle, and of my coming so hard, I cry out around his cock. Which leads to a groan that's so deep, it seems to emerge from his balls. And then his cock jerks, and he spills down my throat.

He seems to keep coming and coming, and when I gag, he shudders.

He licks up the evidence of my climax. When he finally pulls out of me, cum spills down my chin.

He stands, walks around the sun lounger, then covers me with his big body so he's nose-to-nose with me.

He peers into my eyes, his blue irises iridescent and glinting like lightning trapped in a bottle, and with as much energy humming in the air around us, between us, enclosing us like we're trapped in the eye of a storm.

I try to speak but feel too overwhelmed. My vocal cords seize up. My diaphragm spasms. It's like my autonomic nervous system's misfiring, flooding me with adrenaline and short-circuiting higher function. A trembling seizes me.

He instantly presses his chest into mine, and it's like a living blanket of heat is wrapped around me.

"Wow." That feels very inadequate to express what I experienced. But given my brain is mush, it's the best I can manage. Plus, I'm not ready to utter the words that beg to emerge: *I love you.*

One side of his mouth kicks up. He lowers his chin and kisses me tenderly. My lips cling to his, and when he slips his tongue inside my mouth to softly couple with mine, I sigh.

He reaches up to undo the knots around my wrists, and suddenly, I'm free. I wrap my arms around him and hug him tightly. He deepens the kiss, enveloping me in his arms.

I'll never get used to the taste of my cum on his tongue. *Never.* He tilts his head, and the kiss catches fire. My heart thrums in my chest, my pulse bangs against my wrists and my ankles, and my ears buzz. The buzzing sound increases in intensity until a shadow falls over us.

We pull apart and look up to find a sea plane come in for a landing.

"What the hell?" He rises to his feet, then bends and frees my legs. He snatches up his trunks. I jump up to my feet, pull on my bikini, then the sarong I placed nearby, and tie it halter-style around my neck so it covers me.

"Who's that?" I shade my eyes so I can follow the seaplane as it comes to a stop in the strip of water between the yacht and the shore. Whoever's navigating it must be extremely skilled to make the landing. Even before the propellors have come to a stop, the door opens, and a figure of a man waves at us.

"I'll be damned." Connor rubs at his temple.

Then, the figure turns and fiddles around, reaching for something I can now see is attached to the pontoon of the seaplane.

"What's he doing?" I wonder aloud.

As if in answer, he tugs free something like a Jet Ski, which he lowers into the water.

"It's a pod, which he's going to use to get to us." He sighs aloud. "That's my brother Brody, by the way."

"Why is he here?" I ask the obvious question as he jets over. In seconds, he's reached us and anchored his nifty gizmo to the side of the boat. Then, he grabs hold of the ladder set into the side of the craft and pulls himself aboard.

He walks toward me, arms outstretched. "Congratulations."

Before I can take his hand, possessive Connor makes a warning noise at the back of his throat. Then, he steps in front of me. "She's my wife."

Brody seems taken aback. "I'm aware," he drawls.

"Connor," I hiss, embarrassed by his show of possessiveness. I step around him.

"Mrs. Connor Davenport." Brody inclines his head. "You two sure took all of us by surprise. Not that I blame you for eloping. It's the best way to avoid the circus that is a Davenport wedding."

"What are you doing here?" Connor interjects, sounding pissed.

Brody's expression grows even more serious. "Gramps asked me to come to you."

"I know you prefer to keep your truce with the old man, but seriously. Tracking us down on our honeymoon is going a bit too far, don't you think?" Connor scoffs.

Brody's features lose all humor. His expression grows serious. "The old man isn't well."

"He isn't?" Connor scowls.

"Is Arthur okay?" I ask at the same time. Sure, he seemed fine the last time I saw him, but I also know that Connor's grandfather is nearly eighty-three. The kind of age where even small health issues need to be taken seriously.

"He suffered from a bout of food poisoning. He's stable, but insistent that the entire family get together."

Connor firms his lips. "You sure he isn't faking, just so he has an excuse to intrude on everyone's lives and be the center of attention?"

"Connor." I turn on him shocked. "How could you say that?"

"Because, sadly, Arthur isn't above that." Connor rubs the back of his neck.

"I was the one who called the ambulance. I can vouch it was real." Brody widens his stance. "I thought you'd want to know."

Connor blows out a breath. "You should have called."

"I did; neither of you answered your phones. I figured this was as good a time as any to give this little baby a ride." He nods in the direction of the seaplane.

"You came. You spoke to us. You can tell the old man we couldn't make it," Connor drawls.

Brody frowns. "You sure about this?"

"As you said, Arthur is fine, so there's no real reason for us to go, is there?"

I fold my arms across our chest. "We should go."

Connor searches my features. "I don't want to cut our honeymoon short."

"We can have another honeymoon." I touch his arm. "But this is your grandfather, and he's unwell and asking for you. We shouldn't ignore him."

He searches my face. "Are you sure?"

46

Connor

"I still think we should have stayed on our honeymoon." I button up my shirt in front of the mirror in the closet.

"We're doing the right thing. If we didn't come, and if something were to happen to your grandfather, you'd always regret it."

She's right, I suppose.

"Nothing's going to happen to that old bastard. He loves attention, is all."

It's a very domestic situation. I've just showered and am getting dressed on my side of the closet in front of the mirror with my back to her. I watch her reflection as she picks out the clothes, she needs from her side of the closet.

"He's old. Any setback to his health should be treated seriously," she admonishes me, then reaches up to grab a dress. "Regardless of the differences between the two of you, he's still family." She turns to me and stares at the strip of skin exposed by the lapels of my shirt in the mirror.

Then she meets my gaze, realizes I caught her staring, flushes, and glances away.

Considering everything I've done to her body, it's cute that she's blushing because she's seeing me getting dressed.

She has no idea how much I enjoy having her eyes on me.

To prove a point, I begin to roll up the cuffs of my shirt. She peeks at me from the corners of her eyes, and her gaze widens. She seems entranced by my actions and unable to tear her gaze away from my exposed forearms. Just to test out my theory, I raise my hand and run it through my hair, finger combing back the damp hair on my head.

It makes my biceps bulge and stretches the shirt across my chest. She swallows.

I stifle a smile. Yes, I'm using my body to distract her, and damn, if that doesn't feel brilliant. The fact that I can stop her in her tracks and make her forget what she's saying is top-notch.

"You were saying?" I prompt her.

"Uh, so uh, I was saying that—" She shakes her head. "That— It doesn't matter." She grabs underwear from the drawer before she turns and scurries off.

I called ahead and asked for a personal shopper to stock the closet with enough clothes to tide her over until she's had a chance to move her clothes over from her place.

Once we reached London, I asked Brody to drop us off at my place so we could shower and change into a fresh pair of clothes before meeting him and the rest of the family at Arthur's place for an early dinner.

Turns out, Arthur recovered enough to be discharged from the hospital. But in honor of our return, he decided to host a dinner for us. *Damn, that was one quick recovery.*

Perhaps he really was unwell, but it's typical of the old man to milk any occasion for sympathy and use it as an excuse to get the family together.

Tucking my shirt into the waistband of my pants, I follow her out of the closet.

I walk across the floor of our bedroom to the en suite. The shower's already running. I can see the outline of her curvy body through the clear glass of the shower cubicle. I pull the door to the cubicle open and position myself at the entrance.

She looks over her shoulder and when she sees me, her mouth falls open. "I'm showering," she says over the sound of the water.

"I'm very aware of that." I allow myself to follow the flow of the water down her back, over the flare of her spectacular hips and her thick thighs.

"Stop," she says in a breathless voice.

"Can't I admire how beautiful my wife is?" I fold my arms across my chest and lean a shoulder against the doorframe.

She hesitates.

"We're going to be late. You'd better hurry. Don't want to keep the family waiting, do you?"

Truthfully, asking Brody to drop us off at home so we could change was my way of delaying things. I'm not in any hurry to see my family. A day and a half are nothing in terms of everything I want to do to my wife. I barely whetted my appetite in all the ways I mean to have her.

I'm just getting to know her body and what she loves, just beginning to win her trust.

She turns back to the shower and quickly soaps herself. I'm distracted by the foam sliding over her luscious body. My phone vibrates. I ignore it. It vibrates with another message, so I reluctantly pull it from my pocket and take a look.

It's the third one from Save the Kids. Apparently, donating money comes with a new set of expectations. It's my responsibility to ensure the money is spent properly. With a final glance at her reaching for the towel to dry herself off, I turn and head out into the bedroom. Sitting on the bed, I exchange a flurry of messages with the CEO of the charity.

When she emerges ten minutes later, I'm just wrapping up my conversation. I look up to find she's already dressed and has even dried her hair.

"You're quick," I say in surprise.

"Comes from being a doctor and having to always get dressed in record time." Then she nods toward my phone. "Everything okay?"

"It is now." I'm aware there's a thread of lust running through my voice. And there's heat in my gaze.

She tosses her head. "Is that all you can think of?"

"When my wife's standing there looking like a siren, I think I can be forgiven for having a one-track mind."

She blushes, a pleased look in her eyes. Then she grows serious. "But really, is everything okay? I saw you frowning at the phone."

I blow out a breath and roll my shoulders. This isn't a mission, so I can share the highlights with her.

She *is* my wife. And I want to start the new relationship by being as open as possible with her. Perhaps, that will help in her being open with me, too?

"Turns out, there's been a coup in a country where Save the Kids operates. It's led to a border lockdown. Their convoy carrying life-saving medication is being detained. They've also been taken as prisoners."

"Oh, no," she gasps.

"They need help mediating the release of both."

"So, they want you to help with the negotiations?"

I nod slowly. "My connections within MI5 give me unique leverage."

She wrinkles her forehead. "It sounds serious."

"Not more than usual."

She tilts her head. "Are you still taking on undercover assignments?"

"Do you not want me to?"

She blinks. "Would you stop if I asked you to?"

"After this one, yes."

"Oh." Her jaw drops. "You'd do that…for me?"

I rise to my feet and pocket my phone, then walk over to her. "The last thing I want is for you to worry when I'm gone. When I realized I was serious about us getting married, I told the MI5 that I was retiring."

"So, no more undercover assignments?" Relief fills her eyes, and I know, I made the right decision.

"You experience enough pressure in the ER. I don't want to add to that. I don't want you to worry about me, in addition to everything else. I don't want to spend any more time in the field. Besides, taking on dangerous missions has lost its appeal. It's why I'm retiring from the MI5."

"You are?" Her eyes grow wide.

I nod. "I don't want to be away from you. After this last mission for the charity, which happens to be a personal one—and the only reason I'm doing it is because it's for a good cause—I won't be taking on others."

She swallows and seems on the verge of crying.

My chest tightens, "Hey, what's wrong?"

"I don't deserve you." She looks away. "I'm not sure I deserve this kind of empathy from you."

"What are you talking about? You're my wife. Of course, I'll make sure your life is as stress-free as possible."

She takes my hand between her much smaller ones, then brings it to her mouth and kisses my knuckles. "You're a good man."

"Except when I'm bad." I curl my lips.

She rolls her eyes. "That ego of yours! Unfortunately, you have the goods to back it up, so I can't begrudge you that."

"Is that right?" I turn her around and slap her butt. "Come on, let's get going before Brody calls, wondering where we are."

"You shouldn't have cut short your honeymoon, but..." Arthur calls out from his armchair in front of the fire. His voice is strong, his tone amused as he looks from me to my wife, then back at me. A smile curves his lips. "Seeing the two of you married makes me feel stronger."

He's seated in his usual place in the armchair by the fireplace. Tiny is on the floor next to him. Imelda is on the settee to his left. As soon as she sees us near the doorway, she rises to her feet and walks toward us with arms outstretched.

"Congratulations!" She hugs Phe. "I am so happy for the both of you. And I'm so sorry you had to cut your honeymoon short. I'd say you shouldn't have, except—" Imelda steps back and takes my hand in hers. "I know Arthur is very happy to see the two of you. And I suppose, I'm old enough to be selfish and know that seeing the two of you has, possibly, extended his life span."

"Are you okay?" I search Imelda's features and see the dark circles under her eyes. The impact of someone being sick is mostly borne by those closest to them. Imelda always seems so strong and confident; it's easy to forget that Arthur's brush with the Big C would have impacted her more than the rest of us. Probably more than Arthur himself. The old geezer doesn't deserve a woman like her being at his side.

"I'm fine." She pastes a smile on her face that doesn't quite reach her eyes. "I admit, when he collapsed, I was worried; but thankfully, he's better now. And happy to be the center of attention."

She looks over her shoulder. I follow her line of sight to where my family is seated on chairs and sofas around Arthur.

Nathan holds Skylar's hand. He's saying something that Arthur is listening to with great attention.

Brody leans back in an armchair beside Nathan's. He's drumming his fingers on the armrest. His body language says he'd rather be somewhere else, but his features wear a look of patience. He, too, is humoring Gramps.

James walks over to join us. He was at the far end of the room talking to Adrian Sovrano and Toren Whittington, who seem to have joined the ranks of our family.

I'm guessing it's because Arthur's worried he's going to run out of grandsons to marry off after Brody. Bet he's charming them by providing them a family-like atmosphere away from home, so he also has the chance to manipulate them into getting married before too long.

The other reason is because they come from business families whose contacts could prove beneficial to growing the Davenports' influence. Perhaps, the latter more than the former. And no, I'm not being petty when I say that.

"Congratulations." James hugs Phe.

He glares at me over her shoulder.

"You take care of her, or you'll have me to contend with."

"I don't need you telling me how to take care of my wife. I suggest you watch out for yourself."

James frowns. "What do you mean?"

I nod in Arthur's direction. "The old goat loves having projects to work on. If you're not careful, you're going to find yourself next on the list to get married off."

James snorts. "He can try, but I'm good at avoiding such machinations." He looks from me to his sister, then back at me. "Unlike you, apparently. But since it's my sister you married, I'd say Gramps is onto something. Of course, Phe is too good for you, but since I know you to be an honorable man, I'm confident you'll do everything in your power to keep her happy. If not—" He doesn't complete the sentence.

"Her happiness is my priority. She'll never want for anything. I'll do everything in my power to ensure she's taken care of."

James' shoulders seem to relax. A smile curves his lips.

"I'm tempted not to forgive you yet for intruding in my life, but given I wouldn't have met my husband otherwise... I suppose, I should give you the benefit of doubt." She sniffs.

He grins at her with relief and kisses her temple. "Thanks, Sis. You know the family and I only have your best interests at heart."

"Speaking of." She steps back from his embrace. "Did you tell..."

James must guess who she's referring to, for he nods. "They're our parents; I had to inform them."

Phe stiffens, then seems to force herself to relax.

I hold her close. "You okay?"

She nods. "I'm good." Her smile is too bright.

Clearly, she's lying. Why is she so tense at the mention of her parents?

She nods at James. "It's only right that you told our parents. Saves me the need to do so."

Just then, Arthur beckons us over. Best to get this over with. I let Imelda lead us to Arthur, with James trailing behind.

She takes her seat in the chair that's next to Arthur's.

Arthur holds out his hand to Phe, and she takes it.

"I'm glad you're feeling better, Grandad."

His faces softens. "I can see why Connor wanted to elope and seal the deal. He finally showed some good sense." He nods in my direction. "Best to put your ring on her finger before someone else beat you to it."

Phe stiffens. The tension rippling off her turns the air sharp. I track the strain tightening her jaw, the way her shoulders lock—and I know whatever Arthur said has rattled her. The idea that she's still thinking about Drew? That the ghost of that man might still hold any part of her? It burns through me like acid.

He may have asked to marry her, but she didn't say yes. She didn't belong to him.

She belongs to me.

And if she hasn't realized that yet, if she still holds onto memories of him, then I haven't gone far enough.

Not yet.

But I will.

I'll make damn sure there's no room left in her for anyone but me.

I shift closer, put my arm around her, and pull her into my side. She resists for a few seconds, then melts into my side. Her muscles relax.

Arthur lets go of her hand and looks at us with sharp eyes which haven't missed a thing.

Phe raises her hand and places it on my chest. I cover it with my hand, unable to stop myself from rubbing her wedding ring. It feels good that the entire world knows now that she's mine.

"You make sure you're good to her." Arthur scowls at me.

"Instead of worrying about me, why not worry about your own relationship."

"Connor"—Phe nudges me, her eyes wide with surprise—"don't be rude."

I blow out a breath. She's right, of course. "Sorry about that," I say stiffly to Arthur.

He chuckles. "Getting married is already making you a better man. Which is why"—he turns his attention to Brody, who's busy on his phone—"it's my hope that my last single grandson will also be married before the year is out."

"Sure, Gramps." Brody raises a shoulder. "If that's what you want."

Arthur seems taken aback. "You're open to getting married?"

"You won't rest easy until the lot of us have settled down. And you certainly won't let me access my trust fund or confirm my position as CEO unless I do. So, I figure, why resist?" He turns a bland gaze on Arthur. "I plan to save us all time and step up to the altar as soon as I find someone who fits my specifications."

I exchange glances with Nathan.

Brody is determined to pursue his ill-conceived course of action. I don't imagine anyone can talk him out of it. *Stubborn bastard*. He thinks he's immune to love, despite watching us fall for our soul mates.

Arthur's face, which had been wan, is now flushed with color. His eyes gleam. Whereas, he's been sitting back, seemingly listless, he's fairly bouncing in his seat with excitement now.

If this was Brody's intention, he's achieved it. Arthur definitely looks like he's been given a new lease of life.

Imelda spots it, too. She leans over and tucks the blanket around his knees. This, despite the fact it's the height of summer in August, but Arthur doesn't protest.

"You worry too much, old girl." He squeezes her arm. "What I needed to get a fresh infusion of energy was this new project."

"He means you," I mutter in Brody's direction.

"I'm aware." He merely gives me a mild look.

"Dodged that bullet." James pretends to mop his brow.

Famous last words. But I don't say that aloud. I have enough drama of my own to sort through. Starting with why my wife seems so tense at the thought of speaking to her parents. As if my thought conjured them, a voice calls out from the doorway.

"Phoenix?"

47

Phoenix

"Mom?"

Oh no, I thought I'd have more time before I met her.

When I catch sight of her, for a heartbeat, I'm a child again.

The girl who fell asleep to her mother's voice reading bedtime stories. The ten-year-old who got her first period and was met with pads, a hot water bottle, and gentle reassurance.

"Phe, honey, there you are!"

A former model, she carries herself with the same grace and elegance she's always been known for. Growing up, her poise only magnified my sense of awkwardness—my stubborn curls, my book-ishness, my obsession with all things nerdy. She never judged, but I always felt like I didn't quite match her shine.

The old insecurities surge up, clawing at my chest.

I press my palm to my sternum and tap it three times. Breathe in. Breathe out. Some of the tension eases.

Connor is watching me closely. "Are you okay?"

"I'm fine." I take another breath and pull myself together.

"Oh sweetheart, you look radiant!" She folds me into her arms. I'm engulfed in Chanel No. 5. That scent is her—more than her voice, her clothes, even her smile. That's what always lingered, long after she left a room.

And just like that, the dread I've carried—about this moment, this conversation—loosens its grip. I forget the phone calls I ignored. The birthdays I skipped. The quiet ache of absence. I forget that I rehearsed how to tell her about the elopement. Thanks to James, she already knows.

So, I let myself sink into the hug. "I missed you, Mom." And when I whisper, "I'm sorry I didn't call to tell you I was eloping," I mean every word.

"Well then, it wouldn't be eloping if you did." She kisses my cheek.

I hear the disappointment in her voice, though she's trying to hide it.

"I didn't mean to hurt you; things took on a life of their own, and—"

"It felt easier to go with it." She nods. "It's easier to make sense after the fact, rather than when you're in the midst of emotional turmoil."

I step back and survey her features. I expected her to be upset that I didn't inform her in advance of the wedding, but she doesn't seem angry. A little sad maybe, but not as overcome as I expected her to be.

And she understands why I prefer to ride out events, rather than try to confront them. *She and I are more similar than I realized.* I swallow. She'd have understood what happened with Drew. I should have told her. I shouldn't have resented her all these years and allowed my own insecurities to drive a wedge between us.

"Honey, we are so proud of you," my father says gently.

"Dad." I throw myself in his arms and am rewarded by that same bear hug that enchanted me growing up. Every time I was upset, or fell down and hurt myself, my father was there to comfort me.

"I've missed you, Dad." I swallow back my tears. I wonder if I've been hiding from my parents because of my insecurities.

"We're so happy you found your life partner." My dad rubs soothing circles over my back.

"I'm sorry I didn't tell you in advance."

"I'd have been more upset if Arthur"—my mother nods toward him—"hadn't asked us to dinner to celebrate your wedding."

"I'm glad you're here," I say sincerely. "I should have called you anyway, to let you know about the wedding."

"You should have." My mother blinks rapidly. "I'm your mom. The woman who brought you up and—"

"Now, Lana, we spoke about this." My father squeezes her shoulder.

To my surprise, my mother firms her lips. "I'm sorry. I didn't mean to get so emotional." She pulls a handkerchief from her handbag and dabs under her eyes.

I wring my hands in distress. It's typical that my mother makes this about herself, but perhaps, not having seen her in almost three years has given me some perspective. Now I realize, she's upset.

"I'd feel the same if I were in your shoes," I murmur.

She blinks, then looks at me as if seeing me for the first time. "I didn't mean to barge in today and be a drama queen."

"I don't think you could have stopped yourself," I say wryly.

Her lips twitch, and I'm sure she's trying to stop herself from smiling.

Connor drapes his arm around my shoulders. I flinch—not because I don't want his touch, but because it catches me off guard. Then the warmth of him seeps into me. That solid, unyielding weight grounding me. For the first time today, I feel like I'm not standing alone.

He extends his hand. "Mrs. Hamilton."

My mother smiles as she takes it. Elegant as ever, composed as always.

Then he turns to my father. "Mr. Hamilton."

My father grips his hand, eyes steady. "So, you're the man my daughter chose." A beat. "I trust you'll take good care of her."

"She's everything to me," Connor says quietly. "I'd burn the world down before I let anything touch her. She'll never be alone again."

The muscle in my father's jaw softens. His stance shifts, shoulders easing a fraction. "I'll hold you to that."

Connor inclines his head, that unshakable confidence in him radiating like heat.

"James speaks highly of you," my mother says, her voice gentle now. "Anyone James trusts... I trust."

Of course, she does. James is her golden boy. The first of us they adopted. The one she's leaned on through every family crisis. She's always looked to him—his loyalty, his steadiness. And he's always given it to her. Maybe, I've resented that closeness more than I ever admitted. That quiet bond she shares with my brothers, her sons, has always left me just outside the circle. Watching. Wanting.

She glances my way, and something in my eyes must give me away. She hastens to add, "Of course, even if James didn't know you, we wouldn't have been too worried. Phoenix has always had good head on her shoulders. I always knew she'd choose someone worthy of her."

For a moment, I'm struck speechless. Finally, I choke out, "Thanks, Mom."

OMG! Her words have scrambled my brain. I'm not sure how to process what she just said. It's the confirmation I've always wanted from her, and... I don't want to cry, but I can feel the tears building.

Connor's lips brush my temple, jarring me from the spiral of old wounds.

"Mind if I steal my wife for a moment?" he asks.

His voice is low, intimate. Like he's already mine in every way that counts.

And just like that, I can breathe again.

Without waiting for their agreement, he pulls me aside, out of earshot of my parents.

He studies my face, gaze sweeping over every inch like he's trying to read beneath the surface. "You okay?" he asks, his voice low, tender.

I nod.

But the flicker of concern in his eyes says he doesn't buy it.

"I didn't know Arthur invited them," he murmurs. "If I had, I'd have made sure he ran it past you first."

"It's okay," I whisper. My throat's too tight for more.

"It's not." His jaw tightens. That protective edge I've come to rely on flashes in his eyes. "Unfortunately, that's Arthur. He's obsessed with this idea of one big happy family. If I tell him not to —"

"Don't." I lay a hand on his forearm, grounding him. "He's a man staring down time. All he wants is to believe he's brought his family together. Let him have that comfort. I don't want to take it away from him."

He holds my gaze, eyes narrowing slightly like he's weighing whether to push the point. "You sure?"

"I'm sure," I say, firmer this time. "I needed to talk to my parents eventually. There was no point putting it off. I'm glad they're here. I've missed them."

He lifts a hand to my cheek, his palm warm and steady. "You're extraordinary, Phe. Strong. Resilient. The strongest woman I've ever known."

The words hit deeply. I lean in and brush a kiss against his cheek, the roughness of his stubble a sudden comfort. He feels like my anchor in a world that keeps shifting under my feet.

"Thanks," I murmur. Then, softer, "Would it be okay if I spoke to my mother alone?"

"Of course."

He leans in and kisses me hard—firm, possessive, promising everything without a single word—then steps back.

His absence is immediate. Like a shadow being ripped away. I already miss the weight of his presence beside me. I almost call out to him but stop myself. I need to do this. Alone.

I've handled worse, haven't I? Before him, I faced the dark on my own. I can do it again. I have to.

I square my shoulders and turn to my mother. "Mom, can we talk? Somewhere private."

My mom nods right away. "I would love that."

Imelda comes forward. "Why don't I show you to our conservatory?"

"I know you're not happy to see me —" my mother begins, but I hold up my hand.

"Mom, don't. I'm surprised to see you, but that doesn't mean I'm not happy."

She looks into my face. "You don't seem happy," she finally says.

I throw up my hands. "It's taking me a minute to get used to all the events of the past week, okay? We didn't plan to elope; it just happened. And then, having my family descend on me when I haven't seen you and Dad in years is... It's just emotional, is all." Tears press in on my eyeballs, and I try to swallow them down.

"Oh, sweetie." My mum walks over to the chaise I'm sitting on and seats herself next to me. "Marriage is a big step. It's a big change in your life. Of course, you're feeling out of sorts."

"Thanks." I take a tissue from the box she offers me and crumple it in my hand. "I... I didn't expect to see you," I finally say.

She wrings her fingers, and I realize, she's not as composed as she's projecting herself to be.

"When you left home, we didn't part on the best of terms. I wanted a daughter who was more like me. I would have loved for you to follow a career in the arts, or something in fashion, perhaps."

"Instead, you got me." I smile sadly. "I never cared about makeup, or modelling, or dresses."

"And really, that was fine. I think what I found difficult to cope with was how independent you were. You were your own person. You knew what you wanted. And I felt... Like you didn't need me."

"Oh, Mom." I search her features. "That's not true. I did need you. I always wanted you to notice me. To approve of me."

"I realize that now." She blinks rapidly. "When you chose medicine over magazines, it felt like you were rejecting me. You weren't, of course. But it felt like that to me. It's why I didn't reach out to you after you left. Even though, not a day has gone by when I didn't want to call you and ask you how you were."

She touches my hand.

"I'm ashamed to admit, my pride got in the way. You were the daughter; I was the mother. I was adamant that it was you who should apologize to me for not staying in touch." She swallows hard. "Then I realized, if I didn't talk to you, I was the one missing out. If I wanted a relationship with you, then it was up to me to take the first step in healing the gap in our relationship."

She notices me staring and smiles a little. "I know, I sound so mature, right?"

"Umm…" I wonder if I should speak my mind and realize it's best I do. Clearly, my mother's had a change of heart, and if I want any kind of relationship with her, it's best to start off being as honest with her as possible. Besides, she just complimented my judgment. "You do, actually. Surprisingly so," I admit.

It's her turn to look taken aback, then she chuckles. "You've always had more courage than me when it comes to speaking your mind."

"I don't think so." If only she knew how many things I've hidden, even from myself. I shake my head. "It wasn't all your fault that we didn't speak for all this time. I, too, wanted to pick up the phone and call and apologize to you, but I couldn't bring myself to do so. Somehow, every time I reached for the phone"—I swallow—"I couldn't get past how uncomfortable I felt all through the time I was growing up at home."

She looks at me with wide eyes. "You…were uncomfortable?" She looks so upset.

"Forget I said that… I don't know what's causing me to be more open than usual."

"Probably, because you're mirroring me, and I'm trying not to hide my thoughts from you, either."

Again, I stare, astounded. "Wow… You sound like you're—"

"—in therapy." She blows out a breath. "I am. I had to be. I had to understand why you and I never did get along when you were growing up."

"That's not true. When I was little, you were my best friend," I point out.

"I know," she says softly. "Watching Audrey Hepburn movies with ice cream late into the night and being warned by your father that I was spoiling you."

"I still can't pass a Tiffany shop or see a Tiffany packaging or hear about it without thinking of you."

"We did have some good times." She nods, eyes shining.

"Then I hit puberty—"

"—and overnight, I was your worst enemy." She flinches. "Apparently, it's not uncommon that mothers and daughters don't get along. Anything from boundary issues to generational patterns."

The words trip off her tongue like she's said them many times, or read about them a lot.

"Wow, you really are in therapy." I look at her, wide-eyed.

"Mind you, it wasn't voluntary, not at first. But your father told me it was time for me to sort out my relationship with you. He'd had enough of me moping around the house and feeling sorry for myself." She laughs. "And it wasn't easy. I had to go through a few therapists before I found someone I vibed with. But now, I'm one of those obnoxious people who can't complete a conversation without bringing my therapist into it."

She rolls her beautiful, kohl-lined eyes. I've always admired how she always looks so put together. And how she takes pains with her appearance. Maybe, that's why I chose a profession where I don't have time to dress up, or style my hair, or take care of my nails, the way I remember my mom spending time on those things.

"How are you, darling?" She takes my hand in hers. "Are you happy?"

"I am." I hesitate.

She frowns. "You did want to get married, didn't you?"

"Of course." I look at her, surprised. "He didn't force me to elope. In fact, it was my idea."

"Oh." Her shoulders sag. "You didn't want us to be at the wedding?"

"It wasn't that... It was—" It's my turn to lower my chin. "Yeah, that was part of it. But really, I wasn't ready to be the center of attention. I didn't feel ready to have everyone important in my life there while I vowed myself to a man who I was figuring out my feelings for."

"So, if you weren't ready, why did you get married?" She frowns.

"It's not like that. I knew I trusted him—" *And I do trust him.* Until I said it aloud, I didn't realize how much. "I wanted to be with him. I guess, in a way, I didn't want to second-guess myself. I wanted to follow my instinct to the logical conclusion and not give myself a chance to wriggle out of it. Because I knew he'd be good for me." If only, I could also share everything about my past with him? And I should be able to, because I just admitted to myself that I do trust him. "It didn't hurt that he had the necessary influence to stop the ER where I work from closing down."

"Is that why you married him? So, he could help your career."

I shake my head. "I thought that was the reason, but I was kidding myself. No, I married him because—"

"You love him." My mom completes my statement.

"What? No—" My voice tapers off. Do I love him? I know I have feelings for him, but... Love? Could I have fallen in love with my husband so quickly? Sure, he knows how to bring me pleasure and fulfillment, but it's not that, really... It's because... There's something about him that makes me want to believe that I can live out the rest of my days with him. An instinctual reaction where I'm drawn to him. Where I feel like he'll be there for me, no matter what. *Unlike Drew.*

Oh my God. When did my feelings got all confused?

Did a part of me hope I could keep a distance from him? Is that why I agreed to marry him? Thinking I wouldn't let myself fall for him. But I did. My head spins. I let myself be open to being hurt again. How could I do this? I jump to my feet. "I... I need to get back to the hospital."

My mum rises with me. "But honey, they're all waiting for you for dinner."

"I... I can't." To my relief my phone vibrates. I pull it out of my bag and hold it up. "See, the hospital needs me; it's an emergency."

48

Connor

"Where's Fever?"

"Fever?" Her mother knits her eyebrows.

Phe was visibly agitated at the thought of meeting her parents. When her mother returned without her, I realized the meeting must have upset her.

I should have been next to her when she spoke to her mother.

But I didn't want to come off as being intrusive. This is her mother, after all.

In the future, it doesn't matter who she's meeting, if I feel the person will compromise Phe's peace of mind, I'll insist on being present.

"Phoenix. Where is she?" I try to keep the annoyance from my voice and fail.

"She left." Her mother sounds confused.

I stiffen.

"She left?" *Without telling me?* "Did she mention where she's headed?"

"There was an emergency at the hospital," her mother finally adds.

That should make me feel better but instead leaves me more confused. They know she's on her honeymoon. *And why would she not tell me she had to leave?* I'd have driven her there.

"She seemed upset —" Her mother hesitates.

"Upset?"

"I told her it was clear she loves you, which is why, I assumed, she couldn't wait to marry you." She shakes her head. "But it seemed to disturb her."

That would do it.

"I hope I wasn't overstepping. I didn't think so, but my daughter…" She wrings her hands. "She hasn't had it easy, because of me."

I tilt my head. I want to cut her short and run after my wife, but surely, whatever her mother tells me is going to help me understand my wife? I decide to stay silent and listen.

"I might have been overprotective about her in her teenage years. And demanding, at the same time. My Phe is very different from me. Far more creative and introspective, while I'm an extrovert. I couldn't quite understand her and might have pushed her to do things she might not have liked. I couldn't fathom why she wanted to spend her time reading or looking at things through her toy microscope. She was curious about the world and, while I encouraged it, I couldn't understand it."

Her husband comes over and puts his arm about her. She looks at him gratefully. A look of understanding passes between them.

"When she told me she wanted to become a doctor…" She swallows. "I was both horrified, and also, so proud. Then she told me she wanted to leave home and put herself through university on her own merit. Needless to say, I was alarmed."

"She always was an independent person, our Phe," her father says fondly.

"I'm afraid I was angry with him for encouraging her." She casts a sideways glance at her husband. "And when she left home, and he let her and didn't try to help her financially through medical school, I was not happy." She leans into her husband. "It took me a few years to come to grips with how this was probably the best thing for her. By then, my relations with our daughter were strained."

She clenches and unclenches her fingers.

"The reason I'm telling you all this is to say, I hope I have a chance at repairing things with her. I thought, with her getting married, this could be the start of a new relationship between my daughter and me, but perhaps, I was too hasty. Perhaps, I should have called her first, met with her, and tried to smooth things over, instead of arriving unannounced."

She rubs at her temple.

"My excitement at seeing her again overshadowed everything else." She blows out a breath. Her color has faded, leaving her looking pale and much older than when she arrived. "I'm sorry if our conversation distressed her. That wasn't my intention."

But you did unsettle her. Whatever you said triggered something, and now she's hurting.

Anger burns low in my gut. I wrestle it into submission. No use directing it here. What's done is done.

Would I have chosen for her parents to show up like this? Hell no.

But maybe, Arthur had a point. Maybe, she needed this. Maybe, facing them is the first step toward healing.

Still, if I'd known what he had planned, I would've warned her.

I would've prepared her.

I'm glad I'm here for her. No matter what she's facing, she's not going through this alone.

My wife is the center of my world.

I nod at my mother-in-law, then turn to her husband. "I'm going after her, if you'll excuse me."

I didn't realize how strained her relationship is with her parents. And that's on me. I shouldn't have assumed. I'll make sure to find out everything there is about my wife, so I don't commit such a mistake again.

Trust Arthur to invite them without a thought for how it might impact my wife. To him they're valuable business and society contacts who'd help further the Davenport Group's influence.

Again, my bad. I should have seen this coming and warned her. But I was too wrapped up in my new wife to think clearly. I was distracted and not thinking straight. A shiver of unease crawls up my spine.

Why did she rush out without telling me?

"You alright?" Brody walks over to me. "You don't look good, Bro."

I shake my head. "Phoenix left; I'm going after her."

One glance at my face, and he sets his jaw. "I'm coming with."

"What? No. You don't need to—"

"You look shaken. It's best you let Brody drive you," James, who walked over to joins us, chimes in, having caught the end of the conversation.

Both look resolute. Rather than waste time arguing with them, I nod. "If you can let Arthur know that we had to leave—"

"Of course." James looks over at Arthur and sets his jaw. "You two go on. Leave Arthur to me."

"She's not here?" That frisson of unease turns into a warning tingle.

The nurse in charge of the ER operations shakes her head. I came in through the main entrance and was directed to her when I asked to speak with Phoenix.

"She hasn't come in today." She checked her computer. "In fact, she isn't expected back for the rest of the week."

I'm aware of that. I'm the one who used the Davenport name to talk to the senior management of the hospital and have them sign her off the rotation so she could rest up on our honeymoon.

Which is why I was surprised to hear that she'd been called into the hospital. I assumed she called for a ride-share to bring her here.

But she's not here. Where could she have gone? More to the point, why did she tell her mother she was coming here if she never intended to?

The supervisor must see the confusion on my face. She opens her mouth to ask me a question, when there's a commotion behind me. A nurse in scrubs comes running over to the reception table. "Three teenagers just brought in—stab wounds. We need a trauma doctor in Resus, stat."

Instantly, the supervisor reaches for the internal phone system. She speaks into her mouthpiece, "Hi, it's Kenzie on the floor. We have three teens. Multiple stab wounds. Please alert Dr. Vora and have him meet the trauma team in Resus."

I turn to leave, then turn back to find she's disconnected her call. Her fingers fly over her keyboard. I wait until she's done, then she looks up with a curious expression.

"I'm Dr. Hamilton's husband."

She looks at me with mild curiosity. "Didn't realize she'd gotten married."

Right, because Phe didn't have a chance to mention it to anyone yet.

I turn on my most charming expression. "I don't suppose Dr. Drew is around?"

She blinks again. "Dr. Drew?"

I nod. "He was Dr. Hamilton's…ex?"

I curse myself. This was a bad idea. The last thing I need is setting off the grapevine here. If I have a question for Phe, I should ask it of her. It's fucking beneath me, and her, to ask someone else, not to mention, at her workplace.

"Forget I asked."

I turn to leave again.

She calls out after me. "Dr. Drew Carmichael, is that who you mean? He passed away in a cycling accident nearly six months ago."

49

Phoenix

I watch as Drew wheels his suitcase with his clothes and personal effects into the living room. I'm huddled on the chair at the breakfast counter watching him take a last look around the space.

It's clear that he has a fondness for my home and is gutted to leave. But I won't lie. I'm glad he's moving out.

When I walked in here after meeting my mother, it was to find Drew packing. He told me he'd found a place and was leaving. I was so relieved.

These last few weeks have been the best and the worst of my life.

I found my true love. I found Connor. And it gave me the strength to let go of my past. To allow the guilt which has engulfed me for so long to melt away.

He heads for the bookcase, pulls out a few of the books which are his, and slides them into his backpack. He heaves it over his shoulder, then returns to his suitcase.

I am seated with my back to the main door, so I can hear him wheel his suitcase to the door. Hear it creak open. Then there's a pause.

My heart somersaults in my throat. Will he stop? Will he say he changed his mind? I grip the edge of the breakfast counter.

I hear the brush of his shoe as he steps over the threshold. The door snicks shut behind him. He's gone.

Finally.

I slump back and close my eyes. It's over. That part of my life is behind me. I run my fingers over my wedding ring. I'm ready to start my married life with a fresh slate. With a clear conscience.

I'm ready to tell Connor everything about Drew.

Then the door opens again. My pulse rate ratchets up, I look straight forward. Frozen. Unable to move. Footsteps approach. They sound like... *Connor.* Then his dark smoky scent reaches me. Something inside me unwinds. Connor! He's here.

My stomach ties itself in knots. Nervousness grips me. Yet, I can't stop my heart from leaping in my chest.

I clutch my hands together, fingers aching with the force of it. I've never felt this way about anyone before. No one has ever looked at me the way Connor does. Like I'm it. Like I'm his. Like he sees me —all of me—and still wants more.

Terror. Relief. Love. Shame. Desire. The storm of emotion rising inside me makes my head spin. Oh God. *Oh God.* Now is the time to tell him everything. I lock my fingers together so tightly, they hurt.

The way I'm attracted to him surpasses anything else I've felt in my life. I'll never have what I have with Connor with anyone else.

The way he looks at me like I'm the only person in the world. His tenderness, his understanding for me, how he cares for me. The way his touch brings my body to life. The way he knows exactly what I want. How he orders me to bend, knowing it turns me on in a way that guarantees an earthshaking orgasm. The kind only he can draw from me. All of it tells me, Connor's the one for me.

I hope I haven't spoiled any chance of a real relationship with him because I was such a coward.

I hear his footsteps come closer, then there's a soft touch on my shoulders. "Oh, baby"—his voice is anguished—"you didn't need to hide anything from me."

There's no anger in his tone. No judgment. Just a gentle invitation to lean on him.

I draw in a shuddering breath, lower my hands and turn around to face him.

He cups my cheek. "You don't have to explain anything. Though if you did, it would help me understand what you're going through."

I look up into his blue eyes, which have turned almost indigo. In their depths is patience but also, a question mark. Then, as if he's unable to stop himself, he raises his gaze to look at something beyond me. I flinch. I know he's looking at a man's shirt draped on the chair opposite me at the counter. "Is that—" He swallows. "Is that—"

I nod. "It's Drew's," I say softly.

Understanding flashes in his eyes, then his expression grows sad. "Have you had that there since—"

"—the day Drew left the house, never to return."

My throat feels like it's lined with glass. My voice feels like it's being dragged out of a corner of my body where I've hidden so much. "We…we had a fight. I told him I didn't love him. That I never was in love with him. That it was all a mistake. That he should have never moved in with me. He was very upset. We exchanged words. He walked out of the house. I shouldn't have let him cycle to work that day.

"I could tell he wasn't in the right frame of mind. But I was pissed off with him, and with myself. I should have told him earlier. I never should have allowed him to move in with me. But I was a coward… I couldn't find the courage to tell him that we weren't right for each other. The next thing I know, my phone rings, asking me to come into work right away. There was a spate of accidents, and they were overrun in the ER."

"No one told you about…what had happened to him?"

I shake my head. "In the confusion, the person who called me didn't make the connection between Drew and me. Neither did the supervisor on duty. But then, we weren't that open about our relationship, either. I didn't want our colleagues to know about us. Drew was senior to me. I worried I'd be called out for getting preferential treatment." I raise a shoulder. "So, I got into work and went into the trauma bay, just as he went into cardiac arrest."

"Jesus Christ." He wraps his arm about me and pulls me into him. I rest my head against his chest, hearing his heart thump, hearing his breathing, feeling the solidness of him, and greedily taking every bit of strength he can offer.

Again, I'm thinking only of myself, but I can't stop myself from leaning on him. I need him. I do. I rub my cheek against his shirt.

"I… I was the one to defibrillate him. I—" I swallow. "I tried my best to revive him. I did. I kept trying. I didn't give up. Not even after he flatlined and it was clear he wasn't coming back. I wouldn't —couldn't stop. I had to keep trying. Finally, they had to pull me off of him. At which point, I went into a rage and tried to break free to go back to him. They…they had to carry me out of there and sedate me."

"Fucking hell, Fever. You're breaking my heart." He scoops me up in his arms, walks out into the living room, and sits down on my couch with me in his lap. He holds me closely in his arms, like I'm something precious and delicate and I… I don't deserve it. I don't.

The tears trickle down my cheeks. First slowly, then like the rainclouds have burst and it's a monsoon deluge. All the emotions I've closeted inside of myself come to the surface and boil over. I'm not sure how long I cry, but he holds me through it. When the tears finally slow, I slump against him, eyes closed, adrenaline fading, leaving me weak and shaky.

"I'm sorry." I clear my throat, then wince when it hurts.

"Don't apologize. Never apologize for your feelings." He rises to his feet and takes me into the kitchen.

He places me on the counter next to the sink, keeping a hold on to me as if he's scared that if he lets go, I'll collapse. Which I might, to be honest.

It's his touch that gives me the courage to keep my head up and stay upright. He fills a glass with water from the sink and hands it to me. I take a sip, then drain it when I find I'm parched.

He sets it aside, then tucks a strand of hair behind my ear. "Better?"

I nod mutely, staring at the strip of skin on his chest revealed between the lapels of his shirt. I take in the strands of hair on his chest—I know how they feel against my skin.

"Hey, you have nothing to be ashamed of."

I swallow, still unable to meet his gaze. For some reason, I feel so very shy. And embarrassed. "I'm sorry." I find myself repeating that word because, really… I do owe him an apology, regardless of his insisting otherwise.

He opens his mouth to, no doubt, protest, but I place my finger over his lips. "No, let me say it. Please?" I finally raise my eyes to his, and whatever he sees there has him nodding.

I jerk my chin.

"I knew what happened with Drew was a shock. What compounded it was that I hadn't told my family or anyone at work about him."

"Why?" His forehead wrinkles.

"He was older than me, and my superior at the ER. Not my direct boss, but his evaluations would have made a difference on my promotions. I was embarrassed… Maybe—" I hunch my shoulders. "No, that's not right." I look away and gather myself. "It wasn't just that… It was the fact that, deep inside, I knew we weren't quite right. But I wasn't brave enough to face it. I stayed in the relationship, hoping it would run its course and peter out. Only, I hadn't counted on him moving in with me and then wanting to marry me—"

Connor's jaw hardens, but he stays silent.

"The morning, he proposed to me, I knew things had gone too far. I had to…tell him that I couldn't go on like that. That we were over. I guess, it was a surprise to him—guess I'm a better actress than I realized—because apparently, he thought everything was fine with us. But I knew it wasn't. I knew we were spending most of our time apart. Both of us working too hard, barely meeting, even on weekends. We drifted apart and had nothing in common. And then —I suspected he was having an affair at work."

He stiffens, then seems to bring himself under control. "And was he?"

I swallow around the thickness in my throat and nod. "He never had feelings for me. I was simply the woman who paid for all his living expenses. I was his free ride. He took advantage of me, and I let him. I let him convince me that I wasn't good enough to be in a relationship with anyone else. I'm such a cliché.

"You're not," he says in a fierce voice. "You're strong. And brave. And courageous. And you've faced everything life has thrown at you. Look at you. Facing up to everything that happened and telling me about it. That takes guts."

I chuckle because this man... He's always on my side. In my corner. He has my back. And me—I'm still trying to tease out the real reason I couldn't tell him about Drew.

"My friends knew about him, and I told them we'd split up, but they don't know just how haunted by my actions... How haunted by him, I was."

I shift in my seat.

"If I'd had any guts, I would've come clean to you when you first proposed. I should've told you about Drew."

His knuckles notch under my chin, forcing me to meet his eyes.

"You're telling me now," he says, quiet but firm.

"After the accident... When Drew was killed, word got out. About his affair with one of the residents. About me."

His expression shifts—shock giving way to fury.

"Fuck, Fever... That's soul destroying."

I press my forehead into his chest. I can't bear the weight in his gaze.

"Maybe. But it doesn't excuse the fact that I never asked for help. I blamed myself for the accident. Still do. He'd just proposed, and I'd turned him down. He was upset. Distracted. And on his bike when he met with the accident..." I exhale shakily. "I told myself it was my fault he didn't see the car coming."

"You can't do that," he says, his voice rough. "You didn't kill him, Phe."

"Logically, I know that. But logic doesn't stop the guilt. I've replayed it so many times—telling him earlier, ending it cleanly, not letting it drag on. If I'd been braver, maybe none of it would've happened."

I look up at him, my eyes burning.

"I couldn't let go. Not of the guilt. Not of him." My voice cracks.

"His clothes are still in the closet—exactly where he left them. His toothbrush is in the holder. His books are still lined up beside mine, like nothing ever happened."

I swallow hard, but the knot in my throat won't budge.

"I kept it all. Every damn thing. As if I deserved to live inside the wreckage. Like I *needed* to suffer through the reminders—needed to feel the weight of what I did. What I *didn't* do."

My chest tightens.

"I barely sleep here. I can't stand this house. Every corner echoes with the choices I didn't make. Every drawer's a coffin stuffed with everything I buried—grief, shame, regret. Me."

"God, baby, it's making me so fucking angry that you didn't ask me for help."

"I wasn't...in a position to ask anyone. I subconsciously was punishing myself." When he stiffens, I hug him closer. "Not that you're just anyone. You're very important to me, Connor. I knew if I told you, you'd understand, that you'd get me the help I needed... But I had to work my way up to it. But meeting you started me on the path of coming to grips with what had happened and moving on with my life..."

I search his beloved features.

"I wanted to move on with you. I knew you were my salvation. That your touch was what I needed to help me get over what had happened. That how you took charge was what I needed to give myself up completely to you. To find a pocket of not having to think or make decisions and leave it up to you. I knew allowing you to dominate me was the only way to heal myself and find myself again."

He cups my face with such tenderness, the calluses of his fingers rubbing up against my skin and igniting little sparks of heat in their wake.

His eye color deepens until it's almost black, except for the flashes of silver in them. Incredible. I feel like I'm drowning in them, like I can give myself up to him completely, and find myself again... And I want to do that. I need to do that. As if he senses that yearning in me, he wraps my hair around his fingers and tugs.

He exerts enough force that I gasp. That I have to lean my head back and bare my throat to him. He's my husband, the man who knows how to play my body with expertise, so he can make me give him the exact response he wants.

Tendrils of pain spark at my hair follicles, then radiate down my spine, and straight to my pussy. "Connor, I—"

There's a knock on the main door. "Connor, Phoenix, you guys, okay?"

I startle and begin to pull away, but Connor doesn't let me. "That's Brody. When I found out you'd left without telling me... I knew something was wrong. It probably showed on my face; Brody insisted on driving me here."

"We're good," Connor calls out.

"Right, I'll make myself scarce," he replies.

That Connor—the man who has biotech discoveries which literally save lives to his credit; the undercover agent who's undertaken missions for his country—was blindsided, enough to not be in any state to drive—wow! It makes me realize how much my actions upset him.

"I am so sorry." I reach up to cup his firm jaw. "Sorry I didn't tell you everything about Drew. Sorry I didn't tell you how I needed help to get over what happened between us. Sorry I left without telling you. Sorry that—"

"Hush." He lowers his head and brushes his lips over mine, effectively shutting me up. "You don't need to apologize to me. You were coming to terms with your own ghosts."

"Literally," a tear squeezes out the corner of my eye.

"But you had the courage to tell me—with your actions—about what was happening. Your leaving without telling me was a call for help. I went to the hospital first, and that's where I found out what had happened to him."

"Oh." I glance away, revisited by images of walking into the trauma bay and finding him fighting for life, then the desperate fight to save him, and ultimately, the despair. The helplessness. The guilt.

More than anything, I remember being angry with myself for not having called off my relationship with Drew earlier. I'd been a coward, and I was paying the price. Then, I felt embarrassed about having these thoughts just after he died. It was scary and confusing.

I was so perturbed by Drew's death, it became clear to everyone that I'd been involved with him.

I came clean about our relationship to the senior consultant at the hospital. And then, I learned about Drew's affair. That shattered any chance of my being able to move on from the incident unscathed.

I blamed myself for him cheating. We'd drifted apart. We'd spent all our time at work. Of course, he was going to cheat on me. On and on, the thoughts circled in my head. It made me tired just thinking about it. No wonder, I'd been close to a nervous breakdown. No wonder, I had tried to punish myself for what had happened. No wonder, I hadn't been able to bring myself to face the fact that Drew was dead.

"That must have come as a surprise to you," I finally offer.

"It was, but also, maybe, it wasn't."

I angle my head.

"It felt like you wanted me to find out about Drew."

I absorb what he said, then nod slowly. "I did want you to find out about Drew. I guess, I was ready. I suppose, I rushed out, knowing you'd come after me. I didn't go to the hospital because I hoped you'd get there and find out about Drew; then, I wouldn't have to tell you. Honestly, I don't know. Seeing my Ma hit me like a punch to the chest.

"Talking to her made me realize, I could have confided in her about Drew. She would have understood. I wasted so many months drowning in guilt and embarrassment, convincing myself she'd judge me or be disappointed. If I'd just opened my mouth earlier—back when things first started going wrong with Drew—I could have spared myself so much anguish. I know it's not my fault, but maybe he'd still be alive."

I glance sideways at my phone on the counter. There are no messages from Drew.

That knot of tension at the base of my neck fades.

He won't interrupt me again.

He won't make me feel guilty for moving on. A flush of happiness blooms in my chest. I really am free of him.

My heart soars. I can finally belong to Connor, body and soul, the way I never could be before this moment.

He rubs away the moisture on my cheek, "I'm sorry I didn't warn you about Arthur's machinations and that your parents might be there."

I push my forehead into his chest. "No more apologies, remember?"

50

Connor

"No apologies." I allow myself a smirk. "Not even for what I'm going to do to you."

She barely has time to register my words, when I scoop her up in my arms.

Surprise widens her eyes. Lust stains her cheeks. She looks at me in a way that tells me she knows what I want to do to her and that she welcomes it. Damn, if that doesn't turn my groin to granite.

I head out of her kitchen down the hallway and into the bedroom. I walk over to the bed, then pause. "Are you okay if—"

"Yes." She nods. "I want you to show me how much I belong to you. I want you to wipe away all the memories that hold me back. I want you to make me yours again."

A possessiveness squeezes my soul and turns my stomach into a writhing mass of need. My heart booms in my chest. My blood pounds in my ears.

"Say it." I set my jaw. "Tell me what I want to hear."

"I… I want you to fuck me on this bed."

Barely are the words out, when I drop her on the mattress. She bounces once, then shoves the hair that's fallen into her eyes out of her face.

"On your hands and knees," I snap.

"Wh-a-a-t?" Her eyes bug out.

"You heard me." I narrow my gaze on her. "Don't make me repeat myself."

She swallows, then slowly turns over. I grab her waist and pull her close, until her feet are at the edge of the bed. When I flatten my palm on the middle of her back and push down, she gasps, but obligingly slides down, so her cheek is pressed into the mattress and her butt is extended up in the air. I keep a hold of her waist, and cup her arse cheek through the skirt of her dress.

She shudders but otherwise stays still.

"Good girl." I squeeze her butt.

A breathless moan spills from her lips, revealing how turned on she is.

"If I touch your pussy, will I find you wet and needy for your husband's cock?"

She nods.

"Too bad, you're going to have to wait until I'm done with you."

"What are you —" She gasps as I flip up the skirt of her dress. And when I grab hold of her panties and tear them off, a full body shudder grips her.

"Connor," she whines.

"Stay still," I order.

Instantly, she freezes, toes tucked in as she grasps hold of the mattress.

"This is going to hurt." I bring my hand down on her butt. The crack of my palm connecting with the smooth skin of her behind has her entire body jolting. She cries out and grabs hold of the blanket with white-skinned knuckles.

"Count the slaps," I growl.

"One," she says in a breathless voice. Then groans when I follow up with a slap to her other butt cheek.

"Two," she whimpers.

I slap the first again.

"Three," she says on a rush.

And the next. I alternate between her arse cheeks. Her voice follows each hit of my palm on her behind. She counts until I reach twenty. When her voice breaks, I stop with my palm on her heated skin. I massage the curve of her behind. Another moan spills from her lips. I lower my hand, admiring my palm prints on the creamy expanse.

"So fucking gorgeous."

Her knees threaten to give way at my praise. I squeeze her hip and hold her up. And when I trail my fingers down the cleavage bisecting her rump to the valley between her pussy lips, she almost topples over.

"You're so wet, your cum is trickling down your inner thigh."

She tries to pull her legs together in response, but I squeeze each of her outer thighs and stop her. And when I bend and lick down her melting slit, she cries out in surprise. "Connor, it's...too much."

"Good." I lick up her pussy lips, then pull them apart and curl my tongue around her swollen clit.

"Connor, ohmigod," she pleads.

I stuff my tongue inside her trembling slit. She makes a huffing sound. I massage her reddened backside then eat her out. I slurp on her pussy, lick up the cum drenching her inner thighs, all the time holding her open at my mercy. She writhes and tries to pull away. With my tongue still pushed into her tight slit, I slap her cunt. A long, low sound emerges from her lips, and she orgasms.

Her back curves, and her body shudders as she climaxes.

When the aftershocks ripple up her spine, I lean over her. I grip her chin, so she's forced to look up at me.

"Who do you belong to?"

"You," she says without hesitation.

"Who does your pussy belong to?"

"You."

I curl her long strands of hair around my hand and tug. She whimpers. Goosebumps pop on the back of her neck. "Who do you trust more than anyone in this world?" Perhaps, it's wrong of me to ask this question. But she's my wife. My soul mate. My other half. I want...need her to come to me first, when... If she needs anything. "Answer me, Fever."

"You," she moans. "You. Connor. I trust you more than I trust myself."

"Good answer."

I use her hair as leverage to maneuver her up on her knees. It causes her scalp to hurt. It causes her to feel the twinges all the way down her spine and to her cunt. It causes her to lower yet another barrier as she finds herself at my mercy. Releasing my hold on her hair, I pull her dress up. She automatically raises her arms, and I pull it off. Then I relieve her of her bra, so she's naked.

With only her glorious hair cascading down her back, I make short work of my clothes and my shoes, leaving her in her heels.

Then I urge her to bend over again. Another trembling undulates up her spine. And when I grasp her hips and fit my cock against her slit, a full body shudder grips her. "I'm going to fuck you now."

I thrust into her. Her entire body jolts. She throws her head back and pants, mouth open, eyes closed, ecstasy on her features.

Seeing the pleasure I bring her makes my dick swell even more, pushing against the walls of her channel.

Her warm, snug pussy clamps around my cock, and when she squeezes down with her inner muscles, it's my turn to groan.

She's so fucking tight. So wet. So, everything. Despite the fact that I've already been inside her, I need to give her time to adjust to my size again. I set my jaw, plant my feet on the floor, and stop myself from ramming into her. When I feel her relax, I pull out until I'm balanced at the entrance to her gorgeous slit, then in one smooth move, I impale her.

My balls slap against her pussy, and I brush up against the entrance to her cervix.

She whimpers and shudders and slaps her hand into the mattress.

The way her entire body shudders, and her hips undulate, and her arms tremble like they're barely able to hold up her weight, I know she's close. I reach down to where we're connected, and scooping up her cum, I smear it around her forbidden entrance.

She shivers, curves her back, and I slide further inside of her. "You take me so beautifully, baby."

I work my finger inside her forbidden hole, and she mewls. "Connor," she says on a breathy cry.

"Hearing my name from your lips is the most beautiful sound in the entire world," I praise her.

I work my finger in and out of her, then add another. She shudders again. Sweat glistens on her skin.

"That's it." I squeeze her fleshy rump, and she begins to pant.

"OMG, I think, I'm going to come."

I spank her butt. "Not without me."

I pull out of her and plunge inside with enough force that the entire bed jolts. Once more, I hit that spot inside of her, again and again. I pick up my pace until she tries to pull away, trying to escape the orgasm that's about to break over her.

That's when I pull out completely and replace my fingers with my cock at her puckered hole. A tilt of my hips, and I punch through the ring of muscle at the entrance.

She cries out. Her arms go out from under her. She pushes her cheek into the mattress and pleads, "Let me come, please."

In answer, I plunge into her again bottoming out inside of her. A lusty cry emerges from her.

I set a punishing rhythm. Thrusting into her with enough force for my balls to slap against her pussy.

"You hit the anterior fornix erogenous zone—"

Slap.

"—the pleasure point located between the cervix and the bladder," she chokes out.

Slap.

"It is one of five deep vaginal erogenous zones that research associates with the female orgasm."

"Good to know." I pick up my pace even more, making sure she can feel every millimeter of my extended cock, then reach around to rub on her clit.

"Connor," she yells. "Connor please —"

I lean over her and growl in her ear, "Come."

51

Phoenix

To say this is the most intense orgasm I've had so far does not do it justice.

The sensations pound through my body, jangling my nerve endings, thrumming up my spine, until they bounce around my head and push me over a cliff. I ride what seems to be a Niagara Falls force of waterfall over a sharp edge. I feel his heat at my back, his cock still thick and heavy inside me. I feel him give a guttural cry and follow me down.

Then I'm floating, sinking, slowly coming into myself. Feeling the heat of his body pinning me down, even though he's got his arms planted on either side of me so he's barely leaning on me. But the flickers of electricity which seem to sizzle off him, cause the hair on my arms and back of my neck to rise.

My eyelids feel weighed down, my arms and legs so heavy. I'm unable to stop myself from slumping into the bed. For a few seconds, he leans more of his weight on me. The ridges of his chest dig into my back. The warmth rolling off of him scorches my skin. He's still inside me. On me. All around me.

His body holding me down is the most secure feeling in the world. I revel in that absolute bliss that comes with a postcoital glow. A sensation even more intense than the last few times he made love to me. This time... There was abandon. As if he lost control and showed more of himself to me.

Perhaps, the secrets I kept from him were holding me back, but his finding out the most vulnerable aspects of me seems to have pushed him to open himself fully to me. My bones feel like they've melted. I'm wrapped up in him, and floating in a sensation which can only be described as completely being at peace.

The sound of his breathing intertwines with mine. The vibrations of his heart beating against mine sink into my blood, surrounding my heart in a nest of serenity.

The rasp of the hair on his legs as he moves them against mine. The power in his thighs. The ridge of his pelvic bone digging into the raw skin of my butt, the corded tendons of his biceps bracketing my body... All of it is imprinted into my flesh and seared into my brain cells.

The silence stretches, and then something vibrates as if from far away. It infiltrates my consciousness and sends a tremor of uncertainty down my spine.

I push up through the layers of comfort cocooning me. Then wince when he pulls out of me. He kisses the back of my head.

"I should take this." He rolls off, and there's a sucking sound as he peels his skin off mine. Instantly, I feel like I've lost a part of myself, the heat replaced by the cooler air in the room as the sweat on my back begins to dry.

I sense him moving around. There's the rustle of fabric as he reaches for the phone in his pants.

"Davenport."

I listen to the sound of someone speaking on the other side, the words illegible.

"Now?" I sense him snapping to attention. "You sure about that?"

Something in his voice makes me roll over on my back and sit up.

Ouch. Let's just say my gluteus maximus is registering a level of discomfort consistent with a low-grade contusion. Meaning: my ass hurts.

He rubs the back of his neck. "Right. Of course." He holds the phone between his chin and shoulder, and steps into his pants. He listens again. "I'll be there."

"What's wrong?" I frown. "Who called you?"

He blows out a breath, then leans up and kisses me firmly. He licks on my lips, and when I part them, he thrusts his tongue inside my mouth. There's something desperate about his actions, something uncontrolled, different from the dominance he exuded earlier... This is...frenzied. Almost urgent. It's why, instead of allowing myself to be distracted by him, I manage to tear my mouth from his and scowl. "Tell me."

He arches an eyebrow. "You don't tell me what to do."

"In this case, I do, because you're hiding something from me."

He seems taken aback. "Oh, yeah? And you know that, how?"

"I *am* your wife. And when you're stressed you have a tell."

"A tell?" he scoffs.

"Here"—I trace the furrow between his eyebrows—"and here"—I rub at the nerve throbbing at his temple.

His face softens. "Damn." He continues to look at me with wonder in his eyes. "No one's noticed that before."

A warm sensation squeezes my chest. "You haven't been married to anyone else before, have you?"

A tenderness fills his gaze. He kisses me again, then sits up. "I have to leave."

What? The starkness of his words dispels the lazy, lusty feelings that were crowding my mind.

I sit up, then swing my legs over and stand up. Walking around the bed, I grab my dress and pull it on.

"Leave? Where?"

"Save the Kids. We received the coordinates of where the rebels are holding the supplies. I need to head there right away and negotiate the release, or else a lot of children will die."

Panic slams into my chest like a defibrillator. I can barely breathe.

You said you wouldn't take on any more missions." My voice cracks.

"This isn't a mission for the government. This is something I'm undertaking on my own."

I stare at him, disbelief mixing with dread. Of course, he's doing this. It's who he is. The man who can't walk away from a fight when innocent lives are on the line. It's what drew me to him. His integrity. His relentless drive to do good, no matter the cost. To use his money to help those in need.

But to put himself at risk now? When I just got him. When I'm finally free to be with him in every way.

Why does it have to be now?

Why does it have to be him?

A chill races down my spine. I sink down next to him, my legs unable to hold me up any longer.

"Can't...someone else do this?"

He shakes his head. "I'm the only with the experience, the resources, and the influence to negotiate something like this."

"Of course. I have no doubt you're the best person for the job. And of course, the children need you, but—" I take his hand in mine. "I don't want you to go."

"Eh?" He seems surprised.

"It's just... I can't explain it. I have a bad feeling about this."

Once again, his expression melts into something gentler. Something unguarded. I can see the love in his eyes. The vulnerability. The feelings he has for me. I reach up and wrap my arm about his neck and burrow into him. I want to tell him, "I love you" because I do. But something stops me. Maybe, it's because I'm burned from my last relationship. Maybe, I'm having to teach myself how to trust all over again. Though I do trust him. More than anyone else. I open my mouth to tell him, but nothing comes out. Instead, I hug him tightly and burst out, "Don't go, please."

"Hey, hey, it's okay. I know what I'm doing."

"I have no doubt. But it sounds dangerous. Which country are you going to, anyway?"

He hesitates. "I can't tell you. It's better I don't, for your safety."

I nod. "Either way, you'll be putting yourself in danger."

"For a good cause. If anyone can get them to release the supplies needed, it's me." He hesitates. "I won't lie and say it's completely safe; it's not. But I've carried out plenty of such assignments in the past. I'll be in and out in no time. Besides, I won't be going alone."

"You won't?"

He shakes his head. "I'll have the best team from my uncle Quentin's security agency with me."

"But you'll be the one actually negotiating with the terrorists."

"I'm the most skilled at it." He cups my cheek. "I'm sorry for putting you through this. But I'm already committed. I can't back out."

Of course, I understand. Right? "I want to say I'm selfless enough to say, of course, you're right, and you should do it. And I know you should, but"—I frame his beloved face and look into those startling blue eyes—"Connor, I wish you didn't have to go." I swallow. "Not that I'll stop you. I know those children are counting on you."

A tear runs down my cheek. He wipes it away. "I'll be back so soon. You won't even realize I'm gone."

Not likely, but I'm going to put on a brave front. I'm going to wish him luck and send him off, and then I'm going to spend every second praying for his safe return.

"Promise me." I take both of his hands in mine and kiss him hard. "Promise me, you'll come back to me."

52

Phoenix

"Dr. Hamilton?" The receptionist at the doctors' station in the ER looks at me in surprise. "Don't you have the day off?"

It's been ten days since I returned from my cut-short honeymoon. Ten days since my husband left on his mission. And yes, it's my day off, but rather than stay home and stress about the safety of my husband's assignment I decided to come into work. No, I don't plan to continue with this bad habit when my husband is around.

Besides, no way would Connor let me work without taking proper breaks.

Unlike my relationship with my ex, I don't want to hide my new status. I want the world to know I'm married to Connor.

"It's Dr. Davenport now," I remind her.

It feels amazing to say that. Makes me feel closer to Connor to share his surname.

Yes, I worked hard for my career, and now it has his name on it. But if it weren't for Connor, I wouldn't have come to grips with my past. It's thanks to him; I've been able to face the trauma of what happened. I'm a new person.

I'm happy to take his name. It doesn't take away from my accomplishments or makes me less of a feminist. I'm still me, with all my faults and insecurities. I'm also deeply in love with a man who understands me in a way I never thought another person could.

"Of course, my bad," she checks the rota, "and I see you asked to be added to the schedule."

I nod. "I asked to come in today because my husband is away on a work trip. Didn't want to stay home in an empty apartment."

Her gaze grows wistful. "Ah, young love." The phone on her desk rings. With an apologetic look, she reaches for it.

I pivot and head into the triage area. For the next six hours, I'm busy, attending to cases.

A pregnant woman suffering from gas and worried she was miscarrying—which she wasn't, thankfully. An elderly woman with stomach pain and a diagnosis of gallstones. A man suffering from a panic attack.

Luckily, none of them were of the life and death variety. But they kept me so busy that I didn't have time to think of my husband, far away in some country where his life is at risk. How do wives and loved ones of those in the military put up with this kind of distance and waiting?

It takes a special kind of person who's resilient enough to go about their day-to-day life and live with such a high degree of uncertainty when someone they care for is putting their life on the line for them and their country. Thankfully, the rush of patients slows down to a trickle, so I'm able to take a breather.

I head down to the staff canteen. It's also frequented by guests of patients. And not very crowded, for a change.

I grab a coffee and a sandwich, barely noticing what I've picked. I head to a table tucked away at the back of the space. The moment I sit, I yank out my phone and check my messages.

There's one from the Prime Minister's Chief of Staff.

I freeze. My pulse spikes. My vision narrows. Oh my God. *Oh my God.*

Connor sent off that email with my proposal, but I've been so lost in missing him, aching for his voice, his arms, his impossible arrogance, that I almost forgot about it.

I click on the message. My breath shudders out. My eyes skim the first line. Then the second.

The Chief of Staff, thanks me for the proposal. Thanks. *Me*. She also confirms they've already initiated contact with the relevant decision makers in the health service. Archway Hospital's ER is deemed critical to the community, and will continue to operate for the foreseeable future.

I can't breathe. Relief floods my limbs like I've just been pulled from drowning. My shoulders shake as I clutch the phone to my chest.

A sound escapes my throat. Half gasp, half sob. Tears sting my lashes. I want to scream. Laugh. Cry. All at once.

"We did it, honey." I press a hand to my chest. "We. Did. It."

I calm myself, then open the message app and type as fast as I can, my thumbs flying. I send the news to my husband. *My* Connor.

Who's managed to message me every day since he left, using a burner phone to keep the rebels off his trail.

I press send.

Then draw in deep breaths and let the emotions wash over me—gratitude, elation a sense of being overwhelmed.

We saved the ER. Together. Connor and me.

It's been ten days since he left. A few days ago, he warned me he'd be out of communication range.

He also said the mission was reaching a critical stage, so it wouldn't be long now until he'd be done and, hopefully, on his way back.

Meanwhile, I've started the process of renting out my apartment. It's a way to keep myself busy, so I don't spend every moment missing my husband. I've moved all of my stuff into his apartment. It made me feel closer to him to be surrounded by his things and to sleep in his bed, surrounded by bedclothes that smell of him.

A voice interrupts my thoughts, "Phe?"

I smile and jump up. "Zoey, what are you doing here?"

"We haven't seen you since you got married." My friend reaches me. "And knowing you must have gone straight back to work, we figured it was best we come visit you here." I hold out my arms, and she crushes me in a hug.

"We're so glad we caught you on a break." Harper elbows Zoey aside and hugs me.

The faint scent of tomatoes laced with oregano fills my senses. "Mmm, you smell like pasta sauce."

Harper grimaces. "The boss made me cook it over and over again, until I got it right. That was ten days ago. Not that it ever reached his standards." She tosses her head. "I understand why he did it. He's a perfectionist. That's why he's so successful. But I swear, I'll never get the smell out of my skin."

Then a flush creeps up her cheeks.

"No offense."

Of course, she's talking about James. I'm not blind to my brother's faults. "None taken."

"Another one bites the dust, huh?" As always, Grace is impeccably dressed in a designer pantsuit and a single string of pearls, with her hair pulled back in a French chignon. She looks totally out of place among the standard-issue clothing many of the occupants at the other tables are wearing.

Not that anyone pays us the slightest bit of attention. When medics take a break, you better believe, they're too busy catching up on their personal lives… And gossip amongst the staff, of course.

"Did you come straight from the studio?" I ask.

"Had to see you and congratulate you." She squeezes my shoulder.

"In case you were wondering, we heard from Skylar that you cut your honeymoon short." Zoey adds.

Clearly, the Davenport clan have their own established lines of communication, and since the girls know many of them, it's to be expected that they'd know of my whereabouts.

Strangely, it doesn't feel invasive. If anything, it feels…safe. Like a web of quiet protection. Unlike the gossip at work, which always seems to grow legs and twist the truth, the Davenports seem to share information with one purpose: looking out for each other.

It's comforting. Especially now—with Connor gone and off the grid. No updates. No messages. No way to know if he's safe. I feel so helpless... If it weren't for the Davenports I don't know what I'd do. I didn't expect to feel this...held. Not by a family that isn't mine.

Or maybe it's just that I never gave my own family a chance. If I had confided more in James and in my friends, they'd have done everything in their power to help me. And I'm coming to realize, even my parents would do anything for me. I didn't feel like I could trust anyone. And that's on me. But no more.

I'm done letting old wounds dictate how I show up. I'll face my fears, not bury them. I'll do the work. *Starting now.*

Whatever I'm feeling must show on my face, because Zoey slides into the seat beside me and gently squeezes my shoulder.

"Oh, honey, are you okay?"

Harper pulls up a chair on my other side. "What's going on, Phe?"

"Do you want something else?" Grace glances at my half-eaten sandwich and barely touched coffee. "A fresh cup?"

Their concern wraps around me like a blanket. And it's exactly what I need—this warmth, this gentle attention. Especially when worry is clawing at my chest, refusing to let go.

This is supposed to be Connor's final trip. He promised. But I can't shake this feeling. This tightness in my ribs. This dread pooling in my gut.

He's done this many times. He's trained. Experienced. Careful. So what, if he's going to a conflict zone. He knows what he's doing. He'll be fine.

He has to be.

I tap my chest, trying to rub away the panic pressing against my rib cage. Then take a breath and manage a smile.

"I'm okay. Really. But thank you." I nod toward another empty chair. "Why don't you sit? I have something to tell all of you."

Grace settles in, crossing her legs. Zoey leans forward slightly.

Harper looks at me with curiosity and a touch of worry in her eyes. "What is it?"

I look at their faces and steel myself, "I told you I broke up with Drew."

The nod.

"What I didn't mention was that he died in a cycling accident six months ago."

"What?" Harper slaps her hand over her mouth.

Zoey's eyes widen in shock. "What are you talking about?"

Only Grace seems more contemplative than surprised.

Trust her to be a few steps ahead of me. I lower my chin and study her. "You were expecting me to say something like this?"

"Not that he's dead no. But yeah, I wondered if there was something you weren't telling us."

"I should have told you guys. But his accident took place the same day I broke up with him. I'm afraid, I blamed myself for it."

"Oh, Phe." Harper leans over and wraps her arm about my shoulder. "I'm so sorry."

"You do know you're not responsible for what happened, right?" Zoey holds my gaze.

I nod. "I know that, now, thanks to Connor. He made me feel secure enough that I could accept my own shortcomings and learn to be kinder to myself." I rub at my temple. "I realize, I was being hard on myself. I have… Had a habit of taking on guilt and feeling responsible for things that aren't my fault."

Grace nods slowly. "I don't want to talk ill about the dead, but Drew made you feel less than yourself. He diminished you in your own eyes. You felt responsible for him when he was alive, and that extended to when he wasn't."

I nod. "You're right on all those counts. When Connor found out what had happened, he was very understanding. He calmed me, helped me deal with the guilt I'd been carrying. Made me realize I need to be kinder to myself and give myself all the time I need come to terms with what happened."

"He sounds like exactly the kind of man who'd build you up, support you, and believe in you."

"Oh, he does." I lock my fingers together. "I can't tell you what a difference it makes to have someone like him in my corner. Someone who respects me and makes me feel so good about myself." I look between them.

"I'm sorry I didn't tell you guys earlier. I guess... I knew Drew wasn't right for me. And I was ashamed that I couldn't end my relationship with him. And when I did, he died. It made me feel like breaking up with him caused his death, which is silly, I know. But tell that to my psyche. I felt like if I'd cut ties with him sooner, he'd still be alive."

Grace looks at me with speculation. "So, when you told us that you had ended things with Drew, he—"

"He was dead already. I know, it makes me look like I'm delusional—"

"Oh, you're not delusional." Grace waves a hand. "You were hurting. And you were finding it difficult to deal with what seemed to be the outcome of the first time you tried to set up boundaries with him. And given how he was gaslighting you...I suspect you felt relieved when he died in the accident, which probably made you feel worse about yourself."

Tears fill my eyes, and I look at Grace with both admiration and gratitude that I didn't have to explain every single nuance of what I went through. She cut right to the heart of it. I nod. "I really am sorry I didn't confide in you earlier. I realize now, I'd have been able to cope with things better if I'd shared with you."

Grace shakes her head. "You did what you thought was right for you. Never apologize for that. You know yourself better than anyone."

Zoey nods. "I second that. And you're telling us now, when you're ready to share with the world."

"I wish we could have been there for you, sweetie, instead of you going through this alone, but I'm so happy you emerged stronger and found your Mr. Right," Harper's eyes glisten.

"Thanks." I look at them gratefully. "Trust me when I tell you that I won't keep anything from you guys again. I'm so pleased to see you." I rub at my chest. "Especially with Connor being away. I miss him more than I thought I would."

"Aww, look at you, so much in love." There are little hearts in Harper's eyes.

This woman is a real romantic. And for the first time, I understand the appeal. This melting feeling inside me every time I think of Connor is a strange kind of high.

It makes everything I see sparkle—like the world's been dusted in light, sharper, more vivid, too beautiful to bear. And when he's away, my chest aches with a hollowness so fierce, it's hard to breathe. If I don't see him soon, I think I might shatter.

"I am, aren't I?" I name these sensations which have been building inside of me like pressure inside the earth's crust.

"What's that supposed to mean?" A questioning look comes into Zoey's eyes.

Thankfully, she and my other friends stay silent, allowing me to formulate my thoughts. Another reason I love these women. They know when to push and when to back off. Something I can't quite say about my mother. Although, after the last time I saw her, I can honestly say, I think she's trying.

I rub at my temple. "This might sound strange, but I wish I had been more open about my emotions before he left. I wish, I'd told him how I really felt before he went on his trip."

Harper exchanges a look with Zoey. "Is his trip...dangerous?" Her voice is hesitant. "Skylar didn't give us the details, except it was to help a charity."

I nod slowly. I guess, there's no harm in sharing what Connor told me? "The reason we got married so quickly is so Connor could get access to his trust."

"Something to do with the grandfather wanting each of the Davenport brothers to get married before he lets them access their individual fortunes." Zoey nods.

When she sees the confusion on my face she holds up her hand. "I know, only because I held Skylar's hand in the time leading up to her wedding with Nathan Davenport. She's told me a little bit about Arthur's machinations."

"Seems like he's quite the character." Grace shakes her hair back from her face.

"He's doing his best to protect his family's legacy," Harper protests.

"You're probably right." I glance around the table. "The reason Connor wanted to access his money is so he could donate a chunk of it to Save the Kids."

"That's the charity which provides aid to children in conflict regions," Harper exclaims.

I nod again. "In this case, just money wasn't enough. They also needed him to negotiate the release of supplies which had been held up by rebels. It was time critical. He had to rush there."

"But he's, okay? He's been in touch, hasn't he?" Grace asks.

The wrinkles on her forehead tell me her journalist's mind is working overtime. She's probably trying to place which country he's gone to. Guess this is why Connor didn't share more details with me.

If I knew, I'd be tempted to tell my friend, and that would make things unsafe for both of us.

"He was, until he had to go off the grid."

Grace's eyebrows draw down. I see the question in her eyes and quickly add, "He told me there are inherent dangers in what he's doing, but that he's taking every precaution to make sure he's safe."

"That's fair." Grace's voice carries a hint of admiration. "I'm glad he didn't hide the hazards involved. But he also reassured you." Her lips curve. "I already like this husband of yours."

"He's the most gorgeous, most personable, most charismatic man I've ever met."

I must sound like a fan girl, or someone who's head-over-heels for my man; all three wear knowing smiles on their faces.

"Sorry about that. I'm still in the honeymoon phase," I feel compelled to add.

Harper holds up her hand. "You don't need to apologize or explain yourself. And for the record, I think your feelings are only going to get stronger with time."

"Thank you," I say softly.

"Aww." She reaches over and hugs me.

Harper really is the sweetest. Sometimes, I wonder how she puts up with my brother's well-known temper and his bad attitude on the kitchen floor. I worry he'll walk all over her with his hostile disposition. Or perhaps, it's because she's so sweet and understanding, and such a romantic, she's the perfect foil to his grumpiness?

Grace's phone vibrates. She looks at the screen and sighs. "I'm so sorry, babe. I have to head back to work."

"Thought you were headed home?" Zoey scowls.

Grace hesitates. "I need to prep for a possible new show I'm working on." She pauses. "This time, as a producer."

"That's wonderful news," I exclaim.

"Thanks." She looks pleased. "I've tried so hard to move into being a producer rather than being only on screen. These looks"— she gestures to her face—"won't last forever. I want to avoid hitting thirty and losing out to a fresh face."

"Thirty is hardly old," Harper points out.

"Tell that to the producers and Heads of Programming, most of whom are men, which is why I want to break this ceiling."

I take in the determination on her face. "And you will," I say with certainty.

"Thanks for the vote of confidence." She rises to her feet. "I *am* really sorry to leave so soon."

"Oh, please. I'm just happy you could come. I know how busy your schedule can be."

A shadow passes over her features. "I'm sorry about that. But I'm trying not to let my work consume my life. Trying to make time for what's important, you know?"

I wonder who's put that sad look in her eyes. Hoping to lift her spirits, I respond, "Don't I know it. I've allowed work to take over my life. I'm also learning to make time for a personal life."

Zoey and Harper rise to their feet.

"Are you leaving, too?" I look between them.

"The boss left me in charge of the restaurant. I need to get back to prep for the evening service." Harper's voice is filled with pride.

I'm glad James gave her the responsibility of keeping things running in his absence. She's an amazing chef who deserves every success.

Zoey walks around, and when I rise to my feet, she hugs me. "I'd better get along, as well. "

Harper, too, hugs and kisses my cheek, then the three walk out. I take another sip of my coffee, before abandoning it completely. I take a bite of my sandwich. It tastes like cardboard, but I force myself to finish it. I know better than to go back to my shift on an empty stomach. I need the energy. When I'm done, I walk over to place my tray on a cart at the far end of the canteen.

I'm startled by a voice behind me. "Phoenix?"

I turn to find Brody standing behind me, and James is next to him. James holds a phone in a white-knuckled grasp. The other one is raised, palm face up. His jaw is hard. His face is expressionless, but something in his eyes makes the hair on the back of my neck rise. I shake my head. "No."

James' throat moves as he swallows.

"Phoenix"—his voice is gentle but with an urgency running through it—"it's Connor."

53

Phoenix

They kept him back, in exchange for the prisoners. He sent me that last message right before he left to meet with the rebels.

And somehow, I knew.

Knew his life was in danger before James came to me.

Knew, even before he left, that something was going to go wrong. That gut-deep dread, the kind you can't shake, sank into my bones the second he kissed me and said he'd be back soon.

I knew his life would be in danger, even before he left. That's why I didn't want him to leave.

And now, seven desperate days later, that same unshakable instinct is the only thing keeping me upright.

Because if something had happened—if the worst had happened —I would *know*. I would *feel* it in the hollow where my soul sits waiting for his return.

Each time despair claws at me, I fight it. I stare into the abyss of everything that can go wrong and refuse to give into it.

I can feel him in my heart. In my marrow.

With every breath I take, I know he's alive. He *will* come back to me. I believe in him. In us.

"Your presence made a difference today." The team leader of the Kandor outpost of the Save the Kids charity mops his forehead.

I arrived with James and Brody, to help Quentin facilitate Connor's safe return. And once we arrived, I kept busy, using my training as a trauma specialist to help the wounded.

"We are truly grateful for your help." The team leader smiles tiredly at me. He's employed by the charity and educated in England, though he's originally from a nearby province.

"It's the least I could do." I wrap my arms about my waist.

I've never been more grateful that I'm able to use my skill set to save lives.

The team leader runs his fingers through his graying hair.

"Get some rest. We don't need you running yourself into the ground." He pats my shoulder, then walks in the direction of the nurse who's been hovering in the background.

They're hugely short-staffed. When they found out I was a qualified trauma specialist, they welcomed me with open arms.

I can't remember the last time I slept. Or ate, for that matter.

Each time I close my eyes, I remember the last time I saw Connor's face.

How he lovingly swept his gaze over my features. How I felt something shift inside me. How I wanted to tell him I love him and, yet, held back. I wish I hadn't.

I wish I told him that before he left. Fatigue weighs at my eyelids. The team leader's right. I should rest up, but I'm too restless.

I head for the cabin that the team converted into the rescue operation's command center, to get an update.

I'm so preoccupied, it's only when my brother calls my name, I realize he's standing in front of me.

One look at my face, and his features soften in sympathy.

"He's a survivor. He knows how to think on his feet. This is the kind of situation he's trained for his entire career." James gestures to me to continue walking and falls into step with me.

"You never worked with him, did you?"

My brother shakes his head. The fact that he's left his Michelin-starred restaurant in the hands of his second-in-command and come down here to strategize with Brody and Quentin tells me how important Connor is to my brother.

"He specialized in undercover operations, while I was a Marine. So different proficiencies, but similar mindsets."

"Do you miss it?" I've never thought to ask James that before. But I'm realizing, there's a special edge that comes with being on the front lines. Not that I am... But being here, and seeing him in a different role, brings to mind that he used to be on active missions not very long ago, himself.

He pauses to consider, begins to nod, then stops.

"I don't miss not having the luxuries in life—like clean water and a comfortable bed, and being able to shave— But do I miss the adrenaline rush from being in life and death situations?" He inclines his head. "Hell, yes."

"You're such a jock," I scoff.

"Because I like the thrill of being in the thick of the action?"

"Because... You like being the one doing the rescuing."

"I suppose." He scratches his whiskered beard. "And so does Connor. Which is why I was surprised when he said he wasn't taking on any more missions in the field. He told me that right before he informed me you guys were eloping. That's when I knew he was serious about you."

"That's why you didn't turn up and stop us from eloping."

James looks at me like I've gone crazy. "This is Connor we're talking about. Nothing I said or did would have stopped him. Besides, it wasn't really my place to do so. Not when you're a grown up and know what you're doing with your life."

He winks.

"Besides... Once I was over the shock of Connor and you being together, I realized, there's no one else I'd trust to take better care of you."

A pressure builds at the backs of my eyes. Perhaps, it's because we're talking about Connor, and how we met feels like another lifetime, though it wasn't that long ago. Because now, I miss him even more desperately. And all the worries I've been trying to hide from myself rush to the fore. I've managed not to give in to the fears for Connor. I've refused to cry, even when I was alone. But maybe, it's the knowledge my brother won't judge me, and I can lean on him, which causes a tear to trickle down my cheek.

"Hey." James seems taken aback, then he pulls me into an embrace, "We're doing everything to get through to the rebels. If there's anyone who can bring him back, it's Brody, and Quentin, and—"

"We've got contact."

James and I turn to find one of the team members from the command center beckoning us. He's told me his name, but my state of mind is such, I can't recall it.

James and I quicken our steps and reach the cabin.

"A few minutes ago, we noticed activity at the rebel base."

I know, they've been monitoring it since Connor went inside to negotiate the release of the other hostages and the supplies.

"The gates opened, and an SUV drove out," the other man replies.

"Is he... Is he in it?" My heart somersaults into my throat. I don't want to get my hopes up. But I also want to stay positive. I want to...lean into the glimmer of expectation unfolding in my chest.

"We don't know yet. Brody's already set off, with three of the team, to intercept it." The team member keeps this voice steady. The glint in his eyes indicates he's buzzing with anticipation.

I pant as I keep up with the men's longer strides. I step into the operations room and am instantly hit with the tension that envelops everything and everyone inside like a pea soup fog.

One wall holds an intelligence board. Photos of what I know is the rebel camp, grainy thermal images, and handwritten reports are pinned to it. In the middle, someone's pinned a note. The language is the kind they use to outline missions in the military. I've read it so often, I have it memorized.

. . .

PRIORITY TARGET: CONNOR DAVENPORT
  Status: MIA – Deep Rebel Territory
  ENTRY 17 – LIVE EXTRACTION FEED: TACTICAL OPS

• Location: Sector Delta, Kandor – Pinged 06:14 via Drone 17
  • Visual: Last confirmed sighting—Connor, entering the rebel encampment in his SUV.
  Directive: Hold fire until ID is confirmed.
  Mandate: Whatever it takes. We bring him home.

Home. He's my home. He will be home.

The tears threaten again. I swallow them back. I am not going to cry. I'm going to be strong. For him.

A portable generator thrums outside. A ventilation unit spins in the corner, its blades fighting a losing battle against the heat trapped inside—air saturated with sweat, dust, and unspoken pressure.

Against one wall stands a reinforced table, cluttered with encrypted satellite phones, laptops displaying real-time data streams, and stacks of mission briefs annotated in grease pencil and digital overlays alike. Fiber-optic cables snake across the surface, connecting field routers to portable comms relays, their indicator lights blinking in silent conversation.

The wall above the table features a row of mounted monitors flickering with satellite feeds, heat-mapped terrain, drone footage, and a live comms dashboard. Each screen pulses with data: time-stamps, coordinates, flagged activity in red.

One shows a looping aerial scan of what I now know is the rebel corridor leading to the highway, which is the only route between the rebel camp and this one.

Another tracks NGO supply trucks in real time. On a third, there is live action unfolding. It's grainy, but I can make out an SUV. It's battered and has seen better days. There's a gun fitted to the top of the roof. A fist closes around my heart at that. I try to push the significance of what that gun means from my mind. He's going to be safe. He is.

The SUV crawls up the highway in the direction of our camp. *Hurry up,* I silently urge it along. It comes to a stop. The camera on the drone pulls back to show another SUV. This one carries the colors of Save the Kids. It drives up slowly and comes to a halt, perhaps, half a mile away from the rebels' vehicles.

"Tango-1. Visual on target. Holding position." A voice I recognize as Brody's comes over the comms console.

For a few seconds...minutes...nothing happens. Time stretches.

"What are they doing?" I whisper.

"Assessing the situation," James answers.

More minutes pass. My heartbeat kicks up. Sweat pools under my arms. I have my fingers clasped together so tightly, my hands feel numb.

Then, just when I think I'm going to scream from the tension, one of the doors of the rebel's SUV opens. A man steps out. He has on a desert scarf and wears a flowing shirt and loose pants, the kind of clothes favored by the rebels. But the shape of his shoulders, the way he walks... "Connor," I exclaim.

"Do you see him? Is that Connor?" James asks impatiently.

"It's Connor. Can't you see?" I snap.

"They just want Brody to confirm." James wraps his arm about my shoulder, but I'm so full of tension, I can't bear for anyone else to touch me right now. Unless it's Connor. *Connor!* I shake off James' hand.

I grab the back of the chair on which the operator who's managing the drone sits. "Can you zoom in?" I swallow. "Please."

"Do it," James orders.

He maneuvers a joystick. The camera on screen swoops in closer. There's no mistaking my husband's beloved features.

My knees threaten to collapse. This time, when James grabs my shoulder, I let him support me.

"What the fuck?" There's a surprised comment from the communications channel.

"What is it. What do you see?" James asks impatiently.

"One of the rebel's standing up through the roof hatch. He's reaching for the gun. Fuck —" His voice cuts off.

On screen, the hospital's SUV drives forward, then picks up speed. Connor must realize something is wrong, for he begins to run to meet it. That's when the gun behind him explodes. At the same time, men hang out from the Save the Kids SUV and return fire. I don't take my eyes off Connor.

"Run. Connor. Run."

I'm not aware I'm yelling until I hear my own voice. He's almost at the SUV, which comes to a stop. Arms reach for him. He raises his hand, then stumbles.

54

Connor

Despite the weakness of my body, my training kicks in.

The rebels' harsh treatment dulled my senses but didn't completely cut me off from myself. My mind zeroes in on the target, the way it has a million times before.

All I need to do is catch the hand outstretched before me... I take a few more steps, my fingers brushing those of Brody's.

I stumble and begin to fall, when he leans out, grabs me under my arms, and hauls me inside the SUV and into the footwell between him and the dashboard. My legs hang out. It's a tight fit, but goddamn, I'm so fucking glad to be here.

"Go, go, go," Brody yells at the driver.

The vehicle reverses. Meanwhile, I hear shots being returned. More shots fired. A bullet slams into the windshield, which cracks. Glass pieces shatter over us.

"What I wouldn't give to have a battle-ready, reinforced-armored vehicle," Brody growls. "Get us the fuck out of here."

On command, the driver executes a U-turn. The vehicle leaps forward. Brody hauls the rest of my body inside. I'm doubled up, but this is safer.

The men in the back seat hang out of the vehicle and return fire.

"Not long now. We'll be at camp soon. The rebels won't follow us there."

I know this, but it's good to hear it from someone else, too.

Brody pulls out a trauma bandage from his thigh pouch and jams it into my side. Pain shoots up my spine and explodes behind my eyes. "Fuck," I yell.

"You're shot."

"I'm aware," I say through gritted teeth.

"Best not bleed out. Phoenix won't be happy if you do."

At the mention of my wife's name, everything in me lights up.

Do I regret leaving her? Hell, yes.

Every second since I stepped into that godforsaken compound, I've thought of her. Her face is what's kept me going. The memory of her smile. The sound of her laugh. The way she says my name like it means something.

Has it been her, all this time, pulling me back from the edge? Her voice calling out to me when I've been unable to sleep at night. Her scent teasing me, evoking hope inside me every time I sank into despair.

Maybe, that's why I'm still breathing.

Why I'm still fighting. Because I need to get back to her. Because I want—*need*—to hold her again. To tell her the thing I should've said before I left.

I love her.

And I promised myself, if I make it out of this alive, I'm not wasting another second.

I'm going to tell her. All of it. Every messy, broken, desperate part of me—laid bare at her feet. Because she's it. My reason. My anchor. My home.

And I'm coming back for her. No matter what it takes.

Elation bubbles up in my chest. I can't wait to be reunited with her. *Her.* My wife. *Mine.*

The emotions push aside the pain. The fact that I'll be seeing her soon rushes to the front of my consciousness. I have no doubt, that's why Brody mentioned it.

"Nothing's going to happen to me." My voice weakens, my vision going black around the edges. *Fuck, I must be losing a lot of blood.*

Brody, too, must sense me fading, for he slaps my face.

"What the fuck?"

"Stay with me," he snaps.

"You've been waiting to do that since I kissed Miriam in fourth grade, when really, you had a crush on her all along." I manage to make my tongue form the words. *Why does my face feel numb? And why the fuck am I shivering?*

"That's exactly right." He reaches under the seat, pulls out an emergency blanket, and wraps it around me.

"Hold on, almost there." His voice is calm, but I see the strain on his face.

"If something happens to me—" I touch the sparkly hairband around my wrist.

I brought it with me when I left her.

"Nothing's going to happen to you," Brody growls.

"If something... Happens to me... Tell Phe... I'm sorry... I didn't...keep my promise and—" Darkness overwhelms me. I feel him slap my face again and manage to flutter open my eyes.

"You stay the fuck with me, Connor, you hear me?"

I manage to nod.

Then the vehicle screeches to a stop. Hands descend on me. I give in to the darkness.

My body feels weightless, untethered. The pain is gone. There are no more sensations. No heat, no cold, no breath. Only a vast stillness. And an overwhelming peace. It's so comfortable. Quiet. Serene. A soft, shimmering light in the distance beckons.

I gravitate toward it, reaching for it until—

"Connor."

Her voice lassoes around me, halting my progress. I'm suspended, unable to move.

"Connor!"

Her voice again, calling me back, dragging me to the surface. I don't want to go.

"Open your eyes."

I want to resist, but the insistence in her tone resonates with something deep inside me. I need to return.

I turn to the light one last time. I can't. Won't. Not yet. My eyelids twitch, then flutter open. And I see her.

Hazel eyes drowning in fear. Tears streaming down flushed cheeks. Her chin trembling. "Connor."

"I'm here."

She kisses my mouth.

The taste of her detonates in my bloodstream—a lightning strike of adrenaline, a tidal wave of life exploding through my veins.

With that, the pain returns, slamming into me with such force I gasp and cough.

Something beeps too loudly, too fast. Warmth crashes over my body—and with it, white-hot agony. I feel like I'm being sliced in two.

I groan aloud, closing my eyes against the relentless blows of pain.

"Don't you dare leave me," she cries.

Through the searing hurt, through the sensation of my body being torn in every direction, I snap open my eyes.

"You don't tell me what to do," I grit out.

Her gaze widens.

"Except this time." I try to smirk, end up coughing again.

She leans over me.

My last image is of her bitten lips. My last sensation, the edges of her hair brushing across my face. Then darkness pulls me under.

White. Everything is so white. And it smells of antiseptic. Even before I'm fully conscious, I know I'm in the hospital. Then, I remember seeing her before I passed out, and my eyes snap open. I take in the white walls, the sunshine pouring in through the windows. The muted beeps indicating machines are monitoring my progress. Then, like a heat-seeking missile, my gaze locks onto her and doesn't let go.

She's in a chair next to the bed, her fingers woven through mine. And her head is cushioned on her other arm, which is on the bed next to me. Her thick, dark eyelashes form a fringed crescent over her cheeks. Her luscious lips are slightly parted. There are dark circles underneath her eyes.

She was there when the vehicle arrived back at camp. I've no doubt, she jumped into trauma specialist mode and took care of me. I couldn't be in better hands. And then, she must have stayed up, keeping watch over me until I regained consciousness.

I don't want to disturb her, but she must sense me watching her, for her eyelids lift. She looks up, and our gazes collide.

For a second she freezes, then she jerks upright. "You're awake."

"I am." My voice comes out rough. My throat hurts. When I cough, she reaches for the drinking cup. Sliding her arm under my neck, she holds me, then urges me to drink from the straw. I draw the water in deeply, only stopping when the water runs out. The burn in my throat subsides somewhat.

She places the cup back on the side table, then plumps the pillows behind my head. When she's satisfied that I'm comfortable, she sits back. "How are you feeling?"

"Like I've been shot?" I chuckle, then wince when my ribs ache.

"Take it easy. You took a bullet to your left flank. It missed your vital organs, but it did fracture two of your lower ribs. There was a lot of bleeding. We had to manage the hemorrhage and drain some blood from around your lung. The good news is, the bullet didn't hit anything life-threatening. You're stable now, but we'll keep monitoring for any signs of infection or fluid buildup."

She doesn't meet my gaze as she reels off the diagnosis.

"You have been incredibly lucky." She swallows. "A few more millimeters either side, and you'd have been in critical condition. And thankfully, we had an air-ambulance on standby. We airlifted you to a hospital in Germany where they could operate on you."

"Germany?" I look around. "That's where we are?"

"It was the closest place with all the amenities needed. Once we stabilized you, we made the call to move you."

She keeps her gaze fixed somewhere over my right shoulder. I realize then, this entire experience was even more difficult for her than I imagined.

"Hey, Fever, look at me," I say softly.

She shakes her head.

"Phe, come on. I've been dreaming of looking into your eyes and seeing those gorgeous hazel-green eyes of yours when I kiss you."

"You shouldn't indulge in any such physical activity. Not until you're completely better." Her voice is stern.

"Oh?" I quirk my head. "Taking advantage of the fact that you're my doctor, are you?"

"You bet." Her eyes fill, but she blinks away the tears. "You were lucky. Infuriatingly lucky. You'd better focus on your recovery now."

I reach for her hand, half afraid she'll pull away. To my relief, she doesn't. "I know you're upset with me."

She firms her lips.

My chest tightens. I gave her reason to worry—reason enough to fear the worst. I swore I'd never to go into the field again, but this last assignment dragged me into danger and put my life on the line.

I hurt her. Not on purpose, but the damage is done. I swallow around the thickness in my throat. "I'm sorry I couldn't return to you earlier."

She knits her eyebrows. "You didn't have a choice but to walk into that rebel camp and trade yourself for the hostages. Don't get me wrong. I'm proud of you. But as your wife, it's my right to be upset that it was you who had to go in there and negotiate their release. And then, when you didn't return"—she sets her jaw—"I had every right to be pissed off with you for the danger you put yourself in. And every right to be angry with you for being such a humanitarian. Even though it's one of the things I admire most about you."

She brushes away her tears angrily.

"And when I saw you get shot..." She shakes her head. "It was... Horrible. I thought—" She chokes, then seems to find her voice. "I thought I'd lost you."

"I'm sorry. So sorry." I search her features. "I walked into the rebel camp, knowing I was putting myself in a vulnerable situation. But I knew it was the only way to get them to release the kids and the supplies that the charity so desperately needed. You were foremost in my thoughts. I knew it was going to be hell for you when news of my being taken prisoner reached you. But I was also confident I'd negotiate my way out with the insurgents. I was confident I'd get them to release me... I didn't know how soon that was going to happen, but I kept the faith. In the end, it was much longer than I expected.

"But you have to know, every moment I was in there, I cursed myself for what I was putting you through. This is what I wanted to avoid... This waiting game, when you wouldn't know what had happened to me. The only thing that got me through my time there was—"

I glance down at the now-empty wrist of my left hand.

"Looking for this?"

My head snaps up.

She's holding up her wrist. And wrapped around it—like it never left me—is the sparkly hair tie. Her hair tie. That silly, glitter-dusted, now sand-encrusted scrap I clung to like it was oxygen.

My breath catches, and for a beat, I forget how to move.

"I picked it up at The Sp!cy Booktok," I say through the emotions clogging my throat. "You stopped to peruse some books, and I found it after you left."

"You've had it all this time?" Her voice comes out hoarse, disbelieving.

"And thank God, I did. I wore that thing for luck before I left on the mission. I treated it like it was sacred. Pressed my lips to it when I couldn't sleep. All those days and nights, when everything around me was chaos—filth, noise, silence—it reminded me of you. Of that moment. Of your laugh, your scent, your goddamn stubbornness."

I let out a breath that's half-laugh, half-ache.

"It gave me hope that, come what may, I'd return to you."

I reach for her, fingers brushing the tie on her wrist.

"That little band of sparkles got me through hell. Because it meant you were real. And that somewhere out there, maybe, you were thinking of me too."

She twines her fingers through mine.

"It's inevitable that it happened this way." She sniffles. "I'm not upset with you. You helped free those kids. You saved so many lives. It made me realize how important your job is…and how good you are at it." She lowers her chin. "You shouldn't give it up for me."

"I'm giving it up for *me*." I stroke my thumb over hers.

When she shivers, something inside me relaxes. She might be upset, but her body knows me and can't stop its reaction to my touch.

"I want to spend time with you. I don't want to be away. And I definitely don't want to put you through this agony again."

She tries to smile, but her chin quivers. "I don't want to be so selfish. I don't want to take you away from the difference you can make."

"There are other ways to do it. Ways we could make a difference together."

She stills.

"Save the Kids is only one charity I'm involved with. And it, and many others, could benefit from having a medical doctor on the board. Someone who could better plan how to tackle medical emergencies around the world. As for me? My experience means I can make an even bigger difference by strategizing and deploying teams where needed at flashpoints around the world."

She doesn't seem convinced. "But wouldn't you miss the action. I saw your face when you got out of the rebels' vehicle. You were tired but you had this look about you… Like that of a warrior returning triumphant from battle. You had this swagger, like you knew you could pull it off and you'd done it."

"And then they shot at me anyway," I say wryly.

"You almost got away. You knew the team would be there to help you on the last few feet."

"I did," I confess. "And you're right. I will miss being in the action… But it's something I'll gladly give up so I can be with you."

I weave my fingers through hers.

"I want to spend every minute I can carve out with you. Talking with you. Seeing you smile. Working with you, side-by-side. Making you laugh. Making you cry out when I take you—"

She flushes.

"Holding your hand. Getting to know your secrets and your dreams. Understanding what makes you who you are. Going to sleep every night in the same bed as you. Waking up and seeing your face every morning, and knowing how lucky I am that you're in my life. That I get to have you with me as we navigate life."

"Connor"—she sniffles—"you're killing me,"

I wince. "I hope not."

"Sorry, wrong adjective. I mean... You make it very difficult to be upset with you."

"It's okay to feel that way. What happened wasn't easy on either of us. And while you're right—I felt triumphant that I'd convinced them it was too problematic to keep me and they were better off letting me go—every single second I was in there, I was thinking of you. All I could think was when I got back to you—and I would—I was never going to stop telling you that I love you."

55

Phoenix

The moment the words leave his lips, it's like a dam bursts inside me —everything I've held back, everything I buried to survive—surges free in a rush I can't contain.

It floods the walls I built around my heart, tearing them down, drowning me in the truth I've been too scared to proclaim.

"Every second you were away, I regretted not telling you that I love you. Every second of every day that the rebels kept you, I felt like I died a little inside."

My chest heaves. My fingers tremble. I'm almost giddy with the rightness of what I feel for him, as I clasp his hand.

"I realized, I was one-half of this entity that we became together, and without you, I was only half there. It was as if a vital part of me was missing. I knew, if you didn't come back, I wouldn't be whole again. I couldn't understand how I could feel this...strongly about someone I didn't even know until a month ago. Another part of me wasn't surprised about the intensity of my emotions. It felt almost organic. Predestined, maybe."

Tears burn the backs of my eyes, but I don't look away. Not now. Not when I have him back. Not when I can take in his beloved features to my heart's content and reassure myself that he's here. With me.

My throat tightens, thick with emotion.

"For someone who deals with science, I also know there's an unseen hand guiding everything. It's why I see miracles where none should exist. But I lost my faith when Drew died."

My whole body feels like it's vibrating with the truth of my words. I feel completely bare. Like I'm letting him look into my soul. And...it feels so right. I feel like I'm standing in the middle of a storm, but unafraid.

"I blamed myself for it. It was my way of dealing with my fears and insecurities. And then, when you traded yourself in for the hostages—it felt like that power was playing tricks on me again."

His face flickers—just a twitch of muscle—but I see it.

"Only this time... I knew, I couldn't lose you."

I curl my toes inside my shoes, trying to anchor myself to the moment. *He's fine. He's here. He's safe.*

"I couldn't let that happen to you. I had to...stop myself from being dragged back into that place I'd been after Drew. I had to... I knew, this time was different. I believed you'd come back to me. I believed in you. I believe in *us*. And I knew when you returned, I was never going to hold myself back again. I wouldn't let my insecurities run my life anymore."

My voice catches again.

"I'm never going to give in to my fears again. I'm never going to stop telling you how I feel about you."

"Say that again." His blue eyes deepen to a fierce indigo. The silver sparks seem loaded with intent.

"I'm never going to—"

He shakes his head. "What you said earlier."

I know what he means, but a streak of mischievousness pushes me to tilt my head. "I'm not going to give in to my fears?"

He scowls. "Fever," he says in that dark voice, "being my doctor only gives you so much leeway."

"Oh right—" I snap my fingers. "You mean, the part where I said I couldn't lose you?"

He makes a growling sound at the back of his throat. Then, this man who was shot less than twelve hours ago, who was sedated and operated on, and who still has IVs and various other equipment to monitor his vitals attached to him, tugs on my hand. I'm taken by surprise and lose my balance, falling half across his lap.

"You're hurt," I yelp.

"Not so much that I can't hurt *you*." He brings his hand—the one without the IV needled attached to it—down on my rump.

And he might be woozy from the loss of blood and the sedative, but the weight of his palm is heavy enough and sharp enough across my butt to send a tremor of heat flaring under my skin.

"Connor," I gasp.

"Say it," he demands.

I choose to misunderstand him again. "I believe in us."

Even before I complete the sentence—*Crack. Crack.* He brings his palm down over each of my butt cheeks. A throbbing erupts in my clit. My thighs tremble. Every part of me that turned to ice in the last ten days as I waited for news of him begins to thaw. Needles of pain skitter over my nerve endings. Like blood pouring painfully through extremities gone to sleep, sensations of heat and agony fan to life under my skin. It pushes at the sensations spiraling in my chest and squeezes them up my throat.

"I love you," I burst out.

"Again," he commands.

"I love you." Tears squeeze out from the corners of my eyes. "I love you. Love you. You."

"I fucking love you more than myself. You're my heart. My soul. You're the part of me that lives outside of me; the one I cannot survive without. You're the reason I'm alive. I'm so sorry for everything I put you through. I promise, I'll never cause you pain again. I promise, I'll always take care of you and be there for you. I'll never do anything to make you feel distressed. I love you, Fever, my wife."

He grabs me and hauls me up over his chest, over the bandage that's wrapped around his torso.

"Your ribs," I yelp.

"Fuck that."

This man... He doesn't even wince as he takes my weight on his poor, wounded body. I don't know whether to admire or be upset with him for behaving like a caveman. But then, he takes the choice out of my hands by holding my chin in place—this time with the hand that has the IV attached to it—and fixing his mouth on mine. The kiss...is hot and sweet and hard and demanding.

It's everything I dreamed of, and so much more I was unable to bring myself to hope for in the lonely nights we were apart. Because, yes, I was confident about him returning to me.

But while I couldn't let myself entertain the possibility, there was a small part of me that wondered if the universe had given me everything, only to take it away because I hadn't been properly grateful for it. If this was my punishment for not telling him that I loved him.

And with his hard mouth on mine and his tongue sliding over mine, his strong arms holding me and cradling me close to his beloved body, I allow myself to finally hope.

This. Here. With my man. This is right. With my husband. Mine. The kiss goes on and on. He kisses me like he didn't think he'd see me again. The desperation lights a fuse in my clit and sparks a fire in my belly. Trying not to hurt him more than he already is, I wrap my arm about his neck and pour myself into the kiss.

My head spins, and my heart expands in my chest, until I'm sure it's going to claw its way out. Oh, wait. My heart is outside. I'm holding it in my arms. And I came so closing to losing it all. To losing myself. I wouldn't have been able to go on if something had happened to him.

The realization sucker punches me further. All the fight goes out of me. I don't realize I'm trembling until he raises his head and scrutinizes me closely. "You're shivering."

"D-delayed reaction." I try to stop my teeth from chattering.

He brings me in closer to him, wincing when I press down on his bandages.

"You're not well. You just had surgery."

"As long as I have you in my arms, I'm fine."

He's wearing a thin hospital gown which does nothing to mask the heat of his body. I bask in it, giving in to the temptation of rubbing my cheek against his whiskered one. "Did you know you have gray in your beard?" I murmur.

"I need to shave."

I feel his lips curve.

"I actually like the makings of a beard. I like that it feels abrasive against my skin. And that you're marking me when I do this." I press my face against his stubbled jaw—hard enough for it to leave marks on me. "It feels like proof of life. That you're alive and real and here with me."

"There was no way I wasn't coming back; you know that, right?" He tucks a strand of hair behind my ear.

"I did." I cup the back of his neck, luxuriating in the feel of the soft hair at his nape. "I believed in you, but I also couldn't allow myself to hope, in case I jinxed things. I was trying to find this space where I could live moment-to-moment, not allowing myself to look too far into the future. Not setting myself up for disappointment. Then hating myself for thinking that way. I had to stop thinking and simply focus on putting one foot in front of the other. To keep myself busy working in the hospital and believe... That you'd be home soon."

"I'm sorry I put you through that." He stares deeply into my eyes, the silver sparks in those cerulean depths of his mesmerizing me. Holding me enraptured. Captured in that connection I have only with him.

"I'm sorry I didn't tell you that I love you sooner."

"You said it when you were ready. And that means more to me than anything."

"And you"—I lean in and bump my nose against his—"mean everything to me."

He presses his lips to mine, when the door to the room swings open.

I'm aware of someone stepping in but can't bring myself to pull away.

Brody clears his throat. "I guess that means he's on the mend?"

56

Phoenix

My cheeks flame, and I bury my face in Connor's neck.

"I know you two are married, but seriously, could you keep these activities behind locked doors?"

Eek, that's my brother.

"The door was closed, until you two walked in," Connor growls.

I should pull out his embrace, but I can't bear to be physically separated from him.

He must feel the same way for he draws me closer. "This isn't over." He kisses me again. The kiss seems to go on and on, until someone — Brody, I think, clears his throat.

Finally, Connor, lets me retreat to the chair. But he insists on holding my hand. I cling to his, like if I release him for even a few seconds he might disappear.

"I would have asked how you're feeling, but clearly —" James shoots us both a pained look. "I may have given your union my blessing, but can you two please avoid shocking me like this?" He lurks near the door, as if he doesn't want to risk coming too close for fear of being infected.

Brody, on the other hand, walks in and stands by the foot of the bed. "Good to know you're not dying."

"I have a long way to go." Connor scoffs. "Besides, I have a wife. I'm not going *anywhere* in a hurry...again."

We exchange a look, which instantly heats the air and spikes the energy in the room.

"Cut it out, you two," James snaps in a disgruntled voice.

I giggle. Connor smirks. I look at my brother over my shoulder. "Wait until you fall in love."

"That's never happening." He says it with the confidence of a bachelor who's hit forty and never managed to maintain a relationship of any significance.

"Only because you haven't met the right girl."

"Quit trying to get me paired off, just because you and Connor, here, can't stop making googly eyes at each other. I'm happy for the two of you. But leave me out of this love and marriage shit."

"Amen, bro." Brody raises a fist.

James finally ambles forward and bumps it with his. "When they started shooting at you, I thought you were a goner, ol' chap."

I make a sound at the back of my throat.

James' gaze widens. "Sorry about that, Phe. Didn't mean to upset you."

"It's...ah, okay."

"It's not." His features soften. "I didn't mean to upset you further. You've been a trooper these last few weeks. You held your own. Didn't break down. Kept yourself busy and useful at the hospital. You must have been beside yourself with worry, but you didn't let it show. Didn't let it get you down."

He smiles, a proud look in his eyes.

"I knew you were a determined girl, but I didn't realize you'd grown into a woman to be admired."

My cheeks flush scarlet. To detract from that, I tip up my chin. "My brother, the grim, forbidding, bad-tempered chef, showering me with praise. If only the rest of your team could see you now."

"Better not tell them. It would only spoil my reputation." He grimaces. "Speaking of, I need to fly back to London. I've left my kitchen too long."

"I'm sure your kitchen is in safe hands. Didn't you ask Harper to run it in your absence?"

"Exactly." His gaze grows thunderous. "There was no one else, so it had to be her." He curls his fingers into fists. "Trust me, if I had anyone else I could have asked to take over, I would have. But sadly, my sous-chef was the only one available. I'm not sure what state it's going to be in when I get back."

My brother is demanding, but I've never seen him this agitated. "Is it the fact that you don't trust her that's the issue, or is it her that's bothering you?"

He looks at me like he has no idea what I'm talking about. Oh, well. This is something James and Harper have to sort out. And for the record, my money's on Harper.

"Either way, I'm glad you made it back in one piece," he says.

"Thanks for coming, man, and for being there for Phe, and for supporting Quentin and Brody."

"Yep, you were there when we needed a safe pair of hands." Brody slaps James' back.

"You're welcome." James walks over and kisses my forehead. "You take care of yourself, Sis. Get some rest, huh? And you—" He holds out a hand to Connor, who squeezes it. "I'm looking forward to seeing you at my restaurant for a celebratory wedding dinner, on me."

The food at James restaurant is pretty amazing, and except for the one time that Connor took me, I've never been, so I'm happy to go ahead.

"I'll come on one condition," I say slyly.

"Uh-oh, why do I think I'm going to regret this already?" James asks mildly. "But go ahead." He jerks his chin at me. "What's the condition?"

"You let Harper cook for us."

He seems taken aback, then nods. "Why not, eh?" A wicked

gleam comes into his eyes before he schools his expression into a nonchalant one.

"Uh-oh, why do I think I'm going to regret this already?" I murmur.

Connor chuckles.

Brody laughs.

James merely shakes his head. "You better watch out, Davenport"—he smirks at Connor—"this one is going to be a handful."

"Why do you think I fell in love with her?" Connor kisses my forehead.

"On that note…" James steps back, spins around, and heads to the door. "See you back in London, folks."

He shuts the door after him.

"How long do I have to be here?" Connor turns to me.

"Until the doctors discharge you?"

"You're enjoying having me helpless, at your mercy, aren't you?" he asks silkily.

"You're as helpless as an apex predator." I toss my head. "I conferred with the consultant in charge, and we feel you should be here for at least another twenty-four hours. Once your pain level reduces, and we're satisfied with your progress, we'll get you home, okay?"

"You should listen to her." Brody smiles widely. "I, for one, am enjoying seeing you being brought to heel."

"Only because I'm enjoying it, too." Connor gives me a look which can only be described as sultry.

I can't stop smiling because everything feels so easy between us. And yet, there's this undercurrent of chemistry between us that turns every interaction into a game. A very sexy, very arousing, and very stimulating game.

The sound of a phone vibrating reaches us. We turn in Brody's direction to find he's pulled out his phone. He checks it, then groans. "The old man is at it again."

"What does Arthur want?" Connor asks in resignation.

"Another excuse to get everyone together. This one, to mark your safe return and also, because he never got to throw the two of you a wedding celebration."

57

A month later

Connor

"He wants us to play...croquet?" I pause on the patio of Arthur's villa in Primrose Hill. On the sprawling lawn in the backyard which faces the expanse of the Hill, is a set up with six mallets of different colors.

Six corresponding balls, six hoops—which is what they call the metal arches the ball passes through, and one center peg, or the stake, placed at the far end of the lawn, which in this case, doubles up as the court.

"Croquet?" Brody's jaw drops.

"Cro-fucking-quet?" James, who's walked in behind us, scowls.

"Croquet? How charming." My wife beams at the setup.

She no longer has dark circles under her eyes. Her shoulders are no longer tense. I attribute that to my doing my duty as her husband and making sure I make sweet love to her every night.

Thanks to the money I donated to the ER, there's a new crop of residents to help carry Phe's load in the trauma bay. She no longer has to worry about the ER closing, either. I'm chuffed I was partly responsible for that too.

Anything I can do to make her life easier gets priority.

She's my priority.

"The old man expects us to play croquet as some kind of bonding exercise?" Brody scratches at his whiskered chin. "It's fucking irritating, is what it is."

"Everything okay?" I eye him closely.

His eyes are bloodshot. He hasn't shaved. His hair is standing up on end like he's run his fingers through the strands. It's the first time I've seen him look this disheveled.

"It's been brutal at work. My assistant managed to keep things going while I was away, but since I've been back, she seems to be distracted. Enough that I have to pick up the slack." He yawns.

"Thank you for coming to my rescue. I wouldn't be here without you."

He draws himself up to his full height, then pushes his forefinger into my chest. "Firstly, you'd have done the same. And secondly—" He smirks. "This way, you owe me one."

"Anytime, Brother." I hold up my hand, and he squeezes.

We half hug, slap each other on the back.

"You must have an exceptional assistant if she kept the company running in your absence," my wife remarks.

"Hmm." He cracks his neck. "She was only doing her job. But you're right, I should probably give her a raise."

Phe's forehead furrows. "You should definitely let her know how much you appreciate her contribution. Good employees are hard to come by."

"What's she going to do, leave?" His voice is light, but a troubled expression flits across his features.

My wife and I exchange a glance. Brody has a good heart, but between his cavalier attitude to finding love and his brush off when it comes to his assistant, I have a feeling my brother has some tough lessons to learn.

James eyes him closely. "Is that a gray hair at your temple?"

"I believe, the word you're looking for is distinguished, as in, 'You look distinguished.'" Brody straightens to his full height.

"It suits you," Phe assures him.

When I scowl, her features soften. "You have nothing to be jealous about, honey. You know I only have eyes for you."

She runs a finger down the front of my button-down shirt sleeve, my concession to coming to see my grandfather, when I'd much rather be in shorts and T-shirt, sprawled on my couch with my wife at my side. My idea of heaven.

Previously, I'd have looked down on the idea of being home instead of gallivanting around the world on another of my missions, or working in the lab on another scientific discovery I could patent.

Now that I've met her, I realize how hollow those endeavors truly are without someone by my side to share them.

I promised her I won't be in the field, and I'm sticking to that.

At Phe's insistence I have, however, begun discussions with the MI5 to work as a consultant. I'll put my expertise to good use by making missions safer for those in the field. Running missions is part of my DNA. My wife was wise enough to recognize that. And I'd be doing myself, and her, a disservice if I ignored that part of me completely.

Now that I control my patents, I can be assured that the royalties they generate—along with funds from my trust—are used to fund charities that need help. This gives me a deep sense of satisfaction.

It also allows me to feel more complete, which means, I can better care for my wife.

She slides her arms around my waist, then goes up on tiptoes and offers me her mouth. I pull her close, dip my head, and kiss her. As soon as our mouths meet, I'm lost. Her taste, the sweetness, that familiar softness, interspersed with the lick of lust gathering at the base of my spine. Fuck. I want to throw her over my shoulder, walk out of here, and go home. I want to fuck her, then make sweet love to her.

"I know she's your wife, but she's also my sister, and it's taking everything in me not to tear you from her and bash your face in," James growls.

I can understand how uncomfortable it is for James to watch the two of us. Not that I fucking care. She's mine. And it's time everyone, especially her own family, get used to the idea. On the other hand, if it weren't for James, I wouldn't have met her. That's the only reason I step back from my wife.

"Get a room." Brody walks past us.

I wrap my arm about Fever and tug her forward. "Might as well as get this over with."

"A bit like pulling off a bandage, then." James grimaces, then squares his shoulders. "Perhaps, some strong refreshments are called for?" He follows Brody.

I realize they're headed toward the farthermost corner of the garden, where a bar has been set up.

"Is that the single men's commiseration corner?" My wife follows James' progress. He steps to where Brody huddles with Toren, Adrian, and Viktor.

"From what I hear, these men have struck up a friendship outside of these gatherings which Arthur instigated," she adds.

"That's an interesting and very powerful mix of men. I wouldn't want to fuck with them individually. Put them together, side-by-side, and they're invincible in the business world." I purse my lips and contemplate the lot of them, then shake my head.

"Nah, not possible."

"What?" My wife shoots me a sideways glance.

"It's nothing. A passing thought." I shake my head.

"Aww, come on. You can't leave me hanging like that, surely?"

I shrug. "One would almost think that's why Arthur invites them to these family functions."

She surveys them. "You mean, Arthur keeps throwing them together, so they'll turn to each other and form some form of alliance?"

"Sounds far-fetched, right?" I chuckle. "Not even my cantankerous gramps is smart enough to have anticipated this…" *Right?*

Milling about on the lawn are the rest of my brothers and their wives. Nathan nods in my direction. My uncle Quentin, who's standing nearby with his wife tucked into his side, flashes me a thumbs-up sign. I head for him, with Phoenix in tow. "I never got to thank you for the role you played in helping me get home safely."

He rushed off while I was in recovery, as he wanted to return home. Seeing how Vivian is wrapped around him like they can't bear to be parted, I get why.

"Glad I could be of help." He smiles at us. "And very happy to see the two of you together."

"All right, gather up, everyone." Imelda's voice reaches us.

All of us look in the direction of the patio, where Imelda stands with Arthur next to her. He uses a cane nowadays—apparently, Imelda coaxed him to do so—and while he looks gaunt, he still seems sturdy and happy as he surveys us, his family.

"He loves his role as patriarch of the family," Nathan muses.

"I don't see him relinquishing it anytime soon," I affirm.

"He deserves it. Let the old man bask in the glory of his machinations." Quentin chuckles. "After all, the lot of us are married and happy, thanks in no small part to his devious calculations."

Much as I hate to agree, he has a point.

Imelda nods in the direction of the croquet pitch.

"We're going to play a doubles tournament. Two teams of two each. Each player will have one ball. Choose your sides peeps, and—"

The ringing of a phone cuts through her sentence.

Arthur glowers.

All of us turn in the direction of Brody, who holds up his phone. "Sorry, chaps. It's work. They'd only call if it were an emergency."

He answers, voice clipped. "Davenport."

Silence blankets the group as we listen.

"Calm down. Speak slowly, so I can understand what you're saying."

A pause.

"It is?" His jaw tightens.

More silence. Then—

"Ask my assistant to take care of it."

Another beat. His shoulders go rigid. "She *what?*"

He rubs the back of his neck. "I'll be there."

He pockets his phone, nods once to the group. "Office emergency. I need to go."

As he strides past us, he pauses and half bows to Fever and me. "I've no doubt, you'll keep each other out of trouble."

I arch a brow. "Looks like *you're* the one with trouble brewing."

"Don't you have a team for this kind of thing?" Fever asks.

Brody scowls. "I do. And normally they're solid. But this time..." He drags his palm down his jaw. "This time, *my team* is the emergency."

To find out what happens next read Brody and Lark's story in The Christmas Trap

Read an excerpt

Brody

"You're breaking up with me?"

My assistant's voice seems to detonate. Sharp, clear, devastating.

Her back is ramrod straight; fury carved into every line of her petite frame. Her shoulders are drawn so tightly, they could slice through steel. And her tush—that wicked, perfect curve I've tried damned hard not to fixate on every time she walks into my office—trembles with suppressed rage.

I clench my fists at my sides. I want to palm those full, trembling cheeks—yes, the ones I've admired far too long under the guise of professional detachment—and anchor her to something steady. Something safe. Something like me.

I want to march over, haul her into my arms, and press her up against my chest until every hard, angry breath she takes syncs with mine.

The bastard she's talking to stands there, eyes downcast, wearing the dumb, apologetic expression of a man who doesn't deserve to breathe the same air as her. I want to rip his head off. Want to put myself between them like a damn human shield.

I'm lurking at the entrance to her office, which adjoins mine. I listen in on her conversation because, apparently, she also turns me into someone who lacks basic courtesy. Because where Lark Monroe is concerned, I can't help but get involved.

She's going to be furious I didn't even afford her the privacy of not watching her personal life implode. Because I am the only person who can save her from the disappointment that's so palpable, it shimmers off her like rays of light bouncing off a windshield.

I've made her exasperated. I've pushed her to the edge with impossible deadlines, outrageous demands, tight turnarounds. I've gotten my twisted kicks watching her struggle, fluster, then pull off the impossible with a silent glare and a twitch of those arched brows.

But this isn't one of those moments.

This isn't a game.

This is personal.

To hear someone else be the reason she sounds so upset draws a line of fire through my veins. No one gets to draw such extreme emotion from her but me.

I've never hated anyone more than I hate the man standing in front of her, breaking her heart in the most humiliating way possible.

"You've turned me into a living cliché." Her voice cracks, raw with betrayal.

Something primal snarls awake inside me.

Because Lark is my employee. She's mine to protect. Mine to comfort. *Mine.* I'm done pretending otherwise.

I stalk inside her office. The two are so caught up in their drama, they don't notice me.

"You have some nerve, telling me that you're in love with my bridesmaid and want to marry her instead of me. Ugh!" She digs her fingers through the hair piled up on top of her head.

The pencil she stabbed through the rich blonde mass to hold it up slides to the ground. Her hair comes tumbling down. I freeze.

She was about to get married?

My personal assistant, who I speak to more times a day than

anyone else—yes, it's largely by email, but still, I type out her name more than anyone else's—was on the verge of getting hitched? How was I not aware?

If she gets married, who'll take care of the day-to-day operations of my business?

Yes, that's a selfish thought, but I'm a CEO. My company takes priority. And she's invaluable to my company. Ergo, she's invaluable to me. Only because I care about the bottom line of my business, of course.

I take another step forward.

I'm aware of the exact moment Lark notices me, for her entire body snaps to attention. Her spine turns even more rigid. I've noticed how on edge she gets around me.

At first, I thought it was because I overwhelmed her—because the weight of my presence, my authority, was too much for her.

But I see it now. It's not intimidation. It's awareness. Acute. Unavoidable. Electric.

That hum I keep brushing off—the one I feel every time we share air—isn't about her being unnerved by the control I carry.

It's the current between us. Chemistry, sharp as static electricity.

She feels it just as much as I do. And it's not fear I see in her eyes—it's recognition. Of me. Of this.

She angles her body slightly away from the stranger and in my direction. As if she's seeking my help?

She's doing it unconsciously, not aware of the plea for help she's sending out. Unable to resist, I draw abreast and wrap my arm about her waist.

I sense the shock ripple through her. She stiffens, growing so still, she could be mistaken for a pillar of stone.

"How dare you walk in here and insult her?" I glare at the man opposite.

He grows so pale, I wonder if he's going to puke. What a pussy. And this...this sorry excuse for a human was the person she was going to marry. Seriously, she could do better. Much, much better. In fact, I can't think of anyone who'd make a good husband for her. She's incomparable. There's no one who'd be good enough for her.

"Wh-Who're you?" The other man swallows.

"I'm her boss."

As if the sound of my voice pulls her out of her reverie, Lark tries to pull away.

I tighten my arm around her and hold her in place. "I'm also the man who's madly in love with her."

What the — Where did that come from? I did want to say or do something that'd wipe that smug expression off his face, but...

"Love?" The other man's jaw drops.

"Love?" She jerks her chin in my direction. The shock on her face is almost comical. Only, it's followed by panic and horror. *Is the thought of my being in love with her such a terrible thought?*

I glance down at her angelic face. "Yes, baby. I'm sorry if this comes as a surprise. But from the moment I saw you, I knew there was no one else for me."

"Wh-what?"

She draws in a breath. Another. Opens her mouth to, no doubt, protest, so I place a finger over her mouth. "Shh, it's okay darling. I understand how overwhelming this must be for you. But I want you. I understand your value in my life. Unlike this clown." I aim a disgusted look at him before looking back into her eyes. "I can't do without you, sweetheart."

She makes a gurgling sound. Her eyes behind her specs grow so big, they seem to fill her face.

"I want you to come home with me, so I can introduce you to my family."

She blinks rapidly, her face growing a shade of pink which is, frankly, adorable. Then she seems to pull herself together and scowls. "This is not funny," she hisses under her breath.

"No, it's not." I shoot an angry sideways glance at the asshole who's staring at us. "I should bash this wanker's head in for the grief he's caused you."

"Why are you making fun of my predicament?" She makes this growling noise at the back of her throat, which makes her sound like an angry kitten. She's so darn cute. Best not let her know that's what I'm thinking.

I say aloud, "I'm serious."

The expression in my eyes must back up my intent, for she blinks. "I have no idea what you're up to, but it's completely inappropriate."

"Why would it be when I'm going to marry you?" Uh... Okay... Didn't know I was going to say that until this moment.

She gapes at me. "Did you fall down and knock your head? Is that why you're spewing this crazy stuff at me?"

"Do I sound like I'm crazy?"

She searches my features and consternation filters into her expression. "You're not making any sense. You're my boss. I'm your assistant. You barely look at me, except for when there's work to be done. Even then, you barely seem to acknowledge my existence."

"Oh, I acknowledged your existence, all right. I just couldn't let on to you how much it affected me. After all, as you pointed out, I'm your boss. And I didn't want you to feel uncomfortable. Besides, you were getting married, so what could I say? But now that I know you're not, I can tell you the truth. I love you."

She shakes her head. "This is crazy."

"It is," I murmur, my gaze locked on hers. "I'm *crazily* in love with you."

The words hang there, shocking even me with how right they feel. I said them to mess with her head. To get under her skin. To make her ex wish he'd never drawn breath, let alone walked away from her. But now? Now, they feel real. And true.

Because, luckily for me, that asshole did walk.

And now she's free.

Free—and mine.

Mine to help. Mine to protect. Mine to heal. That's what I tell myself. What I need to believe. That I'm doing this only to take care of my employee. Which is all she is. Right?

She throws up her hands, eyes flaring. "I don't know what's gotten into you, but you need to stop this travesty."

Her voice is sharp, but it's the fire behind her words that slices straight through me. That fury. That fight. Something inside me frac-

tures and reforms around it. Like a bone breaking just so it can heal
stronger.

Maybe it's this moment—this exact second—when I start falling
for her for real.

"You're right," I say, voice low, deliberate.

She blinks. "I am?"

I nod slowly. "I need to show you how serious I am."

I take her in like I've never seen her before—those lips that look
too soft for someone who fights so hard, the rise and fall of her chest
like she's barely keeping it together. Her pulse flutters at the hollow
of her throat—wild and erratic, like mine.

And even as I lean in—close enough to smell that unique feminine scent of hers—I know I shouldn't be doing this. She's just been
wrecked. She's vulnerable. And I'm walking straight into her life like
I've got a right to fix everything for her.

But hell, maybe I *do*.

Because the second I walked in and saw the devastation in her
eyes, I knew I'd do anything to erase it. I'd burn the world down if it
meant she'd smile again.

Helping her through this breakup isn't just the decent thing to do
—it's essential. I can't have her falling apart on the job. She's the
backbone of my entire operation. But it's more than that.

Because I'm going to make damn sure her ex knows what he lost
when he walked away from her. That he let go of a goddess. And I'm
the one lucky enough to see it now.

I lower my head.

Her gaze snaps to mine—wide, startled. She sees it. Feels it. The
shift in the air. She knows what's coming.

She realizes my intent a heartbeat before I close my mouth over
hers.

Lark

He's going to kiss me.

He's going to kiss me.

He is kissing me.

My boss is kissing me. My hot boss, who I've eyed from a distance but never dared give any sign I had a crush on him, is kissing me. He has his arm about my waist and is holding me close to his big, broad, manly chest. The chest I've peeked glances at because I'd have to be blind not to notice how he fills out his jacket. How his sculpted torso is outlined against that white shirt. The corrugated plane of his pecs threatening to pop the buttons.

The powerful thighs I'm brushing up against leave me with a sense of coiled muscles and unleashed energy, like the turbocharged vibrations swelling from a rocket about to blast off into space. Then, the sensation of his lips on mine takes over. Softness. How could his mouth be this soft when the rest of him is like leaning into a brick wall? He holds me with such care. Like I'm the most precious thing in this world. Like I'm a jewel, and he's the velvet casing enclosing me. Cocooning me from the vagaries of this world.

There's no missing the protectiveness in his stance as he cradles my head with a big hand at the back of my head, the other grasping my waist like we're one of those entwined figures in a music box. And the song playing in my head is, surely, brought on by how tenderly his mouth brushes over mine? Once, twice.

Then, his grasp on my head slides to the back of my neck. A shiver squeezes my spine. The possessiveness is unmistakable, as is how he squeezes the curve of my hip. He pulls me into the cradle of his thighs, the coiled power in them giving me the confidence that he could hold up my weight. He draws me in closer until, *bam-bam-bam*, his heartbeat rocks against mine. That dark, peppery scent of his intensifies in my nostrils.

The heat of his body hits me like a solar flare—bright, blinding, magnetic—rushing through my chest and wrapping around me with the force of gravity itself.

My knees grow weak. I sway forward, and he tightens his hold on the nape of my neck. A full body shudder rolls over me. My stomach seems to bottom out. It's as if I've boarded a roller coaster and am being pulled up that first incline, knowing what's coming up, knowing it's going to swoop down, and being unable to stop that inevitable sinking sensation.

He flattens his fingers so I can feel each individual fingerprint like a brand through the fabric of my dress. Then, he bites down on my lower lip. I feel it all the way to my toes. I gasp, and he licks into my mouth, the touch of his tongue against mine an explosion of emotions. Taste. Dark and complex. Sensations like sparks left in the wake of a shooting star. A sweetness so unexpected, it's mind-blowing. A tenderness, a sense of being cared for that's so surprising, so heady, so unexpected, it cuts through to my core. I didn't expect that.

I fantasized about kissing my boss, of course. About being held in his big brawny arms and pressing my palm into his sweaty chest, feeling the aliveness of the blood throbbing through his veins, and sensing the unforgiving strength of him, which was so evident, even clothed in his expensive suits. But this...gentleness, this sense of safety washing over me in his arms is unexpected.

The world around us recedes. The fact that my ex is watching only turns the sparks coursing through my veins into a full-blown fire. It burns through the barriers I throw up against the world, against him. I forget where I am. That I'm his employee. And he's my boss. I'm only a woman, held against a man who seems to cherish me and want me, and is trying to comfort me. Subconsciously, a part of me realizes that he's doing this to make my ex jealous, that, in all likelihood, all of this is an act, because he noticed the drama he walked in on and is trying to prove I'm desirable. But another part of me doesn't care.

After being dumped in such a cold-blooded fashion, my wounded ego wants to bask in the attention of this gorgeous specimen of the male species who I ogled from afar but knew was never going to be within reach. So, to find myself in his arms is...as much of a surprise as the earth rotating anti-clockwise. And maybe, it's never going to happen again. And who cares if this is inappropriate? The way he makes me feel is like the most beautiful, most wanted woman in this world, and I'm going to make the most of it.

I rise up on my tiptoes, and when I part my lips, he slants his face, slashes his lips over mine, and then the kiss is everything I imagined it would be from the meeting of our lips. Hard, insistent, demanding and so very hot. Sensations zip through my bloodstream. I feel the touch all the way to the roots of my hair, and my fingertips, and the heels of my feet. Ohmigod, it's like I've been caught in the swell of a wave and am being raised higher and higher to the heavens. Like I'm having an out-of-body experience. Like I'm somewhere high up, looking down on the two of us, our breaths entwined, mouths clinging to each other. His self-assured, firm grip on my neck holding me up, and turning me on, and supporting me, at the same time. And me, clutching his shoulders, aware of the smoothness of his jacket under my fingertips, and that bone deep, head spinning sensation of his tongue dancing with mine.

My heart pounds in my chest like a butterfly trapped in a bell jar, my pulse rate spiking so high, I'm scared I'm going to black out. The kiss seems to go on and on, and at the same time, it's too short because it's suddenly over.

I sway and become aware that he's holding me up. His hand is on the nape of my neck, the other on my hip,

My world has tilted, my points of reference changed. My expectations for a kiss dramatically elevated. I know, I'll never be satisfied by meeting my lips with anyone else's.

My palate is coated with his taste, my mouth full of the remembrance of how his tongue swiped against mine. My heart feels like it's in free fall, my emotions swooping over mountains and dipping down into the valleys between them like an eagle riding the air currents.

I stare at him, lips still imprinted with the shape of his.

My ex clears his throat. "Uh… What… What's the meaning of this? Lark… You… What are you doing? This man—"

"Is going to take care of her the way you never would have been able to. You had your opportunity, buster, and you blew it." My boss jerks his chin in the direction of the doorway. "Beat it, will ya?"

"B-b-b-ut, I—"

"Best be gone, before I call security. I'll have you thrown in prison, and I'm sure you'll be someone's bitch before the week is out, so get the hell out before I make good on my promise."

"Look here, there's no need to get personal," my ex blusters.

My boss, without taking his glowing golden gaze from mine, lifts one hand, swipes it out, and grabs the other man's collar. With one quick move, he's pushed him back with enough force that my ex stumbles. He also seems to get the message; he makes tracks toward the doorway. Where he pauses. "Anyway, it's not like she can satisfy any man in bed. She's frigid. So, you can keep —"

My boss turns his head slowly in the direction of my ex, who freezes. Whatever he sees on my boss' face is enough to have him swallowing audibly.

"Leave. Now." My boss's voice is like a whip cracking out in his direction. It seems to catch him with the impact of a bodily blow, for he pushes the door open and lurches out. It swings shut behind him.

I am so mortified. The heat sears my cheeks. My stomach ties itself in knots. The ignominy of what he said... Aloud. Argh. And in the presence of a man who's so virile, he seems to breathe out pheromones. I try to move back, but my boss' hold on my neck tightens... Just for a second. Then he releases me, stuffs his hands into his pockets and stares into my face. "You okay?"

I shake my head.

"Why don't you sit down?"

I'm too much in shock to compute how to place one foot in front of the other.

"I'm going to guide you to your chair, okay?"

I stare at him.

"Nod if you understand."

I nod.

He takes my hand, the touch like a thousand little fireflies fluttering against my skin and leads me to my chair. He pulls it out, turns it to face us and guides me to sit in it. When I'm seated, he picks up the glass of water on the desk and hands it to me.

"Drink it."

I do. I don't stop until it's empty. Then hand it back to him. That's how much in shock I am. But the water does revive me enough to blink. "What was that all about?" I whisper.

"That...was me showing your ex, what he's missing out on."

"I… I guessed that." I swallow.

"Guessed what?" He places the glass down on the table.

"That you were trying to make him jealous. But you heard him, he doesn't think I'm worth marrying anyway."

He glares at me. Those golden eyes of his seem to blaze with an anger arising from the core of his being. I swallow. He looks enraged. Reminding me of why I've kept my distance from him so long. He's not the kind of man who can be tamed. With his shaggy hair and massive build, and those amber eyes, I've nicknamed him The Lion. And now, I'm reminded why.

"You're better than to believe that loser."

"Doesn't change what he said." I hunch my shoulders. "I'm… Uh… Clearly, not good enough to keep him."

"Fuck him."

His voice is so harsh, I flinch.

"He has no idea what he's let go of. It was his good fortune that he even had a chance to have you in his life. He didn't appreciate you, which is why he cheated on you. You're better off without him. Also"—he slides a hand into his pocket, and stares down at me from his superior height—"you forget that I kissed you. And going by your response, I can promise you, you're anything but frigid."

I blush to the roots of my hair, then look down at where I'm twisting my fingers in my lap. I wish I could sink through the floor. I wish I were anywhere but here. Isn't it enough that he kissed me, and instead of pushing him away, I enjoyed it? And now, he has to point out my response to him?

"I realize, you were trying to help me, but I'm not sure what that kiss accomplished."

"Other than making him realize how much of a terrible mistake he made by letting you go, you mean?"

I hear the smugness in his voice and glance up, and further up— God, he's tall. And sitting down, with him towering over me, I'm struck again by the powerful figure he cuts in his immaculate suit.

It also means I'm at the level of his crotch. *Don't look there. Don't.* I manage to keep my gaze on his.

"I suppose, you have a point. But it's not going to help me when I email all the guests I invited to my wedding. Or tell my parents that I'm not getting married, after all. Not to mention, the money I put toward the caterers at the pub where our reception was going to be held." I wince.

That money could have been used toward paying down some of my student loans, or my next month's rent.

But really, the worst thing will be the pity that'll come my way when the news spreads. I sink back in my chair and wrap my arms about my waist.

"This is terrible. What am I going to do now?"

"What do you mean?"

"You have no idea what it means to call off a wedding when you're one of the normal working class, do you?"

"Tell me." He sinks down to one knee in front of me, then rests an arm across his thigh like he's settling in to wait.

"What are you doing?" I laugh nervously.

"I want to understand."

"Umm... Don't you have your next meeting to go to?"

"It can wait."

I flick my gaze to his calendar, open on my computer. "It's the meeting with the CEO of that company whose takeover you've been planning for months."

"It can wait."

I frown. "You've been wanting to seal the deal for months."

"I want to seal this deal too."

"Excuse me?" I whip my head around in his direction. "What does that mean?"

"I mean, I want to understand what's the result of him having broken his deal with you."

"Oh." I swallow as disappointment hits me again. For a minute, I thought he meant to seal the deal with me—by marrying me. Once again, I wring my hands together. Only, he reaches out and places his hand on mine. I freeze.

Instantly, he pulls his arm back. "I'm sorry, I don't want to make you uncomfortable."

"Umm... You kissed me... I think we're way past that."

"Hmm." He drags his thumb under his lip. "Is the fact I kissed you the problem, or that your response took you by surprise?"

I slowly raise my gaze to his. "Both."

He nods. "Thank you for your honesty. I kissed you because I could not bear to see how unhappy you were. And I was pissed off that… That knobhead cheated on you. I wanted to do something to make it better for you. And I thought the best way was to show him what he was missing. I knew that the moment he thought there was someone else interested in you, he'd regret his actions. So—" He shrugs one massive shoulder.

"He was pissed off, all right. And it didn't hurt at all that he watched us kissing," I say with satisfaction. "But it doesn't change anything." Anger squeezes my chest. Frustrations knots my guts. I blow out a breath. "Best I call city hall to cancel our appointment and send out emails to let people know the wedding isn't taking place."

A burning pressure builds behind my eyes, hot and sharp. I'm going to hate myself by the time this is over. Every call. Every email. Every humiliating explanation.

"I wish you didn't have to go through that," he says quietly. But there's a thread of steel running through his words, one which makes me blink.

"There's no way around it." I rub my temple, jaw tight. "I was paying for the wedding. Should've been my first clue about the kind of man he really was."

My head drops back against the chair. "And then he slept with my bridesmaid. My best friend. God—" My voice catches. "I still can't believe she'd do that."

He studies me for a beat. "What if you didn't have to make those calls? Or cancel everything?"

I blink at him. "Then I'd lose the downpayment on the pub. And trust me, I can't afford that."

His eyes narrow slightly, something unreadable flashing across his face. "You wouldn't have to lose anything. You could still have the reception. Somewhere better."

Frustration squeezes my chest. "Can you please stop talking in riddles already?" I frown. "I'm in no condition to figure out what you're saying."

"I mean exactly what I said. You could still have the celebration. Just...not the wedding you planned."

"That doesn't make any sense." I swipe at a tear trailing down my cheek. "Why would I go through with a reception for a wedding that isn't happening?"

"Maybe, because it doesn't have to be canceled at all." His voice is calm. Steady. Loaded with something I can't quite name. "Not if you marry someone else."

I sit up straighter. "Okay, you need to stop. I don't know what this is, or what game you're playing, but it's not funny."

He leans in just enough to make my pulse stutter. "It's not a game." He holds out his hand.

And automatically, and probably because my brain is too tired to make decisions, I follow his lead and place my palm in his. Instantly, mine is dwarfed by his much bigger one. His skin is rough with calluses on the fingers that drag at mine. Little pinpricks of pleasure whisper over my nerve endings.

It was a mistake to kiss him because now, I'm so aware of his nearness. Of how, with me seated, and him on one knee, we're at eye-level. That's how massive he is. I feel so much smaller in comparison, but he's never made me feel unsafe.

In fact, he's always been gentle around me. Like he's very aware of his size and does everything in his power to make me feel secure. And I do feel protected by his bulk. The way he put himself between me and my ex, as if he were using his body to shield me from him. Like he'd do anything to protect me. My head spins. Why is my mind going in this direction? He's my boss. We have a professional relationship—which just went out the window when he kissed me. The enormity of what happened begins to sink in.

1. I'm no longer getting married.

2. My boss. Kissed. Me.

3. Now he's looking at me, like... It meant something more than just a way of saving my pride and helping me get back at my ex.

My heart leaps into my throat. I try to pull my hand from his, but his holds tightens. His gaze intensifies, and I feel like I'm caught in a spiral of emotions emanating from his eyes.

"What... What are you trying to tell me?"

His features grow serious. More serious than I've ever seen in all the time I've known him.

"Marry me."

To find out what happens next read Brody and Lark's, Boss - Assistant marriage of convenience Christmas Romance, in The Christmas Trap

Scan this QR code to get it

How to scan a QR code?

1. Open the camera app on your phone or tablet.
2. Point the camera at the QR code.
3. Tap the banner that appears on your phone or tablet.
4. Follow the instructions on the screen to finish signing in.

Here's a bonus scene with Connor & Phe

Connor

"I'm Dr. Phoenix Davenport." She strides into the triage cubicle, eyes on the clipboard in her hands. Her voice is crisp, all business. "And you are Mr. —" She pauses, brow furrowing, then lifts a brow. "Lovelorn Romeo who can't function without his wife?"

She glances up and spots me. For a second, her face softens, a genuine smile tugging at her lips—then she clamps it down fast, like it never existed. She folds her arms, hugging the clipboard to her chest like a shield. "How did you even get in here?"

I offer her a calm, innocent look.

She narrows her eyes. "Right. You're the guy who single-handedly kept this ER from shutting down. Of course, you can just waltz in whenever you want."

She pivots, about to stalk off.

"Wait," I call.

She pauses, reluctantly.

God, my wife in scrubs and a white coat—with her no-nonsense expression and that undeniable fire in her eyes—is the sexiest thing I've ever seen. If only I could convince her to give me five damn minutes.

"I think something's wrong," I say, lying back dramatically on the examination table. I press a hand to my chest. "My pulse is racing. Through the roof. I'm certain I'm in cardiac distress."

She glances over her shoulder. Her lips twitch again, betraying her amusement before she reins it in.

"Probably all that espresso you insist on guzzling."

"Nope." I shake my head solemnly. "This feels emotional. Psychological. A case of acute wife withdrawal. Haven't seen you in hours. I'm disoriented. Weak." I place my hand on my forehead. "In desperate need of tender loving care," I croak in what I hope is a pathetic voice.

She turns to fully face me now, her mouth tilting despite herself. "You saw me this morning."

"Exactly. That was nine hours, thirty-seven minutes, and"—I pretend to check a nonexistent watch—"twelve seconds ago. I'm clinically deprived. My condition's deteriorating by the minute."

Her eyes glint with amusement. "You want treatment?"

"Desperately."

She rolls her eyes. "I'm working."

"It's time for your break."

She blinks. Then glances at her watch again. When she opens her mouth, I know she's going to hesitate. "And I'm guessing, you didn't take your last break?"

She scowls at me.

"That's what I thought. Come on, Doc. You need to stay healthy, so you can continue working on your feet. And I know just the thing that can help you get your strength back."

She narrows her gaze on me. "I know what you're thinking."

"Oh?"

"Don't act so innocent. I know, you're thinking of getting up to some hanky-panky."

"Hanky-panky?" I chuckle. "That's cute."

"And we're overstretched."

Now, I'm surprised. "Despite the additional funding that was allocated to the hospital?"

She pushes her hair back from her face. "That helped. But we were so understaffed to begin with, even with the extra resources, we're stretched to capacity again."

I lower my chin. "Why didn't you tell me?"

"Why should I?"

"Because I'm your husband? And I have the connections to help?"

She shakes her head. "And that is precisely why I didn't want to involve you. You helped to keep the ER open. You saved the jobs of my colleagues. You ensured this hospital, the only one in this entire borough, stayed open so it could provide vital services for the people in the area. It was an almost impossible task. One I knew needed the influence that your family brought to the table. It's why I entertained your proposal, in the first place. That and—"

She glances away, then back at me.

"That, and the fact I fell for you the day you swept into my life."

"Is that right?"

A warmth squeezes my chest. I know she loves me. Yet each time she tells me, it makes me feel incredibly lucky and brings home just how much my life has changed since I met her.

She nods. "You've done so much already. And I am grateful. You know I am... But really, I don't want to take advantage of your wealth and your family's standing."

I swing my legs over and rise to my feet. "When will you learn that we are partners. We are soulmates. When I married you, I made a vow to love you, and cherish you, and take care of you. And that includes ensuring I do everything in my power, always, to help you."

Her features soften.

I walk over to her. "I know, you're a strong, independent woman who wants to make her own way. And I'm grateful you chose me as your companion in life. But I'm your husband, and what is mine is yours, just like what is yours is mine." I come to a stop in front of her. "Isn't that right?"

She nods slowly.

"So, let me help. Let me give back—to this hospital that's given you so much, to the doctors who've saved countless lives. I have the means to make a real difference, not just for you, but for this entire community. Let me use my power for something that matters, so it makes a difference in the wider society."

A soft smile curves her lips. "You know exactly what to say to make me agree."

Yes, I can be manipulative. But it's for a good cause. It's so I can help a lot more people, of course. But primarily, it's so I can also ease the working conditions for my wife. She works such long hours. She continues to be dedicated to her job. She's a brilliant trauma specialist and takes pride in her work. It also energizes her and challenges her. And she's very good at it. But she also tends to overdo it.

I managed to take her for a short second honeymoon. This time, we managed to get away for an entire two weeks. Of course, by the end of the first she confessed that she was itching to get back to the ER.

She loves being a doctor. And I love that about her.

Her dedication makes me proud of her. I've always attempted to use my money for the betterment of those around me. Hence, my foray into biochemistry, and the financing of critical breakthroughs in curing disease. That, in turn, provided a great cover for my missions.

But since meeting Fever, I've been able to use my money to help her and what's important to her. And that brings me even more satisfaction. I now have a cause. A reason to live. A goal which I didn't realize I'd been missing in life. One that revolves around her.

"You know, what I'm saying is right."

She blows out a breath, then nods. "Okay."

It's my turn to blink. Maybe, I'm learning how to wear her down. Maybe, I'm learning to say the right things so I'm able to convince her faster.

"Okay?" I ask slowly.

She nods. "You're right. If you're able to use the resources you have to impact a wider number of people, then I should not be a hindrance to that."

"Thank you for letting me help you."

Her smile blooms. "Thank you, for being the most incredible, most generous, sexiest husband in the world."

"Thank you for putting your trust in me." I cup her cheek. "And now—" I bend my knees and peer into her eyes. "Meet me in the break room."

Phoenix

I splash water on my face and meet my reflection in the restroom mirror. After Connor left, I tore up the intake form he'd filled out. When I told the ER receptionist, she smirked—clearly, in on the secret.

No point asking how he convinced her to do his bidding. The man only has to smile, and women bend to his will. And with his connections? Of course, he pulled it off.

A part of me is a little pissed off that he came into my place of work again and managed to grab my attention. Because workaholic that I am, I'd rather be using the time I'm here to care for my patients.

On the other hand, I've been working nonstop since we got back from our honeymoon a month ago. I've managed to take Sundays off, but have spent much of the time on those days sleeping, in order to get my energy back. 'Course, Connor wakes me up each morning with an orgasm (or two, or more), and when I reach home, exhausted, he's waiting for me. He massages my feet, draws me a bath, makes sure I eat, and then, of course, has his way with me. After that, I'm so relaxed, I sleep deeply and wake up refreshed.

All of which is to say, I've never been this happy or more content.

But for the fact my conscience tells me, I need to be spending more time with my husband. Not that he's complained. Or tried to make me feel guilty. He's been so very understanding. Which is why, seeing him earlier was a surprise. A coming together of my home and work life. A reminder of how I met him the first time.

And meeting him this time around was just as potent. I met his gaze, and it was a punch to the gut, all over again. But then, every time I see him, every time he touches me, kisses me, holds me, and every time he fucks me, it's like the first time. I don't think I'll ever get used to how it feels to be with him, in his presence, at the receiving end of his attention.

I grab some paper towels and dry my face and hands, then drop them into the recycling bin.

It's stupid to be this nervous. I don't need to be this nervous. I'm only meeting my husband. And I know him well. And I trust him. So why do I feel so flushed? Why do I feel that tell-tale excitement building up inside of me? Those same embers of fire that light up my skin, so no matter how tired I am at the end of the day. When I step into our penthouse, I'm filled with the anticipation of seeing my husband again. Knowing he'll take care of me in every way. Wondering what new way he's going to pull an orgasm from me on that day. Wondering what new, devious way he's going to pleasure me today.

I shake my hair back, square my shoulders, and march toward the break room. I step in and find it's empty. Not a surprise. I knew he'd find a way to get me alone here.

I glance around the rows of lockers, divided by the benches in the center, all of which seem vacant. I go down the first row toward the galley at the far end. My nerves prickle with expectation. A shiver rolls up my spine. I sense him before the sound of the door being locked reaches me. It's loud enough that it echoes through the space. I begin to spine around when his voice orders, "Don't turn."

I stop.

"Keep walking."

A full body shudder grips me. *Oh God.* That decisiveness in his voice, that absolute assurance, that tinge of darkness and meanness... All of it is a whip across my spine. One which spurs me on. I place one foot in front of the other and keep moving.

When I reach the prep station pushed up against the wall of the galley, he snaps, "Bend over and grip the counter."

"What?"

"Do it."

Oh. God. I can sense the intention in his words. And I'd be lying if I said that doesn't excite me further. Besides, no way, am I going to disobey him. I can't disobey him. Without conscious thought, I do as he says. I grip the edge of the counter.

"Good girl."

His words are spoken so close behind me, I draw in a sharp breath. I didn't hear him approach. Yet, here he is. The heat from his body spools around me, ebbing and flowing over my skin, sliding down to the space between my legs, and lapping at my slit. I'm so wet, and he hasn't even touched me.

"Did you miss me?" he asks in a silky tone.

I nod. "You know I did."

"Did you think of me?"

"All the time," I say honestly. No matter how busy I am, there's this low-level awareness of my husband that exists at the back of my mind. It's a hypersensitivity that he exists, and he's mine, and I'm his, and I'm going to see him not very long into the future. It lends a rosy glow to my outlook and takes the edge off even the most stressful days.

"Can't wait to take me inside your tight, hot cunt. If I touch you, will I find you wet, wife?" He cups my butt, and I groan.

And when he pulls down my scrubs, I cry out, then gasp, for he slaps me. One-two-three-four, he spanks me on each butt cheek. Then, massages the heat into my curves. I pant.

"We can't be here too long. The others will want to use the dressing room."

"Then you'd better come fast." He kicks my feet apart—as far as they'll go constrained by the elastic of my scrubs, that is.

I feel him drop to his knees and then, he squeezes my butt cheeks apart. I know what's coming next, and this is not the first time he's done it, but when he flattens his tongue and licks up my pussy lips, I whimper. "That feels so good." I cry out again when he begins to eat me out. He laps, and licks, and sucks on my lower lips. And when he curls his tongue around my clit, a long low whine spills from my lips. "Ohgod. Ohgod," I pant.

"Say my name," he growls against my cunt. The vibrations sink into my blood and spread to my feet. My knees almost give way.

"Connor, please. Please—" I push my ass out, hoping he'll realize how turned on I am. Of course, he knows. I know that. But I want him to take the hint and fuck me. "Fuck me." I push my cheek into the surface of the counter. "Fuck—" I bite off the rest of my words as he rises to his feet. The next second, something big and blunt teases my opening.

He curls his fingers around the nape of my neck. The heavy weight of his hand anchors me, holding me down. It's primal, and exactly what I need. The tension of the day bleeds from my shoulders. My thighs quiver. He must sense my submission, for in one smooth move, he impales me.

Connor

"So, fucking wet. So tight. So hot. You're such a sweet little slut, my wife." Without giving her a chance to recover, I twist my hips and ram into her with enough force that her entire body shakes. As does the counter.

"Don't destroy the place," she gasps.

"If you're aware enough to note that, then I'm not doing my job." I drill into her again and pick up pace. *Slap-slap-slap.* The sound of my balls hitting her pussy, and the give of her wet flesh as I pull back and plunge into her, fills the space. It's erotic and dirty, and completely elemental. Just like her. I curl my fingers around her throat and gently squeeze. A shiver runs up her back. Goosebumps pop on her skin. "I know what you like, wife." I slide the fingers of my other hand down to play with her pussy. I pluck on her clit, and she whimpers.

"Oh, Connor."

"That's the right thing to say." I nod approvingly, continuing to rub on her clit as it swells further. I thrust into her, hitting that spot deep inside of her, and feel her shudder.

She tightens her inner walls around my cock and know she's close. I bend and place my cheek next to hers. "Come." I loosen my fingers around her throat. She draws in a breath and, instantly, orgasms.

Her body jolts. Her spine curves. A low keening cry emerges from her mouth. I place my lips over hers and absorb the sound, continuing to fuck her as the climax grips her.

I kiss her deeply, slowly, until she slumps. Then, I kiss the edge of her mouth. Her cheek. Lick the teardrop that squeezed out of the corner of her eye. "Ready for another?"

A breath escapes her lips. "You're a fiend."

"Your fiend."

A small smile curves her lips. "You didn't come."

"I plan to."

"I'm not on birth control."

I pause. Stay frozen.

She flutters her eyelids open. The look in them is sheer joy. Happiness. A readiness.

"You sure?"

She nods.

I kiss her again, feeling myself grow even bigger inside her. I straighten, holding her gaze, and push into her. Over and over again. The joining of our bodies, somehow, carries even more significance.

If you'd told me a year ago, I'd be fucking my wife with the intention of getting her pregnant, I'd have laughed. Now...I don't question that even the smallest actions in my life take on an entirely new significance with her. Always with her. She's changed my life for the better... And each time I enter her, I feel myself change further... For the better.

I plunge into her, tilt my hips so I'm brushing up against that part deep inside of her again. Her wetness bathes my shaft, turning my balls to stone. My thigh muscles bunch. I push into her slowly, over and over again, making sure her inner walls feel every centimeter of my length. I brush my fingers over her already engorged clit and her pussy lips, so she shivers and pants and moans. And when her eyes roll back in her head, I bend over her, lick the shell of her ear, and murmur, "Come with me, Wife."

This time, when she orgasms, I follow her over the edge and empty myself into her. I dig my teeth into the curve where her shoulder meets her throat. It seems to increase the intensity of her orgasm, for her climax keeps pace with mine. We soar through the air, and I can feel her with me, by my side. My soulmate. My wife. *Mine.*

I come down from my high, making sure to keep her from collapsing. And when she finally opens her eyes, I kiss her again. Then straighten. She stands quietly as I put her clothes to rights. Then my own. I lead her out of the changing room, nodding at one of my men who stood guard outside. He's dressed as one of the cleaning crew, and at my signal, he pulls off the *Maintenance* sign he' placed on the door outside.

"You think of everything," my wife whispers.

I wrap my fingers through hers and bring them to my mouth. I kiss the tips. "I'm glad you approve."

A week later

Phoenix

. . .

"You are the most beautiful woman in the entire world." My husband rakes his gaze down my dress clad body to the fuck-me stilettos with the strap cinched around my ankles.

The three-inch heels mean I can barely walk, given I'm unused to the height. But the discomfort is totally worth it to see the admiration in his eyes.

"You like it?" I gesture to the silk dress which dips low between my breasts to show off the swell of my cleavage. It cinches in at the waist, then flows out in an A-line to my feet. The skirt features a slit which parts all the way to the top of my thigh when I walk. It's more revealing than any dress I've ever worn. But I wanted to surprise my husband. Also, being with him, I felt emboldened. I feel like I can wear anything and get away with it because he's there to protect me.

"I bloody love it." He stalks over to me, his steps measured, his gaze heated. He stops with the tops of his Italian loafers almost brushing my toes. Once again, his eyes rove over my now flushed features, down to the erratic pulse at my throat, sliding further to where my chest rises and falls. "I love you." He raises his gaze to mine. Those blue eyes of his darken to gunmetal. Hungry and heated.

This possessiveness of his is something I'll never get used to.

My heart melts in my chest. My pulse rate shoots up. As always, in his presence, I feel that thrum in the air between us, that suppressed energy which licks up my skin and causes sweat to form at the nape of my neck. An electric current lights up my spine. I feel more alive than I've ever been before. Every time I'm in his presence, it's like I've stuck my finger into an electric socket. I'm subsumed with sensations zinging through my blood.

"I love you." I swallow around the ball of emotion in my throat.

He places his hand on my hip and squeezes gently. Through the satin of my dress, I feel every heated fingerprint of his on my skin. Scorched by his touch. Imprinted by his presence on my soul.

He lowers his chin, and I raise mine. Our breaths mingle. Our eyelashes make love to each other. He holds his mouth directly over mine. Teasing me. Drawing me into those mysterious depths of his eyes. Each time I look into them, it's like I'm discovering another aspect of this man. Surprising and revealing. Exciting and, somehow, also reassuring. For I see the love reaching out to me.

The heat of his body embraces mine. He bends his big body over mine. Protecting me. Cradling me. And when he draws me close, I feel his heart thundering in his chest, giving away how much he feels for me. He brushes his mouth over mine.

I sigh. The kiss. Is. Everything. Hard lips. Soft touch. The jolt of lust when he licks into my mouth.

He tilts his head and deepens the kiss. I feel it all the way to my toes. I moan, and he swallows the sound, and pulls me up on tiptoe. When he nips at my lower lip, I almost lose my balance.

"Jesus, can the two of you restrain yourselves in public?" Brody's disgusted voice reaches us.

I flush and try to pull away, but Connor has other plans. He holds me in place and continues to kiss me. His touch is firm, his lips are authoritative, but the sweetness dripping into my bloodstream makes me feel like I'm swimming through syrup. My head spins.

I promptly forget about where we are, or who is watching us, until Connor slowly gentles the kiss. By the time he pulls back, my brain cells have coalesced into one big, dripping mess. I stare at him bemused. He chuckles, kisses my forehead, and tucks me into his side.

Brody, who's turned his back on us, asks, "Is it safe to turn around yet?"

I giggle.

Connor smirks. "Can't guarantee I won't kiss her again."

Brody looks over his shoulder, his actions exaggerated, then pretends to flick sweat from his forehead. "It's a great thing that the two of you are so much in love. But it's a hell of a predicament for me to walk in on my brother making out with his wife."

His forehead is furrowed, his jaw tight. He seems more stressed than usual.

"Didn't expect to see you here today. Are you one of the bachelor's who's going to be auctioned off?"

Because that's why we're here. To raise money for Save the Kids, Connor and I put together an auction.

Thanks to the Davenports' connections, the guest list includes the First Lady, Zara Whittington, who agreed to be a patron of the charity, and various personalities, including pop star, Solene and her husband, renowned actor Declan Beauchamp, as well as Prince Viktor Verenza, Adrian Sovrano, and Toren Whittington.

The latter three have agreed to take part in a bachelor auction to raise money, along with my brother James. I'm looking forward to seeing James, who I haven't seen or spoken to in weeks.

He's the person in my family I'm close to, more than my other siblings. He played such a key role in bringing Connor and me together; and all because he was worried that I hadn't been in touch with him or attended any family gatherings. And now, I feel compelled to check in on *him*. Maybe, it's because I've found the love of my life. And it feels incredible. It's not like I'm dependent on another person for my happiness—at least, I'd like to think not—but having Connor in my life makes me feel anchored. Grounded.

Having him in my corner makes me feel cherished and protected.

After what happened with Drew, I was sure I would never find someone who'd love me the way I knew I deserved. I thought the kind of happiness I wanted was just out of reach. Then, Connor stalked into my life. And everything changed.

Now, I want my brother to know the kind of love I know he deserves. And Brody, too. My husband is worried about him. Connor thinks Brody's stubbornness that he will not fall in love is concerning. He feels Brody is setting himself up for a fall because he's so focused on the money and finding a way to unlock his trust without trying to find the right woman to marry.

Inviting him to the bachelor auction was one way of trying to get Brody out of his comfort zone and meeting women. Although, judging by the expression on Brody's face, I'm not sure it's going to work.

Connor eyes his brother with a speculative expression. "You didn't read the email invitation."

Brody raises his shoulder. "You told me to turn up, and I'm here."

"But you didn't realize there was a bachelor auction."

He shakes his head.

"Well, now you know." Connor leads me forward. Brody keeps pace.

When he doesn't reply, I take in the considering look on his face. He doesn't look happy. Oh, dear. "It's for a good cause," I offer.

"And I'm going to donate, of course," Brody says in an affable tone.

"You bet, you are. The millions you make need to be put to some good use." Connor scoffs.

I narrow my gaze on him. Really? If he's trying to convince his brother to take part in the auction with that kind of attitude, it's not going to work.

Connor widens his eyes with a *what-did-I-do-wrong now?* look.

Then, he amends his statement in a conciliatory tone, "I need you to open up your purse strings, so the others follow your example." Connor looks back with a *hope-I-redeemed-myself* look.

Not yet babe, is my silent reply to him.

Oh, I will. Soon. And in the bedroom. His eyes say all the words without speaking.

Brody looks between us, his expression a mix of fascination and being grossed out. "You guys are doing that thing again."

"What thing?" Both Connor and I ask at the same time.

"That thing when the two you seem to speak without words." His expression implies it's weird, but his tone has a touch of longing.

Connor and I exchange another look. My husband spotted that too. He gives me an imperceptible nod.

Brody has no idea how comforting it is that I have another person in this world who knows what I'm thinking without having to say it aloud.

And Connor and I want him to have that, too. Another reason Connor wants Brody to take part in the bachelor auction.

He spends all his time at work. He's so focused on growing profits for the company, he has no time to date.

Connor's opinion is that the occasional hookup doesn't count, and I agree.

Brody needs to think about something other than himself to make room in his life for a woman. And I'm hoping something like this bachelor auction will shake things up enough to make that happen.

"It's quite something, huh?" My husband pulls me closer.

"It's not something I expected," Brody confesses.

"Me neither." I look up at Connor. I know my face wears a big cheesy grin, and I probably have hearts in my eyes. And it's probably cringe, but honestly, I don't care. I'm so happy. And I want the world to see it. I want my brother to realize it.

"But it's so fucking incredible." Connor grins down before dipping his chin and pressing his lips to mine.

Brody groans and looks away. "If you two get any sweeter, I'm going to need insulin on a drip."

"Ooh, a medical metaphor." I chuckle.

"Doesn't quite detract from your grumpiness," my husband drawls.

I swiftly pick up the sentiment from where he left off. "That's just his face when someone shows emotion, and he has no idea what to do about it."

My husband smirks. "Or maybe, it's the sound of his control slipping."

Brody turns slowly, eyes cold. "My control never slips."

Connor raises an eyebrow, amused. "That sounds like a dare. Does that sound like a dare to you, Fever?"

"He's definitely tempting fate," I add helpfully.

"Maybe…it has something to do with a certain member of his team?" Connor drawls.

I blink. "Who are you talking about?"

"No one," Brody snaps.

Simultaneously, Connor says, "His assistant. Who I believe Brody has a sweet spot for, but he's too scared to do anything about it."

"Firstly, she's, my employee." Brody rubs his whiskered jaw. "I never get involved with anyone in my company. It would be too messy. And secondly, she's too good at her job. I don't want to do anything that would result in losing her. So yeah — no, I'm not going there."

"Ah, so you have noticed her." I nod.

Brody frowns. "She's my assistant. I noticed her when I hired her."

Connor and I exchange glances.

"And how many of your employees do you 'notice'?" He makes air quotes.

"None. They're my employees. They might as well have numbers instead of names and —" His voice cuts out, a look of consternation on his face.

"That's what I thought," Connor says smugly.

"She's the person I work most closely with. Ms. Monroe is so efficient, I delegate a lot to her."

Connor smirks.

"She keeps my office running when I'm not around, which is a lot. I'm too busy dealing with all of the mergers and acquisitions needed to grow the business. Which means, I'm away from my desk and traveling a lot."

"Of course." Connor's smile grows wider.

Brody scowls. "Which is why I send her the greatest number of emails, and message her, and call her more than anyone else."

Connor grins hugely. "That's all it is."

Brody glares at him. "What the hell are you getting at, you —"

His phone buzzes. He pulls it out and whatever he reads has his gaze narrowing. "What. The. Fuck?"

I blink. Never seen Brody get this…upset in the time I've known him.

Connor wipes the smile off his face. "What's wrong?"

Brody pockets his phone. There's a look of resolve on his face. "Office emergency." He pivots and heads in the direction he came from.

"Wait, what about Ms. Lark Monroe? Can't she handle it?"

He pauses long enough to throw over his shoulder. "Ms. Monroe is the one in the middle of this shitshow this time."

To find out what happens next read Brody and Lark's story in The Christmas Trap.

ABOUT THE AUTHOR

Hello, I'm L. Steele.

I write romance stories with strong powerful men who meet their match in sassy, curvy, spitfire women.

I love to push myself with each book on both the spice and the angst so I can deliver well rounded, multidimensional characters.

I enjoy trading trivia with my husband, watching lots and lots of movies, and walking nature trails. I live in London.

©2025 Laxmi Hariharan. All rights reserved under the International and Pan-American Copyright Conventions. No part of this book may be reproduced or transmitted in any form or by any means, electronic or mechanical, including photocopying, recording, or by any information storage and retrieval system, without permission in writing from the publisher.

This is a work of fiction. Names, places, characters and incidents are either the product of the author's imagination or are used fictitiously, and any resemblance to any actual persons, living or dead, organizations, events or locales is entirely coincidental.

Warning: the unauthorized reproduction or distribution of this copyrighted work is illegal. Criminal copyright infringement, including infringement without monetary gain, is investigated by the FBI and is punishable by up to 5 years in prison and a fine of $250,000.

No part of this publication may be stored, copied, scraped, text-mined, or used in any dataset intended for training machine learning models, artificial intelligence systems, or similar technologies without express written permission from the copyright holder.

Made in the USA
Columbia, SC
18 August 2025

61494997R00235